THE MAN IN THE WINDOW

Kjell Ola Dahl was born in Norway in 1958 and lives with his wife and children in Askim, near Oslo. His first novel *Dødens more investeringer* (*Deadly Investments*) was published in Norway in 1993. *The Fourth Man,* the first Oslo Detectives Mystery, marked his first publication in English.

K. O. DAHL

The Man in the Window

Translated by
DON BARTLETT

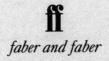

faber and faber

First published in 2008
by Faber and Faber Limited
3 Queen Square London WC1N 3AU

Typeset by Faber and Faber Ltd
Printed in England by CPI Bookmarque, Croydon, CR0 4TD

A CIP record for this book
is available from the British Library

ISBN 978-0-571-23291-8

2 4 6 8 10 9 7 5 3 1

Is this a dagger, which I see before me,
The handle toward my hand? Come, let me
   clutch thee: –
I have thee not, and yet I see thee still.
Art thou not, fatal vision, sensible
To feeling, as to sight? Or art thou but
A dagger of the mind, a false creation,
Proceeding from the heat-oppressed brain?

William Shakespeare, *Macbeth*, Act II, scene i

PART ONE

Friday the 13th

I

Lady in the Rain

In the winter gloom of Friday 13th January, Reidar Folke Jespersen started the way he started every day, at least for the last fifty of his seventy-nine years: on his own with a bowl of porridge in the kitchen, his braces hanging loose behind his back and the rhythmic clinks of the spoon against the bottom of the dish as the sole accompaniment to his solitude. He had big bags beneath two bright blue eyes. His chin was covered with a meticulously trimmed, short, white beard; his hands were large, wrinkled and bore sharply defined veins which wound their way up both forearms to his rolled-up shirtsleeves. His arms were powerful; they could have belonged to a logger or a blacksmith.

Reidar had no appetite. In the morning he never had any appetite, but being the enlightened person he was, he understood the importance of the stomach having something to work on. That was why he began every day with a bowl of porridge, which he made himself. If anyone had asked what he thought about during these minutes, he would not have been able to answer. For as he ate, he always concentrated on counting the number of spoonfuls – 23, clink, swallow, 24, clink, swallow. A long life as a porridge-eater had taught him that a bowl would, on average, provide between thirty-eight and forty-four spoonfuls – and if a trace of wonder lingered in his consciousness during these routine-filled moments of the new day, it was only his curiosity about how many spoonfuls it would take to scrape the bowl clean.

While her husband was eating breakfast, Ingrid Jespersen was in bed. She always stayed in bed longer than her husband. Today she didn't get up until half past eight, then she wrapped a white bathrobe around her and scuttled out to the bathroom where the underfloor heating was on full. The floor was so hot it was almost impossible to stand in bare feet. She tiptoed across, then wriggled into the round shower cabinet where she took a long, hot shower. The central heating ensured that the flat was always nice and warm, but as her husband could not tolerate the same temperature in the bedroom, he always turned off the radiator thermostat before going to bed in the evening. Thus the winter cold sneaked in overnight. And even though Ingrid Jespersen was warmly covered by a thick down duvet, she liked to indulge herself with the luxury of a hot shower to awaken her limbs, get her circulation going and make her blood tingle under the the surface of her skin. Ingrid would be fifty-four this February. She often fretted at the thought of becoming old, but her appearance never bothered her. Her body was still lithe and supple. These were qualities she ascribed to her days as a dancer and her own awareness of the value of keeping yourself in good physical shape. Her waist was still slim, her legs still muscular, and even though her breasts had begun to sag and her hips no longer had their youthful, resilient roundedness, nevertheless she attracted admiring looks

4

on the street. Her hair was still a natural dark colour with a tinge of red. But her teeth worried her. She, like everyone of her generation, had had poor dental treatment when she was a child. And in two places the fifty-year-old patchwork of fillings had been substituted with crowns.

The most pressing cause of this vanity was that she had a lover, Eyolf Strømsted, a man who had once been her ballet pupil and who was younger than her, and she did not want the age difference to become too conspicuous when she was with him. She turned off the water, opened the cabinet door and went towards the mirror where a grey patina of condensation had formed over the glass. There was still a slight touch of uneasiness when she thought about her lover's reaction to her smile. At first she studied her teeth by grimacing to herself in the mirror. Then she regarded the contours of her body through the film of condensation. She pressed her right hand flat against her stomach and spun half round. She looked at the curve of her back, studied her backside and examined her thigh muscles as she completed the manoeuvre.

Today, though, she stopped in mid-swing. She stood motionless in front of the mirror. She heard the outside door slam. Her husband's going to work without saying goodbye caused her to lose a sense of time and place for a few seconds. The bang of the door disconcerted her and she stared with vacant eyes at her own image in the glass. When at last she pulled herself together, it was to avoid looking at her own nakedness. Afterwards she ran the razor slowly down her right calf but it was an automatic, absent-minded movement, without a hint of the well-being and repose the thought of her lover had evoked minutes before.

The husband, who had long finished his porridge, and had therefore put on his coat and trudged out of the flat without a word, hesitated for a few seconds in front of the door, craned his neck and listened to the sound of running water as he conjured up images of his spouse with closed eyes, droplets forming on her eyelashes, breathing through an open mouth in the stream of scalding hot water cascading over her face. For more than ten years Reidar Folke Jespersen had practised sexual abstinence. The marital partners no longer touched each other. They had no intimate physical contact whatsoever. All the same, their love for each other still seemed to others to have a great tenderness and mutual devotion. This façade was not so very different from the truth for as the couple's erotic love dwindled to nothing, the relationship still rested on a tacit agreement – a psychological contract which contained all the elements of mutual respect and a willingness to accept each other's foibles and quirks, such as putting up with each other's snoring at night – an agreement which also included the ability to do so and the extra strain involved in getting along with a person one assumed one wished well for every hour of the day.

Until three years before, Ingrid had regarded her husband's self-imposed celibacy as a caprice of fate, something she would have to endure in order to apportion due value to the time she had lived in tune with her physical urges. But when, about three years earlier, she

6

allowed herself to be mounted by her ex-ballet pupil, and when the self-same slim, muscular man withdrew his penis, after next to no time, supremely aroused, out of control in his excitement and nervousness, spraying large quantities of sperm over her breasts and stomach, Ingrid Jespersen experienced a feeling of purposeful and satisfied calm. Her daily life was given a new dimension, thanks to the lover. A hitherto ignored, but perceived lack had at long last been addressed and met. She embraced Eyolf with passion. She cradled him in her arms. She stroked his supple back and his muscular thighs. She explored him with closed eyes and sensed the satisfaction of knowing a piece of her life had slotted into place. And for the first time for a long time, as once again she felt her ex-pupil's penis swell between her hands, as the low winter sun cleared the neighbouring block, permitting a sharp ray to penetrate two gaps in the blinds to hit the shelf and a glass penguin – an ornament which broke up the sunbeam into a soft carpet of colours, a rainbow effect, which covered their naked bodies and added a symbolic beauty to her physical enjoyment – at that instant Ingrid Jespersen knew that she was experiencing something which would have a decisive impact on her later life.

Taking it as the most natural thing in the world, the two of them repeated the rendezvous the very next week. Now, three years later, they no longer needed to make any written arrangements; they just met in his flat at the same time, every Friday morning at half past eleven. They had no other contact apart from this visit, triggered and maintained by the same rather painful longing for the other's body and caresses. She looked forward to these weekly assignations with Eyolf in the same way that she would have looked forward to a session with a chiropodist or a psychologist. Meeting him was something she did for her well-being and her mental health. And it never occurred to her that the younger man would see it in any other way. As the weeks and months passed, as rendezvous succeeded rendezvous, they adapted to each other physically and psychologically – from which she derived immense, unalloyed pleasure. She assumed at the same time that he would also find pleasure in this, all the days and nights when he was anywhere else but in the same bed as her.

This morning, after taking a shower, washing her hair, shaving her legs, rubbing cream into her body, varnishing her toe-nails and applying make-up to her cheeks, lips, eyelashes and not least the rather swollen, wrinkled part under her eyes, Ingrid Jespersen once again tightened the dressing gown belt around her waist and went for a stroll through the flat. She stood studying the deep bowl on the kitchen table for a few seconds, the one with the rural pattern from Porsgrund porcelain factory. The remains of porridge, thinned with semi-skimmed milk, covered the bottom of the bowl. She automatically picked it up and rinsed it in the sink. Reidar had put the spoon in the dishwasher. He had put the carton of milk back in the door of the refrigerator. On top of the fridge, neatly folded, lay the morning edition of *Aftenposten*. Reidar had not touched it. The coffee machine on the worktop was full. She poured the contents into a coffee jug. It was half past nine, and she was not due to meet

Eyolf for two hours. In half an hour's time, Reidar's son from his first marriage would open his father's antiques shop on the ground floor. It was her intention to take the coffee and go downstairs to the shop, chat to her husband's son and invite him with the rest of his family to dinner that evening. To kill time waiting, she switched on the radio and sat down on the sofa in the living room with the newspaper in front of her.

2

Silk Paper

Today Reidar did not drive to the quiet warehouse in Bertrand Narvesens vei in Ensjø as he usually did on other days. Instead of turning left into the garage to get his 1987 Opel Omega as normal, he walked in the opposite direction. He went into Bygdøy allé and wandered in the freezing winter temperatures down to the Narvesen kiosk at the crossroads by Thomas Heftyes gate. Here, in the taxi rank behind the kiosk, stood three taxis, all in a line with their roof lights lit. Reidar first went to the kiosk and bought *Dagbladet*, *Verdens Gang*, *Dagsavisen* and *Dagens Næringsliv*. There was a lengthy pause while he read the front page of *Aftenposten*. His mind was drawn to his wife, who would soon be reading this newspaper. Nevertheless, he passed on *Aftenposten* and paid for the four newspapers, which he put on the back seat of the first taxi – a Citroën Xantia estate. The driver belonged to the tribe of taxi drivers to whom politicians have learned to listen. But even though he was on top form, full of gold nuggets about international politics plus gossip about the royals, and even though Reidar was strangely partial to street politics and the truths championed by drunks and hairdressers, he remained impassive to all the driver's attempts to get him into conversation. He asked to be driven to an address in Jacob

Aalls gate. Here he went into a little café with a sleepy early-morning atmosphere – several unoccupied tables and just two other guests: two young women drinking café latte out of large glasses at the only table by the window.

A young man dressed in white with inflamed acne on his cheeks and cropped hair in the shape of a ski jump over his forehead, nodded to the new customer whom he recalled from previous visits. He came out from his position behind the counter and asked Reidar whether he wanted to sit at a table. The new customer shook his head. On seeing the bewilderment in the young boy's face, he explained that he wanted to sit by the window and for that reason would wait until the two women were finished. The boy gave an exaggerated nod, thus making it clear that he considered the new customer to be not quite all there, then went back behind the counter where he continued to chop up cucumbers and lettuce. Reidar stood at the counter, staring at the two women who soon sensed his attentions and clearly found them unpleasant. A few minutes later the conversation between them had dried up. Before very long both had finished their coffee and asked for the bill. They let in a cold blast of winter as they battled with the door on their way out. Reidar sat down on a chair which was still warm, took off his gloves with a great deal of fuss, placed his leather document case on the other chair, opened it and took out today's editions of *Dagbladet*, *VG*, *Dagsavisen* and *Dagens Næringsliv*, putting all four newspapers in a pile in front of him. He signalled to the young man, who brought him a huge cup of steaming-hot, black coffee. Folke Jespersen lit a cigarette – Tiedemann's Teddy without filters – and looked at his watch. It showed ten minutes past nine. He inhaled, rested the cigarette on the ashtray and sat staring out of the window. His gaze fell on the front door which Ingrid, his wife, would open in a little over two hours, intending to spend the afternoon in bed with her lover. His mind drifted back to her, who at this moment, he assumed, would be elegantly huddled up on the sofa in her white frotté dressing gown as she finished reading *Aftenposten*. He sat idly smoking while he tried to imagine how she behaved with her lover.

He thought of the various stages he and Ingrid had been through in their life together. He thought about the fragile, vulnerable creature she had been when he first met her. He tried to compare the memory of the person with the quite robust, now very self-assured woman who slept quietly beside him in bed every night. She had packed part of herself away and hidden it. A little packet wrapped in silk paper which he imagined she took out when she was with the man living on the opposite side of the street. Deep down, he wondered whether that part of her soul – to which he had once tried to come close – was in the packet or whether that side of her had disappeared, had vanished into nothingness, along with her former vulnerability and insecurity. He wondered whether the woman he shared flat and bed with every night was the same woman he had once hoped he would succeed in loving. Somewhere in his mind his thoughts revolved around the enigma of human nature, the maturing and developing of a personality. In his mind's eye he saw a sculptor and thought: if you're a sculptor, perhaps you can claim that the final result has always resided in the stone. But, a human being, thought Reidar; human beings are moulded not only by their genes but also by their surroundings, history, by their life experiences and interaction with others. A personality does not reside in a person from birth. In complete seriousness, he considered that his curiosity regarding Ingrid's lover was restricted to the little packet wrapped in silk paper containing Ingrid's soul, and whether she opened it in the man's company. Acknowledging this to himself, Reidar felt something akin to being jealous, but this kind of jealousy was not directed towards the lover as a person – it was a different kind of jealousy – a sort of malaise which had nothing to do with the envy he would feel towards any man to whom Ingrid would reveal her desires. It was more like a raw form of sorrow, something vague and fleeting, the way he imagined people who had had an arm or a leg amputated would feel pain in the absent limb. It was a kind of jealousy he believed he was too old to explore further. With a certain melancholy, he pursued these thoughts, and also with a certain melancholy, he conceded that he cut a sorry figure sitting there as he did now. He tried to find an explanation for his behaviour – why it had become such an obsession to observe with his own eyes how Ingrid routinely cheated on him every Friday with Eyolf Strømsted. However, he allowed this self-examination to wreak havoc in his mind for no more than a few seconds before dismissing it and returning to active enjoyment of his morning cigarette. When it was finished, he stubbed it out in the ashtray and started on the topmost paper.

When, more than two hours later, a shivering Ingrid Folke Jespersen scuttled along the pavement on the opposite side of the street from the café, wrapped in a long, grey, fur-lined coat and went through the front door without even so much as a cursory glance at the café or any other aspect of her surroundings, Reidar had finished reading the papers. He had smoked a few too many cigarettes. He had drunk two cups of coffee and a bottle of mineral water. As the brown door closed behind his spouse, he regarded it with a pained look and almost jumped when the young waiter asked him if he wanted anything else. He checked his watch. And the moment his eyes fell on the round watch face, he caught himself wondering why on earth he always looked at his watch when people asked him questions. With that, he smiled at himself, gave a brief shake of his head and requested the bill. After paying, he left two 10-kroner coins on the table as a tip, which he felt ought to compensate for his rudeness two hours earlier. Then, with an old man's failing agility, he tottered out into the cold and, stiff-legged, walked down towards Uranienborg for a meeting with his brothers.

3

Tired Men

The first thing Reidar noticed on entering his brother's flat was a white screen standing in the corner of the room – in front of Arvid's old Radionette TV with the roll-up door. He saw that all the others were present: the youthful businessman and his wife as well as Reidar's other brother, Emmanuel. The stranger's partner had got up from an armchair by the window and stood ill at ease, nervously wringing her hands. She was in that indefinable age between thirty and forty, with long, dark, curly hair, wearing a navy blue outfit, which created a sense of formality, although her skirt emphasized her legs. Reidar raised his arm and greeted everyone politely. She stuck out a slender hand, which she swiftly retracted, and flicked back her long, dark hair, releasing an aroma of perfume around her. Reidar turned to the three men and shook hands with her middle-aged husband. The latter did not introduce himself; instead he nodded towards his wife and introduced her: 'Iselin Varås,' he said. Reidar turned and looked at the woman as she sat back in the armchair.

'My marital and business partner,' the man added.

He must have been around fifty with short, curly hair, greying at both temples. His looks were the kind that stockbrokers and sports commentators used to have: a brash enthusiasm underpinned by two-day stubble, a small inappropriate earring, jeans and a red suit-jacket. His upper lip was narrow and bared a little of his top teeth, although it was not possible to say whether it was due to a nervous tic or a stiff smile.

'Watch out for her, Reidar,' Arvid mumbled in jest, nodding towards the woman. 'She's tough in the clinches.' Arvid was like August Strindberg in one of the dramatist's less choleric moments: an elderly but dignified man with a goatee, pockmarked skin, lots of grey hair and a watch chain in his waistcoat.

Reidar sat beside his other brother, Emmanuel, who was the only person present who had not stood up. Emmanuel was the sort who liked to sit. He had always been overweight, and a long life as a smoker had given him gurgling emphysema, which meant he had almost no lung capacity. Standing upright for him was a terrible exertion.

'Hermann Kirkenær is in good shape,' Emmanuel wheezed to his brother, nodding towards the man in the red jacket.

Reidar did not answer.

'Do you know Kirkenær?' Arvid asked nervously.

Reidar ignored the question. 'Don't drag this out longer than necessary,' he interjected sourly.

Arvid and Emmanuel exchanged glances in response to this bad-tempered retort. Arvid made an impatient sign to get the meeting started. Emmanuel spoke up in such a loud voice that it sounded formal: 'Now that we are all gathered here, perhaps we had better get on with the matter in hand.' The ensuing silence seemed to catch

Emmanuel off guard. In his confusion, he craned his neck round, sending everyone a good-natured look, and stammered: 'The floor is yours, Kirkenær.'

Kirkenær took a step forwards and folded his hands. 'Thank you, gentlemen,' he responded, moving behind his own chair and grasping the backrest with both hands. Then he nodded to his wife. 'Iselin.'

The woman rose to her feet and passed him a brown folder. Then, with an elegant sway of her hips, she sashayed to the opposite corner and stooped over an overhead projector on the floor. Arvid Folke Jespersen gave an eloquent cough as she bent down and her skirt tightened over her haunches.

She winked at Arvid and smiled in a maternal, indulgent way as she straightened up and put the overhead projector on the table in front of them.

Arvid and Emmanuel scraped their chairs to see better when she switched it on.

'It's always a little special to talk to such a small audience,' Kirkenær began. 'So, let me first emphasize how happy I am to be here.'

Reidar glared at Emmanuel, who had expected this reaction and therefore ignored it, concentrating on Kirkenær instead.

'I would also like to take this opportunity to thank you, Arvid, for our enjoyable and instructive collaboration and also for allowing us to use your flat.'

Arvid gave a gentle, amiable nod.

It had now become obvious to all that Reidar Folke Jespersen was not on the same wavelength as his two brothers. He seemed grumpy and displeased, and he himself was aware of his role in this game. There was a great deal he disliked about the situation. And this displeasure was given greater nourishment as Kirkenær consistently addressed him by his Christian name.

Kirkenær stared straight at Reidar with a broad smile. 'I have, as you know, already informed Arvid and Emmanuel about what I want to say, but let me first present my goals for this little gathering here today: I represent freedom, gentlemen. I represent freedom and security because I have a huge amount of money behind me. But I do not wish money to be at the centre of our conversations. Above all, I am keen to ensure that you trust me. I want everyone to be clear that the fruit of your lives' work is in safe hands.'

He closed his eyes as though devising the formulation of his next nugget:

'Experience is our shared capital. I have cast my eyes over what you have built up with humility and respect. When I, and Iselin . . .' he sent an inclusive glance to the remote, queen-like woman who was smiling at the three aged gentlemen '. . . have got that far, all that will be left to do is to oversee the investment with prudence. Gentlemen, we have explored the charts and sounded out the terrain, we have consulted the financial titans, and we are in total agreement that we should pay *you* in generous measure in order to manage *your* shop in *our* name.'

The man with the red jacket closed his eyes once again – as though tasting what it was like to have let the cat out of the bag. Then he stood in silence watching the three brothers, almost as if he were checking to see how the land lay – until he spun on his heel and placed the first transparency showing his calculations.

Reidar smelt a conspiracy. He and the two brothers followed closely as Kirkenær warmed to his task. None of the three commented on the exact offer when it was revealed at the end of Kirkenær's pitch. The young woman scurried around with refreshments. Arvid had port and Emmanuel took beer while Reidar politely refused a drink. The young lady would not take no for an answer. She delved into a trunk and came up with miniature bottles of Hennessy and Chivas Regal, but Reidar caught Arvid winking to her and gesticulating that she should not press him. This familiarity between the four of them – his two brothers and the two buyers – brought home to Reidar that Kirkenær had already sold the idea to both Arvid and Emmanuel. But that was not what made him cold with fury. There was something else – though this was not a matter about which he could talk to his brothers. Something which was causing him to feel trapped, impatient and a little aggressive. But he refrained from making any further comment to either his brothers or the buyers. He remained impassive. He did not say a word until Kirkenær and Iselin Varås had left.

Arvid let them out. The three of them were making a commotion in the hall; heavy outdoor coats were taken off hangers and remarks exchanged. But Reidar didn't say anything to Emmanuel while Arvid was bundling the two guests out of the flat. The silence between the brothers was palpable; they each stared at their own section of the wall, absent-mindedly listening to Arvid flirting with

Iselin the way old men do, until at last he closed the door.

Reidar realized that the real cause for Kirkenær's prompt, fuss-free departure was that the businessman considered the battle already won. While Reidar sat thinking about the situation, he could feel the anger growing inside him. At the same time he could feel how, yet again, resignation was trying to dampen his rage. It was a feeling he hated more than any other – how apathy had sneaked into his consciousness, with the passing of the years, in the same way that mist seeps into the forest to make it impenetrable and colourless. It was the kind of apathy that tried to deceive the body into thinking that it had neither the inclination nor the energy to take up cudgels. This duality of the senses – aggression mixed with resignation – gave him the fleeting feeling of suffocation. Yet he understood that this meeting was one of the most crucial moments he had experienced for many years. These thoughts churned through his brain as Arvid's whinnying laughter carried through the hall door and Emmanuel glowered darkly at the wall, presumably on account of Reidar's negative body language. At this moment Reidar was planning a strategy with two short-term goals. The first was to torpedo the attempt to sell the shop which the brothers owned in joint partnership. The second was to buy himself time to ponder the situation which had arisen.

The first strike was seconds away. When the hall door opened and Arvid leaned against the doorframe with a studied expression on his face, the old soldier twisted around in his chair, ready for battle.

'And where is the animal?' asked Reidar in measured tones.

As if on cue, the sound of a low, grunting activity came from the hall. A small, black nose appeared in the doorway. It flicked open the door the necessary few centimetres, and a small, fat, panting butterfly dog waddled in. It wagged its tail with half its body and tripped along on thin legs, sniffing like a piglet with a cold. Reidar bent down and pointed a long finger at the creature's snout, causing it to shrink back, retract its head and emit a series of sharp yelps, which in turn made Arvid go down on his knees to protect it. 'There, there, Silvie, there, there.' He picked up the animal and made baby sounds as he rubbed his face against the dog's drooling head. 'She knows you don't like her,' he said in a reproachful, annoyed voice. Reidar grimaced at him, almost as though he had seen his brother handling tainted meat or a grotesque insect.

'This is not going to happen,' Reidar said, to the point.

The other two exchanged glances.

'So there is no more to talk about,' Reidar decided, and stood up.

'We've been preparing this sale for months,' Emmanuel said in a low hiss. 'You can't just torpedo it.'

'I can,' Reidar stated.

'What makes you think that?' Arvid asked pugnaciously.

Reidar did not grace him with a look. He was already on his way towards his coat. 'Now that I've done what you requested,' he said, dismissing them. 'I've listened to the man. I stood it for half an hour. You wanted me to be persuaded. I was not persuaded. Not in the slightest. The man is a nothing.'

'Karsten agrees with us.'

Reidar flinched and glowered at Arvid, who repeated, 'Karsten agrees with us.' Bringing Reidar's son, Karsten, into the conversation made Reidar even angrier because it suggested that the conspiracy he scented was more widespread than he first assumed. It suggested that Arvid and Emmanuel, as well as plotting against him, had also got Karsten on board – his own son.

'Karsten's interests in the matter are of no relevance,' Reidar said, as unmoved as before. 'This is not going to happen,' he repeated.

Arvid's shoulders quivered with annoyance. He sent Emmanuel another look – to gain support – before continuing: 'The long and short of this is that Emmanuel and I are serious. And because he and I know you, and because he and I predicted what would happen if we trusted you to give your opinion, I'm afraid it is your turn to lose.'

Reidar Folke Jespersen regarded his brother with the same unmoved expression.

'You'll have to give in, Reidar. There are three owners. Two against one is an absolute majority.'

Reidar was still silent.

Arvid shot a glance to his brother for support: 'The majority decides – whatever you think.'

'Majority?' Reidar was working his way around the table towards Arvid, who in fear retreated two paces. Both stopped at a signal from Emmanuel, who was in the process of getting to his feet. That is to say, he was panting and manoeuvring his fat body into a semi-upright position, with his stomach resting on the edge of the table. It was a very rare act. Everyone who knew Emmanuel knew what exertions lay behind such a physical movement; both the brothers were aware of the emotional energy that had triggered these contortions. Emmanuel was thus instantly furnished with his special badge of authority which had helped him on several occasions to overcome the younger brother complex he always ran into with Reidar. Now, with assured hand gestures, he tried to exploit the advantage by calming down his two brothers who stood facing each other like boxers in a ring. 'Take it easy, no damage has been done. Kirkenær will stand by his offer and we must stay united . . .'

Reidar twitched at the sound of Kirkenær's name. 'Whether this man stands by his offer or not is immaterial. It will not happen!' Reidar's retort was like the rattle of a machine-gun, and he added weight to the salvo by smacking the table hard with the palm of his right hand.

Arvid put the dog down on a chair and said: 'We'll never get a chance like this again!'

'Exactly!' Reidar thundered. 'Exactly,' he repeated, approaching his brother. 'And has it not occurred to you, in fact, that it's a little odd?'

'Odd?' Arvid looked to Emmanuel for help. He had slumped back into his chair, breathing heavily and wheezing after his efforts. Tiny beads of sweat had broken out on his forehead, but the look he sent his eldest brother showed he was not done for yet. 'That's the problem, Reidar,' he said in a low voice. 'You're getting too old. You've lost your bite. We're not giving in this time. You're going to lose.'

'Lost my bite?'

'Yes,' came a shrill yelp from Arvid. 'You're not what you used to be. You and I and Emmanuel – we are . . .' Arvid gasped for air as if he didn't dare pronounce the word then and there. But he closed his eyes and steadied himself: '. . . we're *old*. Reidar, you're *old*. You're the *eldest*. And you're not bloody immortal!'

Reidar gave a start. Silvie, the dog, in the armchair began to bark loudly.

'Silvie!' Arvid shouted, already nervous. 'Don't be frightened, Silvie!'

Reidar glared from Arvid to Emmanuel and back again.

'There are two of us. You're on your own. This time Emmanuel and I will complete what we started. We're selling the shop and that's that.'

Reidar had turned pale. He grabbed the edge of the table for support. The three men's heavy breathing was drowned by the dog's yapping and high-pitched whimpering.

Reidar Folke Jespersen took a deep breath and was concise: 'I won't sign anything.'

The other two men exchanged glances again. Arvid shuffled to the door, which the little lapdog took as a signal to jump off the chair. Barking and growling, it waddled and panted its way over to Reidar and took a bite at his ankle. Reidar stared down at the dog for a few brief seconds, then a shudder ran through his body. He took aim and kicked the dog as hard as he could. The dog let out a hollow yelp as it took off from the floor, flew through the room and hit the corner of the fireplace with a wet smack. The plump dog's body emitted a rattling noise and lay motionless.

'You monster,' Arvid shrieked, shuffling over to the lifeless animal. He knelt down. 'Silvie!' he called in a reedy voice. 'Silvie!'

Emmanuel rolled his eyes at Arvid's distraction. He hunched his shoulders as he tried to light a slim cigarillo with a hand trembling from tension. The lighter flame grew with every puff he took. Finally satisfied with the glow, he turned to Arvid: 'It was stupid of you to let the animal in, you know that yourself, Arvid. Reidar and the dog have never got on.'

'I'm off right now,' Reidar boomed and pointed to the front door with his long, bony index finger. 'And as things stand, there is very little chance I will return.'

'You've killed Silvie,' Arvid wailed from the fire.

'Cut that whining out now!' Reidar snapped. 'Your pooch isn't dead.'

Emmanuel cleared his throat. But his voice gave way as he inhaled the smoke. 'For us . . .' he mumbled in a semi-strangulated voice, '. . . for Arvid and myself this is pure business, Reidar. Money. It's unprofessional of you to make it into a personal matter.' He coughed and had difficulty breathing. When he resumed speaking, his voice had the same wheeze as a dying godfather in a Mafia film: 'You'll have to give in, that's all there is to it. It would be best for you. Arvid and I will not comply this time. So you might as well just sign.'

'I'll never sign,' Reidar hissed.

'She's not moving,' Arvid shouted, lifting up the lifeless dog. 'Silvie.'

' . . . We're talking about my damned pension!' Emmanuel went on undaunted, though now in his normal voice. 'Karsten also agrees that this is for the best. Arvid, Karsten and I – you cannot let your usual bullheadedness spoil the future for us.'

Reidar stood with lowered gaze for a few moments before peering over at Arvid, who was holding the little dog in his arms. Its two front paws pointed up into the air. One paw convulsed and fell as the dog's head twisted and a pink tongue protruded from its gaping mouth. 'Now the mutt's dead,' Reidar intoned with a crooked, malicious smile playing on his lips. He added: 'You killed it. You shouldn't have picked it up.' Then he turned and marched towards the door.

'Reidar,' Emmanuel chided. 'The war finished more than fifty years ago. You have nothing to gain by going off on your own. For once in your life, admit defeat.'

As Reidar opened the door, he threw a last glance over his shoulder and said: 'I'm not signing. That's it. No signature – no contract.'

Emmanuel shouted at Reidar as he left: 'There's no point resisting, Reidar! Tomorrow the money will be on the table.'

The door slammed shut.

'You've lost,' Emmanuel shouted after him and looked at his brother, Arvid, who slowly raised his head and sent the closed door a furious glare.

Emmanuel puffed away on his cigarillo. 'The vet will fix your dog,' he assured his brother. 'It's another matter with Reidar. We need his name on the contract. Otherwise, we can kiss the money goodbye.'

4

In Medias Res

On the way down the stairs after leaving his two brothers, while stuffing his emotional shock into a dusty old drawer in his psyche, Reidar was planning his next move.

At first he stood still, shivering, in the freezing snow on the pavement in Uranienborgveien as he racked his brain to decide the best way to locate a taxi and a telephone box. That is perhaps the most irritating thing about days like this, he thought. When you are older, breaks in your routine make the days more difficult, almost insurmountable. He started to walk down towards Parkveien. After fifty metres, at the corner of Uranienborgpark, he found a telephone. On unhooking the receiver, he discovered that he needed a card to operate it. He put the handset back and considered whether he should go straight to the office in Bertrand Narvesens vei in Ensjø and ring from there. It was cold, and he was stiff and tired. However, he wanted to call from somewhere anonymous. He regretted not asking Arvid to book him a taxi before he left. A car as a base would have facilitated progress and his actions; on top of that he would have had somewhere warm to operate from. Dramatic exits such as the one he had just made were quite unnecessary, even though the passion underlined his seriousness and created unrest in enemy ranks.

With unbending fingers he extricated a telephone card from the wallet in his pocket, as well as the slip of paper on which he had noted down the telephone number of Ingrid's lover. It rang for a long, long time.

'Yes,' came the response at last.

Reidar hesitated, just for a second and no longer. 'This is Reidar Folke Jespersen,' he said. 'Let me speak to my wife.'

The silence on the phone continued. 'No melodrama – I don't have the time,' Reidar continued in the same calm tone, but with a hint of impatience now. 'It is of the utmost importance that I talk to Ingrid – now.'

'Just a moment,' said the man's voice.

The silence persisted. Reidar was frozen. He looked around him and cursed Ingrid's nervousness, cursed her for not understanding how he disliked this kind of waiting. As he stood there shivering, a white Mercedes with a taxi sign on the roof came up Josefines gate. It stopped a few metres from the traffic lights. Reidar could see the passenger paying. He was keen to be the next passenger. As if in response to his thoughts, his wife's hushed voice came on the line: 'Reidar?'

'Yes,' Reidar intoned. 'I'll be late home today, maybe after seven o'clock.'

The other end of the line was quiet. The rear door of the Mercedes opened, and the passenger got out.

'Are you there?' he asked.

'Yes,' said Ingrid, his wife, in a barely audible voice.

'I assume this will be the last time I find you in the house of another man,' Reidar said. 'But it is your

29

choice. If you wish to stay married, I expect to see you at home at seven. If not, you should not return.'

The white taxi started up and turned into the street where he was standing. Reidar raised his arm and hailed the taxi, which pulled up by the kerb. 'In any event this episode is forgotten and we will never talk about it,' he concluded and hung up. He took his card from the machine and blew on his hands before hunching his shoulders and trudging across the pavement to the car door the driver was holding open from inside. He got in and shut the door after him.

'Where?' asked the driver – a chunky Pakistani, concentrating on the traffic behind him in the mirror.

'Ensjø,' Reidar said and took a deep breath. 'I'm freezing. Would be nice if you could put the heating up a bit.'

5

Ghosts

The anxiety that Reidar Folke Jespersen had not felt for many years lingered – in a way it made him feel restless, which also brought back feelings of youth he had not experienced for a long time either. So it was an anxiety that he both liked and disliked. But he was unsure about what to do next – and that made him annoyed with himself. He just sat at his desk making the essential telephone calls and waiting for five o'clock. As the time approached and it was as dark as night outside, he clumped down the steps from his office to the warehouse. The huge hall was full to the rafters with old furniture and artefacts waiting to be sold at the shop in Thomas Heftyes gate. He stood for a few seconds taking in the chaos of artisanship and old everyday items. For a few seconds he allowed himself to drift into a dream, as he usually did whenever he stood surveying this scene. But on this day he could not hold on to the sensation. So he forced himself to go on, down the stairs. He took a key from his trouser pocket, went to the front door and opened it. It was still icy cold outside. He opened the lid of the green post box hanging on the wall beside the door. The key fell with a faint, almost inaudible clink. Afterwards he went back in and checked that the door was locked. Then he made his way between all the antique furniture, to the very back of the room and stopped in front of a fashionable-looking wardrobe. It was covered with carved mouldings and had decorative flowers painted on the mirrors mounted on the doors. A black dinner suit hung inside. It had hardly been worn, and had an old-fashioned cut. He took off his grey trousers and blue checked flannel shirt, and put on the suit, white shirt and polished shoes.

After changing, he went back to the office and sat smoking at his desk while contemplating the reflection of his upper body in the darkened window pane. What he saw was an elderly man with white hair and a meticulously trimmed white beard covering his chin and mouth. His eyes followed the outline of his suit; the black contrasting with the white of his shirt, and the black bow tie around his neck. To his sorrow, he was forced to accept that he could not meet his own eyes in the window. *I look like my own ghost – in some English drama*, he thought, and rose with apprehension to his feet. He walked over to the window and pulled down the white roller blind. Then he resumed his position at the desk. It was a heavy table and he had covered it with a smooth white cloth from which shone the faint reflection of the ceiling lamp. There were two stem glasses on the cloth. He stared at the ash on the end of his cigarette, reached out for the ashtray between the glasses and noticed how his hand was shaking. Then he flicked off the ash. He stubbed the glow on the ashtray, extinguished the cigarette and rotated his arm to check the time. With sudden impatience he stood up again and went to the mirror hanging beside the door. He adjusted his bow tie, brushed the lapels of the dinner jacket and brushed off tiny specks of dandruff from his shoulders. He studied his shoes, discovered a stain, bent down and rubbed it with his thumb. There was a grandfather clock between the mirror and the door. He opened the door of the clock and checked the time against his wristwatch. All of a sudden he inclined his head and seemed to be listening. There was the sound of a door closing.

He switched off the ceiling light and put on the desk lamp instead. Then he stooped and took a dark bottle from the space under the table, but stopped all of a sudden and angled his head again, as though listening. There was a knock at the door. 'Come in,' he said, spreading out his arm in a gesture of greeting as a woman appeared in the doorway. She was in her twenties, tall, slim and wearing a long, red dress. Leaning against the doorframe, she was in shadow, out of breath.

'Don't be embarrassed,' he said to reassure her.

As he said the last word, the woman raised her chin and looked him in the eyes. He liked the way she fell so easily into the role, liked the self-assurance she displayed, and perhaps this was the moment he liked best of all – when she came into the light from the desk lamp.

'Nice to see you again!' she said, almost in a whisper.

'After far too long,' he answered, feeling his windpipe constrict with self-pity. He stared at the ceiling, swallowed the lump in his throat and, in a dream, repeated: 'Far too long.' He collected himself and went round the table where he sat down on the swivel chair and fixed his eyes on her.

They eyed each other in silence.

At last she coughed and said: 'Coming here is like returning to a secret place.'

He was quiet.

'It's with me all the time, everywhere.'

'What is?'

She considered and said at last: 'Longing.'

'When you're here, I forget what it means to wait,' he said and nodded towards the bottle. 'Sherry?'

'Yes, please.'

He was about to take the bottle, but hesitated and looked up at her. 'Perhaps you would pour?'

She strode across the floor, took the bottle and poured a glass for each of them. Then she raised her glass, swirled the liquid around and inhaled the aroma before gazing dreamily at a point in the distance. She sipped at the sherry and put the glass down. Bit by bit she began to roll down the long glove reaching up over her elbow. 'It was the driver,' she said. 'He wouldn't let me go.'

She articulated every word, with slow emphasis, as though she were worried about how the message would go down. Reidar had closed his eyes, as if in meditation. In the end, he inclined his head, opened his eyes and said in measured tones: 'Well? Why not?' His eyes had taken on a curious yet also caring expression.

'He wanted to have me,' she said, dropping the glove on the floor. Her fingers were long, her nails sharp and painted red. She took off the other glove too – protracted movements, finger by finger, until she had released her forearm from the tight-fitting material. 'He was brutal.'

'Was he a stranger, or did you already know him?'

34

She lowered her gaze and deliberated. At length, she looked up and said: 'Ask me again later.'

Reidar acknowledged this clever response with a smile, drew the glass to his lips, sipped the sherry, swallowed and put it down. With a look of satisfaction he studied the hand resting calmly on the glass. 'There's something I have to talk to you about,' he said in a light tone of voice. 'Something important.'

She took a few paces to the left, walked past the large grandfather clock and stopped in front of the mirror. She gazed at herself. 'I was concerned that you had to wait,' she said, turning back to him. 'But, on the other hand, it appeals to me that a young man shows such obvious interest.'

He reached out and removed the ashtray from the cloth. He put it on the window sill, beside a small cassette player which he switched on. Low, tinny violin tones poured forth from the player's small loudspeaker.

She stood stock still, listening with closed eyes. 'Schubert?'

He nodded as she undid the zip on the waist of her dress. Then she began to undo the row of small, white buttons running down the front of her dress. When she was finished, she freed her shoulders. The dress fell in a bundle around her ankles. She looked down at herself. She was wearing two old-fashioned brown shoes with heels and a string of artificial pearls which she had wound around her neck several times. Otherwise nothing.

Reidar contemplated her from under half-lowered eyelids. When, eventually, he did move, the chair gave a loud, piercing creak. As if the sound were a signal, the woman stepped out of the dress onto the floor. She raised her hand and caressed her breasts. The skin on her upper arms was nubbled. 'What did you want to talk about?' she asked, crossing the floor with long strides.

'Forgiveness,' came the quiet answer.

She stood for a few seconds looking at the table, her mind elsewhere, as though the word was forcing its way inside her, until finally she scrambled up and lay face down on the white cloth. She supported herself on her elbows, took the glass out of his hand and sipped. At last she answered: 'We've talked about that before.'

He nodded.

The silence lingered until she passed back the glass and said: 'You and I should have gone to a concert together. Schubert.'

'Where?' he asked.

She paused.

He regarded her with a blank expression.

'Vienna?' she asked, looking up.

He shook his head.

'Salzburg?'

He shook his head, his eyes closed.

A smile formed on her lips. 'London?'

He nodded.

The woman lay listening to the music with closed eyes until, without undue haste, she rolled over onto her back and stared at the ceiling.

'It's never easy to obtain forgiveness,' she said ruminatively.

He cleared his throat.

'It's a two-way thing,' she said.

He didn't answer.

They both listened to the music without speaking. After a while she got up onto her knees. The warm light from the ceiling light cast a dark, reddish almost, glow on her skin. He pushed the chair back a little and took in the view from the mirror.

'Can you see?' she asked.

'Almost.'

She slid into a better position.

'Perfect.'

He sat observing her in the mirror. He did not move and did not say a word. After a long while she opened her eyes. Then he rose to his feet and whispered in her ear. 'What are you thinking about?'

'Music,' she whispered back.

'What kind of music?'

'Schubert.'

He wrapped both hands around her face. The blue, somewhat grainy eyelids lowered as he kissed her tenderly on the forehead. She bit her lower lip hard. Her breathing was heavy and drowned the sharp violin notes from the cassette player. For a few brief seconds he gazed at the ceiling. But when she later buried her face in his white shirt front, he lowered his head with affection against her soft shoulder and one solitary tear rolled down.

The Night Owl

Outside the warehouse where this scene was unfolding, Richard Ekholt stood leaning against a wire fence and thinking that the window in the building's façade looked like a half-closed eye. The eyelid was a roller blind and beneath it there was a strip of light. His eyes hurt from staring, but he couldn't tear them away.

Even though he was very cold, Richard Ekholt was not aware that he was freezing. He was wearing a taxi driver's uniform and nothing over it. The Oslo Taxis logo was sewn on his left sleeve at the top. The uniform was creased, the trousers unpressed and the soiled jacket lapels bore dark, long-term coffee, hot dog and ketchup stains. On his feet he was wearing brown shoes unsuitable for freezing temperatures. When he noticed the woman's silhouette through the white blind, he closed his eyes for two brief seconds. But the feeling that arose from having his suspicions confirmed was a different pain, different from the jealousy he had felt hitherto. What he experienced was a paralysing hollowness, which was not relieved by turning away. For two brief seconds it felt as though the ground would hit him in the face before he found a fence to grab hold of.

There was just one illuminated window in the row of darkened squares in the wall. Her body became a blurred shadow which soon became a razor-sharp silhouette against the white blind, only to lose its contours in an absurd piece of mute pantomime. The profile of the steep nose, the shape of the top lip and the wig stood out against the blind as she swung round at leisure and began to unbutton her dress. The silhouette was just as sharp as she wriggled one shoulder out and let her dress fall. Her shadow dissolved as, again, she swung around. Then he felt the sensation in his legs go, as though his body were being sucked hollow from seeing her shadow, a torso with straight shoulders and sharply defined breasts, melt into the form of grey mist, as though a film director were sitting somewhere protecting the audience from the spicy scenes. He neither registered the cold on his body nor the icy air in his nostrils. What he felt was the fleeting touch of her skin on his fingers the moment before she pulled away from him and ran out of the car. He staggered towards the door through which she had disappeared. Without taking his eyes off the bizarre shadow theatre going on behind the white blind, he staggered across the tarmac, the patches of ice and trampled snow until he slumped against the iron door which he knew was locked. Nevertheless, he pulled at the handle. He kicked the door. No sign of give. He backed away. How had she got in? he wondered. He searched for a bell, but there was nothing to be seen. She must have known the way, he thought. *She has been here before*, he thought. As though in a trance, he wobbled back to the taxi. All he could hear was the crunching of snow underfoot. He got in and glowered at the clock on the dashboard. Shouts from customers who wanted a taxi seeped through, but he didn't pay any attention; he didn't take his eyes off the minute hand on the clock. Soon he could see his own icy breath. After a while a layer of frozen condensation had covered the inside of the windscreen. His fingers went numb with cold, but all he could think of was her shadow through the blind.

The minute hand moved with infinite slowness. Nevertheless, it crept round half a circuit without his noticing time was passing. It was almost impossible to see out through the layer of ice covering the windscreen. He ground his teeth and blew on his fingers to allay the cold. Then he switched on the engine, revved up and put the defroster and heating on full. He held his hands in front of the heating ducts, which were soon letting luke-warm air into the car. His knuckles were red with cold, his fingers white and bloodless. The ice on the wind-screen soon thawed, leaving small oval patches through which he could see. His fingers began to tingle. But his brain was still churning over her mysterious rendezvous. Whom had she dressed up for? She had been thinking about this man when she was putting on lipstick, when she leaned towards the mirror and put on eye-shadow. The concentrated hand that held the brush – like that – with him sitting in the same room. Her thoughts had been elsewhere, with another man. She had chosen a dress for another man. Already, in front of the mirror, she was practising this deception. She had not been going to do a job – no readings, no dance. She had been preparing herself for a lover. He clenched his fists and glared. There was still light in the window.

The car began to warm up; the ice that had covered

the windscreen disappeared, and when the switchboard finally received the call that had to be hers, he wondered whether he would be cheeky and take the job. But he refrained. He sat there, immobile. Soon afterwards a taxi pulled up a few metres away, with the roof light off. The taxi reversed and waited with the engine idling as the exhaust fumes danced in a line like a grey wad of cotton wool in the cold. His attention was still directed towards the window. That was why he didn't hear them coming at first.

When he did notice them, he grabbed the door handle, then let it go. They came walking in a tight embrace. No. They were supporting each other. She, in her high heels, and he – that was when he discovered it was an elderly man. That became obvious when she opened the taxi door for him. He followed her figure with his eyes as she rounded the taxi on her unsteady heels and got in on the opposite side. The taxi set off and he put his car in gear. They took the ring road – illuminated, almost deserted so early in the evening. He stared at the back of her head in the car window. She did not turn round. She had no idea that she had been found out. His eyes stung as he followed them down towards Carl Berners Plass. They were approaching the lights on red and he hung back so that he would not be seen. He fixed his gaze on the man's white hair. When the taxi moved off, he did not notice where it was going. He only saw the back of the man's head in front of him. He tried to imagine what the man looked like. In his mind, he formulated the question: *Who are you?*

Slowing to a halt, he realized they had stopped outside

her flat in Hegermanns gate. He braked, pulled into the kerb and switched on the roof light – an anonymous taxi in any street in town. Lowering his chin to his chest, he pretended to be making a note while registering her through his eyelashes. She moved to the side, gave the old man a hug as the door opened, set one foot on the road and manoeuvred her body out. The old man was looking ahead. He couldn't even be bothered to look at her. The old man was still gazing into space as the car drove off.

Richard Ekholt instantly switched off the roof light on his car and accelerated. She had crossed the pavement and was now standing in front of the entrance, searching for her key. She turned as he drove past. They exchanged glances. She gave a start and made a movement with her arm when she recognized him. But he drove on. She stared after him. He watched her in the rear-view mirror. The figure became smaller and smaller in the little mirror stained with grease and fingerprints, distorting her features into a hazy shadow. A shadow staring after him, dejected. But he would take care of her later. First, the old boy. He signalled right and followed the taxi along Ringveien.

7

The Glove

Although Jonny Stokmo was small of stature, he was of stocky build; his hands were large and powerful and he had a loose-limbed, bouncing gait that bespoke strong muscles. The thinning hair was combed back as well as it could be and in this cold weather he kept his head hidden in the hood of his quilted anorak. He was smoking a cigarette. As always, it stuck out from the corner of his mouth, a small fag stained reddish-brown, filthy from his own saliva mixed with tobacco juice. He had a moustache which grew downwards in two thin strands either side of his mouth. It had been burnt away by repeated lightings over the right-hand corner of his mouth.

He was waiting for Reidar Folke Jespersen. He paced to and fro on the pavement in Thomas Heftyes gate to keep warm. About half an hour before, he had talked to Ingrid Jespersen, who had said that she was expecting Reidar at any minute. His mind was in turmoil about the imminent meeting. He was unsure as to how he should express himself. On top of that, he was worried about how he should position himself; he would have to try to stand in such a way that he had eye contact with Reidar, who was taller than he was. He wondered whether to go on the attack or to be friendly, or somewhere in between. Perhaps he should be ice-cold, as

Reidar usually was. He rehearsed *We're both adults* in his head, but disliked the choice of words. The last time Jonny Stokmo talked about being adult was when he talked to his ex-wife, Berit, on the telephone.

Reidar, I've been giving this a bit of thought would signal that Jonny had reflected and was willing to see this business from the outside, also that he had considered Reidar's position in an objective light. *Reidar, I've been giving this a bit of thought, and you have to understand there is only one solution . . .* It sounded good. *Only one solution.* It was like saying there was no other way, and then Reidar would be keen to hear what the solution was. Even though, deep down, Reidar had to know the solution. Because Reidar knew Jonny.

Ingrid had invited him to wait inside, but Stokmo did not want to set foot in Reidar Jespersen's flat. He didn't say this, though. She had prattled away like an immature girl, as always. Ingrid Jespersen was a woman with a lot of conversation in her, the type that likes to flirt with lorry drivers and plumbers, someone who gets the hots for men with dirt under their nails, but never leaves her lair and the security of being fettered in a humdrum marriage. Jonny was sure that, whether Ingrid knew anything or not, she was a better person than her husband, something which he had a mind to tell Reidar.

He was freezing cold because he was wearing jeans, with no long underpants underneath, no long johns. He should have put them on when the temperature crept down to minus 20.

The taxi carrying Reidar Folke Jespersen drew into the pavement. Stokmo waited until Jespersen had paid the taxi driver, staggered out and the taxi had driven off. He put both hands in his jacket pockets and went over to meet the man. At first Folke Jespersen stood stoop-shouldered on the pavement. Then he wrapped his coat around him and set off with his old-man-gait, heading for the front door of the building some distance away.

'Oh, it's you,' said the old man, stopping. 'What do you want now?'

Immediately, Stokmo knew how this was going to end. Reidar's intonation, the brief glance, the look of rejection.

'Yes, nice to see you, too,' Stokmo said.

Reidar glared at him over his shoulder. He wanted to pass.

'There's something I want to say,' Stokmo stated.

'The answer's no.'

He knows what it's about, thought Stokmo. *So he's thought about the matter; it has been bothering him; he isn't sure how to tackle it.*

Folke Jespersen shoved Stokmo in the shoulder so he could pass.

'There's only one solution,' Stokmo said with force, standing in his way again.

'Get out of my way,' the old man said.

'I've decided,' Stokmo said. 'And . . .'

' . . . I'm sick of your prattle,' Folke Jespersen interrupted. 'I don't owe you anything – neither you nor your late father.'

Folke Jespersen was about to force his way past, but Stokmo grabbed him by the collar. 'You're going nowhere, old man!'

'I beg your pardon?'

Jonny Stokmo had not envisaged this turn of events, that he would grab the sourpuss by the collar. As he felt the old man's body yield to his muscular strength, he was paralysed by the situation he found himself in. Reidar was not anyone. This was *Folke Jespersen*. The paralysis that overcame Stokmo allowed Folke Jespersen to loosen the other man's grip with ease. 'How dare you!'

'You will pay!' Jonny Stokmo was still angry, but his demand didn't quite have the same power he had expected. The shock of feeling his own anger translate into violence had led to his muscles failing him; he felt weak, his wings had been clipped.

'Creep back down that stinking hole from which you crept!' hissed Folke Jespersen. The old man's jaw quivered. He tore himself loose. Stokmo stood in amazement as Folke Jespersen passed by him with long strides. Then the old man stopped, as though he had changed his mind. He rummaged in his pockets for a pair of gloves. He glowered at one of the gloves for a moment, then slapped Stokmo in the face with it, once, then once again. 'You bloody simpleton!' Folke Jespersen snarled and headed for the door twenty-five metres away.

When the old man had passed him, Stokmo seemed to come back to life. 'You're a thieving bastard!' he yelled and, on his short legs, bounded after the tall, old man. 'And you won't bloody get away with it!'

Folke Jespersen completely ignored him. As they got to the front door, he rang the bell to his flat and stood staring into space as though Jonny Stokmo did not exist.

'You won't get away with this,' Stokmo threatened. 'I'll be back. And it won't be you doing the slapping, you bloody fascist.'

There was a buzz. Folke Jespersen opened the door. 'Do what the hell you like!' he mumbled, letting himself in without so much as a glance in Stokmo's direction. The door slammed in Stokmo's face and he was left looking at it. 'You bastard,' he swore. 'You bastard!' He backed away from the wall and shook his fist at the windows on the floor above.

8

A Nocturne

When Ingrid Jespersen went to bed that evening, she was alone for the first time in many years. She lay thinking. She remembered how the low, cold, white January sun had also on this day pierced her lover's bedroom window and shone on an ornamental glass object, sending out the same multi-coloured fan of playful light – across the bed, across her lover's back and her thighs as she, supine with her hands around Eyolf's hips, had stared at the telephone ringing on his bedside table. That loathsome white telephone which moved to the beat of his rhythmical movements in and out of her, that telephone which never stopped ringing. And for some strange reason she had known, lying there with her head repeatedly banging against the bedstead, known it was Reidar ringing her. She thought of the hours afterwards, the nauseating and humiliating feeling of guilt, which had turned every minute of the day into suffering until the evening meal with Karsten, his wife and Reidar's two grandchildren. She thought of the change that had taken place when Reidar came home and everyone was sitting at the table. She thought of her own role during the meal, how she had succeeded in swallowing the shame, the nervousness, and at the same time how she had managed to grow herself a shell – not a single anxious glance at her husband, not a quiver of her hands. Her mind began to wander and she thought of her time together with Reidar, of twenty-five years of her life married to a man she knew she didn't truly understand. Reidar, who had been married before, who had been a widower when they met, a widower with a son who was not much younger than herself. She thought of the twenty-five years she had shared with her husband, and she concluded that these years had not in fact brought them any closer on an emotional level. The telephone conversation, his monologue, had been a demand for subordination. And the fact that she had dutifully played her role on that evening, converting the subordination into practice, meant that she now experienced a tiny, but very frightening, thought about her own life. For even though it was not the first time she had wondered if she had made a mistake accepting Reidar's proposal twenty-five years ago, this was the first time she had thought that the years had been a total waste. The very idea of choosing a wasted life was so scary that she rejected it outright. However, although she somehow managed to repress the notion, something followed in its wake and made her very nervous as she lay waiting for sleep to overtake her. It was the fact that she was becoming aware of how little she knew about herself. Lying there, listening to the sounds in the house, to Reidar passing to and fro outside her bedroom, and his distant mumble on the telephone, she had a panic attack. The attack brought on a cold sweat; she tossed around in bed and bit into the pillow in desperation. Her physical anxiety was so strong that she got out of bed straightaway, slunk into the bathroom and took an Apodorm sleeping tablet.

Although the physical unease continued to bother her, at some point she fell asleep and heard nothing until she awoke with a start – she had no idea what woke her, just that there had been *something*.

It was night outside. The doziness caused by the sleeping pill lay like a heavy cloud over her temples while her body was tense with fear. The experience of two dissimilar states – crippling fear and wakefulness (she was not capable of experiencing either of them fully) – filled her with an oppressive feeling of nausea somewhere in the pit of her stomach. She lay still fearing *whatever it was* that had woken her. She lay rigid, stone still, not daring to move. She didn't dare to move her head because she sensed that *someone* was in the room. *Someone* might hear her breathing. *Someone* might hear the duvet rustle if she moved.

If only it weren't so cold, she thought, and stiffened even more. The air she was inhaling was ice-cold. The air in the bedroom should not be so cold. With infinite care, trying not to make a sound, she turned her head. And then she saw two things: the bedroom door was open, and Reidar was not in his bed. The light from the room outside fell through the open doorway forming a broad, grey trapezium of shadow across the floor and the end of Reidar's bed; the eerie, shadowy light further revealed that Reidar's duvet was as neat and untouched as when she had fallen asleep.

He had not been to bed at all. This had never happened before. If Ingrid had been paralysed with fear until now, from this moment she sank into an even worse, even more acute, physical state, a state which caused a cold sweat to break out and her fingers to feel like stiff, insensate lumps of wood. As her eyes feverishly scanned the room, there was a part of her hovering above her body. A part of her saw herself lying in bed, as rigid as a pole, with wild eyes. The same part of her observed her body beginning to sit up. *What are you doing?* said this part of her. *Are you crazy?* But her body was not listening. With infinite slowness she raised herself, petrified that she would make a sound, that *someone* would hear what she was doing. Her eyelids were heavy; her brain was still numb from the sleeping tablet. For two or three seconds this nightmare still felt dream-like. If her heart had not been pounding in her body, so out of control, she would have turned over and gone back to sleep, sedated. But that didn't happen. What happened was she that she sat up and swung her legs onto the floor. Despite her sluggish state, she felt the cool air in the room brush against her nightdress, penetrate the fibres of the material and spread a light shiver through her body. And the instant her feet met the wooden floorboards, she received a new shock. Her bare foot encountered something chill and damp. The floor was wet. And as though she were being charged with power from a generator – still outside herself – she saw her long forefinger reach for the switch on the bedside table lamp. A dry click and the lamp came on, casting a warm, yellow light over the brown, mahogany table and around the bed. There was a white patch on the floor, a small puddle of water with snow in the middle. It was the type of mess left by someone coming in from outdoors with snow on their shoes.

The snow came off and after a while began to melt because the temperature was higher indoors. Now, at this moment, as her brain struggled because her senses were still dulled by the strong medication, she realized what must have woken her up. *Someone*, a person, had tiptoed in and stood over her bed, watching her as she slept. It must have been Reidar. But where was he now?

She stood up and staggered through the doorway into the bathroom. She stared at the front door, which was wide open – an open door letting in the cold air from the stairs and making the flat cold. She closed the door. As the door clicked into place, the thought struck her that perhaps she was not alone.

She scoured the darkened flat through the open door. The idea of venturing through the door and into the darkness was repellent.

She turned uneasily to the telephone on the low table and caught a glimpse of herself in the mirror. A pale figure with lifeless eyes. She slumped down on the stool beside the mirror and allowed her fingers to tap in a number she knew by heart. It rang and rang. In the end it was Susanne who answered.

She whispered into the mouthpiece: 'Could you ask Karsten to come over? Reidar is not here and I think there has been a break-in.'

'Is there anyone in your flat?'

'Not sure, but the doors are open. I was woken up. You must ask Karsten to come!'

'But Karsten isn't here!'

'Isn't he?'

'No.' The silence hung in the air. She didn't know

what to say. It was Susanne who ought to say something, who ought to explain why Karsten wasn't at home in bed with his wife. But Susanne said nothing, and Ingrid couldn't bring herself to ask about that of all things. She was confused. The numbing tiredness caused by the pill was making her mind function in slow motion. 'Can you come then, Susanne? I'm so scared.'

'The children are sleeping.'

The silence that persisted now, after the woman's answer, oppressed Ingrid still further. She raised her head and looked round at the darkened flat where danger lurked. She cleared her throat and whispered: 'Can't you wake them up and come here?'

'Ingrid.' Susanne's voice was more awake now. 'What are you going on about? A break-in? Have you been having nightmares?'

'No,' Ingrid snapped, peering over her shoulder in panic – because this conversation was unpleasant and because someone might be listening to her. *Someone . . .* 'I have not been having nightmares. Would you wake Karsten so that I can talk to him?'

'Karsten's not here, I said.'

'You're lying.'

Ingrid instantly regretted her outburst. But it was too late. Susanne's voice was as cold as ice as she articulated her response with slow emphasis: 'No, I'm not, you hysterical old bag. I am not lying and Karsten is not here. I cannot run around like a flunkey for you. I have two children here and they need all the sleep they can get. If you're so frightened, get dressed, switch on the radio and make yourself a cup of tea which you . . .'

'Susanne, don't ring off!'

' . . . which you can drink until Reidar gets back. Goodbye.'

She was standing with her back to the wall and the receiver in her hand. Annoying engaged signals were coming from it. Her eyes glazed over and she took a step forward so as not to lose her balance.

At that moment there was a bang.

It was a door slamming on the floor below.

It had to be Reidar. He was downstairs in the shop. She took another step and listened. There were footsteps downstairs. It had to be Reidar. Then there were footsteps on the staircase. Slow, heavy footsteps. She concentrated. Was his walk that heavy? *Dear God*, she thought. *Let it be Reidar.* And now someone was coming up the stairs. The footsteps came closer and stopped. Outside her door.

PART TWO

A Man in a Window

9

Frozen in Motion

'It's me.' The loud, clear telephone voice of Police Inspector Gunnarstranda cut through the quiet winter-morning air. There was that hint of tetchiness that Frank Frølich had learned to treat with forbearance.

'Right,' he answered, pressing the mobile phone to his ear and tightening his scarf as the cold snow swept across the bridge and held him in its grip again. 'Frogner Park,' he explained. His fingers were frozen. He squeezed the phone tight and buried both it and his hand deeper in the scarf. 'I've just crossed the bridge over the lake,' he added, walking down the last avenue, leading to the metal gate and Kirkeveien. He blinked. The contrasts became clear in the light of the morning sun which hung low and was blinding. In the park, where Oslo Highways' salting lorries never came, the snow was still white, not greyish-brown and compressed as it was everywhere else in town.

'I'm on foot, of course,' Frølich continued laconically. He knew that at this very minute his boss would be fidgeting with a cigarette, walking around in circles out of agitation because Gunnarstranda never knew how to control the stream of energy that was surging through his limbs. Frølich knew that Gunnarstranda would not be in the slightest bit interested in the fact that he had slept at Eva-Britt's – yesterday was Friday and after a huge, painful row he had felt obliged to spend the night with her – or that he had accepted a wager with Eva-Britt's daughter, Julie, that he would lose five kilos before the winter holidays, a bet that he intended to win, for the simple reason that he was sick of the girl's bully-ing. He had also decided to walk to work every day in the belief that walking in the freezing cold accelerated calorie consumption, so the colder the better. Frølich's personal experience of Vigeland's sculptures in the morning sun would have not have interested his boss, either. Frank liked to contemplate the rigid statues that seemed to have been frozen in motion, either throwing or wrestling. He seemed to be moving in a surrealistic landscape of forms, particularly because the low temper-atures gave the frozen-metaphor an extra subtlety on a day like this.

'We have a body,' Gunnarstranda said.

'Where?'

'Turn right at the metal gate, toddle down Thomas Heftyes gate and you'll see us.'

And then the line went dead. It was so cold that his nostrils were stuck together. Frølich buried the lower half of his face under the thick woollen scarf; his breath formed condensation and left tiny beads of ice on the wool. He felt like a wandering tree trunk in his thick woollen jumper, thick jacket and long johns under his trousers. On his feet he wore army boots which squeaked at every step he took on the hard-packed snow.

Ten minutes later, after turning down Thomas Heftyes gate, he found the road almost deserted. There were very few curious onlookers, which could have been for a number of reasons: the cold; the late onset of daylight in January; or the fact that a swarm of police cars in front of a building does not necessarily interest the better inhabitants of West Oslo early on a Saturday morning.

Frank Frølich walked past Inspector Gunnarstranda's new Skoda Octavia and wriggled his way through the road blocks, but came to an involuntary halt at the sight of the body in the shop window. The dead man was naked, a white body sitting in an armchair – between an old wooden globe and a light blue chest covered with faded decorative flowers. A woman in white overalls was busy covering the window with grey paper. Through a covered section of the window Frank could make out the outline of Inspector Gunnarstranda's face. They nodded to each other and Gunnarstranda's glasses caught the morning sun.

The front door was still closed. A sign with yellowish-white plastic letters on a blue felt background gave the opening times. The shop was closed on Saturdays.

Frølich followed the flow of forensics officers towards the staircase, where he found the back door into the shop open. The room inside was no longer warm. The constant traffic in and out caused the breath of all those inside to freeze. Uniformed police and forensics officers in white nylon suits were going through the premises with a fine-tooth comb. Gunnarstranda was crouched in front of the low shop window studying the body in the chair.

A woman was briefing him: 'The chair hasn't moved,' she said, pointing. 'It's been on display for a good while, I suppose. Someone dragged the body from over there

. . .' She pointed to the back of the room. '. . . and put him on show here.'

'One or more?' Gunnarstranda asked.

'Impossible to say.'

'But could a single person have done this?'

The woman just shrugged. 'Haven't the slightest.'

The woman and Frank Frølich exchanged looks. He hadn't seen her for three weeks when she had slept at his place.

They lowered their eyes, both of them, at the same time.

'But you must have an idea,' grunted Gunnarstranda with irritation.

She stared into space, giving herself time to think.

'Hi, Anna,' Frank said. She looked up, and again they had eye contact for two seconds, which was at once picked up by Gunnarstranda and occasioned an angry shake of the head.

'Yes, I do,' Anna said quickly, and added: 'It could have been one person, could have been more. In fact, it is impossible to say much more than that at the present moment.'

Gunnarstranda got to his feet.

A dramatic lock of Anna's hair stuck out from under the white hood, bisecting her forehead and giving her a passionate, Mediterranean appearance.

Frølich looked away and concentrated on the corpse, the shop window, the coagulated blood down the chair leg and the dark stain on the carpet. He tried to imagine the shock he himself would have had if he had been passing by at daybreak. But for the blood, the dead man would have looked like a papier mâché figure. His skin was white, and something akin to frost had settled in the wrinkles and hollows of the body. 'Well, a decent age,' Frølich mumbled, studying the dead man's mask-like face.

'Seventy-nine years old – according to his bank card,' Anna said, a hundred per cent formal now.

'A cut?' Frølich asked, pointing to a red stripe around the dead man's neck.

'Took me in, too,' Gunnarstranda said. 'But it's thread.'

Frank realized at that moment: red cotton tightened around the man's neck.

'Graffiti on the forehead?' Frølich asked.

'Crosses,' Anna said. 'Put there with a pen.' She turned around and indicated a small cylindrical object on the shop floor. 'Probably that one – it's an indelible pen and the right colour.'

Gunnarstranda nodded and once again turned to the corpse, pointing. Frølich followed his boss's gaze, to the blood-stained chest area. Someone had written numbers and letters in blue on the dead man's chest – in the middle between the nipples, which were both covered in bushy hair.

Gunnarstranda stood up. 'That's what we need to look at when they do the autopsy.'

Frølich's eye fell on the wooden globe and the misshapen carving of Africa. Large swathes of the African continent were unlabelled.

Gunnarstranda walked between the tables and chairs with Frølich behind him. 'Antiques,' Frølich muttered, pointing to a red upholstered chair, and called out to Anna: 'Can I touch this?'

She looked up. 'Nice to see you again,' she whispered and disappeared through the door to the little office.

Frølich couldn't think of anything to say.

Gunnarstranda yawned out loud. 'I'm tired now,' he mumbled. 'Yttergjerde,' he shouted to a uniformed officer leaning against a door frame at the back of the shop. Yttergjerde shuffled over.

'Tell Frølich our thoughts about a break-in,' Gunnarstranda said.

Yttergjerde shook his head. 'No alarm activated, no window panes smashed, not a single mark on the woodwork around the doors – on top of that, nothing seems to have been stolen.' He nodded towards the counter by the door leading to the street. 'Wallet intact in his jacket, cash till untouched.'

Frølich went over to the cash till. It was one of the antique variety with a pattern hammered into the metal and a jungle of buttons and levers at the front.

Yttergjerde was a man with unusually long arms and large hands. He pointed a big, fat finger: 'Two doors,' he went on. 'The front door beside the shop window over there is pretty secure. There's a security grille in front.' Yttergjerde pointed to the second door: 'That way leads to the staircase. It was unlocked when we arrived.'

Gunnarstranda pulled out a roll-up from his coat pocket and began to fiddle with it. Frølich noticed that it had been fiddled with before; it was disintegrating.

Yttergjerde went towards them. 'There was one thing I forgot to say,' he mumbled. 'A woman who delivers newspapers discovered the body. She's wondering if she can go.'

Yttergjerde indicated a motionless figure with spikey hair and a fringe above a pair of glasses as round as saucers. She was standing with her hands buried deep in the pockets of a ski suit.

'Take her name and address,' Gunnarstranda said curtly.

'The old boy – the corpse – Reidar Folke Jespersen owned the shop,' Yttergjerde whispered. 'He and the woman . . . his missus . . .' he gestured to the ceiling. 'They live in the flat.' He flicked his head back. 'The floor above.'

Gunnarstranda nodded pensively. 'Priest?'

'Came half an hour ago and is still up there,' Yttergjerde nodded.

'The woman . . .' Yttergjerde continued to whisper; '. . . Her face went grey with shock. She had to lie down, but that was before the priest came.'

Yttergjerde joined the woman who had found the body.

Frølich yawned and went for a walk to look for Anna. Eventually he found her. She was coming out of the little office at the back of the shop.

'Yes?' she said.

'Nice to see you again, too,' Frank said, feeling foolish.

She looked at him askance. 'Interested in the crime scene?' she asked with a faint smile.

'Yes, of course.'

'Keep your ears open,' she grinned, and grimaced as Gunnarstranda's brusque voice carried from the little

63

office. 'Frølich!'

'Yes?'

'Here,' Gunnarstranda muttered with annoyance, pointing to the floor in front of the desk. The carpet had soaked up a lot of blood. Beside the blood lay a bayonet with red stains on the blade.

Frank Frølich exchanged glances with Anna before looking down at the bayonet. Not long afterwards they were interrupted by a solemn-looking uniformed police officer standing in the doorway and motioning towards Gunnarstranda. 'We have a Karsten Jespersen here,' the policeman gabbled. 'And he insists on coming in.'

The man who met them on the stairs was pale and his chin twitched; they were tics, obvious signs of a nervous affliction. He seemed to be trying to shake tiny insects off his cheek.

'Gunnarstranda,' the policeman said by way of introduction, leaning his head back to survey the man. 'Police Inspector, Murder Squad.'

Karsten Jespersen was wearing a corduroy suit under a winter coat. He was tall and lean, thinning on top, with a small, narrow mouth and an obvious receding chin, which seemed to disappear in a concertina of wrinkles and folds of skin every time his body recoiled from the periodic convulsions of his lower face.

'Well,' the policeman said, looking around the narrow stairwell. 'Is there somewhere we can sit?' he asked.

Karsten Jespersen composed himself and nodded towards the office door in the shop. 'We have an office in there.'

Inspector Gunnarstranda sadly shook his head. 'I'm afraid we cannot allow anyone to enter the crime scene.'

Jespersen stood staring at him, puzzled.

'I understand your father lived in this building?'

Karsten Jespersen looked up at the stairs, as though considering something. 'I suppose you can come with me,' he said at last, and forged ahead. The footsteps of the three men marching upstairs resounded between the walls. On reaching the landing, Jespersen ransacked his pockets for keys. 'Just a moment,' he murmured. 'You see . . .' At last he found a bunch of keys, pulled them out and fumbled for the right key: 'Ingrid, my father's wife – I've had a few words with her on the phone.'

Frølich sent an understanding nod to Jespersen, who disappeared into the flat, closing the door behind him with care. The landing was about three metres broad. Originally there had been two doors leading into two flats, but door number two had been closed off. There was no door handle and it was painted the same colour as the walls. An ailing green plant in a terracotta pot had been placed in the recess in front of the door.

'The whole floor to themselves,' Frølich mumbled.

'The widow – Ingrid – must have broken down,' Gunnarstranda mumbled in a low voice.

Then Karsten Jespersen appeared in the doorway. 'Come in,' he mumbled softly, as though frightened someone would hear him. 'There's a lady from the medical centre here, and the priest. But we won't be disturbed in my old room.' He held the door open and gave an embarrassed cough. 'Would you mind taking off your boots?'

Gunnarstranda unzipped his old snow over-boots and shook them off. Under them he was wearing polished leather shoes. He stood and watched Frølich breathing hard as he knelt down in his thick winter gear. With tangled hair hanging over his forehead, he loosened the laces of his army boots, pulled them off and revealed two odd woollen socks. Jespersen opened the door and they could hear low voices in the distance.

Gunnarstranda took stock. A mirror dominated the hallway. It went from floor to ceiling, in a gilt wooden frame. There were patches where the surface was flaking off. The mirror reflected three framed photographs adorning the facing wall. Gunnarstranda turned to study the pictures. They were photographs of erect young men in canvas and frieze breeches with bold curls over their foreheads and Sten guns hanging loose from their shoulders. 'The Palace Square . . . liberation,' Gunnarstranda said to the man in the door. 'Anyone from the family there?'

Karsten Jespersen nodded. 'My father,' he said, pointing to a young athlete standing at ease in front of the Royal Palace.

Gunnarstranda studied the photograph. 'Of course,' he said, taking off his glasses to inspect the man's features close up. 'I can see that now.'

'Shall we . . .?' Jespersen held the door open.

They padded through a room furnished with heavy wooden furniture and beyond to a sliding door which the young man opened. They went through another room, past a huge dining room table. On the wall was a large painting with a national-romantic motif: a fjord, shafts of sunlight shining down on the mountains and a farm where a dairy maid dressed in national costume was carrying buckets slung from a yoke over her shoulders.

The man in the corduroy suit led them on to a further sliding door. He hesitated before opening it, turned towards them and cleared his throat: 'Well, here – is where I grew up.'

Gunnarstranda followed Jespersen in. The room was three metres by three metres, a cross between a boy's room and a bachelor's pad. There was a desk beneath the window along one wall. A sofa bed was the other item of furniture in the room. Family photographs on the wall above it. Jespersen sat on the swivel chair by the desk. 'Please, do sit down,' he said, indicating the low sofa.

Gunnarstranda stayed on his feet.

Frølich had to stoop to avoid hitting his head on the door frame when he joined them. The room seemed cramped all of a sudden. Frølich's jacket, doubtless size XXL, stuck to him like a boy's blazer on a wine barrel. The face hiding behind the bedraggled beard was, as always, a model of expressionless composure. He was wearing a striped sweater under the jacket. He slumped down onto the sofa. When he crossed his legs, his feet collided with the wall opposite.

Gunnarstranda stared at Frølich, then at Karsten Jespersen.

'Fire away,' Jespersen said in a low whisper of a voice.

The Inspector turned, made a show of stepping over Frølich's denim-clad legs and marched out through the door and back to the dining room from where he shouted: 'Has the family lived here long?'

'As long as I can remember,' Jespersen answered, getting up with alacrity and going to the door. 'Since some time in the fifties.' He eyed the detective nervously: 'Don't you want to come in here?'

'No,' Gunnarstranda answered. He stood contemplating the large painting with the motifs of fjord and milkmaid. The picture frame was broad and gilt with carvings. He turned and took a chair from the table. 'I'll sit here; you sit in there – so that we can shout to each other.'

Jespersen stood in the doorway. His face had taken on a sad expression. The continuous nervous twitches around his jaw made his chin tremble.

'What do you do?' the policeman asked.

'I run the shop – downstairs.'

'And your father?'

'He takes – took care of the administrative side.'

'And that means?'

'Accounts, budget – we have a warehouse . . .'

'Go on,' Gunnarstranda said, composed, as the other man fell into a reverie.

'Yes, we have the shop here and, in Ensjø, a warehouse and an office.'

'I'd like to take a look at the warehouse.'

'No problem. It's in Bertrand Narvesens vei.'

Gunnarstranda nodded slowly. 'But I could do with a key,' he thought out loud.

Jespersen gave a start. 'Now?'

'Have you any objection to me searching the place?'

'Of course not.' Jespersen let go of the door frame, shrugged his shoulders and crossed the floor. He sat down on one of the chairs by the table, with his back to the painting and opposite the policeman. He rummaged through his pockets, pulled out the bunch of keys and found a short Yale key, which he took off the ring. 'You just have to unlock . . .'

Gunnarstranda accepted the key and put it in his pocket. 'And you sell antiques, second-hand goods?'

Jespersen gave a deep sigh, rested his temples on both hands and sat with his head bowed and his eyes fixed firmly on the table. 'This is just so awful,' he said at length. 'I seem to be wading through cotton wool. I ought to have checked if anything had been stolen downstairs . . .'

'You can do that when we've done . . .'

Jespersen, bewildered, stared back. His head quivered until he lowered his gaze, discovered a stain on the polished table and rubbed it with his forefinger. 'The one thing I know for sure is that he's dead,' he murmured.

'He was killed,' Gunnarstranda said. 'It's our job to determine the facts of the case,' he added after reflection, and cleared his throat. 'But you and your family will of course be kept fully informed.' He straightened his back and crossed his legs.

Frank Frølich had managed to struggle out of the cramped boy's room and joined them now. He settled carefully into a seat at the table, wriggled out of his enormous jacket and took out his notebook.

Gunnarstranda inclined his head and said: 'It makes everything much harder for the bereaved when sad news has to be followed by a criminal investigation. But I hope you and your family will have some understanding of our role in this.'

Karsten, faraway, nodded.

Gunnarstranda cleared his throat. 'What branch are you in?'

'How do you mean?'

'What kind of antiques do you sell?'

'Exclusive items for the most part.'

'And that means?'

'They don't have to be a special style or design. It's all about the object as such, whether it's in good condition, whether it has appeal. It might be a Remington typewriter from the 1920s or a well-preserved tea table from Victorian times. We judge each case on its merits . . .'

Gunnarstranda nodded. 'What about books?'

'No.'

'I saw Thackeray on one of the shelves we were passing.'

Jespersen indulged himself in a little gesture. 'You saw them? That was observant. Yes, indeed,' he nodded. 'But the books in this house are Ingrid's. She's fond of reading. In general, though, we do not deal with books . . . there is no money in them – for us at least. We're not running an antiquarian bookshop.'

'How do you acquire your objects?'

'Buying job lots, auctions . . . importing . . . well . . . brokering might be a more precise term. We're in the upmarket sector.'

'And that is?'

'What?' Jespersen said, puzzled.

'What is the upmarket sector?'

'Could be anything, in fact. We are just as likely to stock goods from England or Germany as from

Gudbrandsdalen.'

'What about exports?'

'Nothing.'

'How old was your father?'

'Seventy-nine. He would have been eighty in March.'

'And he enjoyed rude health?'

'Oh yes – like a man of fifty, working every day.'

'Fit man.'

Karsten Jespersen pursed his lips in a sardonic grimace. 'You could say that.'

'Had he any plans for slowing down?'

'No.'

The answer was forthright. Without qualification. The two policemen exchanged glances.

'A family business?'

'You could say that.'

'Is his death a loss to the operation?'

'Of course.'

'Who buys the goods for the shop? You? Your father?'

'I do.'

'You alone?'

Karsten Jespersen inclined his head and added: 'It goes without saying that he was involved in the buying, but he always consulted me. By and large, I get on well with customers. That was more or less how we divided the work.'

'What sort of man was your father?'

Jespersen raised his head and sent him a quizzical look.

Gunnarstranda gestured with his hands: 'Was he a kind man? A firm man? Someone with enemies?'

'Of course not.'

'Did he have any enemies?'

'None that I can think of, offhand.'

'Anyone at loggerheads with your father?'

'Several people – even I was at loggerheads with him in a way.'

'How?'

'It was his nature. You know, the type who always wanted the last word.'

'In private too?'

'In private and in business.'

'What's your position now? Will you take over?'

'I would assume so – the shop is a limited company, and so from an administrative point of view the settlement of a deceased's estate has less significance.' He coughed. 'But I'm the only person who can run the shop – who can run it,' he mumbled, repeating himself and gazing into the air, lost in thought.

'What did you think about your father not wanting to retire?'

'You're wondering if he didn't have full confidence in me?' Karsten forced a wry grin.

Gunnarstranda did not answer.

'You could look at it like that,' the other man said. 'Part of the picture has to do with me. I'm tied to the business – but I also have a sideline to take care of . . .' He coughed with embarrassment. 'I'm trying to do a bit of writing – freelance – and that takes time.'

'Freelance?'

'I write small articles for weeklies . . . now and then I try my hand at short stories, too. That sort of thing requires time and dedication.'

'Do you write under your own name?'

'Yes, I do.'

'So you were happy that your father was still going strong and didn't retire?'

Jespersen sighed. 'What can I say? Of course he made a valuable contribution, but I suppose he should have done something else.' He hesitated. 'People in their latter years should – rest, enjoy life in other ways – but not him; I think he was happy, I mean . . . he enjoyed rude health, as you put it.'

Gunnarstranda nodded his head slowly.

'No one would have dreamt of asking him to retire,' Jespersen added. 'He loved working.'

'Can you put a name to anyone who was at logger-heads with your father?'

'It would be easier to put a name to those who weren't. My father was determined and . . . stubborn.' Jespersen found the word he was searching for.

'So your father was difficult, quarrelsome?'

'I would prefer to say he was a resolute person. A strong person. Forgive me, but it feels odd to talk about him in this way.'

'He lived in this flat, together with your mother?'

Jespersen nodded and scowled with embarrassment. 'She isn't my mother; she's my father's wife.'

'Your mother? Is she alive?'

'No . . . She died when I was small,' he added when the police officers said nothing. 'Dad married Ingrid more than twenty years ago, and, in fact, she is only seven years older than me. I'm sure you will understand that your mention of Ingrid as my mother sounds odd.'

'Have you any brothers or sisters?'

Jespersen shook his head.

'So you're the sole heir?'

'Ingrid will inherit as well, of course, and the benefici-aries in the will, if there are any.'

'But you don't know anything about that?'

'About what?'

'About whether he wrote a will.'

'I don't think he did. At any rate, I haven't heard any-thing about a will. But I can give you the telephone num-ber of the solicitor he used. She should know.'

'Was your father a wealthy man?'

'What do you mean by wealthy?'

'Was it well known that he had money?'

Jespersen's face quivered. 'I can't believe that. He had a pension – he didn't get much of a wage. He split the profit with my two uncles – Arvid and Emmanuel. There were three owners, three brothers . . . and then there must be a bit of money in his account, this flat . . .'

'Lots of valuable objects?'

'Hmm,' Jespersen smiled, the dealer's lop-sided smile: 'Must be the odd bijou there . . .'

'The assets, or the inheritance, are basically the chat-tels in the flat and the shop then?'

'I haven't given it a lot of thought . . .'

'But don't you have some idea of your father's assets?'

'Well . . . I would assume the assets are the flat and the chattels, as you call them, a bit of art and, well – money in various bank accounts.'

The policeman changed the subject: 'We understood

that the first thing Ingrid Jespersen did, after confirming the dead man's identity, was to ring you?'

'Yes. I came here as soon as I could.'

Gunnarstranda nodded slowly.

'She rang us earlier in the night as well.' Jespersen put on an apologetic smile. 'Ingrid wanted to get hold of me – in fact. She woke up when she realized Dad was not in his bed. Her first thought was that there was a break-in downstairs, in the shop, that is. But Susanne, my wife, calmed her down. Then she went back to sleep.'

Gunnarstranda observed him and summarized what the man had just said: 'She woke up on her own last night, rang to speak to you, but talked to your wife, who sent her back to bed. What time was it when she rang?'

'Half past two.'

Gunnarstranda stared into space. 'We're going to talk to fru Jespersen about these events too, but why did she ring you in the middle of the night?'

'There's been a spate of burglaries around here. In fact we have . . .' Jespersen heaved a deep sigh '. . . been waiting for something like this.'

Gunnarstranda coughed. 'For what?'

'Break-ins.'

The two policemen eyed him.

Karsten Jespersen tentatively cleared his throat.

Gunnarstranda waited a bit longer before asking: 'Have you put any specific measures in place in the shop to prevent burglaries?'

'We have the obligatory security shutters in the windows facing the street, and of course we have an alarm. I suppose what was new was Dad doing his occasional

75

round of inspection.'

'No alarm went off last night.'

'No,' Jespersen said after some hesitation.

'Where do you think your father was when Ingrid woke up alone?'

'That's pretty obvious, isn't it? He was downstairs.' Jespersen tapped the tip of his forefinger on the table. 'Downstairs, in the shop.'

'In the middle of the night?'

'Of course.'

'But wouldn't it be unusual for your father to be rushing around downstairs in the middle of the night. After all, he was almost eighty.'

'My father was an unusual person.'

Gunnarstranda nodded, deep in thought. At length he looked over at Karsten Jespersen, who was staring blankly into the air. 'Where were you?' the policeman enquired.

'Hm?'

'Where were you when Ingrid phoned last night?'

Jespersen was still staring blankly into the air. 'It's quite odd,' he said in a soft voice. 'My father's dead in the room beneath us. Not easy to disentangle, my feelings I mean, grief and bereavement . . .' He went quiet, took a deep breath, then heaved a sigh and continued: 'Ingrid, my father's wife, here with a priest. Me, sitting here with the police – round the table where we had dinner yesterday, having a nice time, and now sitting here and trying – not just to recall the image of my father, but to pass this image on to you.'

He folded his hands on the table. 'I can feel an atmosphere here now – a feeling of . . . perhaps it's not hostility as such, perhaps it's more a business-like efficiency. But what is dawning on me now is that while I have been trying to determine what it is I feel deep down, in the chaos I have within me, what I have been dreading, as long as we have been talking is precisely that question: *Where were you?* Where was I? All of a sudden the answer to that question has taken on a sort of meaning, a significance, the impact of which I had never imagined.'

He went quiet. The policemen exchanged glances. Jespersen sat chewing his lower lip and thinking. He didn't give the impression that he was going to continue.

Gunnarstranda broke the silence. He coughed, which caused the other man to raise his head. 'Where were you?' the policeman repeated, looking him straight in the eye.

'I was at home. It wasn't the first time we had received calls of this kind. Susanne knew that Ingrid would have nagged and nagged to haul me out of bed and come here. Ingrid is a little highly strung and besides she has a morbid fear of something happening to my father.'

'Did you hear the phone?'

'No. I was asleep.'

'So you didn't discuss Ingrid's call then – afterwards?'

'No, that is, we talked about it early this morning.'

'But, your wife, she wasn't alarmed by Ingrid's fears when she called last night. Did she dismiss them as nonsense?'

'Of course not, but Ingrid was . . . Ingrid is . . . she's a little hysterical at times.'

Gunnarstranda nodded. 'Do you know if your father

had been receiving threats from anyone of late?'

'No, that is . . .'

'Yes?'

Jespersen laid both hands flat on the table. 'It's a somewhat delicate matter,' he started.

Gunnarstranda nodded politely.

'We had a man in Ensjø – who worked at the warehouse. A man who was with us for as long as I can remember – Jonny.'

'Jonny – what?'

'His name is Jonny Stokmo. Something happened a few weeks ago. I don't know what it was. Something happened which led to my father dismissing him on the spot.'

'He was given the boot?'

'Jonny had to leave that day, after being employed, well, for years.'

'So this antagonism is quite recent?'

'I've no idea. Neither of them would talk about it. But I assume it must have been very serious and very private. Otherwise, I would have known what happened.'

'Did Stokmo come to you about this?'

'No.'

There was a long silence until Jespersen continued: 'That was why I thought this state of affairs – the row – was a private matter, between them. Otherwise I would have known what it was about.'

'Do you know if Stokmo threatened your father?'

'No. All I know is that Jonny was standing outside the front door last night.'

'When?'

'Half an hour before my father came home at seven.'

Gunnarstranda nodded slowly to himself.

'Seven p.m.?' Frølich asked with raised pen.

'Bit later, about a quarter past.'

'What is Stokmo living off now?' Gunnarstranda asked.

'I don't know . . . he has a son who runs a kind of workshop in Torshov. He might be working there.'

Silence fell again. Frank Frølich cleared his throat. He flicked through his notebook. 'You say . . .' he mumbled. 'You say your father had guests here yesterday. Who were they?'

'It wasn't a party. It was dinner. We were invited, I mean, me, my wife and the children.'

'How long were you here?'

'Well, it began just after seven. My father arrived late, at about a quarter past. We went home at around eleven.'

'Where had he been until seven in the evening?'

'In Ensjø, at the office.'

'Are you sure?'

'Yes, he was seldom anywhere else.'

'Did he usually work late?'

'He was always working.'

'So it wasn't unusual for him to work late?' Gunnarstranda asked.

'It was neither usual nor unusual. He did work late on occasion. But Ingrid can tell you more about this sort of thing than I can.'

Gunnarstranda sat staring, in silence. 'Do you stock a lot of weapons in this shop?'

'A few. And that's one of the most important reasons

for having security shutters. Antique weapons are sought-after collectors' items.'

'What sort of weapons?'

'A musket, a halberd, a few front-loading revolvers, a variety of edged weapons . . .'

'A bayonet?'

'Two. Why?'

They were interrupted as a door was thrust open and a patter of feet followed. A small boy came running in. He must have been three or four years old, wearing blue dungarees and a jumper with stains down the front. He came to a sudden halt at the sight of the people around the table, but after a few moments' hesitation marched up to Karsten Jespersen, who stared at him in bewilderment. The boy had blond curls and a round, open face with a runny nose. He stuffed several fingers from his left hand in his mouth as he pressed against his father's knee. 'Grandad's dead,' he told Gunnarstranda.

'Looks like Susanne has come, too,' Jespersen said in apology and turned to the boy: 'Where's Mummy?'

The little boy ignored him. He lifted his right arm to shake hands with Gunnarstranda. 'Min,' said the little boy.

'Benjamin,' Jespersen said, winking at the policeman.

'*Just* Min,' the boy called Benjamin said, wafting his hand in front of Gunnarstranda again.

'Show me,' the father said. 'Have you got a coin?' Jespersen's smile was stiff, strained, and he held out an authoritative hand. 'Are you going to give Daddy the coin?'

'Grandad's dead,' the boy repeated, turning to his father with great big, round eyes. 'All dead.'

'Yes,' Jespersen said, winking conspiratorially at the two policemen. 'Are you going to let Daddy see your coin?'

The boy shook his head.

'Are you going to show Daddy?'

'No,' said the boy.

'I think we've finished for the time being,' Gunnarstranda said, addressing Frank Frølich.

'Are you going to give Daddy the coin?'

'No!' the boy screamed with a voice that cut through the air like the whine of a saw.

The look in Jespersen's eyes was ominous. 'Are you going to give Daddy the coin?' He made another grab at the little boy's hand.

'No!' the boy cried with the same piercing scream. 'Daddy's stupid.'

'The coin!' his father repeated sharply, grabbing the little boy's hand and forcing his fingers open, one by one. The boy struggled. His fingers were white and he was crying. His hand lurched. Something like a brooch or a hatpin shot out of his hand onto the floor.

'Shhh now,' Jespersen said and was all smiles again. 'It wasn't a coin, was it! It wasn't money!'

Karsten Jespersen took the badge and held it up in front of Benjamin. It was made of dark metal with an elaborate motif. The boy had stopped crying. He rubbed his eyes.

The two policemen looked at each other.

'Give me,' said the boy and made a grab for the badge. The father withdrew his hand as quick as lightning and laughed aloud, making his chin twitch.

The boy let out another squeal.

'Take it then,' the father yelled in irritation, giving him the badge.

The boy burst into a low whine and took it.

'Shall we go?' Karsten Jespersen said and stood up.

On the way out Gunnarstranda stopped in front of a large glass cabinet displaying the spines of blue and brown leather-bound books. Jespersen was courteous enough to stop and wait. The little boy ran out through the nearest door.

Frølich also stood and gazed at a number of small, white figures in a glass case on the wall. At first he thought it was the usual ornaments, but he had a shock when he saw what the figures were doing. It was Chinese and pornographic: men and women embroiled in sexual games, carved with infinite care. But it did not stop there: a woman was enthusiastically copulating with a zebra; another woman was having sex with a turtle. One of the carvings was of two grinning men coiled up and posing as they masturbated each other. The figures left nothing to the imagination and were carved with an intricacy of detail that Frølich had never seen before.

'My God,' he mumbled.

Karsten Jespersen sent him a condescending look. 'Collectors' items,' he sighed and added: 'Ivory. One, by the way, is made of rhino horn.'

'Are they antiques?'

'Of course.' Jespersen went to the cabinet and pointed

to the woman and the turtle. 'That one is a thousand years old.'

Frankie looked at him. Jespersen was standing with his arms folded on his chest and had an impatient expression on his quivering face.

'What do these things symbolize?' the policeman asked.

'I beg your pardon?'

'The symbolism,' Frank Frølich enquired.

Jespersen splayed his palms. 'It's art. They don't have any significance.'

'But these motifs,' Frølich insisted, pointing to the woman and the turtle. 'They must symbolize something.'

Jespersen, irritated: 'They don't have any significance. Either you think they're beautiful, or you don't.'

Frank studied the figurines again. There was no doubting that they were beautiful. The sexuality was portrayed in a humorous way, emphasizing the aesthetics of the human body – however fanciful the sexual act. The ornament that Jespersen had indicated was carved from rhino horn and portrayed athletes performing group sex. A number of very happy-looking people were intertwined in sexual gymnastics that, from a physiological perspective, scarcely seemed feasible. This means, he thought, I know next to nothing about China.

'Are they yours?' he asked Jespersen.

'No, they belong here, to the house.'

'Are they worth much?'

'Of course.'

'How much would you say?' He straightened up as a

middle-aged woman opened a door and entered.

'There you are,' she said to Jespersen. 'You'll have to look after your children, I can't . . .' She stopped in mid-flow when she saw the two police officers.

Gunnarstranda proffered his hand. 'Inspector Gunnarstranda. Murder Squad.'

The woman shook his hand. Frølich could see that she had been attractive once, and that she still looked good, even though her face was marked with tiny wrinkles and age lines. For a few seconds Frølich was unsure what it was that made her so appealing – the clean-cut face under the fashionable haircut or the figure and the ter-rific legs. It was the latter, he decided, her body – her back was arched like a schoolgirl's – and the dress, which was tight in the right places.

Jespersen was about to say something. But Gunnarstranda got in first: 'Ingrid Folke Jespersen?'

She nodded.

'May I offer my condolences?'

She nodded again and stared calmly into the eyes of her contemporary. Frank noticed that he did not release her hand.

Frølich stepped forward and proffered his hand: 'Frank Frølich.'

'We were just on our way out,' Inspector Gunnar-stranda said by way of reassurance. But she didn't hear what he was saying. The two policemen followed her eyes. She was staring at Karsten Jespersen and her eyes were filling. 'Karsten,' she whispered in a quiet, sorrow-filled voice. There was despair in her almost inaudible outburst. She was staring at her husband's son, who

84

stiffly returned her gaze. He was struggling to control his feelings. She let hers flow. Karsten Jespersen was at the centre of everyone's attention: the woman and the men hung on his lips as if he were going to say a timely word.

'He's jealous of your Thackeray books,' Jespersen stuttered, pointing to Gunnarstranda.

Three heads turned to the Inspector, who contemplated the widow and her stepson for a long time before he took it upon himself to bring the silence to an end. 'Right,' said Gunnarstranda, without any elaboration, angling his head towards the glass cabinet: 'I couldn't find *Barry Lyndon*.'

'I always thought the film was better,' the woman in the doorway said in response.

The dramatic silence still hung in the air. No one said anything. Everyone was looking at her. 'Well, you're right,' she said at length. '*Barry Lyndon* is missing. To Reidar's great annoyance. He was a perfectionist, you know, and could never understand that I wanted a series of books that was incomplete.'

'Have you got a couple of minutes?' the Police Inspector asked.

'Reidar had very little time for reading,' she added, seemingly lost in thought.

The silence had changed. The unspoken words and the tension between her and her stepson were no longer there.

'I don't feel like talking very much now,' Ingrid whispered. 'I'm worn out. I hardly slept last night.'

'We can come back tomorrow,' Gunnarstranda

replied. 'Just a couple of things, though. Did your husband go to bed last night?'

She shook her head. 'I woke up when I became aware that he wasn't there . . . I think. I had taken a sleeping tablet.'

'When did you go to bed?'

'Between eleven and half past.'

'You rang . . .' Gunnarstranda tossed his head towards Jespersen.

'Yes,' she said. 'Last night, when I woke up. But Karsten was not at home.'

Ingrid and Karsten Jespersen stood eyeing each other.

'I was asleep,' Karsten said at length.

'I realized,' she said. Her eyes were shiny and her lips quivered. She wanted to say more, but hesitated.

Gunnarstranda broke the silence: 'Why did you ring?'

'I panicked. Reidar wasn't here.'

The policeman studied her. 'Did you hear any noises from the shop?'

'I don't know,' she said.

Gunnarstranda let her answer hang in the air. He interlaced his fingers behind his back, but she didn't expand.

'You think you heard something?' the Inspector asked finally.

'I don't know,' she repeated, and started to concentrate on cleaning her fingernails. She had small hands; they were pale, with chunky rings on two of the fingers. The nails had once been rust-red, but now the varnish was flaking off. 'I panicked,' she added in a distant voice. 'Can't understand what got into me.'

'Why did you panic?'

'Because Reidar was nowhere around.' Her lips began to tremble again – and tears were in her dark eyes. She wiped her face with her hand.

Jespersen stepped forward and cleared his throat with authority. However, the Inspector raised his palm to restrain him.

'After you rang Karsten Jespersen did you go back to sleep?'

'No,' she said quickly. Something had happened to her. The police officer's questions about her deceased husband seemed to have caused her to lose composure. The apparent calm façade that commanded her face when she strode into the room had been translucent, like the shiny surface of a calm forest lake. Now, with the surface ruffled, you could discern the vulnerability which lay hidden beneath. 'I lay awake until the traffic started moving in the streets,' she said. 'This morning . . . early, very early, while it was still dark.' She paused and eyed her stepson, who returned her look. Frølich did not quite know how to interpret these signals between them.

'And then?' Gunnarstranda interrupted.

Ingrid Jespersen turned to him. 'Then I decided that I had just been having nightmares, that I had imagined all the sounds and everything. So then . . .'

She closed her eyes.

'Yes?'

She pointed downstairs. 'I was on the point of falling asleep when . . .'

'He was seen by a passer-by,' Gunnarstranda said. 'I was given to understand that you joined our colleague

Yttergjerde in the shop and identified your late husband.'

'Yes.'

All three of them stared at her. She was staring at a point in the distant corner of the room and scratching the varnish off her nails.

'The shop door was open,' Gunnarstranda said.

She nodded.

'Who had the keys to the shop?'

'My father and I,' Jespersen interrupted.

'I also have keys,' she said in a tired voice.

Gunnarstranda turned to the son. 'Any others?'

He reflected.

'Maybe Arvid and Emmanuel,' Ingrid Jespersen said.

Karsten reflected. 'It's possible,' he said at length. 'Yes, indeed,' he concluded. 'They definitely have keys, both of them.'

'And they are?' Gunnarstranda asked the widow.

'Reidar's two brothers,' she answered.

'Did your husband have a habit of leaving the door unlocked when he was in the shop in the evening?'

'No idea,' she said.

'When the police arrived, the shop was dark,' the policeman said. 'Did he usually switch off the lights when he was in the shop after opening hours?'

'If he had had a light on, it would have been in the office, at the back of the shop,' interjected Karsten Jespersen.

Ingrid hurried over to the armchair beside the bookcase. She sat down and vigorously adjusted the hem of her skirt which had ridden up so far that her knees were visible as she took a seat. 'The strange thing is that I knew what had happened straightaway. Since the phone calls were from the police.'

Frølich watched Jespersen. He was observing Ingrid with a fixed expression in his eyes.

'I know I'm pathetic,' she went on. 'But it was so terrible . . .' She wiped her eyes with her fingers once again and sniffed.

Jespersen's face was red – from anger, Frølich surmised, as the man asked Gunnarstranda: 'Had enough yet?'

The short policeman sent him a blank look. 'Not quite,' he said.

'I saw that he was dead,' she said. 'I don't know what I was thinking. I just wanted to get away.'

Gunnarstranda observed her. 'Thank you,' he said. 'I have to instruct you to keep anything you saw in the shop to yourself,' he said, calmly bringing things to a close.

'The same constraint of silence applies to you,' he said to Karsten Jespersen. 'It is regrettable,' the policeman said formally, 'but those are the rules. I'm afraid we will have to . . .' He paused, then said: 'We will do whatever we can not to intrude and I hope you will bear with us.'

10

Graffiti

In the autopsy room Frank Frølich was, as always, almost overpowered by the poorly ventilated air. He breathed through his mouth as he searched for a chair. In the end he gave up and joined the others scrutinizing the body of Reidar Folke Jespersen. The white corpse lay stretched out on a metal table beneath the surgical lamp. Frølich fixed his gaze on the other two, Dr Schwenke and Inspector Gunnarstranda.

'And the material around his neck?' Gunnarstranda enquired.

'Sewing thread,' Schwenke said. 'Cotton. Looks like it anyway.' In the light he held up the snipped thread with a pair of scissors and added: 'Description: red, tied in a reef knot.'

Gunnarstranda had clasped his hands behind his back and appeared transfixed, as though reading a letter from a divorce lawyer. The lab assistant took out a scalpel and sent an expectant look from the dead man to Dr Schwenke, who was putting on plastic gloves. Schwenke winked at Frølich. 'Rembrandt, isn't it? Men in black around the corpse. Just wait and in a moment I'll be pulling red tubes out of his arms.' Schwenke parted the wrinkled skin on the corpse's stomach and poked his fingers in the relatively clean cut under the right nipple. 'A single stab wound,' he muttered and ran his fingers across the other injuries. 'Otherwise, there are superficial scratches.' The wound gaped open. In the middle of the man's chest, numbers and letters had been written with a blue pen. Blood and scratches made it difficult to read the writing.

The Professor carefully scraped away the blood covering the writing. 'They look like numbers, don't they?' Schwenke said, running his fingers over one of the inscriptions. 'This squiggle is a number one. But the first symbol is a letter, J for Jørgen.'

'J one-nine-five,' Frølich read out.

'Indeed.' Schwenke was in agreement.

'A code?' Gunnarstranda wondered, resigned, and repeated: 'J one-nine-five.' To Schwenke he said: 'What about the crosses on his forehead?'

'Three crosses. And the same colour. Must be the same ink as on the chest.'

Frølich stooped over the dead man's forehead.

Schwenke straightened up. 'Same cut in the clothing which is soaked in blood. So he was killed wearing clothes,' he concluded with a wry smile, and spoke several medical terms into the Dictaphone. Thereafter he said to the policemen in a low voice: 'The graffiti was added afterwards.'

Frølich made way for the woman who was taking photographs of the dead man on the autopsy table. Schwenke was still talking into the Dictaphone.

Gunnarstranda stood with his eyes fixed on the dead man's chest. 'A code,' he mumbled to himself, rapt in thought. 'The perpetrator takes the trouble to undress the man, write the code on the body and display it in the window.'

They made way for the lab assistant who was washing the corpse.

'Satanists,' Schwenke interjected from the right. He sent Frølich a good-natured wink.

'What are you talking about now?' Gunnarstranda asked in an irritated tone.

'I was just joking.' Schwenke sent Frølich another wink. 'But there is something ritualistic about this, isn't there? Soon only masons and Satanists will have rituals.' He chuckled. 'Hanging from sewing thread, with three crosses on his forehead. All that was missing was a fish sticking out of his gob.' Schwenke laughed louder. 'Perhaps that's what we will find now,' he said, going over to the table where the assistant had finished. He flourished the scalpel before making the classic cut, from the neck down the stomach, left of the navel and down to the edge of the pubis.

He moved to the side as the assistant began to cut through the dead man's ribs. It sounded as though some-one was cracking thick roots in wet mud. Frølich had to lean against the wall, as always.

'Queasy, Frølich?' Schwenke asked, in cheery mood. At a signal from the assistant he turned round, folded back the softer tissue and took a good hold before raising the sternum.

Schwenke lifted out the internal organs and placed them all on the organ table. The assistant hosed them down very thoroughly. Frølich avoided the jets of water and once again breathed through his mouth because of the nauseous stench filling the room.

'Well, what do you know,' Schwenke mumbled. 'What do you know!'

Gunnarstranda woke up: 'What?'

Schwenke: 'The question is how long he would have lasted.'

'Why's that?'

Schwenke pointed to the man's intestines. 'There.'

'And what's that?'

'A kidney riddled with cancer.'

'I can't see any cancer.'

'And this?' Schwenke held up something which looked like a half-chewed, regurgitated blood orange. 'Does this look like cancer?'

'All right. But he must have felt it, mustn't he?'

'I don't know. This type of cancer is hard to detect. If I'm not much mistaken, it has spread to his lungs.'

'He was dying?'

'Looks like it.'

'But he might not have known?'

'Well, we don't know that. I don't have the man's records. Check with his doctor and the usual hospitals. What I'm saying is that finding this type of cancer during an autopsy is not uncommon.'

Gunnarstranda nodded pensively. 'And the wound?' he asked at length. 'The angle?'

Schwenke studied the passage of the weapon through the dead man's internal organs. 'It looks like it was an upward thrust from an acute angle. A punctured lung. Vital blood vessels ruptured.'

'But just one stab?'

'A single stab wound,' Schwenke confirmed, working on the dead man's abdominal organs.

Frølich looked away, at Gunnarstranda, who was intently studying Schwenke's hands at work. 'Is there anything else you can tell me?' the Inspector barked.

Schwenke looked up: 'Like what?'

'Forget it!' Gunnarstranda rummaged furiously through his pockets.

'No smoking in here,' Schwenke said.

'Am I smoking?' asked the policeman in an irritated tone of voice, holding out two empty hands.

Schwenke stood up and beamed a guilty smile. 'Sorry. Well – there must have been quite a fountain of blood as the blade cut into blood vessels under a fair amount of pressure,' he mumbled and added: 'But then you said the crime scene was surprisingly clean. I assume he fell straight to the floor. But,' he continued, 'since the clothing is drenched in blood, the perpetrator's garments must have got pretty red, too.'

'Cause of death?'

'Nine to one it's the stab wound. But I can tell you more in a couple of hours.'

'Time of death?'

Schwenke turned. 'Death is a process, Gunnarstranda. Life is not some digital mechanism that stops working.'

'But you can say something about when . . .'

'The brain might be dead, but there can still be life in the digestive wall and white blood corpuscles,' Schwenke interrupted.

' . . . he was stabbed and fell to the floor, can't you?' the policeman continued undeterred.

'We'll have to see what his body temperature was when we arrived and measure it against the temperature taken by the window, then we'll have to examine the food in his stomach, find out what his last meal was and when he ate it. The problem is the room he was in was freezing. If the temperature of the brain is the same as in the room, the thermometer can't tell us anything. Besides, rigor mortis has not subsided yet. My understanding was that your forensics people had a struggle with his limbs when they brought him in. Do you know what his last meal was?'

'Reindeer steak,' Gunnarstranda said. 'Somewhere between seven-thirty and ten o'clock last night.'

Schwenke looked up from the dead man's stomach. 'With chanterelle sauce,' he added. 'Washed down with red wine. I would guess Spanish, tempranillo, a Rioja.'

Schwenke grinned when he saw Frølich's expression. 'Just joking.' He became serious and reflected. 'We don't know how cold it was in the room and that might cause problems.'

Helter Skelter

After the autopsy they drove back in silence to Police HQ in Grønland and settled in their office. Frølich logged on to the computer network and wrote his report. Gunnarstranda noted down the cryptic message written on the dead man's chest. He stood up and poured himself the dregs of the coffee in the flask. It was cold. He grimaced, went to the sink by the door and poured it down the drain. He repeated the grimace in front of the mirror. 'At times my teeth irritate me,' he said. 'You can see the crowns so clearly. And the older you get, the clearer they are. If I reach seventy, I'll look like a row of teeth someone hung a body on.'

Frølich straightened up. 'Let me have a look,' Frølich said.

Gunnarstranda turned to him and spread his lips wide in a way which made the other man start with surprise. 'You look like a row of teeth with a body on,' Frølich confirmed.

'It was a joke,' he tried to explain to the older policeman, who was still glaring at him.

Gunnarstranda turned away, went back to his chair and lifted up the slip of paper with the code on.

'Might be a road number,' Frølich suggested.

'A road starting with a J?'

'It doesn't have to be a J. It might have been a U once. In England they call major roads A-roads, such as A1, A2 . . .'

'But an A isn't a U.'

'No, but there must be roads beginning with a U, just as there are roads beginning with an A, or an E. We say *Europavei*, don't we?'

'This is a J,' retorted Gunnarstranda. 'It's not an A or an E. It says *J-one hundred and ninety-five*. If you think that's a road, then find out if there are any roads in the world starting with a J or a U. That's fine by me, except for one thing: there isn't a road like that in Oslo, there isn't one in Norway even, and we have no authority outside Oslo's city limits.'

'Could be a perfume,' said Frølich, still persevering. 'There's a perfume called 4711.'

Gunnarstranda lifted the piece of paper into the air and tapped the numbers with his forefinger. 'What does it say here?' he asked in a menacingly gentle voice.

'Fine,' Frølich said, acquiescent. 'But we have to think of a few ideas if we're going to have any chance of discovering what the symbols mean. It's called brainstorming – you suggest something and one thing leads to another.'

'Oh, really?'

'This code could mean anything at all – it could be a trademark, an abbreviation, a code . . .'

'Indeed.'

'But these scribbles could also be a red herring,' Frølich said. 'A code that is intended to confuse.'

Doubtful, Gunnarstranda shook his head. 'What kind

97

of person would stab an old man, leave him bleeding to death and be so cold-blooded as to remain in that room with the huge window looking out onto the street, cold-blooded enough to strip the man when at last he dies, cold-blooded enough to take a pen and leave messages on the dead man's body to confuse us and then place his body in the shop window?' Gunnarstranda said. 'No, it must have been planned.' He regarded the other policeman for a few moments before carrying on: 'Just think of the risk. The window, the writing, and as Schwenke says, the man must have been covered in blood from head to toe. If the intention was to confuse, it could have been done in other, easier ways.'

'Such as?'

'Well, think of Charles Manson – he was the one who wrote *Helter Skelter* in blood over the walls of the pad belonging to . . . to . . . to . . .'

For a few seconds Frølich was fascinated by the dry flicking sounds Gunnarstranda was making with his fingers, but then he helped him out: 'Sharon Tate, Roman Polanski's wife.'

'Right, something like that.' Gunnarstranda stood up and paced to and fro. 'The murderer could have painted a skull on an old coat-of-arms in there, pissed on the body, whatever he wanted.'

'The wife,' Frølich said in a low voice.

'Hm?'

'The wife lives in the first-floor flat. She can nip upstairs, have a shower and wash, wash her clothes. She serves us up all this stuff about not sleeping at night . . .'

'She's almost thirty years younger than the old boy,'

98

Gunnarstranda said. 'The odds are she's having it off with someone.'

'The wife has a lover?'

Gunnarstranda: 'This bollocks about ringing Karsten Jespersen in the middle of the night. If she killed her husband, she rings the son for two reasons: to corroborate the break-in story and to get a kind of alibi.'

'Is that the main lead?' Frølich asked.

'It is a lead at any rate. I'd like to know who she's having it off with . . .'

'If he exists,' Frølich objected with a smile.

'He exists. It's a dead cert.'

'How do you know?'

'You can see it a mile off.'

'A mile off? She's over fifty!'

'Does that mean to say that you begrudge people over fifty a sex life?'

Frølich was on thin ice: 'I didn't mean it like that . . .'

Gunnarstranda, sarcastic: 'No?'

'I meant that things like that . . .' Frølich went quiet and glanced over at his boss who had a deadpan expression on his face.

'What sort of things?'

'For God's sake,' Frølich burst out, his nerves on edge. 'It's all tied up with hormones, isn't it! Working late tonight, darling . . . and infidelity. That's for people in their thirties, isn't it?'

'Working late tonight, darling?' Gunnarstranda queried with a frown. 'Do I detect a reason for your not changing your marital status?'

'Forget it,' Frølich said.

'No, the point is that I saw his wife and my immediate thought was she was having it off with someone. Why didn't you think that?'

'I have no idea . . .' Frølich mused. 'She seemed a bit . . . I don't know . . . she seemed refined.'

'Refined?'

'Yes,' Frølich nodded. 'Refined and nice.'

'Honestly, Frølich, do you think a man of eighty . . .?'

'Does that mean to say you begrudge people over seventy a sex life?' Frølich parried.

'I bet you a hundred kroner,' Gunnarstranda said, responding to the other's patronizing tone. 'No,' he went on. 'I'm not going to bet. I will personally present you with a hundred kroner if we do not turn up a little soulmate for this lady before the case is over.'

'A little soulmate is not the same as a lover.'

'A lover. A hundred kroner. Sight unseen.'

Later, when Frølich had gone, Gunnarstranda sat looking at the telephone. The last time Gunnarstranda had met Tove Granaas, she had invited him out for a meal. It was the third time he had dined out with a woman on his own in as many years. Police Inspector Gunnarstranda did not wish to humiliate himself by counting up how many years it had been. But it was a long time.

Tove had taken him to a sushi restaurant by Lapsetorvet. Gunnarstranda was one of those people who had never tried that sort of food. He admitted that freely. But he had no intention of playing either the narrow-minded or the ignorant peasant. Thus he gave Tove a free hand when she ordered. The meal was not a complete disaster. True enough he dropped some rice in the soya sauce, and true enough he had difficulty getting his teeth through some of the pieces of raw fish in the sushi, but the taste itself was nigh on a religious experience. The heated saki tasted like moonshine with sugar in, and went straight to his head, just like moonshine. They were sitting next to a group of Japanese men who had ordered the most adventurous dish on the menu. All sorts of fried and flambé things arrived at their table. Then the cook left the kitchen, went over to the Japanese table and made a huge spectacle with knives and food. But even the Japanese got drunk on the rice wine. One of the men gave the Inspector a course in using chopsticks. Afterwards he thought that, all in all, the evening had been a success. Even though he staggered out of the restaurant, even though he was unable to remember all the things he had said. Nor even where or how Tove and he parted company. But in some mysterious way he did remember arranging a repeat performance.

Now, however, with this murder enquiry hanging over him, he had to accept that the planned evening with Tove would not come to anything.

He checked his watch. Tove worked as a ward sister. It was late afternoon. He took a chance on her being at home.

His nerves were ajitter at the thought of ringing. As he picked up the receiver, his hand was shaking

'Hello,' came her cheerful answer.

'Hello,' he said with a nervous smile to himself in the window. 'Can you hear who it is?'

'I can. Thank you for the nice evening.'

'Yes, it was . . . good.'

'It certainly was,' she said.

'A man has been murdered,' he said without pausing.

'So we'll have to wait for the anchovies?'

'The anchovies?'

'Your words. You called the food we ate anchovies and the saki firewater.'

'Did I?'

'But we had a great time. What shall we do instead?'

Gunnarstranda cleared his throat. 'I hadn't given that any thought,' he confessed.

Tove Granaas grinned. 'Coffee,' she said. 'I'm sure you'll have enough time for a cup of coffee.'

12

East of Eden

Arvid Folke Jespersen lived in Uranienborg, just off Oslo city centre, in one of those old flats with a view which were so often home to elderly inhabitants born in the area, if their offspring hadn't managed to sell it, lock, stock and barrel, to an advertising agency.

It was late afternoon when Frank Frølich idly contemplated the front entrance from his car. He switched on his mobile phone, called Eva-Britt and cancelled the plans for the evening, although he needn't have done. Even though she was very annoyed, it felt like freedom to evade TV entertainment and the other sad pastimes into which they had slipped. He sat in the car for a while staring into space. A few days ago he had seen *The Getaway* again – Sam Peckinpah's original film with Steve McQueen and Ali MacGraw. The funny thing was that Doc's wife was the spitting image of Anna. The black hair, the brown eyes and the long, slender limbs. It was true that Anna had more meat on her, but otherwise they were strangely similar. What he could not get out of his head was whether this was chance – meeting Anna again today. It was odd, almost as though seeing the film had been part of a greater scheme. But, he told himself, you have no real reason to ring her and you have a lot on your plate with Eva-Britt. With a heavy sigh he struggled out of the car and up the steps to the old man waiting for him.

'Of course I'll try to help as much as I can,' said Arvid Folke Jespersen, letting Frølich into a flat with the stale odour of dust and old books. Like a second-hand bookshop, he thought, taking off his winter boots after some exertion. A little grunt came from behind a curtain. Arvid pushed the curtain to the side. Among a multitude of shoes lay a basket full of old rugs. In the basket was a small tremulous dog. It had a bandage wrapped around its body. 'Goodness, you have hurt yourself, haven't you?' Frølich said to the dog which lay trembling with its ears flattened against its head.

'Silvie has two broken ribs,' Arvid said, opening the living-room door. 'She has to rest, poor thing.'

Frølich followed Arvid into a room with a high ceiling and elegant furniture. The dust collected in balls along the skirting boards. Thick curtains took up most of the space by the windows and let scant light into the room. They seated themselves at a table on which there was a tray of coffee cups, a coffee flask, a sugar bowl, glasses and bottles.

'Even though he was the eldest, I had always thought that Reidar would outlive me,' Frølich's host said dourly. He was wearing a suit with a broad stripe and had a watch chain in his waistcoat pocket. Around his neck he had tied a dark red silk scarf. 'He survived everything, Reidar did. He was even shot down over Germany in 1944, but escaped without a scratch. Reidar only seemed to grow older on the outside; I suppose I must have thought he was immortal. Would you like a glass of port with your coffee?'

Frølich shook his head.

'You're quite right,' Arvid sighed, holding an empty glass in front of his eyes. He found a stain and wiped it with his handkerchief before pouring himself a drink. 'I have port now instead of cognac; port is milder.'

Frølich leaned forward and reached for a bulbous, yellow thermal coffee flask. As he touched the lid, it burst open with a damp pop. He poured himself some coffee. 'But how do you see his murder? It's one thing being surprised by your brother's death, but a murder . . .'

Arvid shook his head. 'Mm,' he mumbled. 'It's beyond me.'

'If Reidar had caught a burglar red-handed, what do you think he would have done?'

Arvid put the bottle of port down on the table and considered. 'I wouldn't begin to know. Nowadays there are so many desperate drug addicts and so on. People you just can't work out. You know much more about this than me, of course. But Reidar was aware of this too. He read newspapers and watched TV like everyone else.'

'How do you think he would have reacted? Would he have kept out of the way, would he have talked to the person, or . . .?

'I think he would have kept out of the way or – maybe not. Reidar was a very determined character. Once he had an idea in his head, it took a lot to dissuade him. Personally, I am a bit different, I'm a little cautious and don't like tense atmospheres. I know I would have kept out of the way or stayed quiet. Reidar never seemed to be afraid, or he became like that, I suppose. He had to maintain this image of himself. Of course, he might have told this intruder to clear off, or threatened him in some other way.' Arvid took a sip from his glass. 'A terrible business,' he mumbled. 'Terrible business . . .'

Frølich sipped at his coffee, which was thin, light brown. Two grains of coffee floated around on the surface. One of them went in his mouth. After he had taken it out, it stuck to the tip of his forefinger. 'Is it long since you last saw your brother?' the police officer asked, discreetly wiping the coffee grain onto the saucer.

The man on the other side of the table gave a start, as though awakened from profound thoughts. 'No, no, he was round here yesterday, with Emmanuel. That reminds me, I promised to ring him. Would you please remind me? Mention it before you leave?'

'When did he come here?'

'At about twelve, maybe just after.'

'About?'

'Yes, he may have come a few minutes later. I think we had been waiting for a while.'

'And when did he leave?'

'He must have been here for just under an hour.'

'How did he seem?'

Arvid stroked his chin. 'He was not himself at all; he seemed quite off-kilter.'

Frølich's eyebrows rose in surprise.

'Yes. You saw Silvie, my poor dog. He tried to kill her. It was fortunate that things turned out as they did.'

'He tried to kill your dog?'

Arvid nodded. 'I know it sounds crazy – Reidar

kicked her. A lot of internal bleeding and two broken ribs. It was a miracle she survived.'

'Did he kick her that hard? Did she bite him?'

'No, Reidar just wasn't himself. He seemed quite agitated. I don't think I've seen him like that before. When I think of how he behaved with the dog, I daren't imagine what would have happened if there had been a break-in. Has Karsten worked out what was stolen?'

Frølich consulted his notepad before saying anything. 'Why was he agitated? Had you been quarrelling?'

'Goodness me, no. That is, we were discussing business. You understand, there are three of us: Emmanuel and Reidar and I. We three own the shares; well, we've all been involved with the shop. Emmanuel and me, too, but now we've accepted that we're old and have retired, both of us. Reidar never wanted to stop working.'

'Hm, now he doesn't have any choice,' Frølich said dryly. He was at once aware of how inappropriate this comment might seem and hastened to add: 'This was a special occasion then – this business meeting of yours?'

'Business is right. The shop is up for sale and we have some purchasers, a married couple. They came, too. A herr Kirkenær and his wife. I think they're married anyway. They've got rings. This man knows a fair bit about antiques, and she does, too, of course.'

'So there was a row?'

Arvid shook his head. 'Not a row. Disagreement is a better word.'

'What sort of disagreement?'

'About the deal. Emmanuel and I are more than happy with the offer made, but . . .'

'But not Reidar?'

'Yes. I thought he wanted to sell. Reidar has never said no to more money but, on the other hand, he has never tolerated the rest of us having opinions. Reidar was a bit odd like that, you know. He was the eldest and always had to call the shots. Well, we suspected, Emmanuel and I, that he would jump up and down a bit, but we had never imagined that he would get himself into such a lather. That was after the buyers had gone. The plan was that we would discuss the offer, but we didn't get round to it.'

Arvid sat sunk in deep thought as he twirled his port wine glass between his fingers. 'In fact that was the last time I saw him.'

'Was he well?'

Arvid raised both eyebrows.

'Was your brother ill?'

Arvid opened his mouth in a soundless laugh. 'Reidar has never been ill. Are you trying to tell me he died from an illness?'

Frølich shook his head and poured himself more coffee. 'And now you and Emmanuel are the sole owners?'

'Hmm, I suppose Ingrid will take over now. She can pay off Karsten and take Reidar's share. Great lady, Ingrid is, very good-looking.'

'She's much younger than him.'

'Right. He was an old goat, Reidar was, no doubt about that.'

'You're sure the wife will take Reidar's share?'

'I would assume so.'

Frank Frølich waited.

'It's Karsten's big problem that Reidar and Ingrid had joint ownership.'

'What do you mean by that?'

'Eh?'

' . . . Karsten's big problem . . .'

Arvid smiled mirthlessly. 'One would assume that Karsten would have preferred to handle things on his own . . .'

'You mean Karsten wanted to be the sole beneficiary?'

'That's not so improbable, is it?'

'I don't know,' Frølich said. 'Are you suggesting there's an inheritance dispute here?'

Arvid stared at him for quite some time before asking in a monotone: 'What do you mean?'

Frølich observed him. Perhaps the suggestion of a disagreement between the widow and the murdered man's son had been meant seriously. The old man seemed to have woken up and realized he was talking to a policeman, and therefore ought to consider what he was saying. It was a familiar reaction. Frølich repeated: 'Is there an inheritance dispute as a result of your brother's death?'

'I don't know.'

'So I've misunderstood what you said about Karsten's big problem?'

Arvid went quiet. He seemed befuddled.

'What did you mean?' Frølich repeated.

'I meant that . . . I've got myself tied in knots now. I don't want to put anyone in a difficult spot, do I? Karsten and Ingrid are good friends. The wolf in sheep's clothing – if such a thing exists – the person who is most upset that Karsten is not the sole heir – is probably Susanne, Karsten's wife. This happens in all families, though. You know . . .'

'Fine.' Frølich cut him short. 'But is the ownership of the shop a cut-and-dried matter?'

'I assume so – so long as a will does not appear, I would expect Ingrid to take over from Reidar.'

'Will you try to get her to agree to work with . . .?'

'Kirkenær. It's written as it sounds: K-I-R.'

'I've got it,' Frølich said with a flourish of his pen to move the man on.

'What was it you asked again?'

'Whether she would agree to what Reidar rejected – the sale of the shop.'

'Of course.'

'And his son, Karsten?'

'What about Karsten?'

'Well, he works there, doesn't he? In the shop?'

'We had aired the proposal with Karsten beforehand, and I believe he was happy with it.'

'But he would lose his job, wouldn't he?'

'It's questionable how important the job is to him. You see, Karsten has other ambitions. He works as a writer on the side. That's what he does when there are no customers in the shop, sitting in the backroom, banging away on the typewriter. When we talked about the sale, he was far from hostile to the idea.'

'Do you think that was why Reidar turned down the deal? Because he wanted to protect Karsten's interests – his son's job in the shop.'

'No, I don't think so,' Arvid said bluntly.

'You seem very sure,' the detective said, peering up.

'If Reidar had refused for Karsten's sake, he wouldn't have made a secret of it. Reidar was not the reticent kind.'

'But why do you think Reidar would not agree to the sale?'

'So that he would have one over us, I think. And because he couldn't stand the idea of not working. That's perhaps the most important reason. Reidar never accepted that he was getting old. Reidar was a man who denied the existence of death.'

Frølich jotted down the last phrase and sat for a few seconds formulating his next question: 'Jonny Stokmo. I've heard he was employed by the shop.'

'He isn't any longer.'

'He was given the boot by Reidar. Why was that?'

'More like the opposite,' said Arvid with a faint smile. 'I would guess – I don't have a clue really – but I would guess that it was Jonny being difficult. He's a hard nut, you know. There was nothing personal between Reidar and Jonny. They are two proud men. It was a kind of affair of honour.'

'But what did they quarrel about?'

'God knows. I don't, anyway.'

'Was Reidar the type to have lots of enemies?'

Arvid grinned. 'If you're thinking about the business with Jonny, then it was just childish. Reidar must have said or done something. We reckoned that time would pass and Jonny would come back with his tail between his legs.'

'Why antiques?' Frølich asked politely.

'More coffee?'

'No, thank you.' Frølich sat looking at the man as he poured himself another port. Two curly white hairs stood out on the tip of his bluish-purple nose. Frølich repeated the question.

'Oh, it's a long story. It started with paper.' Folke Jespersen folded his hands over his stomach.

'Paper?'

'Yes, in those days none of us had any education. Emmanuel did an apprenticeship as a bricklayer. By the way, he built the house next door, which you passed as you came up the hill. Not on his own, of course. He was just one of many. And I began at a bank which disappeared long ago. Reidar was the brightest of us, but he was the one with least education. He worked as a newspaper boy on *Aftenposten*. As a young man, Reidar had idealistic tendencies. For a long time he was one of those few foolish types who think they can get rich by honest means.'

Frølich looked up and was met by a good-natured smile from the opposite side of the table. 'For example, it always irritated Reidar that things were thrown away, and then he found out that newspaper companies threw away those rolls of paper – that is, they had to change rolls on the presses and afterwards there were a few metres of paper left on the roll, quite a lot actually, because newspaper is so thin, of course. There was perhaps that much on the roll.' Arvid demonstrated with his fingers. 'Waste paper, a pile of excellent raw materials which were just chucked out.'

Frølich nodded.

Warming to the topic, Arvid leaned forward in his

chair: 'And no one gave a damn about this wasted paper. Reidar got it for free; he undertook to remove it and the newspapers were happy. And at that time, you know, paper was in short supply in many places in the world.'

'He sold the paper on?'

Folke Jespersen nodded. 'A business grew out of it. He earned money from waste. Then he moved on to antiques.'

'Who bought the paper?'

'Anyone who needed it. There were newspaper businesses in South America, in African states . . .'

Frølich nodded. 'But then he turned to antiques?'

'Exactly.' Arvid nodded.

'Why?'

'Well . . .' Arvid straightened up again. 'There were several reasons, I suppose. But the most important were financial. The paper had to be re-mounted – in other words, put on a new roll so that it could be used for newspaper production. As long as Reidar got the paper free, the production and transport costs could be covered, but one day the free paper came to an end. And then there was an economic downturn – this was before the exploitation of the rain forests. Nowadays they make paper from eucalyptus trees in the jungle and cheap Russian timber . . . Anyway, it stopped.'

'But why antiques?'

Arvid cocked his head.

'Why not something else?' Frølich asked. 'Why antiques of all things?'

Arvid shrugged and spread his hands. 'You tell me,' he said with a grin.

Frølich observed him in silence. Arvid sipped his port and smiled behind the glass. 'I think, firstly, it had something to do with Reidar's love for objects, fine objects,' he said. 'Then there was Margrethe – Karsten's mother, who died a long time ago – she was a terrible snob. She liked to surround herself with beautiful, expensive things. On top of that, Reidar had this idea of making money from waste, that is, from the things that others throw away. He was ahead of his time, Reidar was. Now it's recycling and reclaiming and re-I don't know what. But you're right. It must have begun with something specific. I don't remember what. All of a sudden Reidar began to buy and sell curios, and then it turned out that all three of us were making good money out of it. But how it actually started? I do not remember.'

Frølich jotted down: Why antiques? *Arvid F.J. doesn't give an answer*. He chewed on his pencil thoughtfully, and asked:

'Did you contact your brother later that day?'

'Which brother?'

'Reidar. Did you get in touch at any point afterwards?'

Arvid slowly shook his head.

Frølich formed a tentative smile, unsure how to express himself. 'That's a bit strange, isn't it?' he suggested in a soft voice.

'Oh?'

'Yes, he had spoiled your deal, injured your dog . . .'

'I didn't contact him.'

'Did Emmanuel?'

'You'll have to ask Emmanuel.'

Frølich observed the man on the other side of the table. All of a sudden he seemed sulky and very distant. 'You and Emmanuel didn't hatch any other specific plans with regard to Reidar that day?'

'What do you mean by hatch?'

'I mean,' Frølich said, putting his notes down. 'If I had met this kind of resistance from my sister – I don't have a brother – I think I would have tried to talk to her. That's quite natural, I imagine.'

'Of course we made plans.'

'Yes? But you didn't carry them out?'

'No.'

'So you didn't try to contact Reidar?'

'No.'

Frølich picked up his notepad. 'This is a little awkward,' he said warily. 'But it's part of the job I have been assigned. I have to ask you where you were on Friday night.'

'I was here.'

'In this flat? On your own?'

'My dog – Silvie – was here.'

'Is there anyone who can confirm that?'

'Do you think I would be capable of murdering my own brother?'

Frølich pulled a guilt-stricken grimace. 'I apologize, but this is a question I need to have answered.'

'I don't think anyone can confirm it, no.'

'Did anyone ring you?'

Jespersen shook his head.

'Did you take the dog for a walk? Did anyone see you?'

'Silvie does her daily business in the box on the veranda . . .'

'How long were you at the vet's?'

'It was already dark. I must have got back at about five or half past, I suppose.'

'Fine,' Frølich mumbled, looking up. 'There is one last thing I was wondering. Does the number one hundred and ninety-five mean anything to you?

'One hundred and ninety-five . . .?' Arvid turned his head gravely from side to side. 'No. Don't think so.'

'Do you think the number had any significance for your brother?'

'Haven't a clue,' Jespersen said, tossing his hands in the air. 'Why do you ask?'

Frølich didn't answer.

Arvid Folke Jespersen was lost in thought. 'One hundred and ninety-five,' he mumbled. 'No, I really have no idea. Sorry.'

13

An Old Photograph

That same afternoon Inspector Gunnarstranda drove straight to Folke Jespersen's warehouse in Bertrand Narvesens vei. The key he had requisitioned from Karsten Jespersen worked like a charm. He stepped over the high doorsill and went inside. The spring-loaded door closed with a bang, creating an echo in the room. He looked around. There were tables and chairs piled up, rocking chairs, trunks, cases, cupboards, clock machinery in wonderful, exquisitely made casings. He stood scanning the walls until his gaze fell on a window high up. There was a light on. He walked down the corridor leading through the clutter. A staircase led up to a landing in front of a door. He turned on the landing and cast an eye over the antiques. Between two cupboards with rusty hinges he noticed a cast-iron coke-burning stove beside a stained wood carving of a negro boy. Inspector Gunnarstranda wondered if these items might be worth anything. A fortune maybe, but for all he knew – nothing.

He opened the door and went into an ante-room which appeared to function as a kitchen and dining room. Through another door and into an office. Gunnarstranda studied the table. It was big and heavy, English style; the wood was dark, almost red. The table top was polished and bare apart from a smallish plastic desk pad and an old-fashioned-looking lamp. He advanced further into the room and caught a reflection of himself in a wide mirror with a wooden frame. He stopped to have a look and adjusted his scant hair, then turned to let his eyes wander from the desk to the window sill, on which stood a telephone, and a filing cabinet. The top of the cabinet was a complete mess: a bust of Bjørnstjerne Bjørnson, a Nobel Prize winner, towered over lots of other things. Someone had put a Stetson hat on Bjørnson's head. It suited him. There was a portable radio on its side, a cassette player from the seventies, a hole-punch, a stapler, a roll of tape, a box of paper clips and a pile of loose papers. Gunnarstranda looked from the filing cabinet to the desk and back again. Why were the stapler and the hole-punch on the filing cabinet and not on the desk?

He moved towards a grandfather clock next to the mirror. A quarter past ten, it said. None of its machinery was working. The weights hanging inside the case looked like pine cones. He walked back to the desk and sat in the swivel chair, an expensive number made of wood and upholstered in leather. It was comfortable. The Inspector swung from side to side as he alternated between studying the filing cabinet and the desk. He pulled out the top drawer. It was full to overflowing with pens, pencils, rubbers, correction tape, bottles of Tipp-Ex, rulers and lots of loose, ancient-looking rubber stamps. He picked out one at random, turned it upside-down and peered from under his glasses to read the mirror-image letters:

Another stamp had a big letter 'B' for second-class post. On a third he read:

CONFIDENTIAL

He slammed the drawer shut and opened the next. This one was full of screwdrivers, spanners and various kinds of pliers. In the corner of the drawer there was an old tea caddy without a lid. He read the label: Ridgeway's. In the caddy were screws, used nails, nuts and hooks.

Gunnarstranda opened the next drawer. It contained a folded white tablecloth and a bottle, half full. He took out the bottle and read the label: Bristol Cream. After pulling off the cork, he had a sniff. A potent aroma. He sat looking into the air and musing. Sherry, he thought, and tried to remember if he had ever bought sherry. Perhaps once or twice. Sherry was not a drink he liked. He put the bottle back.

It was warm inside the office. Extra hot in his thick winter coat. He stood up, went to the window and felt the electric radiator. It was on full, burning-hot. Outside it was dark. Between two buildings he caught sight of a road behind a wire fence. Two figures in winter coats ambled towards a car and got in. The car lights were switched on and it drove out of view. Soon the car reappeared between the two buildings. The rear lights cast a red glow across the banks of snow. He moved away, went to the door and opened it. The ante-room to the office contained a kitchen sink area and a pale wooden dining table. In the sink there were two stem glasses. The dregs had dried at the bottom. He stooped down and smelt. There was a residual scent of fortified wine. It had to be the same smell as in the bottle. He craned his head towards the office. Slowly he walked back to the office where he sat down again in the splendid swivel chair. He opened the bottom drawer.

The table has been cleared, he thought, and looked at all the desk items piled up on the window sill and on the top of the filing cabinet.

Someone spreads out a cloth and puts two glasses on the table, he thought. *Someone drinks sherry. Reidar Folke Jespersen and another person drink sherry. Another person. A woman.* It had to be a woman. The cloth. The sherry. He took his mobile phone from his coat pocket and tapped in a number. The chair creaked in time with the dial tone in his ear. He told the woman who answered the reason for his call and gave her the address. After putting the phone back, he took out a ballpoint pen from an inside pocket. With the pen he closed the drawer containing the bottle and the cloth. Then, also with the pen, he pushed the desk pad to one side. Underneath was a faded business envelope and under the envelope a photograph. The policeman stared; it was a faded black and white photograph – a picture of a woman with thick, dark hair cascading over her shoulders. She had a knowing smile on her face; it was as though she had caught him in the act and was mildly reproving him. She was young, no more than twenty-five years old, maybe younger, with a conspicuous mole on her right cheek, midway between jawbone and lower lip.

The policeman scrutinized the photograph for a long time. He angled his head and tried to imagine the same face after the ravages of the passing years, with less strength in the cheek muscles, furrows on either side of her mouth and a shadowy hollow in that indefinable area from the nostrils and corners of the mouth where the cheeks fan out flatly. He tried to imagine her with deeper-set eyes, perhaps with age-related bags under the eyes, wrinkles around her mouth. But he was quite sure. This was a woman he had never seen. He pushed the pen under the photograph and flipped it over. There was something written on the back: four words in a line, looped writing, in pencil, written many years ago: *Because I love you.*

Gunnarstranda gave a jump when he heard the echo of the front door slamming downstairs. He got to his feet and scuttled out to the staircase. There he saw a head he recognized. It was Karsten Jespersen and he was pushing a sack trolley. Jespersen had not seen the policeman. He was pushing the trolley in front of him and didn't stop until he reached the back of the warehouse. There he parked the trolley and began to manoeuvre a wardrobe covered in carvings. 'Hello!' the police officer shouted.

Jespersen started and spun on his heel.

'What are you up to?' Gunnarstranda shouted.

'That's what I was going to ask you,' Jespersen said calmly. 'This is private property.'

Gunnarstranda shook his head. 'Out,' he ordered.

'What did you say?'

'This area will be sealed off and searched in a little

while. We're looking for evidence. You will have to wait. What are you doing with the trolley?'

'Picking something up,' Jespersen said unhelpfully.

'What?'

'That's my business.'

'What were you going to pick up?'

'Something that was mine.'

'Right,' the Inspector said, still annoyed. 'I'm not going to get mixed up in your inheritance rows. But you are kindly requested to wait.' He descended the stairs with authority. 'Out.'

Jespersen did not move. A swathe of antique objects separated them.

'Come on,' the policeman said, impatient now.

Jespersen coughed. 'My father gave me this wardrobe,' he said after a pause.

'You'll have to take that up with others, not with me. Don't touch anything. Just leave. You and the other beneficiaries will be informed when this property can be released.'

'But surely it doesn't matter . . .'

'Out!'

Karsten Jespersen's chin quivered out of control. His mouth was contorted in a grimace. 'You can't treat me in this way,' he hissed as he slunk towards the exit.

'Take the sack trolley with you,' the inspector said tersely.

A Toyota van stood outside with the motor running. Someone was sitting in it. Gunnarstranda went closer. A strapping woman sat in the passenger seat. She rolled down the window. 'The wardrobe,' she shouted to

Karsten Jespersen. 'Where's the wardrobe?'

The detective officer bent down to the window and reached in his gloved hand. 'Susanne Jespersen?'

She didn't seem to register his existence. Her head was bent towards Karsten. 'The wardrobe?' she said to her husband as he opened the sliding door and lifted the trolley in. Her next outburst was drowned in the noise of the side door being slammed shut. Her head moved as her eyes followed her husband. 'Can't you do anything?'

'Would it suit you to appear at Police HQ tomorrow morning at eleven to give a statement?' Gunnarstranda said to the back of her head. She had twisted her whole body round to face Jespersen who was sitting in the driver's seat. 'What? Are we going to leave here empty-handed? Answer me, you oaf!'

Jespersen sat sullenly with his body bent over the steering wheel. He ignored her and put the van into gear. 'Eleven o'clock!' shouted the Inspector as the van drove off. His shout was drowned in the roar of the engine and the cursing and swearing from the cab. Gunnarstranda peered up at the sky. Snow was falling. A snowflake landed on the left-hand lens of his glasses, but didn't melt. He looked at his feet. The snowflakes lay on the tarmac like down. It was the kind of snow that did not stick and form drifts, the kind that fluttered away when you trudged through it, the kind that would disappoint all the children with sledges. Inspector Gunnarstranda walked back to the warehouse to wait for forensics.

Two hours later Gunnarstranda met Tove Granaas in

Café Justisen. After coming through the tinkling door, she stood scouring the café for him. Gunnarstranda rose from his seat in the corner. Tove returned his smile. She was wearing a grey-white woollen poncho and a beret of the same colour. He was about to say she looked elegant, but it didn't come out. Instead he waved to a waitress. He ordered another beer for himself and a coffee for her. They sat chatting about inconsequential matters; he knew this was a preamble. Tove Granaas would never be satisfied with talking about the working day; sooner or later she would home in on *them*.

He had been waiting for quite a long time when the question finally came. Gunnarstranda raised his eyes and looked up at the row of pictures by the Oslo-born Hermansen as he examined his emotions. That particular question would have annoyed and alienated him if it had come from anyone else. He was somewhat surprised not to feel annoyance. He straightened the tablecloth and downed the last of his half-litre before making his reluctant admission: 'Yes, I think it is difficult to talk about Edel.'

Tove raised her cup and swirled the dregs of her coffee around and up the side; then she leaned back in her chair. The hands holding the cup were slim, the nails short and unvarnished. She wasn't wearing any rings. A small gold watch on a slim band adorned her left wrist. She took her time, studying the tablecloth, until she looked up and waited for them to have eye-contact again, and asked:

'Why?'

To his surprise, Gunnarstranda heard himself say: 'I

find it difficult to come to terms with this kind of sentimentality.'

'Sentimentality?'

'Her death has become something which we shared – it is very private. In a way, it would feel like a betrayal to change or modify anything of what we shared.'

Tove studied the cloth again. 'Who said you should change or modify anything?'

He sent her a weak smile. '*Taboo* may be a better word. It feels like a taboo to evaluate or . . . re-work what she and I had together.'

'Talking? Is that re-working?'

He reflected before answering: 'I would have to search for words, weigh them. Talking about her is bound to be an evaluation.'

'Where is the boundary?' she asked with a lop-sided smile. 'Somewhere this sensitivity has to stop, doesn't it? Some of your past must be your own. Some of it must be private enough or sturdy enough to be . . . evaluated. After all you're sitting here with me,' she said.

He looked up. She wasn't smiling any more, but looking into his eyes.

He cleared his throat. 'What do you mean?'

'Well, you don't invite me out to avoid getting to know me, do you?'

'You're very direct.'

'Of course.'

It was Tove who broke the silence. 'You are also very direct.'

'But I'm not sure where you're going.'

She put down her cup and leaned forward. 'You say

you don't want to betray your late wife,' she said. 'Betrayal: that was your word. Are you betraying her by inviting me out?'

'Of course not.'

'If your late wife is hanging over us, is there a chance you will betray her the next time we meet?'

'No, you misunderstand,' he said. 'I mean the years – the time I had with Edel – the years and the things I experienced with her are not something I can easily share with others. You and I . . .' He stopped with a wry smile on his face.

'What's the matter?'

'Nothing, except that I am well over fifty and that . . .' He shook his head from side to side.

'And that I'm also over fifty and we're talking like two teenagers?' Tove suggested.

He nodded. 'Yes, perhaps that's it.'

'What about your husband?' asked the Inspector.

'Do you mean my ex-husband?'

He nodded.

'He thinks birdsong is edible, and that he will be happy if he can eat it.'

'Really?'

'He's crazy,' she explained.

They exchanged looks. 'Are you disappointed?' she asked.

'Am I disappointed?'

'Yes, you seem disappointed.'

'I'm not disappointed,' he said. 'But you don't need to paint a negative image of your ex-husband, not for my sake.'

Tove smiled. 'I'm good friends with Torstein. He is thus far in my life the best friend I have and have had. And I'm the first to complain that he's crazy.'

'In what way is he crazy?'

'He's a realist, a mathematician – very talented as well – perhaps a little too talented. What I call crazy – apart from such cracked ideas as eating birdsong – is that he's trying to develop a theory about super-sensory phenomena.'

'A realist researching super-sensory phenomena?'

'Yes, by preference, ghosts.' She smiled. 'The thing about ghosts is – they like to hang around cemeteries, don't they? And they show themselves at night. So they're not there during the day. Torstein's theory is based on the notion that when a dead person's *essence* or *soul* leaves the flesh – the body – and becomes a ghost, then ghostly activities tend to take place in cemeteries at night – or ghosts haunt the places where they met their tragic death. What Torstein devotes his mathematical talent to is finding a mathematical formula. He is searching for the points around the cemetery or the haunted zone – and the time-segments during the day – that demarcate ghostly activity. In other words, whatever it is that regulates the energy of the ghosts. Imagine you're a ghost – the idea is you are active within certain limits: this is where I spook, this far and no further; I don't haunt areas outside these limits. Torstein's theory is based on the notion that if ghosts are active in specified areas and at specified times, then it is his task to find these limits. And his aim is to position himself on the boundary and drive the ghost mad, that is, to tease the ghost.'

She went quiet.

'You're kidding?'

'No. Torstein has filled several files with his calculations.'

Gunnarstranda cleared his throat and ogled his empty beer glass. He didn't know what to say.

Tove stifled a chuckle. 'Torstein's real aim,' she said, 'which is the basis of his application for a scholarship, is to find energy; he believes there have to be energy fields at these points that delimit ghosts' activity, and this energy is what most occupies his interest. He believes that if he can solve the mystery of this energy, he will be able to solve the parapsychological enigma.'

She lapsed back into silence. Her eyes were both expectant and brimming with mischief. 'It is only after living with him for fifteen years that you realize he's crazy. The problem is that he appears to be able to think and act normally, but something isn't right – and then you end up with border values for ghosts.'

Gunnarstranda pulled a face. 'I think I understand you,' he said. 'I think I understand.'

He waved an arm in the air to attract the waitress's attention. 'Bill,' he said.

'You're not getting away so easily,' she said.

He stared at her.

'Investigation or no investigation – you can make time for the cinema.' She delved into her bag with a hand and pulled out two tickets.

'I see,' he wavered and then took one of the tickets. 'What's it about?'

She looked up with a smile: 'Ghosts.'

14

The Black Widow

Frank Frølich rang the bell by Ingrid Jespersen's door at half past eight in the morning. She explained over the intercom that she wasn't up yet. 'I can wait,' Frølich said obligingly.

'In fact I am up,' she said. 'But I'm only wearing my dressing gown.'

Frølich bent his knees to be able to speak through the two-way loudspeaker. 'That's fine,' he said. 'I'll wait.'

'But it's so cold outside,' she said. 'You can wait indoors.'

'That's kind of you,' Frølich said, an image of Mr Bean flashing through his mind because his knees were splayed and he was talking to the wall.

'The door's open,' she said and pressed the button to buzz him in.

She kept Frølich waiting twenty minutes. He found himself a chair in the kitchen and soon confirmed that the lady had the same taste as Eva-Britt as far as fitted kitchens were concerned. The cupboard doors were co-ordinated and many were made of glass. When Ingrid came out of the bathroom, there was a strong fragrance of perfume. Even though the bags under her eyes were still big and dark, her face seemed less strained today. 'I don't sleep well,' she explained. 'I keep thinking that he died downstairs and I might have been lying awake while he was bleeding to death . . .' She looked around. 'But we can't sit here.'

She took him to a living room in a wing of the flat he didn't remember seeing on the previous visit. She cleared away a glass and an empty bottle of wine from the round table. 'I haven't turned to drink,' she assured him. 'But I get so twitchy in the evening. The flat's so big.'

He nodded.

'I look in all the cupboards and check under all the beds before I go to bed. I lock all the rooms which have keys. I'm afraid someone might be there.'

He nodded again.

'I daren't take sleeping pills because I'm afraid I won't wake up if . . .'

Frølich waited for her to continue.

She sent him an apologetic smile and nervously stroked the back of her hand with two fingers.

'If . . . what?'

She shuddered. 'If someone came.'

'Who?' he asked.

'Mm?'

'Who would come?'

She stared stiffly in front of her.

He waited.

'I'm considering moving into a hotel,' she said at length.

Frølich still said nothing.

'And I get such a guilty conscience, I mean . . . being frightened for myself when Reidar is the one who is dead. Do you understand?'

Frank Frølich nodded.

She leaned towards him and looked into his eyes. 'I don't know if he was attacked or . . .'

Frølich held eye-contact and waited for her to go on.

'I don't know if I'm in danger, do I?'

'Why would you be in any danger?'

She shivered. She glared at him. 'It was a break-in, wasn't it?'

Frølich said nothing.

'I want to know if I'm in danger!' she snarled.

'Are you frightened of being attacked here at home?'

'Should I be?' she retorted. 'Can you tell me?'

Frank Frølich cleared his throat and considered his words. 'We have no reason to suspect that anyone in your husband's circle is in any danger,' he said. 'If, on the other hand, you feel threatened . . .'

'But I don't know anything!' she interrupted. 'You're not telling me anything!'

'Do you feel threatened?' he repeated.

She lowered her eyes, silent.

He sat watching her. Black suited her. Furthermore there was a patch of transparent, patterned material at the front of her dress. The white skin underneath the black made her look incredibly sexy. Her figure was lithe, graceful. She reminded him of something. She had the same effortless control of her limbs that cats have, he thought, and tried not to reveal this sudden interest in her feminine charms. But at once he was clear that she had not noticed anything; she was in another world, immersed in thought. She broke loose with a shudder and folded her arms in front of her chest – as though remembering in a flash that he was present.

'Originally you were a professional dancer, weren't you?' he asked.

She didn't seem to hear. 'I think I'm going to move,' she said in a distant voice. 'Yes indeed, I will move.'

Frølich tried for a couple of seconds to put himself in her position. He wondered if he should repeat what he had said and tell her that there was no reason to feel threatened. 'Do you know if your husband had any reason to feel threatened?' he asked.

'No,' she said.

'Do you wish us to adopt any special measures, to give you protection?'

She stared at him.

'If that would reassure you . . .'

'Do you think I'm being ridiculous?'

'Not at all. It's an offer. We're happy to discuss measures that might improve your situation.'

'No,' she said. 'I don't need any protection.'

Frølich observed her for a moment before repeating: 'Originally you were a professional dancer, weren't you?'

'Oh, that's many years ago,' she said wearily. 'But as a matter of fact you're right. I used to dance ballet. Then I taught for a few years, working as a dancing teacher, not far from here. I had a little room in Frognerveien. There's a restaurant there now, and a coffee bar. I often have my lunch there, from time to time anyway. It's nice to sit there, you know. Nice to think about how things change over time, isn't it? It's been a supermarket too, if you can remember the chain of shops called IRMA. They took the place over from me. But, as I said, that came to an end, the dance school that is. I got fed up and with my lack of economic sense it could only go one way.'

'And you've never been involved in the antiques business?'

'Not at all.' She half-smiled. 'I'm an old-fashioned housewife. Boring.'

'Don't say that,' Frølich said and caught himself thinking how to make a move on her. A seam in her stockings led his attentions upwards. Her dress was tight on her supple hips. He coughed and pulled himself together: 'What made your husband so interested in antiques?'

'He's always been interested', she said, 'in a sense of form, aesthetics – at least that was what brought us together. My sister was working for local government in the seventies. She had a job as a secretary in Oslo Auctions, down in Brugata, you know, where fine ladies can pawn wedding rings if they have a burning need for a dram . . .' She opened her palms. 'Unbelievably, that was how we met.'

'Pawning something?'

'No. Through my sister. Reidar bought up the pawned goods that had not been redeemed. You know, if you pawn something, it has to be redeemed within a certain time. If it isn't, it is sold off at the auction. Reidar bought clocks and old jewellery and violins and I don't know what. My sister and I were invited to a party there once; that is, she was invited, but Ragnhild, my sister, got the heebie-jeebies. She was nervous because Reidar was a widower and so much older. I went as a chaperone and because I was kind of interested in design and so on, well, one thing led to another.'

Frølich grabbed at the chance and bent down to pick up his notepad. The widow seemed to be keen to answer questions now. 'So antiques brought you together?'

'I usually say form, or design. A word like *antiques* seems so dusty. By the way, you should know that for Reidar antiques were all about good taste.'

Frølich nodded and chewed the top of his biro before saying: 'He didn't dabble in the second-hand market, as some people call it?'

'You should be glad that Reidar didn't hear you using the word,' she said in a careworn tone. 'Second-hand – he hated the word. No, the objects we surround ourselves with signal who we are,' she explained in a matter-of-fact way.

Frølich nodded again.

'That's the problem with us Norwegians,' she continued with sudden passion. 'We don't understand the significance of being surrounded by beauty. Look at our churches. They are so boring. Yes, I know it is all tied up with the Reformation and Protestantism and the idea that gold and glitter are said to detract from the message. That's right, isn't it? But I believe . . . that if we had had cathedrals in this country, I'm sure we would have had a healthier relationship with religion. The things you like, the things you surround yourself with, say something about the person,' she added.

Frølich coughed politely and circled his pen in the air to excuse his lack of interest in cathedrals and to get to the point. 'You ate here – on the evening before the murder,' he said cautiously.

Ingrid nodded, but didn't say anything.

'Karsten and Susanne – plus grandchildren – ate with you two?'

'You think I'm skirting the issue,' Ingrid answered. 'But in order to understand my husband you have to understand his feeling for form.'

Frølich took a deep breath. 'It's also very important for us to know what happened on the days leading up to his death. Can you give me your version of events on Friday?'

'Reidar got up early,' she began and faltered.

'What time?' Frølich said to move her on.

It startled her. 'At about half past seven, I think. He went to work before I got up. After that I didn't hear or see anything of him until seven or half past in the evening – when he came home and dinner was waiting.'

'And you were at home the whole time?'

'No, I must have got back here at about two or half past. I went shopping.'

'Shopping?'

She nodded and repeated: 'Shopping.'

Frølich watched her, but she showed no signs of wanting to expand. He met her eyes: 'Just a general shopping trip – you weren't looking for anything in particular?'

She stared back. 'Of course, but is that of any interest?'

He shrugged.

'I went to GlasMagasinet amongst other places.' She fell quiet and did not appear to want to enlarge on her trip. He said:

'When did you go shopping?'

'At about half past eleven in the morning.'

'And what did you do before – until half past eleven?'

'I had a shower, read the paper . . . and at ten, maybe five minutes past, I went down to see Karsten in the shop. He opens the shop at ten, you see, and we usually have a cup of coffee together in the morning.'

'You and Karsten Jespersen?'

'Yes, if there are not many customers. There were none around, so we chatted over a cup of coffee.' She pursed her lips as though reflecting. 'For three quarters of an hour perhaps. He had Benjamin with him. The kindergarten had a planning day, I think. Benjamin flitted around, doing drawings. I came back upstairs, put on warmer clothes to go out and left at some time between eleven and half past . . .'

Frølich wondered if he should ask what she and the dead man's son talked about, but he decided against it. Instead he asked:

'Did you find anything?'

'What do you mean?'

'Did you find anything when you were out shopping?'

'Oh yes.'

Frølich waited for her to go on. He waited in vain.

'And during the day,' he asked, 'did you hear from your husband at all?'

'Yes, he rang,' she said.

'Here?'

'Hm?'

'Did he ring here?'

'Of course,' she snapped. 'Where else?'

'Well . . .' Frølich stared at her. 'He could have called you while you were out shopping,' he suggested. 'On your mobile.'

'He rang me here.'

'When?' Frølich asked.

'In the afternoon, around three. As a rule he comes home at about four. And Karsten and Susanne were coming here that day. But he called a bit before three and said he would be late. He said he would be home at about seven.'

'Did he say why?'

'No.'

'Was that strange?'

'What do you mean?'

'Well, was it unusual for him to be late or did he never tell you why he had been held up?'

'No, I knew it was something to do with business. He might have been talking to his brothers – Arvid and Emmanuel. Arvid lives in Uranienborg and Emmanuel lives a long way out, in Bærum.' She sighed. 'I'm dreading talking to Arvid and Emmanuel. I know they have rung, but I can't bring myself to answer the phone.'

'But do you remember exactly when Reidar returned home?'

'At a quarter past seven. I checked the time. You know Jonny Stokmo was here at ten past? Perhaps you don't know who he is? Well, Jonny is a man who works with Reidar, and he didn't want to come inside and wait, but as dinner was ready and we were waiting I kept looking out of the window for Reidar, and I saw Jonny waiting for Reidar too. That did worry me a bit. I mean it was so cold, almost minus twenty.'

'The two of them worked together?'

'Jonny is Jonny,' Ingrid smiled. 'Jonny is . . . well, you were interested in how Reidar started in antiques. I think Reidar and Jonny's father set out together, a long time ago.'

She nodded as she read the expression on Frølich's face. 'Jonny's father worked with Reidar, but that was before I met him. I've never met Jonny's father – he died before Reidar and I got married.'

Frølich finished making his notes before looking up at the widow in the chair. 'And what did Stokmo want when he came round here?'

'No idea. I asked him in, but I think he felt there were too many people here, with Karsten and Susanne and the young children. At any rate, he said he didn't have time. Yet he waited outside in the street.'

'And when your husband came?'

'I suppose they talked.'

Frølich nodded.

'What was the relationship between your husband and Jonny Stokmo?' he asked at length.

'Umm . . .' Ingrid deliberated, but ended up shrugging her shoulders.

'I ask because I've heard that Jonny Stokmo was sacked,' Frølich said, looking her straight in the eye, and added, 'on your husband's say-so.'

Ingrid knitted her brows in astonishment. 'Given the boot? Are you sure? No . . .' She shook her head. 'I find that difficult to believe. But why would Reidar keep that from me – I mean, if there was some disagreement between them?'

Frølich shrugged: 'I couldn't say.' He looked at his notes and went on. 'So, Reidar arrived back just before half past seven, and what happened then?'

'We ate.'

'What did you eat?'

'Reindeer steak.'

'What was the atmosphere like around the table?'

'What do you mean by atmosphere?'

'Well, was it as usual, open or strained?'

Ingrid paused for a couple of seconds. 'Just as usual,' she concluded. 'Most of the attention was focused on Reidar's grandchildren, of course. It was a typical family meal.'

'Was Jonny Stokmo's name mentioned?'

She pondered. 'No, I don't think it was, that is . . . I mentioned to Reidar that he had been here, that was all. But that was before we started eating.'

'Anything business-related mentioned?'

'Karsten and Reidar had their usual chat, but that was after the meal. They talked together on their own.'

'On their own?'

'Yes, Susanne helped me to clear the table and put things in the dishwasher. The children floated around – and the two men sat on their own with a cognac. I suppose they were talking about money or politics, that's what they usually do.'

'But the atmosphere was very relaxed, or . . .'

She gave a pensive nod. 'There was one phone call, there may have been more, but Reidar answered it. He seemed very angry.'

'Did you hear what was said?'

She shook her head slowly.

'When was that?'

'At about half past ten, I think. Karsten and Susanne were on the point of leaving, yes, it must have been half past ten. The little one was asleep. Benjamin was grumpy, beyond himself. He usually goes to bed at nine.'

'They left at half past ten?'

Ingrid nodded. 'Perhaps closer to eleven. I didn't look at my watch, but I sat around in the living room and relaxed before the late-night news. I watched the news at eleven.'

'And Reidar?'

'He may have been on the phone, I don't know.'

'You don't know what he was doing?'

'No.'

'Had he gone down to the shop?'

'No, he was sitting and reading or doing something else. I went to the bathroom after the news and I heard him moving about. And afterwards I went to bed and we talked for a bit.'

'Did he normally go to bed after you?'

'No, in fact he didn't, and that was what we were talking about . . . I asked him if he was coming to bed.' She went quiet.

Frølich waited. She was clearly finding it more difficult to speak. A sudden, shrill electronic sound cut through the silence. It was his mobile phone. He sent the woman in the chair an apologetic smile and searched for his phone. Ingrid dried the corner of her eye with a finger. Frølich checked the display. It was a text message from Eva-Britt: *Could you pick up some nice fish on the way home?* He could feel his irritation mounting. The word: *home.* He switched off the phone and put it in his jacket pocket. As soon as he had done that, Ingrid stood up. 'Excuse me,' she said, disappearing through the door. Frølich could hear her tearing paper off a roll. He heard her blowing her nose. Soon afterwards she returned with a handful of white tissues. She sat down with a strained smile. The rims of her eyes were red and moist. 'He said he wanted to sit up reading,' she said, fighting to hold back the tears. A teardrop found its way to the tip of her nose. She wiped it away.

'And you went to sleep?'

She nodded. 'I took a sleeping pill, an Apodorm.'

'Why was that?'

'I couldn't settle. I took a pill to get off.'

'But you woke up later in the night?'

Ingrid was staring into space.

'You woke up?' Frølich repeated.

'It seems like a dream sometimes,' she said, wiping her nose again. 'Now it seems like a dream.'

'What seems like a dream?'

'That I woke up.'

'You rang Karsten Jespersen at half past two that night,' Frølich said patiently.

'I thought someone was in the room.'

Frølich raised both eyebrows.

'The floor was wet, you see.'

'Wet?'

'Yes, wet patches from melted snow, like when some-one has come in without removing their shoes and left snow behind them. I saw it, too: the remains of the snow, the zigzag pattern, the rough pattern of a shoe sole.'

Frølich stared at her. The silence endured. The middle-aged woman sat stiffly staring in front of her. She seemed to be studying a point on the floor. Most probably she was contemplating something within her. She wiped tears from her nose again. 'I was petrified,' she said. 'I've never been so frightened in my life. I was sure someone was standing there, watching me in the dark. I didn't dare move a muscle.'

The silence enveloped them again.

Frølich's attention was focused on his own winter boots. The snow that tended to attach itself to the laces had melted now, and at the extreme tip of one lace a drop of water had collected but refused to let go and fall onto the floor.

'Was anyone there?' he asked brightly.

She shook her head.

'Why do you think it was wet?'

'Reidar . . .' she began, but stopped to fight back the tears.

'Had Reidar been watching you sleep?' Frølich asked.

'It sounds so awful when you say it . . . but it couldn't have been anyone else,' she said. 'There wasn't a sound.'

'And you're sure there was snow and water on the floor? It wasn't something you had been dreaming?'

'I didn't dream I wiped it up.'

'You wiped it up? When?'

'When I got up.'

'And when was that?'

'It must have been just after half two.' She blew her nose on the paper towel. 'I was so tired that night, and I may be mixing things up because of the sleeping pill. But I was out of my mind with fear and couldn't get back to sleep. I had to know if there was someone in the room, so in the end I switched on the light . . .'

'I see.'

'Yes, I'd been lying there for a while – and when the light came on, it didn't seem so bad.'

'Which light was that?'

'The bedside lamp. I can show you. Come . . .'

She got to her feet and Frølich followed her. There was still a strong waft of perfume. He couldn't take his eyes off her lithe hips, and again he was struck by the gracefulness of her movements. 'Did you both sleep in the same room?' he asked, embarrassed.

'We share a bed. We've always shared a bed.'

She came to a sudden halt in the doorway to the bedroom. They collided. The contact sent an echo deep into his solar plexus, but she didn't seem to register it.

Frølich was sweating because she was standing so close to him. He apologized with a smile and stepped forward to scrutinize the room. There was a green bedspread over the double bed. A lush green plant stood on a pedestal beside an armchair in front of the window which let in diffuse light through white blinds. The walls were green and a painting with loud colours adorned the wall behind the bedhead. Frølich was unable to make sense of the motif in the painting, but discovered that he liked it. As he viewed the painting and the high, narrow bookshelf lined with paperbacks and magazines, he felt like a voyeur, especially because he soon found himself imagining what position she lay in when she was reading, what nightclothes she wore, the material, the colour . . .

'That one,' she said, bringing him back to reality. On either side of the bed there was a wooden table. On each table there was a small, round lamp with a wide lampshade. She went round the bed and switched on one of the lamps. 'Like that,' she said, standing lethargically by the large bed.

'And the snow?'

'Here,' she said, taking two steps forward and pointing, 'Here . . . and here.'

Frølich scratched his nose with the pen. 'Did you wash the floor afterwards?'

'Of course.' She looked at him askance.

'I was just wondering if we should have carried out a forensic examination here.'

'My God, don't cordon off my bedroom,' she said in a hushed voice, alarmed.

'You said you were frightened,' Frølich said. 'As I said, we have no reason to believe that either you or anyone else is in danger. We assume that the murder of your husband was motivated by personal circumstances. However, if you are concerned, you should take account of these feelings. If you so desire, we are happy to take measures which . . .'

'No,' she interrupted. 'Out of the question. I want to live here. This is my flat.'

'Of course,' Frølich said. 'I'm just saying this to accommodate your . . .'

'No,' she repeated, shaking her head.

'What did you think when you woke up and your husband was not beside you?'

'I thought it must have been Reidar in the bedroom after an evening walk, to pick something up, a piece of paper or . . .' She got up and walked calmly round the bed. 'Here,' she pointed again. 'There too – that was wet.'

They went back to the chairs where they had been sitting. 'And then?' Frølich asked. 'What happened then?'

'I got out of bed, went into the living room and round the flat looking for Reidar. But, of course, he wasn't there.'

'What did you think then?'

'I don't know what I thought, I was terrified. I called Karsten,' she said.

'Why did you do that?'

'I wanted to ask him to come over. I was scared something had happened to Reidar.'

Frølich said nothing.

'I didn't hear a sound. The whole house was silent.'

Frølich nodded. He looked down at his foot, placed his heel on the same wet patch on the floor and watched another round drop of water forming at the end of the drenched shoelace. 'Mm, you made a phone call.'

'Yes, it rang for a long time, well, after all, it was the middle of the night – until at last she picked up the phone. Susanne . . .' Ingrid pulled a face. 'I suppose she thought I was deranged . . .'

'What did you say to her?'

'I asked to speak to Karsten.'

'And what answer did you receive?'

'That he was not at home.'

'How did you interpret that?'

'I regretted the way I had expressed myself. I should have taken a more pedagogic approach. I didn't think when I was ringing that it was the middle of the night. You know, Susanne is quite special. Now and then she gives the impression that she is jealous. I . . .' She paused.

'Yes,' Frølich tilted his head and waited patiently.

'I know this might sound a bit odd, but in fact I think Susanne is frightened about me and Karsten . . .'

'So your interpretation was that she didn't want to wake her husband because she feared your intentions?'

'I know it sounds sick.'

'Did she have any reason to be jealous?'

'What do you mean?'

'Did she have any reason to be jealous?' Frølich repeated with identical intonation.

'Of course not. Susanne is special. I don't know how else to express it.'

Frølich could feel that he was not sweating any more. Nevertheless he had to make an effort to look into Ingrid Jespersen's eyes, instead of stealing glances at her rounded breasts or her hips. In fact, he could understand Susanne. 'What happened after that?' he asked.

'I said that I was worried about Reidar and asked her to tell Karsten when he came home.'

'And then?'

'I went back to bed.'

'But you had a look around the flat?'

'Of course, I wondered where Reidar was . . .'

'Did you see these puddles of melted snow anywhere else?'

'In the hall.'

'But nowhere else in the flat?'

'No.'

'So someone had walked straight from the hall to the bedroom?'

'I thought Reidar had been in to see me or to take something from a cupboard.'

'When you found the flat empty – didn't it occur to you that Reidar might be in the shop downstairs?'

'Yes, it did, of course. I couldn't sleep, I just lay thinking hundreds of thoughts, imagining all the places he might be, what the snow on the floor might mean . . . I lay awake until I heard the sounds of the morning traffic.'

'Why didn't you go down and check?'

'To be honest, I didn't dare. I was petrified. When the police rang the doorbell, naturally I thought it was Reidar.' A shudder ran through her body and she crossed her arms.

'Did you hear anything unusual?'

'What do you mean?'

Frølich observed her without saying a word. Her eyes were glazed. She coughed.

'Did you hear anything during the night?' the detective officer repeated. 'Noises, someone walking down the stairs . . .'

'Down the stairs?'

'Noises,' Frølich said impatiently. 'Footsteps, doors closing, anything.'

'I don't think so.'

'Don't think so?' Frølich gazed into her eyes. The irises were green and looked like two precious stones on a background of white felt in a display case.

'No,' she said with conviction. 'Nothing.'

'Hm?'

'I am sure I didn't hear anything.'

'But you had to have a think about it.'

'Don't you believe me?' she erupted.

'Of course. It is just that we need to know every detail, and there may be things which you overlook or consider inconsequential, things which we can make sense of. And when I asked . . .'

'I didn't hear any noises!' she interrupted angrily.

'Right.'

They sat looking at each other.

Frølich jotted down: *Interviewee is evasive when asked if she heard any noises.*

'The overwhelming probability then is that the person who killed your husband did it before you woke up?' he reasoned out loud.

She trembled again. 'I don't know anything about that!' she exclaimed.

'But you didn't hear any noises?'

'I was in a coma, knocked out, I had taken a sleeping pill! Loads of things could have happened without my realizing.'

'Fine,' Frølich said. 'There was one thing I was wondering about,' he mumbled with the ballpoint in his mouth. 'You said the person who was in your bedroom might have been Reidar. Were all the doors closed and locked when you woke up?'

Ingrid leapt to her feet. 'As I said, the whole thing seems like a nightmare now. I really don't know. The bedroom door may have been open, but . . .'

She paced to and fro before sitting down again. Frølich revelled in the sight through half-closed eyes.

'But when you got up for the first time, and you were petrified, didn't you check the front door?'

'I think so. I'm not sure.'

'Was it locked?'

'I don't know. I think so. Yes, of course it was. I get so confused . . .'

'So if someone had been in here – he must have been long gone?'

She sent him a suspicious glance. 'What do you mean now?'

'Since you didn't hear anything, the person who left snow on the floor must have gone by the time you woke up – isn't that right?'

She gave him another wary look. 'Of course. I didn't understand what you meant.'

Frølich studied her again. He thought: *Is she lying?* There was definitely something bothering her. The interview had not gone smoothly. 'Is there anything missing from the bedroom?' he asked. 'Has anything been stolen?'

'No. That's one of the things that makes me think it was Reidar who came in to see me.'

'Was your husband in good health?' the policeman asked.

She breathed out. 'I wish we all enjoyed the good health he had!'

'So he didn't have any complaints of any kind?'

'What do you mean?'

'He didn't complain about pains in his back, or kidneys, or legs . . .'

'No.'

Frølich nodded to himself. 'Does the number one hundred and ninety-five mean anything to you?'

He had held the question back, wondering how to phrase it. Now he was happy with the way it had come out, but it fell on stony ground. She shook her head and shrugged.

'Nothing?'

'No.'

'Nothing that connects your husband with this number – one hundred and ninety-five?'

'Sorry,' she said. 'Nothing I can think of.'

'In there . . .' Frølich motioned towards the bedroom she had shown him. 'In your bedroom, have you washed the floors?'

'Yes . . .'

Frølich thought. 'We could just have a quick look . . .'

Ingrid Jespersen heaved a deep sigh.

'Well, let me see,' he mumbled, getting to his feet. 'I suppose it isn't really necessary.'

15

Stray Keys

'You can relax,' Gunnarstranda reassured him. 'We'll keep an eye on Ingrid Jespersen. Round the clock.' He yawned. 'But whether there's any point is another matter. I'm more interested in getting an inventory of registered items in their shop. Karsten Jespersen can go through the list,' he continued and added: 'To see if anything has been stolen.' Gunnarstranda stretched and yawned again. 'But it can't be a burglary. That's out of the question. The only thief we have stumbled across so far is Karsten Jespersen. But that's the classic inheritance squabble.' The Detective Inspector rose to his feet, went to the desk, opened the top drawer and took out his darts.

'Who do you want?' Frølich asked, going through the various newspaper cuttings on his green desk pad.

'What's the choice?'

Frølich studied the cuttings. 'Director of Public Prosecutions, Minister of Justice, Pamela Anderson and various celebs.'

'A super-model who plays the devil in a film about ghosts?'

'No. Why?'

'A film I saw yesterday,' Gunnarstranda said and went on: 'Which celebs?'

Frølich shook his head. 'None you know. They do TV shows on Saturday nights.'

'One of them,' Gunnarstranda said, taking the page from the newspaper. He pinned the page to the board and took five steps back. 'Nose,' he said, throwing a dart which hit the celebrity in the middle of the eye.

'Not bad,' Frølich said.

'Nose,' Gunnarstranda repeated, threw and hit the woman on the chin.

Frølich gave an appreciative nod. 'What do we think about Ingrid Jespersen's story about the uninvited bedroom guest, snow melting on the floor and so on?'

'Might be true,' Gunnarstranda said, taking aim.

'How can it be true if it wasn't her old man?'

'The keys.'

'Which keys?'

'Nose.'

The dart missed the page and Gunnarstranda winced. He said: 'There weren't any keys there.'

'Where?'

'In the pockets of the dead man or in the shop.' He turned to Frølich. 'When the old man went down to the shop he must have unlocked the door, mustn't he? And he must have made sure he had the key on him so that he could return to the flat, don't you think? If there are no keys to be found, the perpetrator must have taken them and so the same person could easily have got into Reidar Folke Jespersen's flat.' He threw the last dart, which hit the smiling celebrity right in the mouth.

'Why would he steal the dead man's keys if he wasn't going to use them? Anyway, the missing keys are a good enough reason to keep a watchful eye on Ingrid Jespersen.'

'You don't think it was the dead man who left the snow on the floor then?'

'Yes, I do. The soles of his shoes had thick tread. But then this business with the keys is a mystery!'

Gunnarstranda went to the board, released the darts, went back five steps and took aim. 'Right eye!'

Missed. He said: 'Ingrid Jespersen says she went to bed between eleven and half past. At that time Reidar was in the flat. She sleeps until half past two and is woken by what she alleges is an uninvited guest in the bedroom . . .'

'No.' Frølich shook his head. 'She was alone, but she thinks Reidar popped in. The most probable explanation is that Folke Jespersen went for an evening walk. He came back to the flat, but realized that he needed to go down to the shop and there must have been something he wanted from the bedroom, the keys to the shop for all we know, and so he went into the bedroom. He still had snow on his shoes. Then he went down to the shop, met the murderer and was killed. My problem is that I feel she is holding something back. When I pushed her, she went very odd. But what she is holding back – I have no idea. Anyway, she insists she lay awake from half past two until seven in the morning and did not hear a sound. According to Schwenke, Jespersen was killed between eleven p.m. and three a.m. If it was Jespersen who left the snow on her floor, she must have been woken up by the sounds of the murder. Anyway, that would fit Schwenke's timescale.'

Gunnarstranda took aim.

'Talking about the keys . . .' Frølich said, 'Karsten Jespersen unlocked the flat for us.'

Gunnarstranda threw, but missed the eye. 'I suppose we ought to ask him if he used his own keys.'

'But that's a bit strange, isn't it?' Frølich said. 'Karsten having keys to the flat?'

'I don't think it's so strange him having keys. After all, the dead man was his father. Don't you have a key to your mother's place?'

'Yes, but my mother lives on her own. Karsten's father had re-married.'

They looked at each other. 'Well, I suppose it doesn't have to mean anything,' Frølich concluded, adding: 'According to Ingrid, Karsten's wife said he wasn't at home at half past two in the morning. And the guy has keys to the flat.'

'We'll have to ask anyway,' Gunnarstranda said, going over to the board and pulling out the darts. 'Even if Karsten Jespersen was at home and asleep, it doesn't hurt to ask.'

16

The Last Will and Testament

Detective Inspector Gunnarstranda was shown into Movinckel's office – the solicitor for Reidar Folke Jespersen – by a young woman. Here he was received by an even younger woman. When she stood up, it turned out she was a little shorter than him. She had short, cropped hair and a round face without a single wrinkle. Her skin was white with rosy red cheeks like his image of dairymaids. When she smiled, she revealed a row of white teeth dominated by two large top incisors. She was wearing dark flared slacks and a yellow cardigan. 'You seem surprised,' she said.

'And you seem young,' Gunnarstranda said, looking around. It didn't look much like a solicitor's office. It was decorated with luxuriant ivy and a number of varieties of the ficus plant on the window sills. On the walls hung art posters in pastel colours: Ferdinand Finne from *Galleri F15* and Carl Larsson from the same Moss gallery.

'You didn't think an elderly man would choose a young solicitor? A woman? Well, you're right,' she said. 'He didn't. Herr Folke Jespersen originally chose my father. When I took over my father's practice, he was one of the customers who took a risk and stayed with me.'

She motioned with her hand to the chair in front of

the desk. 'How can I help you?'

Gunnarstranda took a seat and crossed his legs, 'I was wondering if Reidar Folke Jespersen left a will.'

She looked down. 'No,' she answered at length.

'You hesitate?'

She revealed her teeth again. Her face seemed to have been cut out of a pumpkin, thought Gunnarstranda. She seemed to be bursting with a milky-white freshness. She had to belong to that breed of people who do not feel well until they have been out jogging in the morning. 'You hesitate,' he repeated.

'Yes,' she said, her lips still parted in a pumpkin-smile. 'He had a will until the day before he died.'

Gunnarstranda sucked his teeth and stretched out his legs.

'I can understand your reaction,' she said thoughtfully and looked down. 'Of course, a case like this is somewhat delicate.'

'What happened?' asked the policeman, impatient to move on.

'He phoned me on the afternoon of Friday the thirteenth wanting to revoke his will.'

'Phoned?' the policeman asked darkly.

'Indeed,' she said. 'That's part of what makes it delicate. Perhaps the probate court will have to step in here.'

'You're positive it was him on the phone?'

'No doubt about it. It was him.'

'When did he call?'

'Late afternoon. A bit before five, I think.'

'And how did you answer?'

'The way I answered you. Of course it was fine, but

officially he should have come here in person and presented his request.'

'What did he say?'

'He said he didn't have time.'

'Didn't have time?'

'Yes.'

'How did you interpret that?'

'I think he was ill.'

Gunnarstranda angled his head and waited.

'I don't think he had much time left,' she went on.

'Did he ever talk to you about any illness?'

She sent him a faint smile, as though she had remembered something funny.

'Never. But some time in the autumn – October or November – I met him in Bygdøy allé. He rushed up to me and seemed – erm – ill and very old. He was holding a leaf – from a tree – must have been either maple or chestnut . . .'

'Did it have fingers?'

'Fingers?'

'Was it like a large hand with fingers?'

'Yes, it was.'

'Then it was a horse chestnut.'

'Hm, well, at any rate, the point is that he stopped me. He didn't say hello, he was excited, almost like a boy. "Look," he shouted. "Have you ever seen such a large leaf?" I stood gaping at him and didn't quite know what to say – to me the leaf could have been any leaf in the autumn, yellowing of course, and quite big. "Yes," I said. "It is a nice leaf." He beamed like a young boy. "Isn't it!" he grinned and said: "I'll have to go home and show it to Ingrid." With that he toddled off up the street and home.'

Gunnarstranda sat staring into the beyond with a lined brow. 'And this incident made you think he was ill?'

With a grave expression, she nodded her head. 'I watched him disappear. This proud man who all of a sudden seemed shaky and bent, and then this outburst. I'd never seen him like that, neither before nor after. It was like he was running home to mummy. I remember thinking: he hasn't got long to live now.'

'So he was ill.'

'Not just ill, but at death's door.' She frowned. 'He seemed frail, on his last legs.'

Gunnarstranda nodded. 'And the will?'

'It's here, but officially it has been revoked and won't be presented to the beneficiaries.'

'When was it made?'

'A long time ago, before my time. He was here last summer and went through the wording with me, on his own. That was all. But we didn't make any changes.'

'Did he seem ill then?'

'No,' she smiled. 'Just old.'

'Did he give any reason for revoking the will?'

'No.' She shook her head.

'And the request – it wasn't accompanied by any comments, such as why he chose to ring you at that precise moment?'

Her lips parted in another smile. 'I'm afraid not. I thought you would ask. He went straight to the point. All I did was to ask him if he wanted to make another will. But he said no.'

'Without offering any explanation?'

'That's right.'

'And then?' asked Gunnarstranda, impatiently.

'The will?' she asked and said: 'It's very short. Nothing earth-shattering in it. I think you'll be disappointed.'

'Let me be the judge of that.'

Without another word the solicitor moved away some papers and opened a yellowing envelope on the table. 'Here you are. Feel free,' she said, passing him the document.

17

Evening Mood

Eva-Britt served fried Arctic char and made a lot of fuss about the trouble she had gone to in order to lay her hands on some. At first he ignored the cutting remarks, but he didn't escape. She attacked his complacency, and went on with her usual rant about his lack of commitment to the relationship, and his escapism which manifested itself in indifference since he had not even bothered to buy fish on the way home as she had asked. Of course, she had known he would forget everything and had therefore done the shopping herself. He studied her noticeboard for the duration of the tirade. *Home*, he thought to himself, contemplating the postcard he had once sent her from a course in Bergen, the row of Beaujolais nouveau wine labels, the other cards from her friends, all with the conspicuously similar Mediterranean beach scenes, and right at the bottom a few words of wisdom signed by Piet Hein. He knew he would explode if he made an effort to answer. Her goal was to vent all her pent-up frustration before the meal, an objective which he was generous enough to let her achieve without any interruptions so that he could have the first beer of the evening without her starting up again.

After they had eaten Frank Frølich sat thinking about Ingrid Jespersen. He couldn't get the thought out of his head that she had lived for a quarter of a century with a man who was a quarter of a century older than her. He and Eva-Britt occupied their fixed places in her living room – in front of her new widescreen TV. He turned the volume right down and zapped between channels. But he had picked a bad time. There were advertisements or crap series about young celebs on every channel. On Eurosport there was a boxing match between two roly-poly welterweights waddling around the ring. Every time he pressed the remote control the TV screen flashed, sending bluish-green tints along the walls towards Eva-Britt who was curled up in her new, white armchair from Ikea. She was immersed in a book by a writer called Melissa Banks and immune to his boredom. Frank switched off the television.

'Why do women decide to marry older men?' he asked.

Eva-Britt raised her head and sent him a distant look.

'I was just wondering why young women marry older men.'

'In fact I'm older than you,' Eva-Britt said. 'Eight months.'

'Mm . . .' He considered how to express himself. 'Do you remember Rita?'

Eva-Britt looked up from her book again. 'Rita?'

'She was in the year above us at school.'

'Oh, her.' Eva-Britt flicked through the book absent-mindedly, helping herself to a biscuit from the dish on the table and taking a nibble.

'She was with . . . Anders, the dark-haired guy . . . almost five years older than her . . .'

'Mm.' Eva-Britt smiled at something she was reading.

'There was always such a terrible to-do at parties. No one wanted to invite him while Rita was always nagging and pushing for him to be invited. Do you remember that?'

Eva-Britt was munching the biscuit.

'Weren't you in love with Anders, too?'

'Hey?' She looked up.

'There was something between you and him. At one party . . .'

Eva-Britt put the book down. Frank could see her earlobes going pink. 'What are you going on about now?'

'I was wondering why women choose older men.'

'I'm not in the slightest bit interested in older men!'

'Did I say you were?'

'You're talking about things that happened many years ago!'

Frank sighed. 'When you're with Trude, the only thing you talk about is your schooldays,' he countered. 'Teachers, crushes and all the so-called crazy things you did to celebrate the end of school!'

She took a deep breath. There was an ominous hard look in her eyes. He didn't have the stamina for her to crank it up again so late in the evening. Time to row to the shore, he thought with a diplomatic smile. 'You see, I've interviewed this woman who is twenty-five years younger than her husband. I mean, she's attractive, elegant and all that, but she chose such an old man. I don't understand.'

'That's because you're thinking the wrong way around. Women don't choose older men. It's older men who chase younger women!'

'Mm,' he sighed, trying to imagine Ingrid Jespersen being courted by older men. What did she have in common with the dead man, except for an interest in design, he wondered. The same taste in music? Friends? She had been interested in literature – he hadn't. On the other hand, the son was interested in literature – Karsten.

Eva-Britt had opened her book again, but was looking at him with gentler eyes now. 'Does it have to be a mystery? It could be true love,' she suggested silkily.

He gave an ironic smile. 'True love?'

She sent him a meaningful glance from over the top of the book. 'Like ours.'

He side-stepped the provocation and said: 'If it wasn't true love – like ours – what could it be?'

'Is he rich?'

'Presume so.'

'Has she got a difficult relationship with her father . . . I mean . . . are her parents divorced . . . or is her father a sailor?'

'I have no idea.'

'Money and/or no father figure,' Eva-Britt suggested, searching for the right page in her book. 'Young girls, on the other hand,' she smiled, tucking her legs beneath her on the chair, 'young girls choose slightly older boys because they have fewer pimples, broader shoulders and are a bit more experienced than certain other boys.'

Frank Frølich switched the television back on.

'Are you bored?' she asked.

He lifted the remote control and pressed. 'Bored? No . . .'

18

Salsa

The pick-up arm refused to lift. The sound in the loud-speakers was reminiscent of worn windscreen wipers rubbing against a dry windscreen. At last Gunnar-stranda got out of his chair, went over to the record player, activated the lever to raise the arm and blew away the dust that had gathered on the stylus. Then he lowered the stylus down. The old Tandberg speakers emitted scratching sounds until the first guitar notes of Peggy Lee's 'Love is Just Around the Corner' stole into the room. Gunnarstranda stood for a few reflective moments by the window. He held his hand against the glass and felt the cold penetrating the pane. Then he almost pressed his face against the glass to read the temperature on the outside thermometer with the fading blue numbers. Minus 23. Down on the pavement in Bergensgata a woman wearing a coat walked into the yellow glare of the streetlamp. She was taking a lean setter for its evening walk. The dog did not enjoy the cold weather. Its movements, which would normally be supple and bouncy, were reluctant and stiff; its head and tail trailed along the ground. The woman seemed to be dragging it along. The policeman watched them for a little while until he sat back at his desk. He stared down at the scrap of paper on which he had jotted the code that been written in pen on the murdered man's chest. He rested his head on his hands without taking his eyes off the numbers. In the end he grabbed the almost full bottle of Ballantine's which was on the tray beside the typewriter and twisted off the cork. He poured two centimetres of whisky into a tumbler. As he raised the glass to drink, the telephone rang. He took the receiver.

'Is that you?' It was Yttergjerde's voice.

Gunnarstranda swallowed and felt the spirit burn its way down to his stomach. 'What did you say?' he rasped.

'You're usually so abrupt on the phone,' Yttergjerde said. 'I was beginning to wonder if there was something wrong.'

'What do you want?' Gunnarstranda asked.

'She's got a man,' Yttergjerde said.

'Name?'

'Eyolf Strømsted. Runs a dance school. Looks like that anyway. This evening there was a salsa course and African dance. You should have seen it, a black man with a drum and about fifty Norwegian women shaking their butts.'

'And our lady?'

'At first I thought she was on the course, but she went straight to this guy wearing yellow pants and a silver shirt. He had a microphone round his neck, the kind of loop thing in front of his mouth that TV hosts have. He gyrated and jigged through the dancers, and when he screamed into the mike, you could hear him in the speakers along with the music – what are you listening to you by the way?'

Gunnarstranda looked across at the record player. 'A singer. Jazz ballads.'

'Not quite the same beat, no, this was salsa. When she arrived, there was a bit of a commotion because the guy had to get someone else to take over.'

'Did she see you? Were you in the same room?'

'There were loads of people there. She didn't see me.'

'Go on.'

'They went outside to the car and drove off. So I followed them. They parked in the car lot outside the Munch museum. Sort of discreet, under the trees by the fence around Tøyen Park. And there I watched them sitting and smooching for almost forty minutes, so I guess it must have been more than smooching. She drove the guy back to the dance school and went home.'

'And you?'

'When the widow had gone, I was off duty and went back to the dance school. At last the guy came out and locked up. He walked home. Lives in Jacob Aalls gate, in Majorstua. That's where I found his name. He shot up the stairs about five minutes ago.'

'Good work, Yttergjerde. It's cold. You should go home and get warm.'

'I'm never cold,' whinnied Yttergjerde. 'In this freezing weather people take cod liver oil and vitamins, but there's no point – what counts is eating spicy food. You should remember that. Just add three or four cloves of garlic to your eggs for breakfast, and red chilli peppers, best if they're so hot you can't breathe and break out into sweat. With that kind of firepower on board your hands will never be cold. You can walk around in minus

20 with your shirt off and still the steam will be coming off you. Not one germ, not one virus, will get a hold inside your mouth. Your breath will kill healthy potted plants. You become immortal, man, immortal.'

'Yes, yes,' said Gunnarstranda.

'Yes,' said Yttergjerde.

'Sleep tight,' Gunnarstranda said and put down the telephone before his colleague could give him the recipe for a good night's sleep. He took the tumbler and drank the rest of the whisky. Then he picked up the ballpoint pen and drew a triangle on the scrap of paper. In the two bottom corners he wrote the names Ingrid and Reidar Folke Jespersen. In the top corner he wrote Eyolf Strømsted. Finally, he put three crosses under the triangle. Three crosses, and he was careful to draw them like those on the forehead of Jespersen's body.

19

The Parked Car

When Frølich entered the office, Gunnarstranda was engrossed in the *Aftenposten*. 'Anything about us in there?' he enquired.

Gunnarstranda shook his head.

'And the will?' Frølich asked.

Gunnarstranda lowered his paper. 'Disappointing. Just a list of specific items of property – Karsten would get some wardrobe, that sort of thing. The old boy doesn't say anything about anyone being cut out or favoured. No secret beneficiaries, nothing. There's just a list of about twenty to thirty items and who will get them – that is to say: Ingrid and Karsten.'

'What's the upshot of him revoking the will?'

'It means his estate will be thrown into one big pot. Ingrid will get half of the broth plus her share of the old boy's legacy. Karsten will be paid off. That's all. The revocation of the will just means that Karsten and Ingrid have to argue about who gets what.'

'But why change such a crappy will a few hours before he is murdered?'

Gunnarstranda sighed in response. 'Yet another mystery in our files.'

'What sort of things were on the list?'

'Wardrobes, pornographic Chinese carvings, that sort

of thing. I wrote it all down. What about you?'

Frølich sighed and rubbed his eyes. 'I've interviewed every single occupant of their block,' he said, consulting his notes. 'Interested?'

'Give me the edited highlights.'

'On the ground floor only shops. As far as the first floor is concerned, it's occupied by Ingrid Jespersen. On the second there's a married couple in one flat – herr and fru Holmgren. Both between fifty and sixty. He works for a tool agency. She's his secretary. They didn't hear a thing on Friday. They were watching TV and went to bed at about half past twelve. The man's mother, Aslaug Holmgren, lives in the adjacent flat. She's almost eighty, same age as the dead man, and she thinks Reidar Folke Jespersen was an *arrogant, snobbish buffoon*, but had nothing to tell us about the evening in question. Her hearing isn't so good, and she usually goes to bed after watching a series about the FIB, as she called them. She didn't approve of NRK putting on crime programmes so late. Also, she wanted *Oberinspektor Derrick* back on TV and thought we police could learn a lot from it. Said she went to bed at eleven and didn't hear a thing.'

Inspector Gunnarstranda chewed his lower lip, deep in thought. 'And that's all the people who live in the building?' he asked.

'I crossed the street too,' Frølich said. 'Got a nibble there. A mysterious car.'

'Oh yes?'

'I tried to work out who would have had a view of the shop. Since the killing took place at night, in practice that meant quite a lot of flats.'

'What sort of people?'

'Cross-section of Oslo 3: a typographer who works on a newspaper – *Vårt Land*. He lives on his own with a dog. Then there's a young couple – he's a cameraman with TV Norge; she works for *Dagbladet*. I spoke to a publishing editor who said she would also ask her children. She has two teenagers who weren't there at the time. She thought she had seen a taxi parked outside the antiques shop for at least an hour – that's what she maintained anyway.'

'A taxi?'

Frølich nodded. 'And that's the only hot tip so far. A taxi – I asked whether the roof light was on or not. It was. She said she thought it was strange that the taxi's engine was running, or that it was there for so long.'

'How long?'

'At least an hour, she guessed. The problem is that this was early evening, before ten – she said. Seems she had been working late – she had been to a meeting and didn't get home until eight, half an hour after Jespersen arrived. She wasn't sure whether the taxi was already there when she got in. But after taking a shower she looked through the window and saw it parked beneath her flat with the engine running. At least three quarters of an hour later she looked again and the same car was still there.'

'Had she . . .?'

'I'm coming to that,' Frølich interrupted. 'She looked out again later – before going to bed. There was a Mercedes taxi parked in the road. She thought the taxi with the engine running – the one she had seen before –

had also been a Mercedes. But the car she saw on her way to bed – its engine wasn't running.'

'Colour?'

'Dark.'

The two detectives stared at each other.

'It could have been three different taxis,' Gunnarstranda said. 'Every second taxi in Oslo is a Mercedes – at least. And this is one of the most densely populated areas of the city.'

'Two men live in the top flat,' Frølich continued. 'One of them works in local radio and calls himself "Terje Telemonster". Perhaps you've heard of the guy? He rings people up and is a kind of telephone terrorist. If the victim works in a hotel he rings and says he's on night duty and has been locked in a broom cupboard and he's starving, or he rings the emergency doctor and says he's on top of his wife and can't get his ding-a-ling out of her muff. Very funny guy.'

'Sounds extremely funny,' Gunnarstranda said, deadpan.

'It's popular anyway. And he lives with a sort of drag artist, a guy who's into Egyptian stuff. He does bellydancing. And male belly dancers are a bit special.'

'Well? Had they seen anything?'

'Nothing. The taxi was all I managed to turn up,' Frølich summarized.

'What impression did people have of our old man?'

'Anonymous, elderly. Those who knew who he was connected him with the shop. Only Holmgren and his wife knew he was married to Ingrid. Several people recognize her – because she's kept herself in shape.' Frølich grinned and mimicked them: '*Oh, is that who you mean? The good-looking one, no spring chicken, but she keeps herself in good shape.*'

'Great,' Gunnarstranda mumbled.

'The man who lived alone, with a dog, asked if I knew anything about the person stealing his newspaper. He seemed a bit manic – had put a wide-angle lens in the door to see who was stealing his newspaper every morning.'

'Observant?'

'I thought that too, but the problem is that all his attention is focused on the door. He couldn't tell me anything about activity in the street. And this couple – the man working for TV Norge and the woman for *Dagbladet* – had been out to a seafood evening and didn't come back until five o'clock in the morning.'

'And didn't see anything?'

'Zilch. They returned in a taxi, but neither of them noticed any parked cars when they came home. I have the licence number of the taxi they came home in. The TV cameraman had kept the receipt, so I'll talk to the taxi driver – he may have seen something. But the two of them had been pretty pissed and staggered into bed without noticing the shop window across the street or anything. By the way, they were able to confirm that the window was never lit at night.'

Gunnarstranda wiped his upper lip. 'I came across something the son – Karsten – has written,' he mumbled, wiping his lip again.

'Where?'

'I stumbled across an article in an old journal – amazing what you hang onto really,' Gunnarstranda said. 'A back-copy of *Farmand*.'

'*Farmand*?'

'An old organ for reactionary intellectuals, a journal that died a death many years ago.'

'What did he write about?'

'The prison system.'

'My God. Is he any good? At writing?'

Gunnarstranda opened the top drawer of his desk and rummaged. 'There was quite an interesting bit about a man who went mental in solitary confinement, but the rest was . . .' Gunnarstranda shrugged, produced a pair of tweezers from the drawer, stood up and went to the mirror hanging on the wall beside the door and continued: '. . . banal reflections on the treatment of criminals, but strangely enough there was none of the usual harping on about custody and human rights.'

'Must have been editorial guidelines,' Frølich said. 'If the journal was reactionary, as you say.'

Gunnarstranda took a concentrated hold on the tweezers and pulled out a hair from his nostril. He scrutinized his catch carefully. 'Must have been,' he conceded. 'I think you may well be right.'

20

The Coat

'Where can I hang my coat?' Susanne Jespersen asked, removing a dark, fur-lined garment which she passed to Frank Frølich. She looked around. 'What have you done with that impudent boss of yours?'

Frølich stood for a few moments wondering what he should do with the heavy outdoor coat. In the end he made up his mind, moved a few things off the little table in front of the sofa and put it there.

'I've been to see the solicitor,' Susanne Jespersen said. 'He's not allowed to treat us like this, so there will be repercussions. Mark my words!'

'Of course,' Frølich mumbled. He knew he had put his notepad somewhere. He had had it in his hands, used it when he was writing the report. But he didn't have a clue where it was now.

'I've been finding out about your boss,' Susanne ranted on. 'And I happen to know he is not flavour of the month. I have contacts in high places. And I won't put up with much more from him. You can tell him that from me!'

'Right,' Frølich said, scanning his own and his boss's desks. No notepad in sight.

Susanne studied herself in the mirror and straightened the belt she had put around her waist. 'We'll go and collect our personal property. After all, Karsten is the shop in person. We'll take the property that belongs to us, we will. Don't think this despotic gnome will frighten us away! Got that?'

'Absolutely,' Frølich said, rubbing his nose. 'I took her coat . . .' he muttered to himself.

'And on top of that I have to take a day off work, postpone important meetings, but it won't happen again. I've been making enquiries, I have, and I know you need a court order!'

Frølich found it under the coat. He lifted it up and there was his notepad.

'You see, I've got you there, haven't I!'

'Please take a seat,' Frølich said, pointing to an uncluttered chair.

'As I thought! But now that poor me has made the effort to come here, I may as well stay,' Susanne Jespersen said. 'Get it over with,' she added, folding her arms above the handbag resting on her lap.

'Exactly,' Frølich said. The telephone rang. 'Excuse me,' he said, walking over to Gunnarstranda's desk and lifting the receiver. 'Gunnarstranda's phone.' He watched Susanne Jespersen with his mind elsewhere. She studied herself in the mirror on the wall, adjusted her long hair, plunged into her handbag and pulled out a lipstick which she ran across her lips.

'Yes, she's arrived,' Frølich said. 'Yes, I'll remember that,' he said and cradled the receiver.

Susanne sat down. She pulled a face. Frølich thought at first she was having convulsions – until he recalled her putting on lipstick. For a moment he wondered how old she was. Thirty-five, he thought, between thirty-five and forty, but no older than forty. She was a bit plump and round-shouldered, with thin lips. Now that she had painted them red, they looked like a smudged brush-stroke on an otherwise grey painting.

'Your mother-in-law rang you in the middle of the night?'

'Oh, my God,' Susanne sighed, resigned. 'I assume you mean my late father-in-law's partner – Ingrid Folke Jespersen, née Rasmussen. And, yes, it is correct that she *gave me a buzz* . . .' Susanne pronounced the final words with a pinched expression around her mouth. 'Ingrid Folke Jespersen, née Rasmussen, doesn't phone, you see, she doesn't ring either, she *gives you a buzz* – and she does that whenever it suits her, at six, five, four, three or two o'clock at night. And she was so *scared*!'

'So she did ring?'

'Karsten! I'm so *scared*! Come and hold me, Karsten!'

Frølich calmly observed her. 'Are you suggesting that she and your husband are having an affair?' he asked in a cold voice.

'How dare you!'

'Answer the question,' Frølich said with force.

Susanne Jespersen lost her composure. 'No, I do not mean to suggest anything of the kind.'

Frølich felt some silence would be appropriate. So he took his time noting down her answer.

'But she's an insufferable nag. And sometimes she seems to be trying to catch Karsten on his own. For that reason I did not wake him when she rang that night . . .' Susanne was on the point of slipping into the role as her old self when she added in an angrier tone: 'But I don't regret it! After all, it was half past two in the morning. Like other people, she has to understand that you can't ring in the middle of the night, even though your husband's bed is empty. What would I do if Karsten went out on the town or came home late – ring everybody I know? Eh?'

Frølich regarded the woman sitting on the chair. Imagine being married to her, he thought gloomily. Imagine waking up with her in the morning! Every single morning. Imagine coming home to her after a long, tiring day. He caught himself extending Karsten his sympathies as he said:

'So your husband was at home asleep all night?'

'Yes.'

'Have you or your husband a key to the flat in Thomas Heftyes gate?'

'Karsten has,' she said. 'It's where he grew up, isn't it!'

'But you haven't?'

She shook her head.

'You let Karsten sleep when she rang. What did she say on the phone – word for word?'

'She said: "Susanne, it's me, Ingrid. Could you ask Karsten to come over? Reidar's not here and I'm scared."'

'Did you have the impression she was as scared as she maintained?'

Susanne recoiled and poisoned daggers took up residence in her eyes. 'Do you mean . . .?'

'No,' Frølich said firmly. 'I don't mean anything of the kind. Just describe how you perceived the situation?'

'Well, I was out of it. This was half past two at night. I had been in bed only two or three hours. But I remember what she said. I was pretty shaken myself!'

'And what did you answer?'

'I said I would say she'd rung.'

'Yes?'

'She said something about a break-in and being scared . . .'

Frølich waited for her to go on.

'I don't remember every word. There was something about her being worried about a break-in. I couldn't be bothered to listen. They had been talking about break-ins all evening – I mean the evening before, when we were at their place.'

'They talked about break-ins?'

'Yes, it was a terrible evening – so depressing. Do you know what we talked about? How tender the steak was. We talked about food and how the shop downstairs might be burgled.'

'Was this a departure from the norm?'

'What do you mean?'

'Well, was it always so boring or was there a particular atmosphere that evening?'

'There was a particular atmosphere. Ingrid seemed very nervous – she is not usually. Reidar was just sullen. But he always is.'

'What do you mean she seemed nervous?'

Susanne thought back. 'She knocked a glass of wine over the table cloth. She seemed hyper and clumsy. Nerves, nothing more, nothing less.'

Frølich jotted this down.

'The thing is I thought the way Ingrid spoke that night – being scared about a break-in – it all seemed, well, a little convenient.'

'Convenient?'

'Yes, a little conspicuous, as though she were using it as a pretext to get Karsten up in the middle of the night. I said he wasn't at home and put down the phone.'

'Do you mean that Ingrid is interested in your husband?'

'I didn't say that!'

'My understanding was that Ingrid had a better relationship with your husband than with you!'

'That's true enough. It's a good observation. Exactly. You said it.'

'What's the reason for that?'

'Are you asking me?'

'What do your husband and Ingrid talk about?'

'Books!'

'You don't say. Books.'

'Karsten has a talent, he can write, you know. He's done talks on the radio and written articles for the newspaper. But, Ingrid, she just reads novels. And she has got it into her head that they have something in common.'

'That evening,' Frølich said with emphasis. 'That evening when you were visiting Reidar, do you know if anything unusual happened, if someone came to the door or if someone rang?'

'There were a number of phone calls.'

'A number?'

'Yes, I saw Reidar talking on the phone, but I have no interest in who people phone . . .'

'So Reidar was making the calls?'

'I've no idea. I saw him talking on the phone. That was all.'

'How many calls were there?'

'One, maybe two, perhaps three. I wasn't following.'

'But you must know if it was one or three calls?'

'There were more than one. That's all I can say.'

'Fine,' Frølich said, and hastened to add before she could continue: 'Ingrid rang you in the middle of the night, but she rang you later too – in the morning.'

'Yes, at half past seven. But then Karsten answered the phone. Oh God, I regret taking the children – with Grandad lying there, dead!'

'In fact I met your boy. Nice boy.'

'Hm,' Susanne grunted.

'Did you like your father-in-law?'

'Yes,' came the firm response from the woman on the chair.

'Really?'

'I sometimes helped him with the annual accounts. I can do that – accountancy. I don't have a problem with numbers. You can say what you like, but Reidar Folke Jespersen was a decent person, solid.'

'Do you think he had many enemies?'

'He had friends and enemies. I was a friend. But enemies? No doubt. That doesn't bother me, though. I looked upon him as a friend.'

'So you considered him . . .' Frølich searched for words. 'You considered him to be in good health?'

Susanne bent forward. 'That man would have outlived us all,' she said. 'The lot of us.'

'If I say the numbers one-nine-five, does that mean anything to you?'

She rolled her shoulders.

'Nothing you connect with these numbers? The whole number? Single digits? No relevance to your father-in-law? Accounts? Tax? Anything at all?'

Susanne stared into space. 'No idea,' she said at last.

'And your husband? Was there a good relationship between father and son?' Frølich immediately regretted the question. A suspicious, conspiratorial glint came into the eyes of his witness the moment he said the last word.

'Of course,' Susanne said, and added: 'Are there really no other officers to put on this case? After all, it is a murder and has to be cleared up.'

'Thank you,' Frølich said, standing up and passing her coat. 'I have no further questions for the time being.'

21

Reflection

Emmanuel Folke Jespersen lived in a cul-de-sac in Haslum. Cars were parked higgledy-piggledy alongside the fences, packed in a thick blanket of snow. The snow-ploughs had snaked their way through. Inspector Gunnarstranda parked in a gap between two well-wrapped cars. There was a line of four red terraced houses. Each house had a handkerchief of a garden in front of the door. A black and white cat, tranquil and picturesque, sat on the front doorstep. The step had been swept; the piassava broom was blue and the shaft decorated with roses in Norwegian style. As soon as Gunnarstranda put his foot on the little step and rang the bell, the cat rose and brushed against his left trouser leg.

The door was opened by a chubby, young woman with curly hair and glasses. 'Oh, there you are,' she laughed, a little disorientated, as the cat slipped in. 'Are you the man from the police?' she asked, holding the door open for Gunnarstranda, who nodded. 'My grand-father's in the living room.'

Soft violin music resonated from somewhere inside as Gunnarstranda hung his coat on the peg the woman showed him. 'I'll be off soon,' she assured him. 'I just promised to lend a hand.'

The policeman followed her down a narrow corridor.

They passed a staircase to the first floor and continued into a smallish room furnished with a piano and an English-style leather three piece suite. The violin music came from an old stereo cabinet positioned beneath the window – a comfortable arm's length away from Emmanuel Folke Jespersen, who struggled to his feet and extended his hand in greeting.

Jespersen had two squinting eyes set in a round face dominated by a heavy jaw. His hair was completely white and shone like a Christmas tree decoration.

'I'll be off then,' the young woman said to Folke Jespersen after pouring coffee for him and the policeman.

'Right,' the man said, glancing across the table where a flower-patterned coffee flask, cups and a plate of biscuits had been placed. Jespersen pulled out a slim cigarillo from the breast pocket of his pink shirt. 'Mind if I smoke?'

'Not at all,' Gunnarstranda answered, pulling out his own roll-up tobacco and putting it on the table. Again he screwed up his eyes against the low winter sun bursting in through the window. 'I can't sit here,' he said and moved to the opposite corner of the sofa.

Emmanuel turned and raised his arm in salute to the young woman closing the door behind her. 'Grandchild,' he said in explanation. 'Kristin. Great girl. Helpful.' He flicked a lighter and puffed the cigarillo into life. Through the loudspeakers the music swelled to a crescendo.

'Beautiful,' Gunnarstranda said.

'One of the new rising stars,' Jespersen explained,

blowing a smoke ring, which quivered, rose in the sunlight and slowly disintegrated. He picked up the CD sleeve lying on the table between them. 'She looks good, too – unbelievably beautiful, these young lady violinists. They almost play more on their sexuality than on their music.'

Gunnarstranda took the sleeve. The photograph on the front was of a dark-haired beauty posing with a violin against a sinister background – an urban night scene with dark shadows. Her clothes were provocative and her make-up voluptuous, and she stared at him with moist, parted lips. 'A few years ago I would have thought she was a glamour model, but can you be sure?' he motioned towards the speakers. 'Is it really her playing?'

Emmanuel Folke Jespersen nodded, amused, and rolled the cigarillo between his fingers. 'Indeed, and not just that, apparently at concerts she stands in a swimming costume and plays. Imagine that. That's the way it is now. A gifted violinist has to wear a bikini to make it!'

Gunnarstranda nodded: 'It reminds me of . . .' he began, but paused as Jespersen waved his cigarillo to point out the violinist's virtuosity. Gunnarstranda listened out of courtesy until the orchestra came back in. He went on: 'When I was a young policeman – that must have been in . . . I can't remember exactly when, but it's a long time ago. I was up north. A lady moved up from Oslo and opened a hairdressing salon in her cellar, but she didn't get any customers until she began cutting people's hair in just her swimsuit.'

'Well, there you go . . . coffee?' Jespersen held up the flask.

Gunnarstranda nodded. 'There were single men and schoolboys and swingers, long queues of men who went to have their hair cut, some of them had their hair cut several times a week! No surprises there, she was a good-looking girl, but when the priest went down for a haircut, the women in the district went into action.'

Jespersen gave a deep guffaw. 'Did you have a hair-cut?'

'No, I was sent there because there were allegations that she had started doing bits and bobs in the salon, and sometimes without even a swimsuit on.' Gunnarstranda passed back the CD sleeve. 'So there's nothing new about swimsuits in the food chain,' he concluded, stretching out his legs and making gestures of appreciation as the music flowed out of the speakers: 'She can certainly play.'

'Schubert,' Jespersen said. 'He was Reidar's favourite composer, by the way.'

'You don't say?'

'Yes, he had a side he didn't show to everyone. How should I put it? His soft side – he reserved it for a small band of people.'

'But you were one of them?'

Jespersen answered with a shrug and blew another, less successful, smoke ring towards the ceiling.

Gunnarstranda held his coffee cup and raised it. 'You three had a chat the other day . . . I was told you met at your brother's place, at Arvid's.' He took a sip of coffee and then put down the cup.

'Yes, and it was sad. To part on such terms.'

'What terms?'

'We had a little dispute, and Reidar was upset. It was a shame – that we couldn't make up before he died.'

'A dispute?'

'This couple, Iselin and Hermann, they want to buy the shop. Which I think is wonderful. I mean we're – all three of us – getting on and it would be nice to have a lump sum and be finished with everything.'

'You didn't agree on the price?'

Jespersen nodded his head gravely. 'Reidar did not want to sell.'

'Why not?'

'I have no idea.'

'Had he had a sudden change of heart, or was he never involved in the sale?'

'He knew about it. He hadn't been openly hostile until then, just undecided. That was why we had the meeting.'

'You say you don't know why he turned down the offer. Could it have been to protect his son? Karsten works there, doesn't he?'

The man tilted his head, as though reflecting. 'Of course it's a possibility . . .' he murmured. 'Although it doesn't seem altogether probable. Well, I don't know why. Reidar was so unpredictable, you know. He . . .' Jespersen shook his head again. 'To understand my hesitation you need to have known Reidar.' He panted as he changed position in the chair, put out his arm and turned the volume down low.

The two of them exchanged looks. Jespersen bent forward in the chair. 'Reidar didn't give a shit about Karsten,' he stated. 'Reidar . . .' Jespersen leaned further forward, as though to create confidentiality.

The policeman followed suit.

'Reidar was old school,' Jespersen said. 'Do you understand?'

Gunnarstranda didn't answer.

'Reidar did things during the war about which neither you nor I want to know. Reidar was not a warm-hearted person. He was much too hard on Karsten. You can see that. The boy's crushed. He shakes like a whelp in a thunderstorm. But Karsten is an adult now, with a good marriage, and Karsten and Susanne have enough money. She makes good money, you know – chief accountant and all that. But Reidar – he's never bothered about Karsten's interests. And Karsten? He's never been interested in the shop – not really. He's worked there all these years because he's scared of his father. What Karsten wants is to have a career, as a writer.'

Jespersen straightened up and puffed on his cigarillo.

'Has he had any success?'

'Doing what?'

'Journalism.'

'Well . . . he's written a few reports on things he knows about – a few very interesting articles about Sotheby's in London and that sort of thing. I remember he had an article accepted about the Queen Mother's jewels. That must have been . . . I wonder if it wasn't in the *Aftenposten* magazine.'

'You don't say?'

'Yes, but it's a while ago. In the main he's translated cartoons.' Jespersen grinned with the cigarillo in the corner of his mouth: 'Drop the shooter, you charlatan! Ugh! Argh!' The latter was too much for Jespersen. His face went puce and he had a severe coughing fit.

Gunnarstranda waited politely. 'I get the same myself,' he said with sympathy when the other man's breathing was back to normal. 'I suppose it has something to do with smoking.'

'Yes, it may play a part,' Jespersen replied. 'There's not much bloody point stopping, though, when you're over seventy, is there? I've stopped inhaling. That's fine, so long as the cigarillo is strong enough.'

'Hm, I still inhale,' the policeman conceded.

'And I cheat a bit, too.'

'But back to Karsten,' Gunnarstranda interrupted. 'Wouldn't he have seen the sale as a kind of threat? I mean if a job he had been clinging to for years were to be snatched from him?'

Jespersen sent the other man an amused scowl – to show that he had seen through the policeman's questioning technique – then shook his head again. 'I don't think so, in fact. I think he would look upon it as a kind of – a kind of release.'

'And you?' enquired the Inspector.

'Me?'

'It must have been sad for you that the deal went down the Swanee.'

Jespersen nodded. 'Not *so* sad,' he said guardedly.

'What do you mean?'

'Not so sad that I would hurt my brother.'

Gunnarstranda nodded to himself and looked around in the ensuing silence. The piano was black, one of the old stand-up types, a Brüchner. Above the piano hung a landscape painting of a meadow of flowers with a daisy as the central focus. A picture of boats adorned the other wall. There was a storm and a sailing boat was, symbolically, half a length behind a steam ship going at full speed. 'What sort of relationship did you have with your brother?' he asked.

'Close, but also distant,' Jespersen growled, circling the cigarillo in the ashtray to get rid of the ash. 'We each had our own families, but we kept in regular contact. Close but distant is quite an accurate description.'

'You met in your other brother's flat – Arvid's?'

'Yes. And we had invited our buyers as well, a pleasant married couple. They know all about antiques, and we thought everything was hunky-dory, and then along comes Reidar . . . I could smell trouble as soon as I saw his face. He was in a terrible mood.'

'Was he surprised?'

'What do you mean?'

'Was he surprised . . . by . . . the situation, the two buyers? Hadn't he been involved in the process?'

'Yes, we were all agreed on the sale, but in fact it was Arvid who stepped into the breach.' Jespersen searched for words. 'Who was the driving force.'

'Driving force?'

'Yes, who did the brunt of the work.'

'So your brother, Reidar, was kept out?'

Jespersen shook his head. 'No, it's not right to put it like that. Both Reidar and I left the actual sales pitch to Arvid.'

'So Reidar wasn't against the sale?'

'No, that's what's so strange. I think something must have happened that day. That was why he dug his heels in – he was just in a bad mood.'

Gunnarstranda took his tobacco pouch and began to roll himself a cigarette. 'Just grumpy?'

Jespersen splayed his arms. 'Something must have happened. I saw he was furious the moment he arrived. And then I regretted the whole arrangement – I mean the buyers were there before Reidar came. You know, that meant he was the last to arrive, a kind of outsider, and I don't think he liked that very much.' Jespersen put on a weak smile. 'I *know* he didn't like it at all.' He shook his head in despair. 'The man hated being put last.'

'What do you think put him in such a bad mood?'

'I haven't the foggiest. Perhaps he'd had a row with Ingrid. But . . .' Jespersen shook his head. 'That happened very seldom. No, I don't know.'

'How do you see their relationship? I mean their marriage. Your brother was much older than her.'

'You mean whether she . . .?'

'Yes, whether she flirted with other men.'

Jespersen shook his head gravely. 'Have you met her?'

'Of course. But you know her better than me.'

'She's the loyal type,' Jespersen affirmed. 'She's always been light-headed, liked dancing, you know, but loyal, very loyal.'

'So you don't think she has someone?'

Jespersen gave a shy smile. 'No, that . . .' He shook his head. 'No,' he concluded.

'But, Reidar, was he angry during the meeting?'

'No. He didn't say much, well, while the buyers were there, but as soon as they had gone, all hell broke loose.'

'In what way?'

'He rejected the whole proposal without any discussion, without even *wanting* to enter into any discussion, although that was nothing unusual actually, but what was new was the rest. When we started arguing he got so angry that he kicked Arvid's little dog.' Jespersen grinned. 'I've never seen Reidar react like that, I mean, it was so childish, to smash things and so on, it's what young sweethearts do when they're jealous.' He shook his head. 'It was very strange.'

'He didn't give a hint of what was to come when he arrived?'

Jespersen shook his head. 'That's what's so weird. Because he wasn't play-acting. Arvid, you see, was knocked sideways by what happened to the dog. And it was impossible to go on with our discussions. The meeting had been torpedoed. Afterwards I wondered if that had been Reidar's intention.'

'What do you mean by that – his intention?'

'Well, to bring the meeting to a close, get out and away from us. You see we stood up to him. We were not going to give in, Arvid and I. And it was when we applied pressure, two against one, that he kicked the animal.'

Gunnarstranda ran his fingers across his lips. 'I see,' he murmured and looked around. 'You like crosswords?'

'Yes.' Jespersen followed Gunnarstranda's gaze to the bookcase where there were rows and rows of crossword books and reference works. 'I can see you are a detective . . .' He nodded, and pointed to the magazines under the table: 'Yes, indeed, all my grandchildren come here with magazines and newspapers. Crosswords and puzzles, they're my passion. What about it?'

Gunnarstranda shook his head. 'I was just wondering. You see I have a puzzle I'm still trying to solve, but I can't crack it.'

'Come on then,' Jespersen ventured.

Gunnarstranda looked him in the eye and said: 'There are four symbols. The first is J for Jørgen. Then there's a number, one. Then nine and lastly five: J – one hundred and ninety five.'

Jespersen cocked his head. 'Hm,' he sighed. 'Have to think about that one.'

'Do that,' the policeman said and went on: 'Did you contact Reidar later?'

'Mm . . . there are no other clues . . . there are only four symbols – the letter J and a one and a nine and a five?'

Gunnarstranda nodded. 'J one-nine-five – that's all there is.' He repeated: 'Did you contact him?'

'I tried. I rang him.'

'When was that?'

'At about six, early evening. I tried a couple of times, first at home, but Ingrid said he would be late home – he had rung home to tell her. Then I rang the Ensjø number, but no one answered.'

'What sort of time?'

'At about half past six. I don't remember exactly.'

'Mm?' Gunnarstranda lit one of his roll-ups. 'When did you try next?'

'Half past ten in the evening. Reidar said he didn't want to discuss the matter. Karsten and the family were there and he kept things brief.'

'Did you visit him later?'

Jespersen stared glumly at the policeman and gave an emphatic shake of his head.

'No, I did not.'

'When did you go to bed?'

Jespersen considered the question. 'At one, maybe half past.'

'And you were alone in the house?'

The man nodded.

'How did you find out about the murder?'

'I rang the next day. A priest answered. The one who was with Ingrid.'

Gunnarstranda inhaled and focused for a few moments on the cigarette glow. 'I'm sorry, but I'm afraid I have to ask you these questions,' he apologized and for a second their eyes met. Emmanuel Folke Jespersen understood. At that moment he was a sad man with heavy jowls, a large stomach, doleful eyes and an extinguished cigarillo in his hand.

After calling on Emmanuel Folke Jespersen, on the way back to Oslo, Gunnarstranda took a detour via Røa. He drove down Griniveien, but turned off before Sørkedalsveien, into Røahagan, one of the typical West Oslo streets where the old houses set in large grounds have been cut up and divided over the years, so that an ever-increasing and more status-conscious middle class can build kitsch palaces in what once had been shaded apple orchards. Karsten and Susanne Jespersen's house was red, an obviously ex-functionalist house, built in the

1930s, and converted out of all recognition. The Police Inspector stood hesitating for a while in the drive. Many years ago a colleague and he had developed a secret code. They had given interviewees their own labels when they talked about them in the presence of others. A woman could be LH; a man might be LTP. These codes were used so that witnesses and interviewees would not understand the internal messages they were sending to each other, but also because this kind of categorization is important when you are trying to establish an overview. LH stood for *løgnhals* (liar), LTP stood for *liker trynet på'n* (like the look of him). They had devised a list of such codes and used them to great effect.

Gunnarstranda and Frølich had never worked in that way. The reason, Gunnarstranda thought, was that they were on the same wavelength. Now and then, though, he and Frølich were way off beam. At that moment he was trying to make sense of something which he knew his younger colleague would overlook, on purpose or otherwise. Police Inspector Gunnarstranda took the view that people built up the armour that would benefit them most at all times. He was very conscious that this theory of a self-serving morality had its weaknesses, and so he was constantly trying to test and refine his own conclusions by adopting new angles. The problem here, standing outside Karsten Jespersen's house, was that he could not make sense of one single signal. He knew that a detached house in the west of Oslo at today's prices would be unaffordable for many. On the other hand, he couldn't begin to guess how Karsten and Susanne had acquired this house. For all he knew, it could be the house where Susanne had grown up. Nevertheless, for the time being, the house's geographical location was quite irrelevant. He studied the house front. The steps by the main door were made of brick, but the foundations were poor. Many years of ground frost had caused the steps to move and introduced cracks which had been forced open by snow and ice. But the cracked brickwork showed no signs of collapse. As the house was among the oldest on this road, there were none of the fake status symbols the newer buildings came with: rough wood cladding, grass roofs or Dutch glass tiles. Since there wasn't a car in the drive either, the façade of Karsten Jespersen's residence was as plain and impenetrable as the man himself. He wondered then if this was an important conclusion, whether Jespersen's anonymity was conspicuous and therefore genuinely worthy of his fuller attention.

When at last he rang the bell, it was a long time before the door was answered.

'I dropped by on the off-chance that you were at home,' Gunnarstranda said with good grace. 'As we've closed your shop.'

From the hallway they went straight into Karsten Jespersen's workroom. Very appropriate, Gunnarstranda thought wryly. But the room seemed pleasant. There were full shelves of books reaching up to the ceiling. An old brown writing desk stood in front of the window. On it an old-fashioned, black typewriter, a Royal, a sharp contrast to two enormous loudspeaker columns on the opposite wall. Gunnarstranda turned with satisfaction to the immense hi-fi system, and thought that there he might find an expression of this man's deeper emotions. The low but very wide amplifier rested on a slab of polished marble-like stone. The speaker columns were triangular and almost touched the ceiling. In front of the speakers were two modern designer chairs with adjustable backs.

'I've come by to ask what you discussed with your father on the evening before he was killed,' Gunnar-stranda explained, after taking a seat in one of the reclining chairs.

Jespersen sat at the desk. 'Did I talk to my father that evening?' he asked tentatively.

'When you went to your father's house for dinner.'

'Oh . . . well, just chat, general chitter-chatter – over the meal. We talked about food and whether children should eat everything on the plate – that sort of thing.'

'And afterwards? I was told you and your father had a cognac on your own.'

'That's right, we did. For the most part we talked about the shop – I wondered about prices for various items and we discussed them.'

'What sort of items?'

Jespersen pulled out a drawer from the desk and rested one foot on it. 'A table, an old uniform, two glasses from Nøstetangen. They were new acquisitions and – they're all down in the office.'

'Which office?'

'My office. In the shop.'

'And this was the only thing you talked about?'

'This wasn't such a little thing. You don't price antiques in two minutes. I suggested we took our drinks down to the shop so that he could see the things for himself, but he wasn't in the mood. And that was not so strange. After all, it was a Friday. He said he would have a look in the morning, the day after, that is, Saturday . . .'

'Could that be why he went downstairs after you and your family had left that evening? Might he have gone to the shop to look at these items?'

'Possible,' Jespersen said. 'I don't know.'

'Why do you think he went downstairs?' Gunnarstranda asked.

'He must have wanted to check the items – since they had just arrived . . .'

'But he didn't want to go down with you when you suggested, did he?'

'True, so it is perhaps a little odd that he went downstairs later that evening. I don't know. He was always so unpredictable.'

'But what did you think when you first heard he had been found dead in the shop? What did you think he had been doing there?'

'I suppose I thought he'd been checking everything was all right, that the doors were locked, or he just wanted to get something. I didn't give it a lot of thought.'

'But if we were to work on the reason why he went downstairs, how many options are there?'

'I reckon he must have gone to check the doors. I cannot imagine he was so keen to inspect the few items I had been talking about. After all, he'd said he would do that the following day.'

'Do you think he might have arranged a meeting with his killer?' Gunnarstranda asked.

Jespersen stared back.

'Does that sound bizarre?'

'No, but it means that it wasn't a burglary, doesn't it?'

'There's no sign of a break-in anywhere, but we don't know yet if anything has been taken.'

'If you would let me in, I could tell you on the spot whether anything has been stolen or not.'

Gunnarstranda stretched out his legs and adjusted the back of the chair. It was very comfortable. 'We can't do things in that way. Not yet at any rate. We have to finish the forensic examination of the room. You'll get a list of the objects we log in the shop, then you can have a look.'

'But why . . .?'

Gunnarstranda interrupted him. 'Because the shop is a crime scene. There is nothing to discuss.'

Jespersen went silent.

'You use a typewriter?' the policeman asked, pointing to the black machine on the table. 'Not a computer?'

Jespersen shook his head. 'Typewriter and fountain pen. They have style. I couldn't imagine writing in any other way.'

'But it's ancient.' The policeman nodded towards the machine. 'No correction key, nothing.'

'That's how Hemingway wrote,' Jespersen said.

Gunnarstranda considered this riposte and made a mental note of a new crack in the man's grey façade. 'What else did your father talk about?' he asked.

'Otherwise?' Jespersen shrugged. 'I don't actually remember.'

'Did he mention a meeting he had with his two brothers?'

'Yes, he did mention it. That's right.'

'What did he say?'

'Almost nothing. He said he had turned up at Arvid's and had put an end to the sale of the shop.'

'And you'd forgotten that?'

Jespersen grimaced. His chin quivered with tiny tics. 'No,' he said. 'I hadn't forgotten, but it . . . well . . .'

Gunnarstranda said nothing and waited.

Karsten Jespersen rested his head in the palm of his hand, as though pondering how he could express what he had on his mind. 'If you had met my father when he was alive,' he began, peering at the ceiling. 'You see I knew about these . . . these . . .' He waved his hand in the air while searching for words; '. . . these sale negotiations. Arvid had talked to me. I suppose he and Emmanuel were frightened I would be against selling since I run the shop . . .'

Gunnarstranda said nothing and waited.

'But I wasn't – against it, that is. I can open a shop in my living room if I want. My goodness, I have the contacts . . .'

He sat and reflected.

'So you didn't object to the sale of the shop?'

'Not at all. But when my father went on the attack as he did. This was late at night. We were sitting with a cognac, I was telling him about these engraved glasses, the uniform complete with medals and ribbons, and he just scowled and said – as if he were pouring a bucket of water over my head: *I've torpedoed the sale of the shop. Do you want to ring Arvid and console him?* It was almost comical . . .'

'Were those the words he used?'

'Yes. He knew Arvid had been talking to me about these matters. He said those actual words, and that he was angry with me. He must have thought I had gone behind his back or something like that.'

'But what did you say?'

'Not very much. In fact, he was the one who should have informed me about these negotiations, not Arvid. My father had known about the process the whole time. Until then he hadn't objected. So I said that for me it didn't matter whether the shop was sold or not, which was the truth. If he and Emmanuel and Arvid sold up, I would manage anyway – and in the end I told him that Arvid had sounded me out about any objections I might have had about the sale. And I said that I had told Arvid what I had just told him. Finally I said it was strange that Arvid should be the person to inform me. After that we didn't talk about the matter any more.'

'You finished your conversation?'

'No, we talked, but not a word about Arvid or Emmanuel or the sale.'

Gunnarstranda nodded.

'How was he that evening? Different in any way?'

'No, he was his usual grumpy self.' Karsten gave a faint smile. 'By and large he tended to be bad-tempered.'

'Why was that?'

'Hm?'

'He wasn't ill? I mean he may have been bad-tempered because he was ill.'

Jespersen smiled. 'My father was not often ill.'

Gunnarstranda nodded. 'In fact he was ill,' he said.

'Your father had tumours on the kidneys. The patholo-gist's verdict is that he had malignant cancer. The chances are he didn't know himself.' Gunnarstranda coughed. 'So the question is whether he talked to you about any illness?'

'Never.' Jespersen stared into space. 'Cancer?' he echoed in a hollow voice.

Gunnarstranda cleared his throat. 'Well, back to the evening before he was killed. Did he talk on the phone while you were there?'

'He might have received the odd call, but he didn't make any himself.'

'Do you know who he talked to?'

'No, no idea. My mind was on other things. The chil-dren were beginning to get tired . . . Imagine him having cancer!'

From his inside pocket Gunnarstranda took the old photograph he had found under the pad on Reidar Jespersen's desk. 'Do you know her?' he asked.

Jespersen held the picture, studied it and shrugged his shoulders. 'No idea,' he said and handed back the pho-tograph.

'Never seen this person?'

'Never.'

'I found it in your father's papers. Thought it might be your mother.'

'My mother?' Jespersen shook his head and smiled. 'No. My mother was blonde – quite different from this woman.'

Jespersen got to his feet and wandered over to the wall between the loudspeakers. He took down a picture in a glass frame. He held the photograph in one hand and the frame in the other. 'See for yourself,' he said, passing both to the Inspector.

Jespersen's mother was a woman with short, blonde hair. He thought he could recognize Karsten Jespersen's chin and eyes. The picture had been taken in Bygdøy. She was sitting on a chair in a café. The Fram museum building towered up behind. Gunnarstranda suddenly regretted not having shown the photograph around before. 'I thought it would be your mother,' he reflected. 'It occurred to me that I hadn't seen pictures of her – your mother.'

Jespersen coughed. 'It's not that strange that you haven't seen pictures of her. I don't think Ingrid would have approved of a picture of my mother on the wall. Ingrid is great, but she drew the line there. There are lots of photos of my mother in the flat, but in albums.'

Karsten Jespersen put the photograph of his mother back on the wall.

22

The Inheritance

'What have you had in this? Tar?' Frølich was trying to rinse their cups in the sink before serving coffee from the machine. Gunnarstranda's china cup, purloined from a canteen a long time ago, was almost dark brown on the inside from coffee tannin. His own cup was a green, arty ceramics number which he had been given for Christmas by the same Anna who was recording all the objects at the crime scene. Frølich stood thinking about Anna and the night they had shared after the Christmas dinner almost four weeks ago. Frank Frølich had not often been unfaithful to Eva-Britt. When it had happened on the odd occasion, he was full of remorse and abject fear of sexual diseases or an unwanted pregnancy. But he didn't have this feeling after the night with Anna. As the water from the tap swirled round Gunnarstranda's filthy cup, without making it any cleaner than it had been five minutes earlier, he was thinking he might give her a call to chase up the inventory of items in Reidar Folke Jespersen's shop. He looked at his reflection. 'But why?' he asked himself. 'Why would you want to do that?'

'Eh?' Gunnarstranda said from his chair. He was leafing through the evening edition of *Aftenposten*.

'What?' Frølich asked.

'You were the one who spoke,' Gunnarstranda

answered with his nose in the paper.

Frølich straightened up and knew why he wanted to meet her. She had not hinted at their joint escapade one single time. Although there had been that little glint in her eyes when they had met in Jespersen's antiques shop. He poured coffee into both of their cups. 'I was saying Jonny Stokmo's telephone is dead,' he told Gunnarstranda and placed the full cup of coffee in front of him. 'Stokmo's disappeared, vanished off the face of the earth.'

'All the more reason to check him out.'

'We can start with his son – this scrapdealer in Torshov,' Frølich said, pulling a face as he sipped the black coffee. 'You or me?' he asked.

'Me,' Gunnarstranda said, looking up. 'What do you reckon about the brothers? Have they got a motive?' He folded the newspaper.

Frølich, who was still thinking about Anna and how her hair had tickled his nose one night four weeks ago, tried to repress the thought and instead put on a concentrated expression for Gunnarstranda, who looked up at him from an angle.

'What's up?'

'Reidar and Ingrid owned everything in joint names,' a composed Frølich reasoned. 'No one has objected to that. The Marriage Settlement Office in Brønnøysund has not registered any separate property either for her or for her late husband. The will has been revoked. In practice, if Ingrid Jespersen can sit tight on the old boy's possessions . . .' He left the rest of his reasoning in the air.

'She can't. Karsten Jespersen has a right to his inheritance,' Gunnarstranda said. 'He is not her child. He has a right to part of the settlement.'

'But suppose we imagine that Ingrid has free rein over the old boy's share of the business,' Frølich said. 'She has actually admitted that she wants to get rid of it. In other words, now Reidar is dead the sale should go through without a hitch.'

'Do you mean that gives the two brothers a motive?'

'I mean it would be stupid to overlook that motive,' Frølich said. 'The man who stood in the way of the sale is now off the scene. The two brothers each own a third. Furthermore, everyone insists that Karsten is not interested in the shop. However . . .' said Frølich, 'we don't know who will take over the shop. There's bound to be some discussion between Karsten and the widow – and the two of them seem to get on like a house on fire. From an inheritance point of view, Karsten has a right to a percentage of the assets, and its size is calculated on the basis of Reidar's half of the joint property. Inasmuch as Ingrid and Reidar had joint ownership, it will be Ingrid rather than Karsten who benefits from Reidar's death.'

'We don't know anything about Karsten's late mother,' Gunnarstranda said.

'What?'

'Karsten also has a right to part of the inheritance through her. We don't know if that baton changeover has been effected. Looking at all the things we *don't* know, I think the distribution of the deceased's estate seems so complicated that I doubt . . .'

Gunnarstranda paused.

'What do you doubt?'

Gunnarstranda shook his head. 'I don't know. At any rate it's difficult to see a motive based on the inheritance issue alone.'

'Perhaps we should chase up the shop inventory,' Frølich said upon reflection.

'Why's that?'

Frølich stared into the distance, in a dream. 'Well, I can take care of that at some point.'

'I can't imagine the brothers would bump off Reidar because he delayed the sale of the shop,' Gunnarstranda said sceptically.

'Delayed?'

'Yes. The two brothers were in the majority. Reidar would have been outvoted.'

'But now you're ignoring the dynamics of their relationship,' Frølich interrupted. 'This is a closed circle of family members,' he continued. 'These three brothers know each other inside out. Reidar is the leading light, the man who always calls the shots, who has always called the shots, and who bullies the others into doing what he commands. An offer flutters in through the door. Result: the other two brothers see the chance of a fat pension – and Reidar opposes it. The other two are used to giving in to Reidar. Isn't it a little conspicuous that the eldest brother is killed?'

'Everything is conspicuous, given the right circumstances,' Gunnarstranda replied.

'And in the middle of all this we have the son, Karsten – he's sick of working for a pittance under his father . . .'

'We know nothing about that!'

'But Karsten has grown up in the shadow of a macho

man. Think about that. That boy has never been allowed to be afraid. I'm sure that when he was afraid of shadows behind the door as a small boy he . . .'

Gunnarstranda leaned back and waited for the continuation. It didn't come.

'Yes?' enquired Gunnarstranda.

'You've seen him with your own eyes. Karsten is a wreck!'

'So what?'

'The two brothers know that only Reidar stands between them and the sale. Neither Karsten nor Ingrid will oppose the sale. For the two brothers . . .'

'All they needed to do was raise their hands at a board meeting,' Gunnarstranda said. 'They were in the majority, weren't they!'

'But we know that Reidar let the murderer into the shop,' Frølich persisted.

'But he could have let lots of other people into the shop, and not necessarily the brothers.' Gunnarstranda peered up at his tall colleague: 'There's another thing you're forgetting. You told me about Arvid's dog – Silvie. Doesn't that suggest the man is too soft?'

'No, if we take the dog into account, it would reinforce Arvid's motivation. After all Reidar tried to kick it to death.'

'I don't think so. The dog was one of those poofie types, wasn't it?'

Frølich knitted both eyebrows.

Gunnarstranda threw his arms into the air and searched for words: 'Yes, it was . . . a little rat with fur. Only ageing prostitutes and homosexuals own dogs like that, don't they?'

Frølich eyeballed his boss, speechless. 'My grandmother had a dog like that,' he stammered.

'All right,' Gunnarstranda said, in retreat, pursing his lips and creasing his face into an indescribable expression. 'I'm sure Arvid is a perfectly normal fellow, but I don't think we should get hung up on Reidar Folke Jespersen's inheritance. The only point of interest for us is that the man revoked what seemed an undistinguished will just before he was bumped off.' He coughed and gazed ahead of him for a few moments. 'In any case, it is too early to focus too much attention on the brothers. The one I met – Emmanuel – might perhaps be credited with scribbling a riddle on the body, but he is no fighting man. He could only just raise his body to reach for the ashtray.'

He stole another glance at Frølich. 'Afraid of shadows behind the door?' he asked.

'All children are frightened of the dark.'

'What shadows behind the door?'

'Shadows, things you're afraid of.'

'But behind the door? Can you see shadows through a closed door?'

Frølich stared at him. 'Under the bed – is that better?'

Gunnarstranda threw up his arms in resignation: 'By all means.' He cleared his throat and stood up. 'Well, have to make tracks,' he mumbled and grabbed his coat.

23

Old Friends

Gunnarstranda strolled down Vogts gate searching for the workshop run by Stokmo's son. He flipped a few bits of plastic dangling down at face height to the side – this was an invention whose purpose he could not begin to understand. Were these strips supposed to signify something or were they an aid for blind people to find their way in winter? There was ice on the pavement. He squeezed himself up against the wall as the tram passed. Finally he found the right house number. However, since there was no sign over the entrance, he stood hesitating before going into the back yard. He passed a dirty fork-lift truck with a petrol tank behind the seat and he stopped to eye a rusty iron staircase running diagonally up the end wall of the two-storey building. Every step consisted of three parallel grooves, yet a slippery sausage of ice had attached itself to the edge of most of the steps. Gunnarstranda took a good grip of the hand rail on the way up. The window was dark. He peeped in through the pane and found himself facing an old Singer sewing machine on a workbench. Behind it, a toboggan lay on its side on the floor, and along the walls were cardboard boxes filled with unidentifiable scrap. At the back of the room he could make out the shape of a door. He pulled at the external door. It was locked. He straightened up and scoured the area. The view was limited to the houses around the back yard. They were old buildings; the plaster was crumbling off all of them. The lower part of the walls in the yard was half-timbered. A tram rattled past, and a car hooted its horn in the street. Down in the yard there were two abandoned washing machines stacked on top of a pile of pipes. A wide door opened into a workshop containing gas cylinders for welding apparatus and huge wire-cutters on coiled cables. Gunnarstranda pulled his coat tighter around him and picked his way down the steps with care. The snow had drifted up the walls. Clumps of white snow hung from the plaster. It looked like there had been a snowball fight. He peered in through the half-open workshop door. No one around. He continued round the corner into the yard and found out why the snow was stuck high up on the wall. A Norlett snow-blower was positioned beneath a wire glass window. Inside, there was light.

Three heads turned towards the door as he opened it. Two men wearing oil-stained overalls sat at a table along one wall, with their packed lunches and Thermos flasks between them. The third man in the room, a fierce-looking individual with a bushy moustache, sat behind a desk. On his head he was wearing a back-to-front baseball cap, inscribed with SAMVIRKE ASSURANCE.

'I'm looking for Jonny Stokmo,' Detective Inspector Gunnarstranda said.

'He's not here!' said the man with the moustache good-naturedly, raising a cup to his mouth. The cup was furnished with the same legend as the cap. He slurped his coffee.

'But you know the name?' the policeman said.

One of the overalled men grinned, revealing two teeth in his top set, like a mouse sniffing in the air. The lenses of his glasses were impenetrable.

The moustachioed man took his time to put down the cup before exchanging glances with the other two and starting to grin as well. 'Bloody hell,' he sighed, sucking the coffee off his moustache. His outburst set the third man off. 'Grill them,' he whinnied. 'Grill them with spices.'

The man with the moustache ignored him. 'Would you like some coffee?' he asked the policeman. 'Don't listen to Moses,' he said, inclining his head towards the man with the whinny. 'He's crazy.'

'Barking mad,' said the man with the glasses and the mouse-teeth.

'Half-baked,' replied Moses.

The man at the desk eyed Moses. 'What are you going on about?' he asked. 'No one can understand a word!' The moustache gestured towards Gunnarstranda.

The latter perceived this as a suitable moment to reveal his identity. 'Police Inspector Gunnarstranda,' he said. 'Murder Squad.'

'Oh, shit,' answered the man at the desk, smiling into his moustache.

'Steam them in butter,' said Moses, causing the man with the mouse-teeth to snigger and slap his thigh. 'Steam them in butter,' the man with the mouse-teeth repeated. 'With macaroni.'

'No – pickle them,' Moses said. 'Put them in barrels – in cod-liver oil and salt in the 69 position.'

'Moses is trying to think up horrible ways to eat cod,' the man with the moustache explained. 'Pull yourself together now, you halfwit,' he said to Moses.

'Think of something else for dinner,' the man with the mouse-teeth said.

'Anyone here know Jonny Stokmo?'

'That's my father,' the man with the moustache said, taking off his cap and revealing a shiny pate surrounded by a wreath of grey hair gathered into a long ponytail.

'I need an urgent chat with your father,' Gunnarstranda said.

'Understand,' said Junior. 'Just a shame that he doesn't. What do you reckon, Moses?'

'At the farm,' Moses said.

'Christ, you are crazy,' the man with the moustache replied, swivelling his chair towards Gunnarstranda. 'To hear the truth, listen to drunks and nutters.'

'Where's the farm?' Gunnarstranda asked in a soft voice.

Junior swivelled round on the chair and took a newspaper from the table. 'You look younger in the photo,' he said, showing him the paper.

Gunnarstranda contemplated the picture of himself.

'You've got hair here,' Junior said.

Gunnarstranda had always been irritated by the photograph the newspaper used. He had just returned from a holiday in southern Europe. In the picture he was frowning like an idiot. His face was as red as a lobster, he had bags under his eyes and because he was so short he was looking up at the camera. 'Where's the farm?' he repeated with authority.

'Do you know Bendik Fleming?' the moustachioed man asked.

Gunnarstranda nodded slowly.

'He sends his regards,' the moustachioed man said.

Gunnarstranda nodded again: 'That's a long time ago. I think . . .' Gunnarstranda ruminated. 'It must have been in '92,' he said at length. 'I think he went down for a couple of years . . .'

'No problem with your memory,' the man with the mouse-teeth said, taking a slice of bread from his lunch box with black, oil-stained hands. He bit off a large chunk and began to chew, with thoughtful eyes.

'How is Bendik?' Gunnarstranda asked.

'Drinks a lot.'

'That's not so good,' Gunnarstranda said with sympathy.

'But he doesn't turn nasty any more when he's drunk. He laughs.'

'Better than killing people,' Gunnarstranda said. 'Send him my regards,' he added and cleared his throat.

All three of them stared at him.

'Hasn't your father got a telephone?' Gunnarstranda asked.

'Yes he has, but he's switched it off – a mobile.'

'Why's he switched it off?'

'I imagine he suspects you will ring,' the man with the moustache grinned.

'Where's the farm?' Gunnarstranda repeated gently.

The man called Moses slipped off the table he was sitting on, crossed the floor and pointed to a framed aerial photograph hanging on the opposite wall: a farm from the air. 'There,' he said, grinning at his boss behind the desk.

Gunnarstranda checked his watch. He would be eating out in a short time. So he asked Stokmo Junior if he would mind drawing him a map.

Two hours later he opened the door to Hansken, a restaurant where Tove Granaas was waiting for him, engrossed in a book.

Gunnarstranda's first, and somewhat less private, encounter with Tove had taken place at a meeting of the local garden association. The theme advertised on the posters had been lilies. Since he had known the speaker, and had neither wanted to meet him nor believed the man could teach him anything new, he would probably have stayed at home that evening too, had the chairman not rung him a few hours before and reminded him about the meeting. Old Bøhren, the speaker, was an arrogant, retired bureaucrat who loved to provoke the policeman into trivial rows over botanical phenomena.

He had told the chairman of the garden association there was no point in trying to get him to join; he already subscribed to the magazine, and the chairman knew this very well. Becoming a member was quite out of the question, a point which he had made perfectly clear a month before when giving an association slide show about indicator plants in lime soil.

Nevertheless Gunnarstranda trotted along to the gymnasium where folding tables with the requisite plastic chairs stood in rows alongside the wall bars. He arrived through the emergency exit doors, nodded to the left and right and found a free seat in the far corner. Most of the audience arrived in pairs at such meetings. In fact, it didn't bother him to sit on his own, he thought, so long as he got away from Bøhren – the pompous pensioner from the Department of Justice who loved the sound of his own voice. He was anxiously keeping an eye on the entrance when an arm bearing a coffee flask entered his field of vision. 'Is this seat free?' she asked. But before Gunnarstranda could find his voice, she had sat down.

'Nice to see you again,' she said. He knew he had seen her before and searched the archives of his memory.

'You questioned me concerning a murder,' she explained, on noticing his reaction. 'At work,' she added.

'Tove,' he stammered, once again falling for her smile. 'Tove Granaas.'

'Imagine you not recognizing me when we last met.'

Gunnarstranda was embarrassed to think of her in the audience at his talk. 'Did you come to the last meeting?'

Her hand woke him from his reverie again. 'I've been stalking you,' she said. 'As a murder squad detective, you're almost a celebrity.'

A man at the neighbouring table raised his cup and signalled that it was empty. She grabbed the flask in front of her and passed it to him in one movement. A light waft of perfume brushed his cheek as she whirled back. In her plain knitted sweater and jeans there was something summery about her. Her hands were small with strong fingers and short nails. Hands that have seen work, he thought. When he looked up again, her attentive eyes were still there. She supported her head on her hands and talked about the problems of growing narcissi. 'I put them in a proper bed, set the bulbs in autumn, but something always goes wrong and they never come up.'

'Poor drainage. Dig a deep hole and fill it with leca pellets or sand.'

'How deep?'

'Deep enough for the bulbs to be three bulb lengths under the ground.'

'You make it sound so easy.'

'Put lots in every hole, lots of bulbs, fifteen, twenty, then there'll be a beautiful clump of them.' In his enthusiasm he bent over the table and before he could compose himself, he heard his own voice say: 'I can help you.'

Once the words were said, he could have bitten off his tongue.

'Well, it's too late now anyway,' she answered. 'As it's winter.' Gunnarstranda gulped with gratitude. 'You can get them started indoors and put them out when the ground is frost-free,' he consoled her.

A little later they saw Bøhren come in, without a tie, but with a ridiculous neckerchief around his neck. With his long body supported on a stick, he stood surveying the room with displeasure. The policeman knew he was being watched. But as soon as he felt Bøhren's eyes on him, he looked away.

'There's Bøhren,' Tove said in a loud voice.

He stared right at them, but made no move.

Gunnarstranda nodded slowly.

The measured gaze the pensioner returned was microscopic. The retired department head twisted gently and hobbled off into the room, away from them.

'I hope I haven't taken his seat?' Tove whispered, in a conspiratorial voice.

'For God's sake, stay where you are,' Gunnarstranda whispered back in the same hushed tones. And for the third time in an unusually short time she gave his arm a light squeeze.

Since then neither of them had been to any meetings at the local garden association. However, they had been to the restaurant three times.

As Gunnarstranda sat down and met her smile, he was looking forward to the conversation as much as the meal.

24

The House in the Forest

Company halt, Frølich thought, remembering forced
marches in full army kit many years before. The rain
falling down from the sky, uniform soaked, stiff, cold,
his reluctance to move a single muscle. The only way out
had been to wait, stand still and wait until the sky or an
officer announced a change in their situation. Now: Eva-
Britt and he were at the restaurant. Even though they
had finished eating some time ago, even though he had a
hundred things to do, it behoved him to wait calmly. It
was a ritual the two of them had lapsed into because
Eva-Britt had always hated hurrying. But it was also a
ritual he was beginning to loathe from the bottom of his
heart. There were two similar feelings competing for the
upper hand behind his calm exterior: the feeling of stress
imposed by inactivity and the feeling of annoyance
because he allowed himself to be cowed by her need for
contentment. He stretched his legs, ripped the foil off the
third or fourth toothpick and looked around. At the
adjacent table sat a young chrome-dome listening to a
woman of the same age who gesticulated with both
hands when she talked. Frølich had picked up that she
was a waitress. She was telling stories about insufferable
customers to chrome-dome, who was stifling a yawn
and fiddling with a toothpick, too.

Frølich's eyes searched the room and at length they settled on Eva-Britt's face. She had been talking without stop for quite some time. Frank had no idea what she was talking about.

'How did I end up here?' he thought and drained his glass with enforced patience while watching the talking face; the lower lip he had once longed to nibble to pieces, the eyes he had compared with a dash of the Mediterranean, enclosed behind the lowered eyelids. He asked himself the question: 'How did *we* end up here?'

A few years ago it would have been both natural and feasible to stop this babbling with a kiss. Today she would be angry, offended and ashamed on his behalf. And he may well have knocked the glasses over in the attempt.

He thought of her navel, the hollow in her stomach, the rounding of her stomach when she stretched in the morning. They were images that had to be sought out, which no longer fell into place of their own accord.

'Where's the spark gone?' he thought, looking at one long leg under the table. Knee-length boots, Eva-Britt's trademark, the plinth to carry her body. Footwear emphasizing the erotic mystery that women's legs point towards and men's eyes seek out.

Now he no longer felt any spark. And he imagined she would also have the same feeling of emptiness. 'Why do we pretend?' he wondered.

They had eaten a fillet of lumpsucker fish. The waiter took their plates. And at long last she was quiet as the man cleared the table. For that fragment of a second he detected panic in Eva-Britt's eyes. As soon as the waiter had gone, she started up again. Now she was having a go at TV hosts and the banality flourishing in new TV series.

'Isn't that right?' she asked, and for one split second he caught a hint of aggression in her eyes. She may have thought she had caught him letting his mind wander.

'We had all this in the discussion on TV last night, didn't we?' he answered slowly. 'The topic was done to death.'

She was hurt. Because the answer was too brutal, he thought. In other words, being uninterested, or not feigning interest, is too brutal. However, he could feel his irritation growing and hardening because she was hurt by his sense that he was wasting his time. Eva-Britt was hurt, never angry, but she would not allow herself to reveal too much of the hurt. Instead she fled into a self-constructed state of mind, a sort of wasteland where she did not perceive the essence of a change in mood and the substance of an atmosphere – Eva-Britt's demilitarized zone. Here the important thing was to be disarming, to find neutral ground as soon as possible. As usual she blew out her cheeks. 'I am just *so* full,' she said, imitating a beach ball. 'All blob!' This word was supposed to represent the inflated cheeks. 'All blob!'

Frank Frølich gave a leaden nod.

'That fish almost exploded my *taste buds*!'

Frølich nodded again as the waiter came with coffee and liqueurs. As she sipped her cognac, she rolled her tongue around her mouth. 'Mm,' she said, smacking her lips. 'Mm, mm, now I think my *taste buds* are going *berserk*.'

Frølich nodded.

'The last time we were here, we had snails for starters. Do you remember? And ravioli with sage and pure butter, un-ex-pur-gat-ed fat, and afterwards filet mignon!'

Frølich nodded.

'I was so full. I just sat like this . . .'

Her cheeks bulged.

Frølich sub-vocalized the words.

'All blob!'

He nodded again. Afterwards he looked out of the window because he knew she would be extra hurt if he checked the time too obviously. The jeweller's clock glowed on the other side of the street. It said ten minutes past ten.

He managed to negotiate himself an hour at work, but on condition that he went back to hers afterwards. At midnight he was back. Eva-Britt had just finished in the bathroom. Since she was wearing a nightdress, Julie must have gone to bed. He was tired and took a hot shower. When he had finished she was already in bed. She was lying under the duvet, naked and warm. As soon as he joined her, she grabbed his sex with both hands. They made love in a variety of positions for a long time, but he was fantasizing about Anna. Afterwards he slept like a log, still dreaming about Anna. He dreamt she was lying on top of him, like in the early hours almost a month ago. In the dream she sat up, but when he met her gaze, she had Ingrid Jespersen's face. He shuddered and woke up. It was the middle of the night. He had an erection. For some minutes he lay staring into the darkened bedroom before rolling on top of Eva-Britt again and fondling her into consciousness. That morning he had breakfast in bed. Eva-Britt gave him a warm, gentle smile and said it was fine if they lived apart so long as they were able to work positively at the relationship.

He drove Julie to school before heading for the Swedish border. A new, harsh winter day was dawning. The flawless snow-covered fields of Østfold reposed between swathes of forest and road. The sky was a blue parchment. The trees extended their thick branches into the air and might have looked like Chinese script had it not been for the frost; statues dressed in white armour of rime and ice crystals.

After taking the wrong road several times, he eventually found the ice-covered lake. Occasional tips of yellow stubble protruded through the snow in a field where a flock of crows was holding court. Judging from the activity, it seemed to be a rather tedious affair they were discussing. The snow glittered and reflected the dazzling light; wonderful weather for skiing if it hadn't been so cold. Smoke was coming from the chimney in what had to be Jonny Stokmo's farm. Frølich turned off, up the little incline towards the white house and passed a low barn before swinging into the yard. Beneath the bridge leading to the barn stood a Belarus tractor fitted with a snowplough. Obviously a gasket was leaking somewhere because the snow under the engine was black with oil. A barrel of diesel stood on its end beside a Mazda pick-up truck with rusting joints. Frølich turned to the farmhouse and caught a movement behind the window. At once the front door opened. A man with a checked shirt and two ends of a moustache extending down to his chin appeared on the step.

The room smelt of a mixture of sweat, resin, tobacco smoke and rancid frying fat. The walls were bare, the floor covered with lino. Jonny Stokmo bent down and checked the cylindrical wood-burning stove to see if it was time to add more fuel, then closed the door again. Frølich decided not to take off his shoes when he saw Stokmo was wearing winter boots. 'They're miserable bastards,' Stokmo said in answer to Frølich's question about whether he knew the Folke Jespersen family.

He had sat himself down on a rocking chair in front of the TV set. Frølich headed towards a sofa on the opposite side of the coffee table covered in newspapers and full ashtrays. Stokmo mumbled:

'They'd have the shirt off your back. I may once have had a high opinion of Reidar, but that's got to be a bloody long time ago. He was just like them.'

'Like whom?' Frølich interrupted and took out his worn, old notepad.

'Like those two slobs, his brothers. That's *them,* and his boy, Karsten. He's one of *them*. My father knew Reidar well. I never did, and now they've killed the poor sod. Have you wondered what they're fighting about? A corner shop. Hell, it's nothing more than a kiosk crammed with old lumber. Have you thought about that? That shop is nothing, a pile of crap, apart from a few things Reidar nicked from other people, or rubbish others rejected. Do you understand? They're miserable bastards!' Stokmo pulled a grimace beneath his truck-driver moustache. 'Perhaps I shouldn't say this, you being a policeman, but I'm going to be honest and tell you who Reidar was: a bloody rag-and-bone man who got himself a good-looking tart and a flat in West Oslo. But that's not what you'll hear. No, Reidar Folke Jespersen was a businessman, big guy with white hair and beard, once on first-name terms with our famous resistance fighter, Max Manus, and went around wearing a black beret on Independence Day! You should have seen the old codger, carrying a briefcase down the stairs to the kiosk that was his pride and joy. Just imagine it. Reidar was an old man who thought he could live for ever by doing two workouts a week on a cycle trainer. I saw it with my own eyes, for Christ's sake, and I was the only person who did a stroke of work – who do you think drove to the houses of the bloody deceased or to demo jobs to carry away old desks, corner cabinets or old wood burners, and clean them up for auction or some flea market?'

'But he did keep the family going. His son must have received some sort of income . . .'

'Karsten's pushing fifty. What do you think he does in the shop with two customers a day? He's sitting in the backroom in the shop writing pornographic novels and so-called true stories for magazines. It's not the shop that keeps Karsten going, it's the missus that keeps Karsten going. She's head of accounts for a big firm in Oppegård.'

'Did Karsten work for free?'

Stokmo shook his head. 'You have to understand that nothing was normal about Reidar. He was eighty years old, but refused to hand over the shop to his son. Think about that!'

'But why?' Frølich asked.

'Some posh tart from Frogner,' Stokmo said bitterly, 'might turn up and pay a thousand for a rotten bit of wood, and Reidar was the one who pocketed the kroner, no VAT, black. I'm telling you Reidar was a miserable bastard!'

'You mean he was greedy?'

'The word greedy doesn't quite cover it,' Stokmo snarled. 'Look around here,' he said, encompassing the room with a swing of his strong workman's hand. 'This is nothing much, a smallholding, but anything that has any value in this house Reidar haggled off my father and sold as an antique. Once I picked up an old workbench from a carpenter's workshop up in Gran, then I found a matching stool and I thought of putting it in the cart shed, but before I could get it here, Reidar had sold it as an antique dining table, sold it for ten thousand kroner – of which I got nothing, not one øre. I have seen Reidar sell an old motorbike helmet and claim it was a rice bowl from the Congo. That's the Reidar I knew. Loved money and himself.'

Frølich sent Stokmo a calm look of appraisal. Neither spoke for a few seconds.

'The word greedy,' Stokmo repeated, 'does not cover it.'

'But you,' the policeman said slowly, looking up from his notepad. 'You earned an income from the shop.'

'Yes.'

'Driving goods around, second-hand goods?'

'Second-hand goods and antiques. As I said, clearing houses after the death of the owner or ones up for demolition, that sort of thing. Reidar had a chat on the phone and if he needed me, I jumped in the truck and was there.'

'So it wasn't fixed work?'

'No.'

'But then it finished?'

'Shown the door three weeks ago.'

'Why was that?'

Stokmo hesitated for a few moments. Then came the answer: '*That* is a private matter.'

'It can't be private when one of the parties is dead.'

'It was about money – everything is about money – especially where the Folke Jespersen family is concerned.'

'You'll have to be a bit more precise than that.'

'He never paid me what he owed. And I'd had enough.'

'And you left?'

'Left? I didn't go when the sack of shit phoned me.'

'Some say it was the other way around. That Reidar gave you the boot?'

Stokmo sneered. 'Can you see what I mean? They're miserable bastards, the whole lot of them.'

'So Reidar didn't give you the boot?'

Stokmo's eyebrows shot in the air and he clenched both fists. 'Are you hard of hearing?'

Frølich regarded him coolly until the aggressive expression softened. 'Were you employed by them or did they buy your services?'

Stokmo relaxed again and demonstrated this by crossing his legs. 'Reidar Folke Jespersen would have spotted a 50-øre coin on the opposite side of the street,' he said. 'Do you think a man like that would pay the employer's contribution to social security? The answer is no. I was never employed. I sent him invoices.'

'You said they were fighting about the shop,' Frølich continued, flicking a page over in his notepad.

'As I said, they were quarrelling about this tiny shop. Everyone wanted a slice of the cake and everyone wanted to earn something from junk. But they didn't pay my invoices.'

'How would Reidar's brothers earn anything from the shop?'

'They own the whole caboodle, don't they? The three of them. Now there are two. And it was a limited company, so Ingrid is out of the picture. Smart move, you see. By croaking Reidar they got rid of the missus at the same time. So now there are Karsten, Arvid and Emmanuel left. Now just wait and see if a will turns up, and if it does, you've got your murderer.' Stokmo gave a sly grin and stood up. Then he plodded over to the chest of wood next to the kitchen door, took out two birch logs, sauntered over to the stove and went down on his knees. Frølich watched him place his hands around the logs, make a hole in the glow with the log before forcing the wood into the stove, closing the door and adjusting the draught.

In his mind Frølich tried to follow Stokmo's reasoning, but gave up. He said: 'But if the shop isn't worth anything, as you say, then this theory doesn't hold water.'

Stokmo stood up. His eyes flashed. 'What theory?'

'The theory that one of the heirs might kill Reidar to inherit the shop.'

Stokmo sat back in the rocking chair, took out a packet of tobacco from his breast pocket and rolled himself a cigarette. 'That's the tragedy of it, isn't it? These people are fighting over nothing. It's like watching the heirs to one of the farms round here. Brothers and sisters stop talking, they get into brawls and feud over tiny strips of land which produce bugger-all. In a couple of years, when we're part of the EU, all these smallholdings will be closed down and abandoned, but still they knock ten bells out of each other. Do you remember that case up in Skedsmo, a few years ago, where a whole family was killed, mother, father and daughter? It's like that. Reidar was running a second-hand shop, for Christ's sake, a hole in the wall, less than fifty square metres and they didn't have enough money to settle old debts. That's what they were fighting over, what they killed for.'

'How much did he owe you?'

'That's private.'

'But you think he had enough money to pay you?'

'No comment.'

'Hm?'

'I said: no comment.'

Frølich sat up straight in his chair. 'This is a police interview, Stokmo, not a press conference.'

Stokmo didn't answer.

Frølich nodded. 'What do you think? Did Reidar have a large fortune?'

'I don't imagine so.'

'He must have had money in the bank,' Frølich opined.

Stokmo shrugged his shoulders.

'But you were there on the evening he was killed?'

Stokmo nodded.

'What were you doing there?'

'I wanted to talk to Reidar.'

'What about?'

'About debts.'

'Did you talk to him?'

'No.'

Frølich jotted down the answers and looked up from the pad. He said nothing.

At last Stokmo lit the cigarette he had rolled. He inhaled the smoke deep into his lungs and kept it in. Then he sat forwards in the chair, his hands cupped around the cigarette, staring ahead with vacant eyes, while holding his breath.

Frølich wondered how long Stokmo would manage to stay silent. The man leaned back and almost seemed lost in his own thoughts as he rocked backwards and forwards in the chair. The creaking of the runners against the lino floor, as well as the crackle of burning birch accompanied by the chug of the draught on the wood burner were the only sounds in the room. All of a sudden, Stokmo sat up with a start, as though waking from a dream. 'Was there anything else?' he asked.

'I want to know what happened when you met Reidar that night,' Frølich said.

'He arrived in a taxi and I asked for my money. He

told me to go to hell and went inside and up to the missus.'

'Had you been waiting outside?'

'I went up to the flat first, but he wasn't there and his missus said she was expecting him any minute.'

'What did you do when he went in?'

'I left.'

'Where did you go?'

'To a lady I know.'

'Who?'

'She's called Carina. Lives in Thereses gate.'

'How long did you stay there?'

'Don't remember. We were busy for a few hours. I went to my son's place. I sleep there when I'm in town. I slept at his and came back here the day after.'

'When did you arrive at your son's house?'

'I would guess at around eleven.'

'Did you try to get in touch with Reidar again?'

'Depends what you mean.'

Frølich raised both eyebrows.

'I tried early in the morning.'

'When?'

'I went at eight – to Ensjø. They have a warehouse and an office there.'

Stokmo went quiet.

'You waited for him in Ensjø at eight o'clock on Saturday morning?'

'That's what I said.'

'Was he as unsympathetic then too?'

'He wasn't there at all. I waited until eleven. Sat waiting in my car for three hours. He didn't bloody turn up.'

'Are you sure?'

'Do you think I would sit here and lie? He wasn't there. That was why I tried Thomas Heftyes gate in the evening.'

'Where did you go in the intervening time?'

'I went to Karl-Erik, my son. I gave him a hand until about five. Afterwards we had something to eat and then I went to Reidar's place.'

'Was your son at home when you went there – after you'd been to Thomas Heftyes gate?'

'Think so.'

'What do you mean *think*? Didn't you talk?'

'No. I heard a woman in his flat. He lives over the workshop. I suppose you've been there – in Torshov – since you found your way here without asking for directions. I usually spend the night in the back room in the office shed when he has this lady staying. I went there and snored through till the next morning.'

'You met Folke Jespersen at about a quarter past seven. You left him and went to this Carina. What's her surname?'

'You tell me,' Stokmo mumbled and thought aloud: 'Smidt? Smestad? Something beginning with S. I don't remember.'

'Have you got her telephone number?'

'Yes. And the address.'

'All right. You went to this Carina then and stayed there until about a quarter to eleven?'

'Possible.'

'And you arrived at the workshop in Torshov when? Eleven?'

'More or less.'

'And you went to bed straightaway?'

'I probably had a smoke first, read the paper for a bit . . .'

'When did you go to bed?'

Stokmo shrugged. 'Didn't look at my watch.'

'But you didn't talk to anyone?'

'No.'

'Did you go back to Jespersen's that night?'

'No, I told you!'

Frølich studied him, but didn't quite know what to believe. 'Did you see your son the next morning?'

'For God's sake, this was a Saturday, wasn't it! And he had this woman with him.'

'In other words . . .'

'In other words I don't have an alibi, as you call it!' Stokmo snapped.

'Why are you so aggressive?' Frølich wanted to know.

'I'm not aggressive. I'm just bloody sick of all this beating round the bush. I stopped having anything to do with Reidar because I have had him and his family up to here!' He illustrated with a hand to his throat, and went on: 'But I wanted my money and I was stupid enough to go and get it.'

He slammed his fist down on the table. Frølich watched him. There was no room for anything else but fury in the man's black expression. He tried to imagine this man being given the cold shoulder by an eighty-year-old, but abandoned this line of thought and instead asked:

'You said there was a connection between Reidar and your father, didn't you?'

'They were old pals.'

'So the connection between Reidar and you was through your father?'

'Yes. Have you finished now? I have to chop more wood now – and have a crap.'

Frølich pondered. 'I'm not sure I have what I need. So there's a very good chance we will have to talk again.'

'Then you'd better get it over with now.'

'How much did Reidar owe you?'

Stokmo sent him a dismissive grin.

Frølich stood up, went to the window and gazed across the partially snow-covered field stretching down to the frozen lake. The ridge of a barn roof was visible above the crest of a hill on the opposite side. A herd of deer had collected under some trees. They were grazing on hay. Someone had put a bale out in the snow. It was a very harmonious, idyllic winter landscape. 'It's very nice here, by the way,' he said to the man in the rocking chair. 'If I lived here, I don't think I would be so angry all the time.'

Stokmo didn't answer.

'What do you associate with the number one hundred and ninety-five?' Frølich asked from the window.

'The same as I associate with the numbers one or seven or fifty-two. Nothing.'

Frølich studied him. 'Hmm,' he said. 'You've got previous convictions, haven't you?'

He had waited a long time to deliver this blow because he knew it would hit the mark. Stokmo's shoulders slumped; he scowled and had the eyes of a hunted animal.

They stared at each other: Frank Frølich reclining against the wall and Jonny Stokmo cowed in the chair.

'It doesn't look good you hiding out here, as you were one of the last to see Folke Jespersen alive.'

'It was . . .'

'Shut up,' Frølich said coldly. 'You've admitted you had a score to settle with Folke Jespersen. You were one of the last people to see him alive. You don't have an alibi for the time of his death. And your story is damned thin.'

Stokmo stared at the floor.

'I've given you this opportunity and I won't be coming this way again. Have you got anything to add to your statement?'

Stokmo slowly shook his head.

'I'm instructing you to make yourself available at all times,' Frølich said in a low voice. 'You might be required to appear at the drop of a hat. If I call you and fail to get an answer, just once, I'll send two men round to pick you up and put you on remand. Have you got that?'

Stokmo nodded.

Frølich checked his watch. 'Until then,' he said, 'try and rustle up someone who can confirm your version of events on the night of 13th January.'

25

Through Fire

The car park in Vestre cemetery was quite full and Gunnarstranda was late. The breath around his mouth was frozen as he went to grab the large handle of the heavy chapel door. But before he could pull it open, it was gently pushed open from the inside. An official from the firm of undertakers, dressed in black, let him in.

' . . . *a man who lived a long and eventful life,*' the metallic voice of the priest echoed through the loud-speakers around the chapel. Gunnarstranda entered with as little noise as possible and sat on the chair clos-est to the aisle in the last row. He noticed the gaze of another official and nodded courteously. The man stared back. Reidar Folke Jespersen's coffin was white with decorated brass handles, and it was placed on the catafalque in front of the altar. The little canopy over the coffin was decorated with wreaths and bouquets of flowers. A long ribbon from one of the wreaths was draped down the aisle. Gunnarstranda inched off his gloves. It was warm in the chapel, but most of those attending were still wearing their thick winter coats. His glasses steamed up. He took them off and wiped them with a handkerchief while gazing up and taking in the sight of the frescoes on the walls. He put his glasses back on and scanned the assembled mourners. In the front row he could see the back of Karsten Jespersen's head and Ingrid, the widow. Three small children who couldn't sit still kept jumping off their chairs and were being hauled back by a resolute Susanne Jespersen. She sent frustrated looks to her husband, Karsten, who appeared to be oblivious of her – his gaze was firmly directed towards the seasoned priest conducting the service.

'*As a very young man Reidar Folke Jespersen was no stranger to death and terror in this war-ravaged country of ours,*' the voice intoned through the microphone. The priest was in his forties and spoke the dialect of southern Vestland. The first three rows were full while the other mourners were scattered around. He located the heads of the other two Folke Jespersen brothers, and he continued to search for Jonny Stokmo, but could not see him. His gaze rested on the coffin and he was reminded of how the dead man had looked – first displayed in his own shop window and then on Professor Schwenke's autopsy table.

The door directly behind him opened and he swivelled round on his chair. It was a woman. She also took a seat in the back row, but on the other side of the aisle. Her chair scraped as she sat down. Gunnarstranda stole furtive glances. She was wearing a thick sheepskin jacket down to the middle of her thighs. In her lap she was holding one red rose wrapped in transparent plastic. Her hair was short, blonde, and her hairstyle underlined her young age and chiselled features. Her hair stood up; it was brushed back and looked as though she had been caught in a gale. She was a beauty – a ray of sunshine from a window high up in the wall cut through the room and fell on her, gently setting off the contours of her face. She swallowed. The policeman realized that she sensed he was staring at her and he looked down. The priest was talking about how Folke Jespersen enjoyed mountain walks and unsullied nature. Gunnarstranda stifled a yawn. The grandchildren in the front row were fed up with the whole thing and their spoilt, angry voices were beginning to become audible as they argued with their mother. Susanne's whispered, almost hissed, reprimands carried to the back row. Gunnarstranda became aware of an electric charge in the air and peered to the left. The woman who had been staring at him looked down at once.

When the priest had finished, Karsten Jespersen got up to speak. He fixed his eyes on a point in the ceiling, clasped his hands behind his back and talked about *Dad* in a formal way, free of any pomposity. His chin trembled uncontrollably. He made a lot of his father's famous deeds during the war and his own pride.

There were several speakers. An elderly man with a sharp profile stood to attention before the coffin and paid tribute. When the priest looked to see if anyone else wanted to say something, Gunnarstranda decided to withdraw before the end. In a flash he noticed that the young beauty had risen to her feet. She stood for a few moments, expectant, then strode up the aisle with a light spring in her step and a red scarf flapping from her shoulder. She laid the rose on Reidar Folke Jespersen's coffin, curtseyed and stood still. The official from the firm of undertakers gestured for her to move forward to the microphone. But the woman took no notice of him.

She stood in the same place, silent, composed, with her back to the room and with bowed head, as though meditating. After standing in this position for some time, she spun round and strode back with her eyes firmly fixed ahead of her.

Gunnarstranda observed her face. There was something familiar about that chin and those lips.

Karsten Jespersen, the widow, Ingrid, and the forceful children's mother turned, all of them, and in amazement watched the woman walk out of the chapel. When the heavy door slammed, they turned round. Gunnarstranda got to his feet and made for the door.

The cold hit his cheeks as soon as he was outside. He was blinded by the light from the low sun. With his hand shielding his eyes, he looked for the woman, without any success. He put on his gloves and stalked down the steps, annoyed to have lost her. 'You don't have a phone on you by any chance, do you?' asked a voice from behind him. Gunnarstranda turned on his heels. 'Why's that?' he answered in a soft voice.

She had been leaning against the wall beside the church door. The muffled sounds of the organ and the psalms carried out to them. She took a step forward, and trembled as she lit a cigarette she was holding between long, white fingers. A fat, black ring graced her left thumb. 'I was thinking of calling a taxi,' she answered with a light shiver.

'Where are you going?'

She looked up. 'Have you got a car?'

The policeman nodded.

'Torshov.'

'Fine. Come with me,' Gunnarstranda said, leading the way to the car park.

When, soon afterwards, they were settled in the car, the cold had already managed to form a couple of frost flowers on the front windscreen. Gunnarstranda started the engine, put the de-froster on full, rubbed his hands and fumbled in his pockets for a cigarette. The woman sat stiffly beside him in the passenger seat, without saying a word. Gunnarstranda noticed she had thrown away her cigarette. For a brief moment he considered smoking, then decided to put his roll-up back.

By the time the car had reached the intersection between Skøyenveien and Sørkedalsveien, the warm air had cleared a half moon in the windscreen and improved visibility. A tram passed. The red light was slow to change.

Inspector Gunnarstranda used the wait to offer his hand. 'Gunnarstranda,' he said.

'Wyller,' she replied, looking with condescension at the hand the Inspector left hanging in the air for few seconds before she took it. 'Haven't you got a Christian name?' he asked.

'Haven't you?' She smiled at her own banter without evincing any pleasure from it and stared tight-lipped out of the window.

'I'm a policeman,' Gunnarstranda said as the lights changed to green.

She, to the side window: 'And I'm an actress.'

'Did you know Folke Jespersen?'

'Please shut up,' she said curtly.

Gunnarstranda smiled to himself.

They sat in silence. He bore right at Smestad and joined Ring 3. Not until they had passed the toll station by the research stations did she open her mouth: 'You can drop me by Ullevål stadium. Anywhere.'

'I'll drive you home,' Gunnarstranda insisted.

'Why?'

'I'm investigating the murder of Folke Jespersen.'

She went quiet.

'He knew my father,' she said at length, in a reflective rather than a friendly way.

'Who?'

'Folke. He knew my father.'

'Who is your father?'

'He's dead.'

Gunnarstranda nodded. 'Where do you live?'

'Hegermanns gate.'

'By the bull fountain?'

'Further down. Towards Marcus Thranes gate, Ring 2.'

Gunnarstranda slowed down for the lights at Ullevål stadium. He indicated right. The sun was now so low in the sky that you could only make out the outline of people in the street. The policeman flipped down the sunshield and leaned back to see better.

'How did they come across each other?'

'Who?'

'Jespersen and your father?'

'They were friends.'

Gunnarstranda nodded. 'What's your Christian name?'

'I have two.'

'Me, too,' said the policeman.

240

'Which one do you want?'

'Both.'

'I mean which of *my* two Christian names do you want?'

'The one you like best.'

He had to brake again. She grabbed the dashboard and smiled as she said it: 'Hege.'

Gunnarstranda tasted the name: 'Hege Wyller,' he muttered. 'And your father?'

'Harald Wyller.'

Gunnarstranda shot her a sceptical glance. There was no time for more than a glance – he was doing 80 kilometres an hour.

She stared ahead, smiling, as though she had thought of something amusing.

'And you're an actress?'

She nodded.

They drove on in silence. As they approached Hegermanns gate, Gunnarstranda asked again: 'How well did you know Folke Jespersen?'

'I didn't know him.'

'But you placed a rose on his coffin.'

'Don't you think he deserved it?'

Gunnarstranda didn't answer.

'There,' she said, pointing. 'In front of the drive, behind the red Toyota.'

Gunnarstranda slowed down. She immediately put her hand on the door handle.

'When was the last time you saw Folke Jespersen alive?' Gunnarstranda wanted to know.

She stiffened for an instant, but opened the door a

little anyway.

'When?' the policeman repeated.

'I don't remember.'

'Was it a long time ago?'

'Yes.'

She opened the door wide and got out. Gunnar-stranda also moved to get out. 'Bye,' she said and slammed the door. Gunnarstranda stood up; he had one foot on the ground, the other on the sill. He followed her with his eyes. She headed for the front door in the brick façade. As she unlocked the door she threw a last look at the policeman. They observed each other for two brief seconds before she disappeared inside.

Gunnarstranda left the car and walked slowly to the same door. Next to one of the bells he found her name engraved in white on a small, black nameplate: GRO HEGE WYLLER.

26

Pas de Deux

'One, two, cha-cha-cha, one, two, cha-cha-cha!' There were just two people practising in the room which smelt strongly of stale gymnasium. The man pirouetting in the room had his back arched like a bull-fighter's. He was wearing a short, baggy woollen sweater over a yellow leotard. He was medium height with longish, curly hair and a very athletic build. He was twirling round a young girl of maybe seventeen or eighteen who was trying to follow his movements. The music coming out of the speakers of a stereo-rack on the floor was easily drowned by the man's screaming voice. 'One, two, cha-cha-cha!' The man stamped his feet hard on the floor. 'Oh, come on!' he screamed, theatrically tossing his head and creating a swirl of glamorous locks around his head. 'Don't be so sluggish and slow! Pick up your feet!' The girl was wearing a gym outfit and legwarmers. Her blonde hair, which she had tied up in a ponytail, was beginning to come away from the elastic band. The man let go of her and demonstrated the dance steps once again. He studied his body in the mirror. The man's thigh and buttock muscles stood out through the leotard. For a brief second he exchanged glances with Frank Frølich, who was checking his wristwatch. He had been sitting on a bench in the large hall for twenty minutes. The young girl seemed so exhausted now that he guessed the lesson would soon be over.

Five minutes later the two men were alone in the hall.

'Eyolf Strømsted?' Frølich asked, reaching out his hand. 'This is about Ingrid Jespersen,' he said after introducing himself.

'My God, what a situation,' Strømsted said, wiping the sweat from his face.

'We have reason to believe that you're on very good terms with Ingrid Jespersen,' Frølich said.

'That's one way of putting it,' parried Strømsted with a fixed frontal gaze.

'I'm part of a team investigating the murder of her husband,' Frølich said and nothing more.

Strømsted held his rigid stare.

Frølich took his time. He was looking for the right words.

'We know you and Ingrid Jespersen are on very intimate terms.'

'And whose claim is that?' Strømsted said in a measured voice. 'Is it hers?'

'In fact we have seen you together.' Frølich stood up and rummaged in his bag. 'I have a few photos which would support what I'm saying, but . . .' He abandoned the search. 'I don't seem to have them with me, but you and the widow have been seen in somewhat intimate circumstances in a parked car the night after Reidar Folke Jespersen was found dead.'

Strømsted was breathing hard.

'When did you last meet her?' Frølich asked gently.

'On Sunday. We drove to the car park outside the Munch museum.'

'And before that?'

'The Friday . . . 13th January.'

Frølich took notes and peered up. 'Could you tell me what happened that Friday?'

'She dropped by to see me between half past eleven and twelve – in the morning. Half an hour later we went to bed. We had a cup of tea and chatted for a bit first. That's what we always do – every Friday.'

Frølich looked up when the other man paused.

Strømsted had a steely expression on his face. 'Perhaps half an hour later her husband rang. He rang while we were fucking. How great is that!' the man grinned.

'What did you say?'

'While we were fucking.'

Frølich sent the man with the curls a stern look. The forehead under the curls was sweaty.

'And who rang?'

'Her old man. The murder victim. Reidar Folke Jespersen.'

'What did he want?'

'To talk to his wife.'

'And did he?'

'Yes indeed.'

Strømsted was still staring ahead. Into the mirror on the opposite wall. They exchanged looks in the mirror.

'Has this relationship been going on for a long time?'

'Much too long!'

'What do you mean by that?'

Strømsted ran his fingers through his curly locks. 'I suppose it means I think this situation is quite dreadful.'

'Which situation?'

'To have to stand here answering your embarrassing questions when a pupil can come in the door at any moment.'

'How long has this relationship been going on?'

'About three years.'

'Have you ever met Folke Jespersen?' Frølich enquired.

'Once. Many years ago when I was dancing with Ingrid.'

'Have you seen him since?'

'Never.' Strømsted wiped his forehead with the back of his hand and pulled at the front of his sweater. He wafted it to let air in. 'What's the time?' he asked.

'Five past,' Frølich said.

'Another pupil will be here any minute.'

'That's fine. Did you meet Folke Jespersen that Friday?'

Strømsted blenched. 'Meet her husband? No.' He dried his face with the towel again. As he took it away, he grinned. His upper lip abutted a wide row of impeccable teeth. It was a winning, though also a much practised, smile. Frølich was clear that this man could easily make women go weak at the knees.

'How long was Ingrid with you?'

'Until just after three.'

'What did you do after his call?'

Strømsted grinned. 'What do you think?'

'Just answer the question.'

'We carried on.' Strømsted sent him a provocative glower. 'She was sucking me off,' he said with a fixed smile.

'Did you talk about the phone call?'

'It wasn't so easy for her to talk at that point.'

Frølich, remaining patient, took a deep breath.

Strømsted stared ahead, thoughtful, open-mouthed.

'Hmm, I'm sorry. This situation isn't exactly easy. What we talked about? What we talked about was her husband. For the most part we talked about how much he knew, how long he had known and what the consequences would be.'

'What do you mean by that?'

'By what?'

'What the consequences would be? Of his phone call?'

Strømsted flashed a faint, dreamy smile. 'She'd been caught being unfaithful, hadn't she! So she was pondering the future of her marriage. She was quite distraught.'

'Her husband didn't usually phone her then?'

'Are you insane?'

'So her husband had exposed her activities with this phone call? That's what you're saying?'

'Yes.'

'Do you think she wanted to get out of her marriage?'

'What do you mean by that?'

Frølich: 'Do you think she was sorry she had been caught? Was there a risk of a divorce?'

'Hmm,' Strømsted said. 'Well, you can imagine. Her husband rings while she . . . while she . . . I suppose it must have knocked her off her perch, as they say – in this case, quite literally.' His upper lip spread to reveal his teeth again. Frølich could feel that he was beginning to dislike this smile.

'I think she was dreading the evening,' Strømsted said in a more earnest tone.

'Why was that?'

'Just imagine it, being caught like that, and then having to go home to your husband and spend the whole evening with him.'

'Why did he ring?'

'He wanted to put a stop to our activities.'

'Do you know that for certain?'

'Yes, she told me what he had said. It was a very brief conversation.'

'What did you do – later that evening?' Frølich asked.

'I was at home.'

'Can anyone confirm that you were at home?'

Strømsted stood up and strolled towards the mirror on the opposite wall. He grabbed the wall bar and raised his right leg in one supple movement. It was a classic dance step, a classic pose. 'Is this the moment of truth?' he asked in an exaggerated, theatrical voice while observing Frølich in the mirror. 'Will you let me go if, Mr Policeman, if I answer yes?'

Frølich looked at his image in the mirror. He was all the dancer was not. His grey hair was unkempt and lifeless. His beard made him look down in the mouth. His body was too big and too heavy.

Eyolf Strømsted was a statue. Muscles and sinews wreathed the man's body like yarn around a ball. The man's curly hair emphasized the almost feminine features of his clean-shaven face.

'Does that mean the answer is no?' the policeman asked blithely.

Strømsted took pleasure in the sight of his own body as he lowered his leg without any hurry and continued the slow movement into a glide and the splits. 'Of course not,' he said to his own image. 'I realized after the phone call that Ingrid Jespersen may not have been the smartest move I have ever made.' He grinned: 'And yes indeed. You can have it confirmed any time you like. I was at home all evening and all night.'

27

Lady in Snow

The next morning Gunnarstranda tried to call Ingrid Jespersen on the telephone, without any success. Then he read through reports and was able to establish, after going through Frølich's interview of the widow, that firstly she was somewhat reluctant to pick up the phone and secondly that she liked to take her lunch in a café with which she had been connected earlier.

It took him a further three calls and a few enquiries before, at half past twelve, he was able to park his almost new Skoda Octavia in Frognerveien and stroll the few metres to the café, open the door and hand his winter coat to the Vietnamese-looking woman in the cloakroom. He checked himself over in the mirror behind the attendant, straightened his sparse hair and turned to study the scene. 'Only one person?' asked a woman dressed in dark clothes, the head waitress. 'I'm afraid so,' answered the policeman defensively. 'But I was thinking of joining Ingrid Jespersen.' He motioned towards a window table where Ingrid, engrossed in a newspaper, was eating pasta.

'May I join you?' he asked, although she did not catch what he had said at once. When she peered up she did not seem at all put out. 'Sit down? Of course.' She extended an open hand to the unoccupied chair. Slowly she folded the paper. It was *Verdens Gang*. A youthful photograph of Reidar Folke Jespersen disappeared. 'I've read that you have some leads.'

Gunnarstranda smiled and shook his head to the waiter who came with the menu. 'Just coffee,' he said and added: 'Black.'

To Ingrid: 'I suppose you must have gathered that we are keeping all our options open?'

She nodded. 'How did you know I was here?'

'Because we're keeping all our options open,' he replied lightly.

Taken aback, she grimaced. 'Well, I must say . . .' She stared down at her meal, but seemed to have lost her appetite. 'Are you having me followed?'

Gunnarstranda took the cup of coffee without a word and stirred it with a faraway look. The waiter stretched out a hand for Ingrid's plate with a questioning look. 'Thank you. I've had enough,' she said. The policeman was stirring his coffee as he watched the waiter retreat.

'Are you following me?' Ingrid Jespersen repeated.

'We're looking after you as well as we can.'

'But . . .'

'Do you know the name Eyolf Strømsted?' he interrupted.

Ingrid lowered her eyes. She went quiet. Gunnarstranda leaned back in his chair.

'Is that what they call shooting from the hip?' she asked, her eyes still downcast.

No response from Gunnarstranda.

'Or what?' she went on, with renewed energy in her

voice, and raising her head. Her eyes seemed tired, but aggressive at the same time.

'It's a question,' Gunnarstranda said with composure. 'Either you answer it or you don't. Make sure the answer is honest.'

'Looking after . . .' Ingrid muttered. 'Isn't it simply spying on people?'

Gunnarstranda didn't answer. Instead he sipped his coffee.

'We know each other,' she said in a more controlled tone of voice. 'We know each other very well. But I presume you know that.'

Gunnarstranda nodded.

'We go way back . . . he's . . . he was once a pupil of mine. He used to be a dancer.'

'How long have you two been having an affair?'

'For three years.'

'That's quite a long time, isn't it?'

'There are some that last longer, unknown to anyone.'

'That goes without saying.'

Ingrid reached down and scratched her leg. 'My God, I'm so hot . . .' Gunnarstranda noticed she had a determined furrow between her eyebrows. It made her look severe. 'Have you got any plans?' he asked.

She straightened up.

'What do you mean?'

Gunnarstranda looked into her eyes: 'I was wondering what Strømsted means to you. Is he an erotic dalliance or does he mean much more?'

'Much more?' She lowered her gaze and rested her head on her hand. 'Isn't it enough that we have stayed together for three years?'

'I would like you to answer the question.'

'Whether he's an erotic dalliance or more? Does whether I distinguish between eroticism and love tell you anything about who I am?'

Gunnarstranda patiently sipped his coffee.

'Do you know what I've heard?' she said, gazing out of the window. 'I've heard that however wild your desire there will always be a concomitant feeling of emptiness.'

Composed, she turned to him again.

'Sex,' she began, pausing for a few seconds before taking the plunge. 'Sex is about bodies, a physical phenomenon which can be calculated and defined, a mathematical curve with growth, with peaks and troughs. Sexuality exists by virtue of its form.'

They exchanged glances. The policeman said nothing. She had not yet finished.

'Sexuality is man-made, and like all man-made things it has deficiencies. Sex contains an anticipation of something else and more. All physical matter is bound to reach saturation point – just because it has physical limits. That applies to sex too. Therefore it is the nature of eroticism that you become sated, either with the partner or with the sexual act.'

Rapt in thought, she gazed across the room, and then continued: 'On the other hand, there is an energy which does not depend on physical proximity. The emotional, psychological longing which two people feel for each other is a genuine form of love. Longing is love that knows no boundaries. Longing can never be destroyed or fade away or die.'

Gunnarstranda observed her over the rim of his cup. It was as though she had been giving a lecture learned by rote, and at this moment she was recalling the times when she used to swot for school. He had to swallow hard. Her words had conjured up an image of Edel. He cleared his throat to make his voice heard, so strong had the sensation been that she had been talking directly to him. 'That was well put,' he conceded and coughed again. 'And I may well have heard something similar. But is it like that? Most people would rather try to unite these aspects of their love life. At any rate, those who choose a partner for life through marriage.'

'But if it isn't possible?'

'What?'

'For some it may be impossible to unite the physical with the emotional.' Then she added: 'For Reidar it was like that.'

'Reidar?' the policeman said. 'I thought you were talking about yourself.'

She shook her head. 'I don't know what I think about this. I've never had a consistent policy on such things. But I have long wondered why I should have had to live in abstinence for seven years.'

'Was he impotent?'

'Impotent?' She sent him another weary smile. 'Do you realize you are trying to justify many years of imbalance with one word? Was he impotent, you ask, and you apparently expect me to clarify the situation with a *yes* or a *no*. Well, what sort of clarification? Have you considered at all what it is you're asking? Fine, let me take you at your word. I can say *yes*. Yes, in recent years

Reidar was not capable of performing the physical activity with me which is required to make a child. And so what? Does that make our love less pure or . . .' she contemplated the ceiling as she searched for words . . . 'less tender, less warm? I don't think so. You didn't object when I claimed there was a distinction between eroticism and longing. They were his words. Reidar said it so often, and I have thought about those words so many times that I know the reasoning off by heart. Reidar didn't have any hormonal problems. The distinction between sexuality and longing was an intellectual standpoint on his part. He was finished with eroticism. He didn't want to make love to me, to use a cliché. For a long time I thought he despised me, that he found me unattractive or loathsome. But of course he didn't. Reidar was so straightforward, so uncomplicated – that he told the truth. When he grew older, he made a distinction between physical love and psychological longing. He despised the one and prized the other.'

'But what does it mean?'

She shook her head in desperation. 'What does it mean? It means you know something about me no one else does. It means you have made me declare my love for my husband. It means I feel sordid!'

'Did he have any other women?'

'No. Not at all.'

'Did he use prostitutes?'

'He would rather have died than go to a prostitute.'

'Who did he long for?'

'Well, you tell me.' Ingrid had a faraway look in her eyes, and a furrowed brow. 'I would guess he longed for the wife who died, my predecessor.'

'Did he say that in so many words?'

'No. He never admitted it, if that's what you're asking. It's my guess. On the other hand, it's based on many
years of practical experience. All in all, my marriage was
a fiasco.'

'A fiasco?'

'The word may be an exaggeration. Let's just say you
can rely on my assessment.'

'What about your current relationship? Which cate-
gory of love does that fall under – eroticism or longing?'

'I don't think the same way as Reidar. I do what I feel
is right. And, for me, meeting Eyolf feels right.'

'But then my earlier question is very pertinent: Have
you two got any plans?'

She shook her head. 'No, we have no plans.'

'Have you split up?'

'No, but . . .' She shrugged her shoulders. 'I assume we
will continue as before.'

'And what is that supposed to mean?'

She pulled a wry grin. 'Inspector . . .'

He raised a hand to stop her. 'What is that supposed
to mean?' he repeated with emphasis.

She was at a loss for a few moments.

'We'll meet once a week.'

'Where?'

'In his flat. He lives in Jacob Aalls gate. But you
already know that.' She breathed in and steadied herself.
'Now I think about it, I suppose he could come to my
place as Reidar is . . . no longer there.' She looked into
his eyes, provocatively.

He nodded slowly. 'Well, you wouldn't have to resort to car parks . . .'

She sat up in her chair, glared at the table for a while before raising her eyes to meet his. She was flushed, he realized, flushed with anger.

'I'm investigating a murder,' he said gently. 'What you and Strømsted do in vehicles in Oslo car parks does not interest me.'

'Oh no? Why are there people spying on us then?' she snapped.

'Because I want to solve a crime, a task which entails needing to know more about you and your acquaintances. Also we don't know why your husband was murdered and therefore we need to be close at hand. But above all I want to know what you and your husband were doing on the days before the murder. Did you meet Strømsted during this time?'

'Yes.'

'When?'

'The same day. I visited Eyolf on Friday the 13th.' She looked down as though collecting her strength before staring provocatively into the policeman's eyes again, with a malicious little smile. 'We went to bed at some time between twelve and one, and stayed there . . . for a couple of hours. I dozed off while Eyolf made us lunch. We had pasta. Penne all'arrabbiata. His is better than the one they serve here, in fact. And I left at about three. Happy?'

'I will be soon,' the policeman said, leaning over and resting his elbows on the table. 'You didn't say anything about this in your earlier statement.'

She didn't answer.

Gunnarstranda mused. He was questioning her, but you weren't supposed to question suspects in cafés. Too late to stop now, though. He said:

'Does this mean you will change your statement?'

She stared at him. 'Are you taking my statement here?'

'You could pop into Grønlandsleiret today after five. Your new statement will be ready in reception. You only have to sign. Read it through first. If there is anything which does not accord with what really happened, leave it and get in touch with me immediately.'

'Right.'

'Immediately means that very instant!'

'I've got the point.'

'The day after your husband was found dead in the shop window, you went to this dancing school run by your lover. You took him out and he had to find an instructor to step in for him. You drove to the car park between the Munch museum and the Botanical Gardens – why?'

'Because,' she said dismissively, and pinched her mouth shut.

Gunnarstranda gave a lop-sided smile. 'You mean this is private?'

'Of course.'

'I will repeat the question and you are requested to answer: Why did you visit Eyolf Strømsted on the Sunday in question?'

'Because we have the relationship we do,' she growled. 'I needed to be near him.'

'But why in a car park?'

'Why not?'

They sat eyeing each other in silence. 'I'm sorry if you're not satisfied,' she said at last. 'But that's my answer to the question.'

'What did you say to Reidar when he rang?'

'What?'

Gunnarstranda's eyes flashed. 'You heard what I said. I know Reidar rang when you and Strømsted were in bed that Friday.'

She closed her eyes and blanched as though he had slapped her. 'Has Eyolf . . .?'

'Answer me,' the policeman insisted with force.

'I don't like to talk about this,' she whispered.

'Answer me.'

'He demanded that I . . .'

Gunnarstranda drummed his fingers with impatience.

She breathed in and gazed out of the window. The policeman followed her gaze. A woman in a tight-fitting winter coat got out of a car and slipped into a hairdresser's on the other side of the street.

'It was typical Reidar,' Ingrid said. 'He was efficient in everything he did. He rang me up, presumably to show me he knew. He asked me to stop meeting Eyolf. That was all.'

'He asked you?'

'Well, it was more of a demand.'

'What did you say?'

'Nothing. He rang off.'

'But what did he say when you were alone – later in the evening?'

'We didn't talk about the matter.'

'That's odd.'

'You didn't know Reidar. I neither wanted nor dared to broach the subject.'

'You had been caught in the act.'

'Yes.' She ran a finger under one eye, moved.

'It might have given you a motive.'

'Motive?' She said with a resigned smile. 'Why on earth would it give me a motive? In fact, I was ready to break with Eyolf.'

'That stands and falls on how far you are telling the truth.'

Another weary smile. 'What do you think, Inspector Gunnarstranda? Do you think I'm telling the truth? I know you have discussed this case with others.'

'Let me put it this way,' the detective countered sharply. 'If you fail to present evidence or information which has a bearing on the case, it will not count in your favour.' He took a deep breath. 'You maintain you were on the point of breaking up with Eyolf Strømsted on that Friday, but how does that tally with the fact that you met him a short while after?'

'I needed it. I needed to meet him again.'

'Why?'

'Because my husband had been killed, because I felt alone, because I needed someone to hold me. Is that so damned difficult to understand?'

'Not at all, but there could also be other reasons for meeting him, reasons which you are withholding.'

She shook her head with vehemence.

'You and Reidar might have had a row on Friday

night when you were alone.'

She was quiet.

'If you had a row – there are many outcomes one could envisage.'

She was still quiet.

'Did you have a row that evening?'

'No.'

'The fact that you have a relationship with another man is not something I can ignore in the investigation.'

'I understand that.'

'Then I'm sure you'll understand that we will have to come back to this matter.'

'I don't know if I will understand.'

'Why do you think Reidar did not go to bed that night?'

'I have no idea,' she snarled. 'Perhaps you do.'

'I can only form hypotheses – and have them confirmed or confounded.'

'I didn't have a row with Reidar.'

'Was Strømsted's name mentioned either by you or your husband that evening?'

'No.'

'I also find that very unusual.'

'Sorry, but I can't do anything about that. Eyolf's name was not mentioned at all.'

'You've already had to change your statement once. I'm asking you one more time: Was your infidelity discussed by you and your husband that evening?'

'The answer is no,' she said stiffly, in a low voice and with downcast eyes.

The policeman watched her. 'Do you know if

Strømsted has other lovers?' he asked quietly.

'You'd better ask him, not me.'

'But he's been your lover for a long time. You must have had thoughts of that nature, about whether he meets other people.'

'Of course. I assume he meets other women – on the odd occasion. But whether he sleeps with them . . . I have chosen not to speculate.'

'He lives with someone,' Gunnarstranda said.

For a fraction of a second her eyes bulged, then she looked down, swallowed, shook her head again and gave a disdainful laugh. 'He definitely does not, that much I do know.'

The policeman, surprised, smiled gently. 'You didn't know he lived with someone?'

'I don't believe you.'

'Why the doubt?'

'I've been visiting him every week for three years. I've never so much as seen a pair of knickers or a packet of tampons in that house, no high-heeled shoes . . .'

'Hasn't he got a double bed?'

'All men have double beds.'

'Is that so?' Gunnarstranda swallowed, then pursed his lips, as though he had learned something new, and asked: 'Why do you think he didn't take you to his place on Sunday evening when you turned up at the dance class? Why do you think you ended up in a car park?'

'This is none of your business.'

'He lives with a man,' Gunnarstranda stated baldly.

Ingrid recoiled. She stared out of the window, folded her trembling hands and after a glance down at the table jumped up and snatched her bag. Without another word she turned and strode out between the tables. Inspector Gunnarstranda watched her. The Vietnamese-looking cloakroom attendant searched through a row of winter coats, took one off a hanger and passed it with a smile to Ingrid Jespersen, who donned it with her back to the detective. She spun on her heel and marched out. As she passed the window where Gunnarstranda was sitting, her eyes were fixed in front of her and she didn't even grace him with a look. At that moment she slipped on a patch of ice and fell sideways. She landed on her hip and one arm. A young man with a long fringe ran up to her. She waved him away and struggled up on one knee. It wasn't easy – the soles of her shoes were smooth and had no tread. The back of her dark coat was white with snow. She had snow in her hair. She had snow up her nylons. She stood supporting herself on a parking meter for a few moments. Two small children on the opposite side of the street pointed and laughed. It was all over in less than thirty seconds. Not once did she look in the policeman's direction. When Gunnarstranda finally managed to compose himself, the same waiter was standing there. He was flourishing a slip of paper. 'I've prepared the bill for you,' he said in a soft voice and placed it on the table.

28

Motives

Frølich was lumbering down the corridor when he saw Gunnarstranda switch off the light and close the door behind him. He joined Gunnarstranda back in his office. The acrid smell of many smoked cigarettes hung in the room like the fusty smell of carriages on the Østfold railway line.

Frølich took a seat and put his feet up on the desk, then flicked through Ingrid Jespersen's revised statement.

Gunnarstranda was smoking a cigarette by the partly opened window and said: 'By the way a complaint has been lodged against us.'

'Us?'

'Well, me, to be precise,' Gunnarstranda said. 'Someone has claimed I've been smoking in smoke-free zones.' He flipped over the long-necked ashtray behind his chair and looked down into it. 'It wasn't you, was it?' he asked.

Frølich turned round. 'Me? No.'

'The complaint was anonymous.'

'Does it matter who complains? You could smoke outside, like all the others.'

'I do smoke outside.'

'And you smoke in here.'

'Are you sure you weren't the one who complained?'

'Yes.'

'Hm.' Gunnarstranda sat down, placed the cigarette on the rim of the long-necked ashtray and focused on Frølich, who was still studying the report. 'Suppose it's Ingrid who did her husband in,' Frølich began. 'Her infidelity has been rumbled. Reidar rings her – catches her in the act – threatens her and tells her to finish with the guy. What would he threaten her with? Divorce? But she's fifty-four and he's eighty.'

'Seventy-nine,' Gunnarstranda corrected.

'OK,' Frølich said. 'What I don't understand is why she would be afraid that her adultery would come to light. What could he threaten her with? Or what has she to lose by being divorced? Her share of the inheritance?'

Gunnarstranda looked at him with unseeing eyes. 'Yes,' he said. 'She would lose the inheritance, but that's not an immediate issue. Divorce would give her half anyway.'

Frølich put down the papers. 'Imagine the atmosphere,' he exclaimed. 'The meal must have been a pretty quiet affair. Reidar's son and family are there while the two of them are sending each other signals – but when Karsten, his wife and children leave, Ingrid is bound to have discussed the matter with her husband!'

'Why?'

Frølich sighed with despair. 'But she had to, didn't she! They have to go to bed. They have to share intimacies . . .'

'We don't know that.'

'I'm not thinking of sex. But there is something intimate about going to bed at night. They share a bed. He

– Jespersen – has caught his wife with another man. Strømsted is young and virile – a man his wife must have chosen because she wants sex from the relationship. Think about it! Jespersen is close on eighty and impotent. His wife's choice of a lover is like a slap in the face. Of course they must have talked about her infidelity that night!'

'Not necessarily.'

Frølich, perplexed: 'You don't think they talked?'

'I don't think they necessarily discussed her infidelity,' Gunnarstranda said.

'Why not?'

'There are things we choose not to talk about.'

'But this is adultery.'

'I know it's adultery, but you and Reidar Folke Jespersen may not have the same moral code.'

'Code?'

Gunnarstranda waved him on. 'Oh, never mind. Go on. Where were you?'

'My guess is they started rowing. I think she became aggressive when he refused to talk to her – or when he stuck to his guns and insisted she stopped meeting the other man. Because she had been unfaithful he refused to sleep in the same bed. I assume he went down to the shop to sleep there. She couldn't put up with his sulking and followed – down to the shop where the row continued – and in the end she grabbed a bayonet hanging on the wall and stabbed him!' Frølich illustrated with stabbing motions in the air.

'Sleep in the shop? Why didn't he go to one of the many sofas in the flat?'

'All right, he didn't go downstairs to sleep, he went to the shop to look at the things Karsten had been talking about, or to check the door was locked – or just to sit and meditate for all I know. It doesn't change anything. She ended up stabbing him!'

'And then?'

'Hm?'

'What happened then?' Gunnarstranda asked with interest.

'Well, she undressed him, scribbled those things on his chest and forehead and dragged the body to the shop window. We know all this . . .'

'Yes, but go on. What happened then?'

'Well, then she goes up to her room – and then she panics. She fakes a kind of nervous breakdown and tries to work out how she can get off the hook.' Frølich throws his arms in the air. 'The upshot is she phones Karsten to foist this break-in fantasy on everyone around her.'

'And then?' Gunnarstranda urges his colleague on with a flourish of the hand.

'She could have rung her lover,' Frølich says with triumph in his voice. 'If she really was frightened, she should have phoned her lover. But she doesn't; she rings Reidar's son. Why would she do that – if it wasn't to establish an alibi . . .?'

'But then?'

Frølich: 'Yes, things go wrong. She's rebuffed by Karsten's wife – Susanne – as it is half past two at night. She sits up until the morning biting her nails. But by a stroke of good fortune this paper girl shows up. So she doesn't have to discover the body. Nor does she have to ring the police.'

'There are some flaws in your theory.'

'Fine, but at least it is a theory. And when I asked her whether she had heard any noises that night, she went ashen. I'm sure she's holding something back. Absolutely certain.'

'Possible,' conceded the inspector, thinking. They stared at each other as Gunnarstranda added: 'However, why put the body in the shop window?'

Frølich reflected. 'That's a question we'll have to ask all the suspects,' he said. 'It's irrelevant as a counter-argument to the theory.'

'Irrelevant? The wife displaying her murdered husband in the shop window is illogical. If she were trying to cover up the murder and claim it was the result of a break-in, the logical thing to do would be to leave the body on the shop floor – dressed. It would be logical to damage the door frame or smash a window – much more logical than stripping the body and dragging it to the window.'

They sat gazing into the air.

'He may have threatened her with divorce and loss of the inheritance,' Frølich said at length. 'That would explain why he revoked the original will. It would also explain why he didn't suggest a new will to the solicitor.' Frølich jumped to his feet with excitement. 'Of course. It's obvious. That's how it was! He used divorce and the inheritance to put pressure on his wife.'

Gunnarstranda shook his head. 'We've already been through the inheritance business.'

'Well . . .' Frølich was thinking aloud. 'She must have gone for the old goat for money from the very outset. Women who marry old men do it for money – everyone says that. Assuming this goes for her too, she's stuck it out for almost twenty-five years waiting for riches, and now, all of a sudden, this dream of paradise is jeopardized by her infidelity. That's why she kills Reidar, so that he doesn't have time to leave the money to others in a new will.'

'Two arguments in contra,' Gunnarstranda said. 'First of all, the likelihood is we're not talking big money here. The couple lived in an expensive apartment in Frogner – and I imagine they were quite well off, but there is nothing to suggest that Jespersen was a man of great wealth. The second is that I don't believe Ingrid Jespersen is the type to marry a man for his money. Another thing I'm also a little uncertain about is whether her infidelity unduly bothered Reidar.'

'He made the phone call,' Frølich objected. 'He ordered his wife to stop meeting Strømsted.'

'That's true, but we shouldn't forget that Reidar had lived with this age difference for a very long time. Do you remember what I said when I first met Ingrid? I took it for granted that she had a lover – why would Reidar see things any differently? My guess is he assumed she would take lovers from time to time.'

Frølich considered what Gunnarstranda had said, but also found a counter-argument: 'If Jespersen accepted that his wife would go with other men, he wouldn't have bothered to ring her on precisely that day, would he?'

'We don't know why he rang. Perhaps he rang to give

her a shock, to show her he knew about the relationship,' Gunnarstranda said darkly, 'to tell her to get her act together. Something may . . .'

'Possible,' Frølich interrupted. 'But it's not without significance that he rings his wife when she is in the process of cheating on him and that he rings his solicitor a few hours later to retract a will, which, whatever you say, favours her in some shape or form. The strange thing is that he is killed afterwards. Furthermore, you're overlooking the dirty dog himself: Strømsted. He may be involved.'

'Something,' Gunnarstranda continued undeterred, 'may have happened which caused or provoked the telephone call from Reidar to Strømsted.'

'But what could that have been?'

They were interrupted by the telephone. Gunnarstranda grabbed it, listened for a couple of seconds and said: 'Excellent, Yttergjerde. Stay on their tail.'

'Trouble in paradise,' he said, putting down the receiver. 'That was Yttergjerde. Ingrid is having another tête-à-tête with Eyolf. Driving round in the car.'

'Co-ordinating statements?' Frølich suggested.

'Seemed like they were having a row.'

The two men exchanged looks.

'They do have a relationship, which we have uncovered. It would be strange if they weren't talking.'

Frølich scratched his beard. 'It's not strange that she's angry,' he said. 'Strømsted admitted the relationship to me, whereas she lied when I talked to her.'

'It'll be interesting to see if she signs her new statement,' Gunnarstranda, said, putting on a thoughtful expression. 'This Strømsted person has a long-term relationship with a man. While he is humping Ingrid Jespersen once a week – why?' The Detective Inspector supplied his own answer: 'I suppose to satisfy his bisexual orientation. If he's crazy about Ingrid, he wouldn't be living with someone else, would he?'

'You mean because Strømsted lives with someone he cannot be the murderer?' Frølich asked, and said: 'We don't know much about the feelings between the two of them – for all we know he could be screwing her to get a few kroner from the shop . . .'

Gunnarstranda's brow was still furrowed.

'They drove all the way to Tøyen Park the day after,' Frølich said quietly. 'Both of them live in the best area of Oslo. Why would they drive all the way to Tøyen Park if it wasn't to hide from us and get their stories straight?' He opened his palms. 'And now they're doing it again.'

'I think you have a point. Tøyen is a fair distance away . . .'

'Why did they go all the way to Tøyen if it hadn't been to lose Yttergjerde?' Excited, Frølich sprang to his feet. 'Even if they couldn't go to Strømsted's place, because of his partner, they could have gone to Ingrid's. But why didn't they? Well, first of all there are police outside the house. And second of all they would have to have sex in the flat above the crime scene. Imagine the night of the murder: Ingrid checked all the doors in the house. If she was in this together with Strømsted, she's the Trojan horse.'

Gunnarstranda sighed. 'If Ingrid's the Trojan horse and lets in the murderer, why does she tell us the story about the snow on the floor? If she let him in, why did-n't she keep her mouth shut about the puddles? After all, the puddles mean someone was in the house!'

'But what if she woke up panic-stricken and phoned Karsten, only to receive a surprise visit from the murderer afterwards . . .'

'Then she's not a Trojan horse any more,' Gunnarstranda countered.

'No, but if that's how it was, then she invents the story about the snow on the floor as a red herring! The snow is meant to suggest that somebody had been inside the house *before* she woke up, while the truth was that a guest came *after* she had made the call.'

'Of course that's possible . . .'

'Strømsted may even have killed the old man without her knowing,' Frølich suggested, getting excited. 'Strømsted kills Reidar. Then he takes the keys from the body, goes up to the first floor, lets himself in, meets her, tells her what he has done and . . .'

'Two arguments in contra,' Gunnarstranda cut in.

Frølich was breathing hard.

'First of all, Strømsted immediately told you about the call from Reidar which interrupted the love-in he was having with Ingrid. He needn't have done that. In other words he was serving up a motive on a silver platter. That may suggest he has nothing to hide. Secondly . . .' Gunnarstranda paused.

Frølich sat and observed him.

'There's still the problem of the shop window and the scribble on the man's body.'

'Whoever killed Reidar, that aspect of the case is going

to be a problem,' Frølich said, dismissing the objection with some irritation.

'Fair enough,' Gunnarstranda assented. 'But deep down I know I believe one thing: there was a logic to what someone did with the body! In addition, it seems as if the relationship between Ingrid Jespersen and Strømsted the dance teacher is not straightforward. He's cohabiting with another homosexual man. Ingrid Jespersen didn't seem to "know" anything about this gay relationship.' Gunnarstranda formed the quotation marks with his forefingers. 'You should have seen the way she flounced out of the café. It was worthy of an Oscar. Fittingly enough, she took a nose-dive right in front of me.'

'She doesn't seem the kind to fall flat on her face.'

'Perhaps not, but I'm not sure I believe that she didn't know about Strømsted's orientation. I've never met a woman who hasn't intuited a gay man. Think about it: Ingrid Jespersen has been humping this man once a week for years, in his partner's flat! It's very unlikely that she didn't know he was gay.'

'He's bi, not gay.'

'Yttergjerde said he waggled his bum like Olympic long distance-walkers!'

Frølich raised both eyebrows. 'You don't say,' he mumbled. 'I can't tell gays and heteros apart. Especially not when they're walkers. I would never have guessed Strømsted was bisexual.'

'You aren't a woman!'

'Are you?'

'Well . . .'

Frølich grinned.

Gunnarstranda changed the subject. 'That's enough of that, but she must have known. Ingrid may be behind the murder, but for the time being I think it would be unwise to put all our eggs in that basket. Bearing in mind that Strømsted lives with a man, I think it very unlikely that he would kill for her sake.'

'So that's it?'

'It is, as always, about finding out who did what when,' Gunnarstranda said wearily. He flicked the sheets of paper in his hand with a finger: 'We have to talk to his partner and find out whether he can substantiate the alibi. But first we'll have to see whether the widow will sign this statement or whether she'll show up at all.' He turned and selected another document. 'This is the report on the forensic examination of the office in Bertrand Narvesens vei. There are fingerprints on both of the sherry glasses I found. Reidar drank from one of them. Someone else drank from the other.'

'Who, do you think?

Gunnarstranda grinned. 'We don't have any records on whoever it was. I have a feeling a woman visited him. And it wasn't his wife.'

29

Lady in Red

Gunnarstranda took the route through the city centre. He stood watching the children skating on the ice rink around the fountain in Spikersuppa to disco music. The floodlighting cast a sharp, white light and converted the scene into a setting for a film production; the spray of snow the skates sent up looked like icing sugar. Two blonde women in their twenties floundered on the ice, doing precarious pirouettes and giggling to each other, excited by being in the spotlight.

Gunnarstranda continued along Lille Grensen, turned into Akersgata and ambled through the Parliament area and on to Café Justisen where he drank a leisurely cup of coffee, read two tabloid newspapers and listened to words of wisdom from regular customers. A freshly groomed tramp dressed in Salvation Army clothes sat down at a window table with a grunt. The waitress, who was very attractive, served beer, potatoes and a fried egg. 'Have you washed your hands, Roger?' she asked in a firm voice, like a mother. 'I'm as clean as a Pentecostalist in Philadelphia,' Roger sighed, and wolfed down the food and beer.

Gunnarstranda thought about the reply as the café door slammed shut behind him. Outside, it had grown dark as he strolled down to Storgata to catch the tram to pay a visit to Gro Hege Wyller.

She hesitated when he introduced himself through the intercom. But in the end the front-door lock buzzed. On the way up he inadvertently kicked a metal railing alongside the steps and it emitted a hollow ring.

She didn't seem surprised to see him. 'Thought you would be back,' she said, holding the door open.

Gunnarstranda walked past her and into a one-room flat which bore all the hallmarks of a young woman with economic restraints starting out: a once-spacious flat divided and portioned up into smaller units. The part that Gro Hege Wyller occupied had perhaps been a servant girl's room before or the pantry. The bedsit was just shy of thirty square metres and the ceiling was high. A short mezzanine floor had been built over the sitting room section – a sofa and an armchair over which she had thrown some large, purple cloths. The floor functioned as a bed. Cushions and corners of a sheet were visible up there. Three pairs of knickers and black tights were drying on the radiator beneath the window.

She stood by the door sizing him up. Her jeans were worn and skin-tight. They hung perilously low from her hips and revealed a deep navel decorated with a silver pearl.

Police Inspector Gunnarstranda sat down in the armchair without any ceremony. On the table there was a portable 10-inch TV with the aerial extended. 'When was the last time you saw Reidar Folke Jespersen?' he asked gently.

'The day before he died,' she replied.

'Thursday or Friday?'

'Friday 13th January.'

They exchanged looks. She held his stare, which made Gunnarstranda decide not to comment on the change to her previous statement, which this answer represented. 'What was the purpose of your meeting?'

'Work.'

'Had you worked for him before?'

'Yes.'

'Office work?'

'No.'

Gunnarstranda waited.

'A monthly assignment. As a rule we had a fixed time,' she went on and slid down onto the sofa under the low mezzanine floor. In Ensjø – Bertrand Narvesens vei.'

Hege drew a foot up beneath her on the sofa.

'You both drank sherry,' Gunnarstranda stated.

'Yes, I drank sherry and listened to Schubert.'

'And that was work?'

'Two thousand kroners' worth. An hour's gig.' She made an exaggerated flourish with her hand and rolled her eyes. Then added: 'As you can see, I needed the money.'

'Did you prostitute yourself?'

She sighed and gravely shook her head to emphasize how stupid she thought the question sounded. 'No,' she said. 'I have never prostituted myself. And it would never enter my head to do so.'

'Striptease?'

She sent him a condescending look and shook her head. 'Do I look that cheap?'

The policeman bided his time. 'Well, what did you do?'

'I'm an actress. I perform theatre.' She smiled at the

policeman's facial expression. 'Folke paid me to appear in a play which he had written and directed. Folke never tried it on with me. Never.'

'Why do you call him Folke?' Gunnarstranda asked.

'No idea. I don't like Reidar. Reidar just sounds silly.'

'How long have you been doing this?'

'What?'

'This play-acting stuff.'

'A year and a half.'

'What sort of man was Folke Jespersen?' Gunnarstranda asked.

She deliberated before answering. 'Nice. A decent guy,' she concluded. 'He was old – impotent – which he talked about without any inhibitions. We became very close – by playing the same roles time after time. But he didn't want to be close to me in a physical way.'

'And you?'

'I don't know,' she answered, leaning forwards with her hands folded – concentrated. 'But I would maintain that the feelings we had for each other were . . . a kind of love,' she said, focusing on some point in the far distance. 'A small, pallid love which we re-played again and again in that little room, for an hour or two – after intervals of many weeks.'

Gunnarstranda waited. She wasn't finished.

'He was . . . knowledgeable, had a sense of irony, was mysterious and . . .'

She faltered.

'And . . .?' the policeman asked.

'He was captivated by me. That's important: he was captivated by me.'

A silence descended over them.

'He was proper,' she added. 'Always well turned out. He smelt of coffee and cigarettes and . . . a particular scent . . .' Her lips quivered with emotion for a moment.

'How come you were performing your play on this day of all days?'

'I don't know.'

'Why this day of all days?' he repeated slowly.

'I don't know. It wasn't supposed to have been then.'

'Pardon?' Gunnarstranda's voice deserted him as he leaned forward with sudden interest.

'It wasn't supposed to have been then. Relax, you seem so hyper.'

'What do you mean? It hadn't been planned for that day?'

'No, he called me.'

'When?'

'He rang at about – between two and half past. He asked if we could bring the arrangement forward. In fact, the meeting had been set for the 23rd.'

'Did that often happen – that he would ring you and re-schedule?'

She shook her head. 'Never.'

Gunnarstranda leaned back. His fingers were trembling. 'He never re-scheduled once over eighteen months, never changed an arrangement?'

'Right.'

'Did he give a reason this time?'

'No.'

The policeman waited.

'I didn't ask,' she said.

'Why not?'

'Because I was happy he had asked me to come.'

Gunnarstranda regarded her with scepticism. 'But what kind of play was it?'

'I played a woman and had two chunks of dialogue.'

'And it took you an hour to say two chunks?'

'It was theatre – improvisation. I had fixed lines, two things that had to be said every time – however our conversations developed. There were several conversations, the same framework, the same point of departure, a play that was repeated again and again – but which finished in a different way every time. The two chunks were two fixed points in a larger, unrehearsed performance. But the lines were so important that I was only taken on after an audition. 'Yes,' she nodded and grinned at the policeman's open mouth. 'I went to an audition . . . You think I'm kidding, don't you? But this was serious.'

'So it was just rubbish that your father knew Folke Jespersen?'

'It wasn't rubbish. It was a lie.'

'Well, what were the lines you were given?'

She reclined in the sofa. 'The scene was the same every time. He covered the table with a white cloth and put out two glasses of sherry. On the window sill there was an old cassette player with a terrible sound . . .'

Impatient, Gunnarstranda waved her on.

' . . . and he sits there . . .' She pointed to a chair next to her desk. She got to her feet, crossed the floor, went to the front door and stood with her back to it. '. . . I knock . . .' she said, tapping on the door behind her. She continued: '. . . I walk in . . . and we start any old conversation.

Oh, and I'm wearing a red dress – I can show you it . . .
and a dark wig.'

'A wig?'

'Yes, a wig. Long, black hair down to my shoulders.'

'Anything else?'

'A beauty spot.' She indicated her left cheek. 'A mole,
painted on, here . . .'

The policeman breathed out, whistled. 'A mole on the
cheek,' he repeated.

She nodded.

'And the lines?' he asked, impatient, following her
with his eyes as she flopped onto the sofa.

She spoke with her eyes closed, as though it cost her
an enormous effort: *'When the essence of life is reduced
to memories – they are always fragments of the good
things that have happened. It is these which survive and
make memory your greatest asset – the ability to remember,
not only to retrace your steps, but also to hold onto
your soul and who you are.'*

'And you had to say that every time?'

She nodded. 'At some point during the hour I said
those words – very often I broke them up. One clause
first, the next whenever it fitted. It became a game – he
waited for the following part, put obstacles in my path
and plunged the conversation into directions which
made a conclusion difficult. It was theatre – tough,
demanding – but theatre.'

The inspector flipped over a blank page in his
notepad, and passed her the pen and the pad. 'Write it
down,' he requested. 'The dialogue.'

She took the pen and paper, and wrote. She was left-handed and held the pen in a somewhat awkward manner.

'Was there anything else?' he asked when she had finished.

She hunched her shoulders. 'A lot was left to me – how I started the conversation when I entered – what sort of mood, state of mind I was in. Sometimes it could go off at a complete tangent – almost. But all within the same framework – the sherry, Schubert . . .'

She faltered.

'Schubert?'

'Yes, it was always Schubert's eighth on the cassette player – the Unfinished.'

'What was the topic of conversation that day?'

'Forgiveness.'

'Uhuh,' Gunnarstranda said impatiently.

'We talked about forgiveness, discussed forgiveness as a phenomenon.'

'Were any names mentioned?'

'None at all.'

'Were any specific events mentioned?'

'Not from his side, if that's what you're wondering.'

'But he wanted to be forgiven by you?'

She nodded.

'What for? Why did he want to be forgiven?'

'It was never clear. Apart from . . .'

Gunnarstranda was waiting with bated breath, but she said nothing. She looked away. He cleared his throat. 'Have you any idea what the purpose of this performance was?'

'I speculated at the beginning, of course. But, as time went on, it gave me . . .' She paused.

Gunnarstranda stared at her.

'I suppose it was fairly obvious. He wanted me to be someone else, a woman he dreamed about, but he never attained. I'm not so keen on that sort of thing.'

'Why not?'

She gave him a doleful smile. 'He was dreaming about an unattainable woman, but he had me. A part of my personality which existed at that moment, in that room. At the start he asked me to pretend to be another woman, but – initially I thought that was how it would work, that I would be his secret dream of a woman I didn't know, but it didn't turn out like that. No,' she burst out and shook her head in desperation, as though what she was going to say was stupid.

'Say it,' the detective exhorted.

'Once I was ill. It must have been six or seven meetings back, about six months ago – I had flu – a temperature of almost 40 and I had to cry off.' She smiled. 'He went berserk. I had found a substitute, another actress – excellent, but Folke wouldn't take her. He wanted me.' She looked up. 'Do you understand?' she asked. 'It was me he wanted! No one else but me. Even though I wore the same outfit, the same wig, it wasn't her any longer, it was me!'

Gunnarstranda stood up and paced to and fro in the small bedsit. He stopped by the window and looked out onto the trees lining the road, their heavy, leafless branches stretching into the air.

'But the forgiveness must have had something to do with her,' came the delicate voice behind him.

The Police Inspector turned around.

'I had to forgive him on her behalf. I think he once did something nasty to her, and never managed to make amends.'

Gunnarstranda, sunk in thought, nodded. 'And the last time this happened was the evening before he was killed. What was the other chunk of dialogue?'

He turned, walked around the chair and caught her eye, but she was still looking away.

'What was the last piece of dialogue?'

She hesitated.

Gunnarstranda glanced at her. 'Who was the woman on whose behalf you were supposed to forgive him?'

She shook her head. 'I haven't a clue.'

He sighed. 'Come on, you must know. You had to play someone. You're an actress. You must have asked him about the role!'

'I really don't have a clue who she is.'

'But it must have been tempting to ask – a woman with long hair, the mole, and your figure I suppose, your features,' Gunnarstranda said and added with intrigue in his voice, 'I'll tell you something. I've got a photo of her.'

Gro Hege Wyller blenched. The look she sent the policeman was troubled, riddled with doubt, and there was a forced rigidity about her body he had not seen until now.

'You look like her,' Gunnarstranda said without emotion. 'I noticed – at the funeral.'

'I don't believe you,' she mumbled and, in a rather firmer voice, re-stated her view: 'You're bluffing.'

Gunnarstranda sat back in his chair. He crossed his legs and let her uncertainty rumble about inside her.

'Why should I lie?' he said at last.

'Where is the photo?'

He tapped his breast pocket. 'Here.'

'Let me see then!'

Gunnarstranda hesitated.

'Aren't I allowed to see it?'

'Why do you want to?'

'Let me see the picture,' she repeated peremptorily.

Gunnarstranda beamed a mischievous smile. 'Are you wondering whether you mastered the role, whether you got her likeness?'

'No,' she said with emphasis.

'Sure?' Gunnarstranda smiled coldly. 'But there were two bits of dialogue. They must have something to do with the woman?'

'May I see if I tell you the other line?' she cut in.

'All right.'

'*I love you.*'

'I beg your pardon?'

'That was the other bit of dialogue: *I love you.*' She sat with her eyes closed, in another world. Again there was something about the contours of her profile, how the light met the lustre of her skin that rendered the policeman speechless, and he sat spellbound as she slowly opened her eyes. They exchanged glances. 'And the photo?' she asked.

He put his hand in his inside pocket and pulled out the photograph he had found in Jespersen's office. He concealed it in his hand and gave a tentative cough: 'Are you sure you want to see it?'

Again they exchanged looks. He looked into her blue

eyes; for a few seconds they revealed a vulnerability which made him swallow hard, and he could see that she had noticed, that she was pained by it, he noticed the moment she looked away and whispered: 'No . . . perhaps it's best not to.'

He didn't move.

'Well,' she said in bewilderment. 'Is that it?'

'Did you feel,' he began, running two fingers across his lips. 'Did you feel anything was different on that day?'

'Mm, it was different every single time, but he seemed perhaps a little . . . sad,' she faltered.

'Sad in what way?'

'He started to cry,' she said. 'Not much, a little. And that has never happened before. I don't know. I think he seemed sadder than usual, quieter, a bit distracted.'

Gunnarstranda studied her. She was somewhere else. When, finally, she did look up, she appeared to be emerging from water. She blinked to focus on him. 'What happened afterwards?' he asked in a low voice, putting the photograph back in his pocket.

'We shared a taxi.'

Gunnarstranda waited.

'From the warehouse,' she said. 'From Ensjø.'

'Where to?'

'Here.'

'Both of you?'

'I got out here, he went on. Back home, I assume.'

'Who rang for the taxi?'

'He did.'

'And you didn't notice anything outside the building

286

in Bertrand Narvesens vei when you came out?

She glanced quickly over her shoulder. 'What do you mean now?'

'I don't mean anything. I'm asking – and your reaction tells me you did notice something.'

She didn't answer.

The policeman got to his feet, pushed the table to the side and crouched down in front of the woman on the sofa. 'You have nothing to lose,' he whispered. 'And you have nothing to gain. Once you've said A you have to say B – that's the way the game works. Believe me, I know the rules, I've been playing it half of my life. Don't lie to me. Was the driver someone you knew?'

She cast down her eyes. 'How do you mean?'

'Don't give me the *How do you mean?*' Gunnarstranda barked with irritation. 'Answer my question. Did you know the driver?'

'I came by taxi.'

'Answer my damn question!'

'His name's Richard. He lives in this building – but he drives a taxi.' She added, annoyed: 'I am not lying.'

Gunnarstranda released a little sigh and sat back in the chair. 'Did you ask this taxi driver to take you there – to Jespersen's warehouse in Bertrand Narvesens vei – or was it just a coincidence that his taxi turned up when you needed a lift?'

'I asked him if he felt like taking me – he was here when Folke rang.'

'He was here – with you?'

'Yes.'

'You and this taxi driver here, alone?'

'Yes.'

'But why didn't you say that at once?'

'I don't know.'

'Are you a couple?'

'No.'

The police officer regarded her with a sceptical expression.

She ignored him.

'Richard – what's his surname?'

'Ekholt. His name is Richard Ekholt. He does the evening and night shifts. I once got a lift with him and he gave me his card and I've used him a few times since – when it's hard to get hold of a taxi, late at night and so on, it's great to be able to ring someone you know. Yes, I've done it a few times. And now he's got it into his head that he's in love.'

'Did you see Ekholt again later that day?'

She said nothing.

Gunnarstranda stroked his lips nervously. 'I assure you it is relevant to the case.'

'Something happened, something which means I do not wish to meet him again.'

'What happened?'

'I don't feel like talking about it.'

Gunnarstranda studied her. 'Did he hurt you?' he asked gently.

'Not as such.'

Gunnarstranda waited.

'He wasn't nice – on the way there he was bad-tempered and quarrelsome – and when we arrived he began to paw me and tried to take my clothes off. I had to run.

It was slippery and bloody cold.' She stared at Gunnarstranda as though she were revisiting the scene. 'He went ballistic. I think he was jealous because he knew I was meeting another man.'

'Where did you go?'

'To Folke. The key was in the postbox, as always. Fortunately I managed to unlock the door and slam it shut before he . . .'

'You weren't hurt?'

'No. I was furious though.'

'Did you mention this incident to Jespersen?'

'Yes – it became part of the play. Forgiveness,' she said with a blank expression, looking at her desk. The policeman watched her – without speaking.

'I had a shock afterwards. You see, I never thought he would wait for me, but when I came out, there he was,' she said at length. 'When Folke and I went out to the taxi, Richard's car was in the same place. He was sitting inside and I'm sure he followed us back here.'

'How can you be so sure?'

'I was about to open the door here – I had been dropped off and Folke went on. I had the key in my bag and was rummaging around for it when Richard drove past, following Folke's taxi.'

'Are you sure he was following?'

'Yes.'

'Did you report it?'

'Report?'

'Him harassing you in the car?'

'Nothing to report. The incident showed him up for what he was.'

He put his hand in his inside pocket, took out a biro and asked: 'Have you got any paper?'

She looked around.

'Never mind,' he mumbled and took the newspaper from the table. In the margin he wrote the code that had been scribbled on the chest of the dead man and showed it to her. 'Does this mean anything to you?'

'Are you sure that's the letter?' she asked.

He flinched. 'Why?'

'I think the number of Richard's taxi is 195,' she said. 'But there's an A in front – not a J.'

30

The Missing Uniform

When Inspector Gunnarstranda came home that evening, he stood contemplating the goldfish swimming around in a bowl that was more green than transparent. However, he managed to withstand the baleful eyes of the fish. He went to the kitchen and fried two eggs and half a packet of bacon, which he devoured along with two slices of toast and a glass of milk. Thereafter he took a hot shower before sitting down in front of his desk and reading through the case reports. Finally he went to the old seaman's trunk from which he took one of the bottles of whisky. He poured himself a glass which he emptied while writing the report on his visit to Gro Hege Wyller. Only when he had read it through did he go to the telephone.

Frank Frølich answered with a yawn.

'It's me.'

'Do you know how late it is,' Frølich said.

'Do you remember one of the people in Thomas Heftyes gate talking about a taxi being parked outside with the engine running?' Gunnarstranda asked.

'Yes,' Frølich yawned. 'She works for Egmont, publishers of children's books.'

'I think the driver's name is Richard Ekholt.'

'Uhuh.'

'I'm going to call him in for questioning. But it would be good if you could check the man's record and ask around the central taxi switchboard or use some reliable informers with good contacts in that sort of area.'

'Informers?'

'Ekholt does night shifts. He's bound to know several of our regular customers. On top of that, his taxi number is 195. Were you asleep?'

'What did you say just now?'

'I asked if you had been asleep.'

'You said something about a number.'

'Richard Ekholt's taxi is number A195.'

'Bloody hell!'

'A195, Frølich, not J. An A is not the same as a J.'

'But that can't be chance.'

'Every day you and I survive is chance. The fact that one of your father's cells won the fight for your mother's egg and created you is chance. It's chance that people live on earth and not on Mars. Were you asleep?'

'How can you ask? Do you know how late it is?'

'No, but I can hear music in the background.'

'I didn't say I was in bed.'

'Anything else?'

'Glenn Moseng rang in.'

'And who is Glenn Moseng?'

'He runs a coffee and waffle place in Jacob Aalls gate. And the best bit is that the café faces the building where Ingrid's lover – Strømsted – lives. This Glenn Moseng recognized Folke Jespersen's picture in the paper. Our dead man was sitting in the café from about nine to some time between eleven and twelve on 13th January.'

Gunnarstranda let out a whistle.

'Stokmo is telling the truth,' Frølich went on. 'Reidar Jespersen didn't go straight to work; he went to this café to wait for his wife.'

'But he didn't stop her when she appeared,' Gunnarstranda answered, flopping into a chair with the telephone in his hand. 'What did our man do there – at the waffle café?'

'He drank coffee and read newspapers – for two hours, at least.'

Gunnarstranda considered this information in silence.

Frølich, more animated: 'He quarrels with his brothers and then calls his wife while she is with the lover. We always come back to the wife and the lover,' Frølich continued, with enthusiasm. 'Motive and the opportunity.'

'Anything else?' Gunnarstranda asked, stifling a yawn.

'I got hold of Jonny Stokmo's girlfriend. *Carina*. She's a prostitute operating from a flat in Thereses gate. She confirmed that he had been there that night. But she can't remember the exact time he left.'

'Not the exact time?'

'No, Stokmo had dropped by without warning. But she had an appointment with some TV celeb at midnight and she got shot of Stokmo early, as she put it. She had time to take a shower and clear up before this celeb rang the bell. So it is not impossible that Stokmo went to bed at eleven as he claims.'

Gunnarstranda yawned. 'Looks like we have something to work on tomorrow.' He noticed the accusatory gaze from Kalfatrus the goldfish and felt his conscience prick.

As soon as he had finished the conversation, he set about draining the goldfish bowl. He had to go through a number of cupboards before he found Edel's wine siphon. Equipped with this and a bucket, he put the tube into the bowl. He sucked up some water and pulled a face of disgust, then spat it into the bucket. He let the water run until there was five centimetres left in the bowl. Then he took hold of a jug and a thermometer. Kalfatrus was swimming round the bottom of the bowl with an accusatory expression on his face. 'It's old Folke Jespersen's fault,' Gunnarstranda apologized.

At that moment the telephone rang.

He seized the receiver and yelled: 'Yes!'

'This is Karsten Jespersen speaking.'

'Oh yes?'

'Sorry to ring so late. But I've been through the inventory of registered items – from the shop.'

'And?'

'Nothing of any value seems to be missing.'

'What do you mean?'

'There's only one thing missing in fact. A uniform.'

'A uniform?'

'Yes, it was in a brown cardboard box in my office.'

'What sort of uniform was it?'

'I'm not sure. It hadn't been unpacked. The box was addressed to my father. I mentioned it to him on the last evening. It was one of the things we talked about.'

Gunnarstranda's eyes swept the table, hunting for a cigarette. He patted his pockets. 'I remember,' he mumbled. 'You've mentioned it before, the uniform, and it's not on the inventory we gave you?'

'No.'

'Not even expressed in vague terms? A box of clothes or military paraphernalia or something like that?'

'No. There's nothing.'

'And you hadn't unpacked it? How do you know there was a uniform in the box?'

'I didn't have time to do anything, but I did cut open the box. There was a uniform inside, you know, woollen material, a military colour, bluish.'

'Bluish? Navy blue? Grey-blue?' Gunnarstranda asked, locating a cigarette end in the ashtray on the edge of the desk and lighting it.

'Grey-blue.'

'More air force than navy then?'

'I have no idea.'

'It wasn't a tram conductor's uniform? Even the officers in parliament wear uniforms.'

'It was military; there were stripes and decorations. But I didn't give it more than a cursory glance. I mentioned to my father that it had arrived, and the two glasses from Nøstetangen too – they are on the list – but he didn't seem very interested.'

'So do you think he went down to the shop that evening to have a look at the uniform?'

'Can't imagine him doing that.'

Gunnarstranda inhaled greedily and said: 'You don't know if the uniform had any particular value?'

'As I said, I didn't get a chance to see,' Karsten Jespersen said.

'Who sent the box?'

'I have no idea. Don't remember. Don't think there was a sender's address.'

'But wouldn't it be very odd if someone sent a uniform to your father anonymously?'

'Mm . . .'

'It was anonymous, wasn't it?'

'I don't remember. I didn't pay any attention to it.'

'Did you tell your father?'

'Tell my father what?'

'That there was no sender's address.'

'Yes, I think I did. Or I may have said a uniform had arrived, but I hadn't checked it over. It seemed to be complete with trousers and jacket . . .'

'Is the box still there?'

'No, there's no cardboard box on the inventory.'

'So a uniform and a cardboard box are missing?' Gunnarstranda tried to imagine the two men sitting alone with coffee and cognac, crabby children all over the place and things unspoken in the air: 'He received a number of calls that evening. Perhaps the man who sent the uniform rang?'

'That's certainly a possibility,' Karsten Jespersen admitted. 'But it's hard to know.'

'OK,' Gunnarstranda said. 'Thank you for ringing. You've been a great help.'

After putting down the receiver, he stood still for a few seconds and nervously stroked his lips with his fingers. He came to with a start and went to the kitchen to fill the jug with water. Taking great care, he poured the tepid water into the goldfish bowl. Then he opened the packet of fish food and sprinkled a little food onto the surface of the water. 'Dried fly larvae and smoked spiders' legs,' he muttered to the fish nibbling at the food. 'Food fit for a king.'

Gunnarstranda helped himself to another whisky, sat down and turned over a piece of paper from the pile in front of him on the table. On the topmost sheet lay a copy of the photograph which had been hidden under Reidar Folke Jespersen's desk pad. This time the woman seemed to be laughing – at him.

31

The Sleeping Dog

Next day Frank Frølich got up straight from his breakfast table to search for the driver of taxi number A195 while Gunnarstranda spent a long day at the office going through statements, copying reports and making a number of by and large fruitless telephone calls. By the evening the Inspector had packed his things and set off for Stokmo's Metal Service in Torshov. The windows in the workshop were dark, but the windows of the flat on the first floor shone a welcoming yellow light into the yard. Police Inspector Gunnarstranda stared up at the sky, which was grey with polluted wintry mist, then shivered and grabbed the metal rail on his way up the slippery steps. He had to bang three times before Karl-Erik Stokmo, wearing a track suit and battered trainers, opened the door and said: 'Come in.'

The flat smelled of food. A slim woman of around thirty sat in the sitting room in front of the television with a plate of what looked like fish au gratin on her lap. The screen was showing a TV Shop advertisement of a man spraying something chemical on filthy garden furniture and wiping it clean with a cloth.

Gunnarstranda nodded to her. She was barefoot and wearing skin-tight, white jogging pants and a black singlet. Her skin was unnaturally brown for the time of the year; she boasted a blue-black tattoo on each upper arm and when she smiled you could see a canine was missing. She sneaked into the kitchen when the two men sat down.

On TV Shop a bodybuilder was demonstrating a training machine. Karl-Erik Stokmo took the remote control and turned down the volume. Gunnarstranda got straight to the point: 'Your father doesn't have an alibi for the night of the murder.' Gunnarstranda added: 'That is unfortunate. Your father says he went to bed at eleven on Friday night in the backroom of your work-shop.' The policeman tossed his head to the side: 'Down there.'

Stokmo leaned back in the Stressless chair, raised his legs and placed them on the foot stool.

'Was he here at eleven that night?'

Stokmo sighed. 'I would guess so.'

'Guesses won't do. Can you swear that your father came here and slept through the night in your back-room?'

'No,' Stokmo said. 'I know he was here, but we nei-ther spoke to each other nor saw each other.'

'You can't say then when he arrived or when he left?'

'But I know he was here,' the man repeated. 'Lillian!' he yelled in the direction of the kitchen.

The woman opened the kitchen door and stood in the doorway. She had two yellow washing-up gloves on. They could hear the water running in the sink some-where behind her.

'Did you notice when Dad got here on Friday?' Stokmo asked.

The woman stared at Gunnarstranda. 'I heard the

motor start up – the following morning,' she said.

'That's right,' Stokmo said. 'That was his.'

'What time would that have been?'

The woman rubbed her chin against one shoulder. 'In the morning, before we got up.'

'Before or after twelve?'

'Before twelve – I would guess. No?' Her look questioned Stokmo and he also had to shrug his shoulders.

'But did the two of you see him or the vehicle – with your own eyes?'

Stokmo shook his head.

Gunnarstranda stared after the woman as she hurried into the kitchen to turn off the water. Then she reappeared in the doorway. 'No,' she said. 'But I'm certain it was his pick-up.'

Stokmo nodded. 'Silencer's gone. You can hear the old banger anywhere.'

'You would have heard the pick-up if it had been used in the night?'

The two of them looked at each other and in the end both shrugged.

'Did you hear anything like his pick-up that night?'

Both shook their heads.

'Great,' Gunnarstranda said, looking up at the woman who showed her missing canine again. She said: 'You're the one who knows Bendik, aren't you?'

Gunnarstranda nodded.

'Good,' she said, shutting herself in the kitchen once again.

Stokmo cleared his throat. 'She and Bendik used to live together,' he explained.

'And now she lives here, I can see.' Gunnarstranda surveyed the room. On TV Shop there was a bikini-clad woman with an impeccable figure demonstrating the same training machine.

There was almost nothing on the walls, just a turtle shell over the kitchen door. A brown eagle with a white head was painted on it. He looked at the eagle. Its one eye looked back. 'Do you know why your father was so angry with Folke Jespersen?' he asked Stokmo.

'I would guess it's about my grandfather. He helped people over the border during the war.'

'May I?' Gunnarstranda asked, taking out his pouch of tobacco.

Stokmo nodded and took a cigarette from a packet of Prince lying on the table. 'I've heard Jespersen ran an illegal press in Oslo – printed leaflets with news from London and that kind of thing. But someone informed on him and he had to flee the country.'

'I've heard that, too,' Gunnarstranda said, lighting his cigarette.

'Well, it was my grandfather who took Folke Jespersen to Sweden.' Stokmo inhaled and crossed his legs. 'Towards the end of the war my grandfather was caught by a German border patrol – *die Grepo*. The soldiers almost shot him. He panicked and ran into the forest. The Nazis shouted and ordered him to stop, but he had panicked because he was carrying a gun. When the Nazis shouted, my grandfather had drawn his gun, but fell headlong over a large tree root. He nose-dived into a bog – the hand with the gun buried in the mud. With his hand covered in mud he let go of the gun and stood up –

unarmed. He was searched, but they didn't find anything – he had a guardian angel, didn't he! – and my grandfather said he was out picking blueberries. He was allowed to go but instructed to report to Halden the day after.' Stokmo flicked ash off the cigarette and blew out smoke through puckered lips.

'Did he show up?'

'He did. And he managed to avoid suspicion. And this is the crux, you see. Because my grandfather got off lightly, rumours began to circulate. It's a long story: he was well paid by the people he had secreted out of the country and had received a lot of presents. They were things he had hidden away. I don't know how much there was, but it was worth a good deal. Many of the Jews who were taken across the border were rich, you know, goldsmiths and jewellers, and they were generous. But just after the war there were stories about Jewish refugees being robbed by greedy border guides and so on. There were also rumours about my grandfather because some people were suspicious that he had got off so lightly. For that reason he didn't dare do anything with these presents after the war. Folke Jespersen took on the job of selling these things – of being the middleman.'

Gunnarstranda was rolling himself a cigarette. 'Uhuh,' he said, lighting up with a Zippo. 'So the rumours were that your grandfather was working for the Germans?'

Stokmo gave a rueful nod.

Gunnarstranda inhaled. He mused: 'He helped people to cross the border and had a dubious reputation, I can

302

see that. But the animosity between your grandfather and Jespersen – where does that stem from?'

Stokmo stubbed out his cigarette and leaned back. 'I was talking to my dad a couple of weeks ago,' he began.

'Yes?'

'I knew a lot already. But the story about the arrest in Halden is new. Also about Folke Jespersen selling the presents he got. You see, my father didn't know about that either or about the silver and so on that had been hidden away during the war. But he found some old papers not so long ago – amongst them deals made between my grandfather and Folke Jespersen. The papers tell you how much Folke Jespersen owes. According to my dad those debts were never paid. He thinks Folke Jespersen swindled grandfather out of a stack of money.'

'How?'

'Jespersen agreed to sell things, which he did, but he never settled up with my grandfather.'

Gunnarstranda nodded. 'I see,' he mumbled.

'I don't give a shit by and large, but my dad, Jonny, has really gone to town on this business. I think it has something to do with the bullying he received when he was younger, you know, the stories about him being the son of a Nazi spy and all that. It's the personal stuff that frightens me. You see, my dad demanded money off Folke Jespersen and the time I'm talking about they were almost at each other's throats.'

'Fighting?'

'Folke Jespersen's version is that the goods were stolen from the Jews during the war. That is just awful. First of all, it was my grandfather who took Folke Jespersen to Sweden, and the two of them worked together for years afterwards. But once the man was dead Reidar Folke Jespersen claims my grandfather was an asshole. That's what makes my dad think Folke Jespersen was black-mailing his dad. My grandfather never did anything to force Folke Jespersen to pay up. Pops thinks that Folke Jespersen had a kind of hold over my grandfather – that he threatened to spread all sorts of shit and lies about Grandad robbing Jews during the war and spying for the Germans.'

Gunnarstranda nodded thoughtfully.

'Your father must have been furious with Reidar Jespersen,' he concluded. 'What means most to your father? What does he want to avenge: lost money or lost honour – or both?'

Stokmo shrugged. 'As I said, I don't give a shit about this business. But I think honour has priority over money here.'

'Sounds sensible,' Gunnarstranda said. 'But this story gives your father a motive.'

'You have to think logically. Why would my father kill Folke Jespersen? Now the man's dead, my grandfather will never have his name cleared, and Pops won't receive satisfaction either.'

'Well, your father might have lost control. That sort of thing has happened before. You said yourself that this was personal for your father.'

'But he's no kid,' the other objected. 'He would never be crazy enough to do Folke Jespersen any physical harm.'

Gunnarstranda got to his feet. The kitchen had gone quiet.

'But he's under suspicion?' Stokmo asked, standing up as well. The two men went to the hall. Gunnarstranda put on his coat. 'He'll have to make a statement. That means he's a witness.' He turned to a mirror on the wall, three square mirrors, one on top of the other. His body was divided into three sections: head and neck, upper torso and trousers. He buttoned up his winter coat and adjusted his hair. 'He'll have to put his trust in the truth and us,' he summed up, and opened the door.

As he was driving home ten minutes later, to take a shower and change clothes before going to the theatre with Tove Granaas, Frølich rang.

Gunnarstranda asked the younger man to wait while he pulled into the kerb and parked just in front of Bentse bridge.

'I've just been talking to a Dr Lauritsen in the onco-logical department at Ullevål hospital,' Frølich said.

'I know her,' Gunnarstranda said.

'You know her?'

'Grethe Lauritsen dealt with my wife at the time.'

'Oh.'

'Well?' Gunnarstranda said, unruffled. 'Folke Jespersen must have been her patient, too, I suppose.'

'Something like that,' Frølich said. 'At any rate she told Folke Jespersen he had invasive cancer. But the interesting bit is the timing.'

'Oh yes?'

'Friday the 13th once again, boss. Folke Jespersen

rang Dr Lauritsen at four to hear the results of the tests. She didn't want to say anything on the phone at first and asked him to make an appointment. But then he got angry and began to hassle her. His questions were so direct she had to admit the cancer was malignant and aggressive. She made an appointment for him which he never kept.'

'How aggressive was the cancer?'

'She gave the old man two months to live, maximum. He found that out half an hour before he rang his solicitor and revoked his will.'

32

Brief Encounter

A woman was standing in front of the post office cash-point in Egertorget. Frølich joined the queue and passed the time watching the young man singing and playing guitar in front of the metro subway. He had always wondered how fragile instruments fared in such freezing temperatures, let alone this guitarist's nails. He was wearing fingerless gloves and walked, shivering, around loudspeakers mounted on a shopping trolley while singing to a sparse audience: two sage-like drug addicts and the bouncer from the Tre Brødre bar.

The woman by the cashpoint had finished and turned round abruptly. 'Hi,' she said and gasped with pain as she grabbed her back, dropping her bag in the process. Frølich caught it in mid-air. It was Anna. She stood bent double, laughing and gasping.

'What's up?' he asked.

'My back,' she said, panting for breath. 'I've got such a bad pain in my back. You startled me. You were a bit close behind me.'

'Oh,' Frølich said. They stood facing each other for a few moments. She was wearing a thick, brightly coloured woollen jacket and faded jeans. She wriggled her fingers up the sleeve of her jacket. Frølich instantly became aware of the freezing cold.

'Thanks for the list,' he said. That was all that occurred to him.

'List?' she said, puzzled.

'The items you recorded in the antiques shop,' he said with an embarrassed smile.

'Oh, not at all,' she said with a grin.

Frølich realized that the street musician was singing 'The Streets of London'. A nice voice. From behind Frølich a red-faced man wearing a coat and woollen hat broke in and asked in a brusque manner if he was queueing for the cashpoint.

Frølich let him through. 'It's cold,' he said to Anna, putting down her plastic bag. There was a bottle inside which would have caused it to topple over. He rested the bag against his leg. 'Shall we go somewhere and sit down?'

Slowly and carefully, she craned her neck up to see the Freia clock above the Mamma Rosa restaurant.

He could have bitten off his tongue and tried to smooth over his boldness by saying: 'Perhaps time is a bit tight?'

She went for it. 'In fact, I was on my way to visit someone at hospital – Aker hospital.'

She didn't say who she was going to visit, and he couldn't bring himself to ask. 'Another time then perhaps?'

'I think so,' she said with a light shiver. 'We'll sort something out.'

'When?'

'A beer after work one day?'

He nodded. The non-specific 'one day' was a little discouraging and non-committal. On the other hand, he didn't have anything any more concrete to suggest himself.

They strolled down Akersgata, past the *Aftenposten* and *Dagbladet* newspaper buildings. He carried her bag. They walked at a slow pace. 'Coughing is the worst,' she said. 'Laughing is fine – for my back.'

They tried to speed up and run the last few metres in order to catch the bus coming round the corner from Apotekergata.

'Careful,' he said as they hobbled along.

She grinned at herself.

As she was standing on the step of the bus, he realized they hadn't agreed a time or place. He shouted after her: 'Where?'

The door shut with a thud. It made them burst into laughter as they exchanged looks through the glass door.

She mouthed an answer, pointing to herself and pretending to hold a telephone against her ear.

'Me?' Frølich shouted. 'Shall I phone you?' But the bus had already gone. He was shouting questions into thin air.

33

Manna in the Wilderness

Gunnarstranda collected Tove Granaas at half past seven. He had decided in advance that he would not get out of the car. He had been quite precise about that on the telephone. He had said: 'Come down when you see the car in the drive.' Tove rented the first floor of a house in Sæter, a white detached Swiss-style chalet in the middle of a garden full of old apple trees which, as a result of incorrect and insuffcient pruning, looked like piles of twigs on poles. Tove complained that the apples were always small and riddled with maggots. On trees like those, apples would be small and riddled with maggots. Gunnarstranda knew that. But of course he didn't say so. If he did, he would end up doing the pruning, for which he had neither the energy nor the enthusiasm. The house owners were a couple in their fifties: the kind who go caravanning along the Swedish coast and take an evening constitutional in matching barbecueing outfits. 'The woman runs and hides whenever I come home from work so that she doesn't have to greet me,' Tove had said. 'We've got nothing in common.'

'Can you have a conversation?'

'We talk when they increase the rent, but that's the husband's job. He hates it, but dare not fail her. The wife hides under the stairs before he rings, and as soon as I open the door, she starts prompting him. With all the whispering and hissing going on you would think someone had left a leaky bottle of pop out somewhere.'

However eccentric the house owners were, Gunnarstranda had no desire to meet them. He was too old to wait outside a woman's door, ringing her bell like a schoolboy. But when he turned into the drive and raised his head he could see Tove standing in the window waving. Three minutes later she was in the car.

Beneath them the town twinkled like the reflection of a starry sky as they drove around the bends in Kongsveien. Gunnarstranda switched on the radio. They were lucky with the programme producer – it was someone who liked quiet music. As they approached Ibsen multi-storey car park, Billie Holiday was singing 'I love you, Porgy', but once inside there was just noise coming from the loudspeakers.

Tove glanced at him. 'You're the only person I know who does not have either a cassette or a CD player in their car,' she said.

Gunnarstranda turned down the old car radio with its shiny knobs. 'I bought it in '72,' he said. 'Just because you change your car doesn't mean you have to change your radio.'

As they strolled past a row of parked cars towards the lift Gunnarstranda said, 'The problem is there is no decent radio any more. Years ago you could read what was on in the newspaper and choose a programme. You could look forward to something special, a discussion presented by a writer you respected, or maybe a wonderful voice, like Aase Bye reading Hans E. Kinck's short story "White Anemones on the Mountainside".' He held the door open for her as they went in to the waiting area by the lifts. 'The thing is you used to be able to time your afternoon coffee so that you didn't miss grand radio moments,' he went on. 'But now it's all one big impenetrable barrage of sound. The radio announcers babble away about themselves, broadcast their ignorance diluted with pop songs, then they call it morning radio, afternoon on 2 or traffic round-up. But if there were a pearl in all of that, something worthy of a couple of moments' concentration, respect or reflection, it would pass you by – unless you were lucky enough to be sitting in your car at the exact moment it and the voice traversed the ether. But presumably it is just me who has been left behind.'

'Presumably,' she smiled and went quiet when they were joined in front of the lifts by another couple. The lift door opened. All four went in. They exchanged a glance in the mirror.

She staunchly hooked her arm through his as they strolled down Kristian IVs gate and went through the glass doors into Det Norske Teatret. They stood looking around the theatre foyer. 'We're early,' Gunnarstranda said.

'Are you nervous?' she asked in a low voice – without letting go of his arm.

'What?'

'Are you nervous?' she repeated.

Gunnarstranda coughed and studied himself in the mirror he was standing beside. 'Why do you ask?'

'You seem stiff and a bit stand-offish.'

'I'm not nervous.'

'Is being with me unpleasant?'

'No.' He cleared his throat and added: 'It's nice.'

She let go of his arm and instead stood in front of him and angled her head. 'Shall we do something else? Cinema or a beer in a darkened pub?'

'No, the theatre is fine. But perhaps we could talk about something else.'

She hooked her arm under his and led him towards a group of unoccupied chairs in the foyer. She waved to another woman across the room. 'I haven't seen her for several years,' Tove whispered. 'This is where your old friends are – in the theatre. And I never knew.'

'All grey hair in here,' he answered.

'Your mind's elsewhere, isn't it!' she stated. 'What were you thinking about just then?'

'Numbers and letters.'

'Manna seeds?'

'And that means?'

'I'd like an aperitif,' she exclaimed. 'Could you get me a sherry?'

He shuddered. 'I'll have red wine – can't stand sherry. What did you say about seeds?' He passed her his gloves and slid a hand in his inside pocket for his wallet.

'Manna seeds,' she repeated and explained: 'I assume if they are sown, you get the bread that rained down on the Israelites in the wilderness.'

'But what made you say that?'

'It was what I was thinking when you said numbers and letters. My grandmother was very religious, you see. On top of the kitchen cupboard she always kept a bowl full of small bits of paper, thousands of them. There were numbers and letters printed on them: Ez 5,4 or Luk 8,12. Quotations from the Bible, the Book of Ezekiel . . .'

Gunnarstranda froze. 'Of course,' he whispered.

'Yes, right – manna in the wilderness. The Bible quotation of the day. I think she was a Pentecostalist.'

'From the Bible,' sighed Detective Inspector Gunnarstranda, slumping down onto the bench.

'What's up with you?'

'J for John. Nineteen, five.'

'St. John's Gospel, chapter 19, verse 5,' Tove said with a mischievous smile. 'What happened to the sherry?'

'Bristol Cream,' Gunnarstranda said, preoccupied. 'Do you like it?'

She nodded. 'Whatever. I don't know any brandnames of sherry.'

'Then let's go to the Library bar – in the Bristol Hotel – it's just across the street,' Gunnarstranda said gently. 'Then you can have the whole bottle if you want . . .'

'One glass is enough,' she said. 'Why should we leave here?'

'Because I want to get my paws on a Bible.'

When, five minutes later in the Library bar at the Bristol Hotel, they discovered there wasn't a single seat free, Gunnarstranda began to stroke his lips nervously. 'Bloody hell,' he mumbled.

'Relax,' she said with a smile.

'I should . . .'

'You've got a Bible at home, haven't you?' She turned to the window from where they could see the entrance to the theatre. 'I'm sure the play is as dull as ditchwater.'

'What? *John Gabriel Borkman*? I thought Ibsen was right up your street?' he mumbled.

'Not in our other Norwegian language,' she said. 'Translating Ibsen into nynorsk is the height of all that I consider idiotic in Norwegian culture.'

She slipped her arm into his. 'Let's go to your place,' she said, meeting his eyes. 'If you dare.'

While Gunnarstranda was searching for one of his three Norwegian Bibles on the shelving system he had made in the shoe cupboard in the hall, Tove was standing in the living-room doorway studying the TV with the screen facing the wall, the old botanical prints over the armchair, the old carved standard lamp and the wall itself, covered in books of various heights, hardbacks mixed with paperbacks, lots of magazines and pamphlets and books pushed in everywhere, making the shelf look like an overpopulated block of flats in a flamboyant ghetto. She read the spines, observed the portrait of Edel without a word and allowed her eyes to wander over to the goldfish bowl. 'So this is your pet?' she burst out.

The Inspector had found two Bibles which he placed on the work desk under the window. He flipped through both before looking up. 'I haven't got any sherry,' he said. 'But I have some good whisky.'

She turned, interested. 'Where?'

'In the wooden chest.' He nodded towards the seaman's trunk by the fireplace.

'Here?' She opened the lid and regarded the tightly packed bottles in the chest. 'You've got enough whisky,' she mumbled, lifting out one bottle after the other and reading the labels. 'Which one would you like?'

'One that's already open,' Gunnarstranda answered, his finger following the lines in the bible. 'Luke . . . John,' he muttered.

Tove decided on a quarter-full bottle of Ballantine's, went into the kitchen, found two tumblers and poured.

Gunnarstranda took the glass she passed him, rapt in thought.

'Here,' he said, pointing.

'What does it say?'

'Jesus and Pontius Pilate.'

'*Skål*,' Tove said. 'To my grandmother.'

'And Pontius Pilate,' Gunnarstranda added.

Tove sighed, looking at the whisky tumbler with appreciation.

'Pontius Pilate washes his hands – and the people put a crown of thorns on Jesus's head. The three crosses on the dead man's forehead. The Crown of Thorns! Red thread around the neck, the purple robe.' Gunnarstranda gazed into the distance, pensive, and asked: 'But why?'

'You're the cop,' Tove said. She pulled books down from the shelf and studied the titles while he flicked through the Bible and read. After a while she poured herself another whisky and asked if he wanted any.

Gunnarstranda peered up and shook his head. He hadn't touched his glass while he was reading. 'This is interesting,' he mumbled. 'There are four gospels. But there are only three that describe this precise incident. Luke is the odd one out . . .'

He thumbed through to show her.

'I believe you,' Tove said, taking another sip. 'Damned good whisky, this.'

'Luke doesn't mention the incident at all, not the purple robe nor the crown of thorns nor the jeering. Luke brings in Herod instead. In general, Luke appears to be on the wrong track. Whereas the other three all agree that Jesus was given a purple robe . . .'

'The red thread,' Tove interrupted. 'You've already said that.'

Gunnarstranda nodded. 'Three of them also agree on the crown of thorns and Jesus being shown to the crowds to be mocked. But here John is the odd one out.' Tove peered into the bottom of the glass, to confirm that it was empty yet again. 'I think I'll have another,' she said, taking the bottle. '*Skål*,' she said.

Gunnarstranda raised his glass, sipped and read aloud: '*And the soldiers plaited a crown of thorns and put it on his head, and they threw a purple robe around him, and said "Hail, King of the Jews!" And they hit him in the face. Pilate therefore went out again and said to them, "Look, I bring him to you so that you may know I find no fault in him."*' Gunnarstranda looked up and continued: 'Here's the relevant quotation, John, 19:5: "*Then Jesus came out, wearing the crown of thorns and the purple robe. And he said to them: See the man!*"'

Tove walked along the bookshelf with her glass in hand. Gunnarstranda stood up in his excitement and articulated his thoughts: 'Only John has that line. If there is a reason for the killer quoting John and not Mark, or Matthew, it must be because John has that phrase: "See the man!"

Tove turned a fraction, a genial smile on her face, and sipped her whisky before returning to the bookshelf.

'But then the question is . . .' the Inspector continued, concentrating, 'What does the phrase mean? And who said it?'

'Pilate,' Tove answered. 'It's Pontius Pilate talking.'

Gunnarstranda nodded. 'Pontius Pilate says he finds no fault in him, and then he shows the humiliated prisoner and says: See! See him!' Gunnarstranda frowned. 'But in grammar, if the pronoun *he* appears after the proper noun *Jesus* it would be normal to interpret the sentence as meaning it is the prisoner, Jesus, who utters the words.'

'Right,' she said without a flicker of interest.

'The question is: Who does the writer of this message identify with?!' Gunnarstranda read the quotation from the Bible again: '*Then Jesus came out, wearing the crown of thorns and the purple robe. And he said to them: See the man!* So it is not clear who says it or what it means.'

'Was he crucified?' Tove asked with somewhat slurred speech.

'Jesus?'

'No, the antiquarian!'

'He was an antiques dealer, not an antiquarian. No, Folke Jespersen was not crucified,' Gunnarstranda mumbled fastidiously. 'There were no wounds on the hands or feet – so it must be the exhibiting of him and the quotation which are important. The method of death is irrelevant. The situation, the quotation and the humiliation must be the relevant points. But if Pilate said

318

the line it is as though he is begging for Jesus; he seems to be imploring the crowds to come to their senses: Look – now he has been humiliated, show mercy! But if Jesus said the words, then the line contains a great many levels. After all he claims to be the son of God, immortal and all that, and he is saying: 'See me, see the man!'

Tove stifled an outburst of laughter.

'What?' Gunnarstranda asked, disorientated.

'I hope you won't be damaged by this,' she giggled. 'I hope you won't become religious.' She laughed out loud.

Bewildered, Gunnarstranda stared at her. 'Oooh, dear me,' she said, recovering. 'That must be the whisky. It's just so good. I think I might have one more.'

'But it may be something to do with guilt,' Gunnarstranda reasoned as Tove poured them both another. 'This incident – where Pilate does not want to execute Jesus and offers to release him, but the crowd chooses the other one . . . what's his name?'

'Barabbas,' Tove said, lowering her face over the goldfish. 'Bar a bass,' she said, changing the stress. 'Bass is a type of fish, isn't it?'

'That's it, Barrabas, and Pilate, who washes his hands of the whole business. It might all be tied up with – guilt.'

Tove leered. 'What's his name?'

'Who are you talking about?'

'The fish.'

'The fourth wise man.'

'The fourth?'

'There are three wise men in the Bible. This is the fourth.'

'Your fish?' Tove's face was one big question mark. 'Oh, my God, I can already feel the whisky,' she grinned.

'Kalfatrus,' Gunnarstranda said.

'Pardon?'

Gunnarstranda smiled.

'There you are, you see,' she said. 'You *can* laugh!' They grinned, both of them.

'Sorry,' she said. 'I'm stopping you thinking.' She took two unsteady steps towards the bottle. 'You think; I'll take care of this.'

'Where was I?'

'You were talking about guilt.'

'Yes, Pilate says the man is innocent. It's confusing . . .' Gunnarstranda furrowed his brow. 'The sentence in the Bible may be a reference to the discussion surrounding the Jesus figure. Is he really the son of God, a God or a man? As a king he is mocked. The concept of king – you know, the Jews' idea of a Messiah was a kind of all-powerful emperor who smashes the enemy and proclaims himself king, but then this Jesus figure comes along with his "king" metaphors and uses the concept in a sort of spiritual sense. So the sentence is to do with the relationship between the concepts of king, God, man and father. But the question is whether the fact that he is exhibited in the shop window is significant or whether it is the issue of guilt itself – after all, the section with Pilate is a legal procedure . . .'

'*Skål*,' Tove said.

Gunnarstranda took a sip. 'What about if all the elements are involved here: law, guilt, public humiliation, God's image.'

'Patricide,' Tove said.

Gunnarstranda looked up. She was holding the bottle between thumb and first finger and dangling it in the air. 'Empty,' she said.

'What did you say?' he asked.

'Empty,' she said.

'Before that.'

'You're not that drunk.'

He grinned. 'Find yourself another bottle.'

'Excellent,' she said, bending down to take another bottle from the travel chest. 'What was I saying?'

'You mentioned the word *patricide*. But what would motivate Karsten Jespersen to bump his father off?'

'Revenge,' Tove said, opening a new bottle. She raised it and studied the label. 'Glenlivet. That's sure to be expensive, and good.'

'What sort of revenge?'

'You're the policeman.'

Gunnarstranda drained his glass and rubbed his face in his hands.

Tove fell back onto the sofa. She kicked off her shoes and placed a slim, nylon-clad leg on the table. 'My God, I'm glad you've finished with that Bible stuff,' she sighed and sat watching him with a grin on her face. 'You live here, so I suppose it's best to ask.' She put the bottle and the glass on the table and started rummaging through her bag. 'Do you mind if I smoke?'

34

Two-Step

That night Frank Frølich dreamed about Linn although it had to be at least fifteen years since he had last seen her. In the dream they were in her chalet. Outside the window twittering birds were frenetically busy. He was lying on his side in bed and could feel the sun warming his feet. A sweet smell of summer wafted in through the half-open window. Linn had rolled over. He lay admiring her taut stomach muscles. The sun cast a clearly defined shadow from the crosspieces in the window across the bed. Her hair cascaded over the pillow. A tendril from an ivy plant stretched down towards the floor and touched a pile of underclothes. And then he was no longer in the chalet, he was in a spinney and it was autumn. The air was keen. They had a view of a small lake and the beech leaves on the far side had turned yellow with an orange glow; the reflection in the dark water was so detailed that the reflected image seemed sharper than reality. Now it wasn't Linn he was with, but Eva-Britt. She stole a glance at him with a lock of hair in her mouth as she threw an armful of birch leaves at him. They were dry. Instead of falling to the ground they were picked up by a gust of wind and rose in the air; they became smaller and smaller until they were fine specks in the sky and disappeared. He turned away from her and saw a bookshelf. He couldn't read the titles on the spines. The shelf was too far away. Instead he caught sight of a picture of a motor cycle on the door, a Harley-Davidson Fat Boy ridden by a dark-haired woman with bare breasts and long legs in tight jeans. It was Anna. He woke up and found himself lying in his own bed. No Linn, no Eva-Britt. Just a pile of his clothes lying on the floor. On the cupboard door hung the old poster of the Harley-Davidson Fat Boy – without Anna.

In the end he swung a leg down onto the floor and sat looking at his sorry figure in the mirror. Thank God no one nags me in the morning.

An hour later he opened the front door and left. It had turned milder, around zero degrees, and it had snowed in the night. The snow ploughs had packed all the parked cars into a cloak of wet snow. The rhythmic stroke of a spade at work told him that a determined office worker was set on using his car to go to the office. But when the engine started, the tone was muffled. The air was like wool. Sounds had to drag themselves through the deadening layer of thick falling snow. Frank wished it were summer and that he could wake up one morning with the sun warming his feet.

On arriving at the bar in the Hotel Continental, he found himself a seat on one of the leather sofas at the back of the room. By and large the customers in the bar were men who worked in industry and took off Hugo Boss overcoats. However, ferociously made-up, fur-coated mothers also frequented the place, dragging along ungainly teenage daughters sporting large breasts, sulky lower lips and well-rehearsed doe-eyed glances aimed at the most affluent-looking men. Frank ordered coffee. It was served in a pot. Soon afterwards a man in a red jacket bounced into the hotel foyer.One of the women behind the counter pointed to Frank Frølich, who stood up and shook hands. Hermann Kirkenær had short, curly hair that was beginning to thin on top. He was unshaven and had a ring in his left ear. Once seated, he was served a glass of Coke by the woman who had pointed out the policeman.

Kirkenær said that he and his wife lived in Tønsberg, but they stayed at the Continental when they had business in town, like today, when they had three viewings.

'You're going to move to Oslo, I believe?'

'Yes,' Kirkenær said, looking over Frølich's shoulder. A tall woman with long hair and watchful eyes stood waiting beside the policeman.

'Iselin,' Kirkenær said. 'Meet Frank Frølich.'

Her hand was dry and warm; she had long fingers. She was wearing a short jacket and a skirt which covered her knees.

She took a seat on the sofa beside Kirkenær. Her broad mouth was marred by a nasty sore on her lower lip. Frølich lowered his eyes when she transfixed him with a deep stare.

'Inspector Frølich is investigating Reidar Folke Jespersen's murder,' Kirkenær explained.

'It was so brutal,' Iselin Varås said with sympathy.

'Iselin's reactions are always open-hearted,' Kirkenær said, his sarcasm barely concealed, before going on to address the woman with intonation that lay somewhere in the jarring range between spiteful and arrogant: 'It is a very sweet characteristic, but what the police want to know in fact is whether we had any contact with Reidar before Arvid's meeting on Friday the 13th.'

Iselin Varås was holding a stick of lip salve in her hand. She pressed it cautiously against her cold sore.

'We must have exchanged a few words,' she said. 'You had met Reidar, hadn't you? I hadn't seen him before.'

'The thing was we communicate with Arvid – his brother,' Kirkenær said. 'We wrote to many – I mean several shops. At first we addressed ourselves to Reidar, but it was Arvid – the brother – who contacted us, who reacted to the letter, if I can put it like that.'

If the letter went to Reidar, the brothers must have talked about it, Frølich concluded, and leaned back as the waitress came to the table with a bottle of Ferris mineral water and leisurely poured it into Iselin's glass. Iselin watched the water foam in the glass and said: 'Reidar is the official owner.' When the waitress had gone, she raised her glass to toast with Frølich. He inclined his coffee cup out of politeness.

'In fact, they've been very positive, all three of them. Arvid even said he was very happy we had approached them,' she said and put down the glass. She took hold of her hair with both hands and swiftly formed a thick ponytail which she held in place with an elastic band.

'They haven't said no yet,' Kirkenær continued. 'And of course one can . . .'

'Hermann,' she interrupted with a maternal tone.

'What?'

'The man's dead, Hermann,' she said, glaring reprovingly at him. Then she dabbed the lip-salve on her sore again.

The man didn't like being brushed aside like this.

She went on, undaunted: 'We'll leave it up to them to re-establish contact. It's news to us that Reidar Folke Jespersen was against the sale. We thought all three of them were agreed, but with the situation being as it is . . .'

'All that was missing was the signatures on the contract,' Kirkenær interrupted, sending her a furious look.

'When you met the brothers, you didn't pick up a hint of discord between them?'

Both shook their heads.

'I'm positive about that,' she emphasized, rolling the lip-salve between her fingers. 'And I'm certain he didn't say anything while we were there.' She smiled and shared a look with her husband, perhaps a mutual experience of something amusing. 'Arvid may well have said something.'

'Old Arvid is besotted with Iselin,' Hermann Kirkenær said brightly, and continued in a way calculated to ensure she would also catch his drift: 'You see, I'm married to a woman who flourishes in the company of older men.'

'Nothing wrong with a woman enjoying feeling attractive, is there?' she said, with a tentative dab to her cold sore with her first finger.

'Providing that she doesn't offer herself.'

The comment was direct and personal. Frølich studied the paintings on the walls. He thought of Eva-Britt and how she could on occasion annoy him. The thought of what that annoyance could lead to in others' company brought him out in a sweat.

Iselin Varås spoke with a voice she was clearly struggling to control: 'I've been told Hermann can be so nice.'

The silence that followed was unpleasant. Iselin concentrated on her glass of mineral water.

'You're into antiques, I understand,' Frølich said to ease the atmosphere.

Kirkenær didn't speak.

She raised her eyes and nodded.

'Why this shop in particular?'

Iselin cleared her throat. 'A general evaluation based on the current state of the industry.'

'Many businesses are unprofessional,' Kirkenær added.

'Hence the difficulty of starting from rock bottom,' she said, and it was obvious the cold sore bothered her. She had taken off the top of the lip-salve again. 'We're on the lookout for an established business in one of the town's more prestigious districts,' she went on. 'You know, you buy the reputation as well.'

'Have you had your feelers out anywhere else?'

Kirkenær nodded.

'What sort of reputation are you buying off the Folke Jespersen brothers?'

The two of them looked at each other. 'You answer,' she said.

He flung out his arms. 'They sell good things,' he said.

'Good taste,' she added. 'They have good taste.'

Frølich lifted up his coffee cup. It was empty. He put it down.

'Why risk everything on this?' he asked.

At a loss to know what to say, they stared at him.

'What did you do before?' Frølich asked.

'Teacher,' she said. 'I'm a qualified language and art history teacher.' She looked across at her husband with a smile. 'Your turn.'

'Guess,' he said to Frølich, who shrugged.

Kirkenær provided the answer himself. 'Cars.'

'Car salesman, shall we say,' she amended, with light irony. 'Hermann is of the firm conviction that salesman-ship is what it's all about, not the sale item. A standpoint which means he doesn't have to call himself a car sales-man.'

'She's a kind of expert on the subject,' he interceded. 'An art historian.'

'What sort of cars?' Frølich asked.

'Expensive ones. Mercedes, BMW, the biggest and the most expensive.'

'OK,' Frølich said, becoming irritated by the mud-slinging that was going on. 'There's one thing I was won-dering about: this meeting at Arvid's flat, why was it held at all?'

They exchanged glances. 'You tell me,' Kirkenær said.

'We had to conclude the deal,' she said. 'The arrange-ment was that all three brothers would meet us, hear our ideas and be convinced.'

'So the price wasn't a relevant topic of conversation at the meeting?'

'No,' Kirkenær said. 'The price had been agreed.'

'Reidar already knew about the plans for the sale then and knew what your offer was . . .'

Both nodded. 'Neither the meeting nor its purpose would have come as a surprise to anyone,' Kirkenær said. 'And I cannot recall a negative response from any of them, either,' he added.

'You didn't propose any new conditions, anything which might have caused Reidar Folke Jespersen to change his attitude?'

'Not at all,' said Kirkenær.

'Might the two brothers have held anything back from you?'

Husband and wife exchanged looks. Iselin slowly hunched her shoulders. Kirkenær answered: 'It's possible, in theory. But you'll have to ask them. To me . . .' He glanced at the woman nodding in assent. 'To us it didn't seem as if he felt anything surprising or unfamiliar had come up at the meeting.'

'If he was intent on rejecting a deal, he must have reached that conclusion before he appeared,' Iselin added.

'Did you get in touch with any of the brothers after the meeting?'

'We talked to Arvid,' she said, still playing with the cold sore.

'When?'

'We rang Arvid the same afternoon, didn't we? And he said we should let things settle for a day or two and then everything would fall into place.'

'He didn't say anything to you about Reidar being against the sale?'

'No.'

'Can you remember what he said word for word?'

Iselin coughed. 'That is what he said verbatim: *I think we should let things settle for a few days and then every-*

thing will fall into place.'

'What did you think?'

She shrugged. 'I was a little . . . how shall I put it? . . . I began to get cold feet. So I asked if anything was the matter. Arvid said a small cloud had appeared on the horizon, but it would be gone before the day was over.'

Frølich scrutinized her. 'A cloud which would be gone before the day was over?'

'That's what he said.'

'And when was this?'

'It was the same day we met. It must have been about four in the afternoon, I imagine.'

'And afterwards? Have you talked since?'

'He rang the day after, before we knew anything about the murder. It was in the morning. He told me that his brother Reidar was dead. So they would have to sort out legal formalities amongst themselves before there could be any talk of concluding a deal. And he asked me if we had the patience to wait.'

Both were now staring at Frølich. 'Did you?' he asked.

Kirkenær, puzzled, said: 'Did you what?'

'Have the patience to wait?'

They exchanged glances and smiled. 'That's what we're doing now,' she said. 'We're waiting.'

'How long are you prepared to wait?'

They eyed each other for a long time before Iselin turned to Frølich with a resigned expression on her face. 'That's precisely what we've been discussing,' she said. 'And I don't think it's going to be very much longer.'

35

Cherchez la Femme

Emmanuel Folke Jespersen was thinking. Gunnarstranda endured the long silence by gazing out of the window. His thoughts drifted to Tove while his eyes rested on the view from Jespersen's terrace. The rime frost lay like a layer of melted sugar over the roofs and the veranda railings. The low winter sun hit the window at an angle and showed up grease stains and fingerprints on the glass. Emmanuel fidgeted with the photograph between his fingers, rubbed his eyes, laboriously raised one leg and tried to cross it over the other, but then gave up.

Gunnarstranda let his mind wander. A few hours earlier he had woken up in the same bed as a woman for the first time in ages. He leaned back and gazed at the rays of sun hitting the opposite side of the room. The light appeared to shimmer; the heat radiating from the fireplace made the sunlight restless.

There was no doubt that Emmanuel had seen the woman in the photgraph before, but Gunnarstranda recognized that it would take time to elicit an admission. At first Jespersen took a deep breath as he spread his lips into a melancholy acknowledgement, an expression which he allowed to subside before it had fully developed, and with his face set in a weird grimace, he met the Police Inspector's eyes for two long seconds. Then his lower lip shot forward and with a shake of the head he announced that the photograph of the woman with the mole on the cheek meant nothing to him at all.

'I've been talking to Arvid,' Jespersen said at last. 'He said you police were keen to find out why Reidar became an antique dealer . . .'

The table was awash with weeklies and other magazines. In the middle towered a pile of books including a large crossword dictionary and Aschehoug & Gyldendal's one-volume encyclopaedia. A third book was so creased it was impossible to read the title on the spine. The man's black and white cat had curled up on a cushion on the sofa between them.

Emmanuel took another look at the photograph, shook his head and placed it on the pile of books on the table with care. 'No,' he said with a deep sigh and stroked his chin. 'Such a good-looking lady would have stuck in my memory.'

Gunnarstranda gave a weary smile. 'Perhaps you know why your brother became an antique dealer?' he asked without bothering to conceal a certain forbearance.

After grabbing a good wedge of his trousers, Jespersen finally succeeded in crossing his legs. With one hand resting on his knee, he stole a furtive glance at the picture.

Gunnarstranda bent forward across the table and played with the photograph.

'I think Reidar was carrying around a great void inside himself. Perhaps that was why – he went for antiques. If he didn't own things he was . . . he was nothing.' Jespersen threw out his arms as if to emphasize: 'A void. Reidar was obsessed with collecting.'

'Trophies?'

'Yes, I suppose you can call them trophies. I think he almost lived through objects; he was the objects he owned.' Jespersen glanced down at the picture and said: 'I think it was Reidar's greatest nightmare – almost as though he was trying to justify his existence through possessions. I think that deep down there was a forbidden area, perhaps a wound from some blow, event or experience – at any rate something which caused his life to take the course it did.' Emmanuel closed his eyes and went quiet, as though deep in reflection, then went on: 'On the other hand, Reidar may not have been unique in this respect. I've often thought that we're all like that, that we all have a *fundamental suspicion of ourselves*. Do you understand? If we dare to put morning routines and work to one side – in other words, the *ritual* side of life: cleaning teeth, job, meals, celebrating Christmas and Easter, and as far as I am concerned, the time we spend in the freemasons' lodge, conversations with other people too – we probably all find ourselves being brought up short at some point, don't we? Wherever – in a shop or at home in an armchair. We may hear something said or recognize something from our childhood, a smell or a sound or an atmosphere – and we stop and realize – or can see at a deep level what we have become – the unvarnished truth – and we have to close our eyes and repress the realization – because we can see right through the shield we hide behind, the bonds of friendship, our social life. We stand there with closed eyes and want to flee, perhaps because it is painful to come to a halt, to turn round or to get a grip on this hurt. We soldier on with life as it is, without brooding any further – without – without grabbing the chance we have to make a change there and then. Do you think I'm waffling?'

'Not at all,' Gunnarstranda said. 'I think you're right. Many people will have to confront their dreams sooner or later – hold an annual general assembly on themselves, if we can put it like that. But I suppose some get round to it quicker than others. Many may never experience it.' He straightened the photograph and brushed down his trousers. 'Go on.'

'Well, watching your brother like this – as a *victim* . . . you have to remember that Reidar was my big brother, my model, a person with an aura of irrefutable authority – watching him like this . . .'

Police Inspector Gunnarstranda waited politely as Jespersen searched for words.

'It was very difficult because he understood what I was thinking. Perhaps he didn't notice the concern behind it, but he noticed the *change*. He understood intuitively that he had been seen through, that he had been *unmasked*. But I'm not sure that he understood what I had found out in specific terms. He just noticed the change in the atmosphere between us – he noticed that I felt sorry for him. Which he was incapable of forgiving.'

'Forgiving?'

Jespersen nodded. 'Forgiving.'

'Why couldn't he forgive?'

'Perhaps it was something to do with his internal void, whatever it was he was fleeing from by building this armour around himself. But also because the balance between us had been upset. When he was *unmasked* – the word is appropriate here – I saw through this somewhat abnormal urge to be fit and active, to own – to build a fortress of *objects* around himself, he was unable to maintain the same hold over me as a brother, of course. He just did not like dealing with me.'

Gunnarstranda supported his chin on his bony index finger and said: 'You must have had your own ideas about what this collecting of objects and feverish hyperactivity was meant to redress, I suppose. Was there some ulterior ideology? Was it trauma as a result of horrendous experiences? Was it repressed memories of some kind?'

'Well, yes, I have thought about it a bit . . .'

Gunnarstranda bent forward in his chair. The cat, sitting on the sofa next to Emmanuel Folke Jespersen, twitched its head. It purred softly, stretched its rear legs and reposed on the cushion like an Egyptian queen. Its eyes were open but it wasn't awake; it blinked and slowly lowered its head onto its front paws. 'Tell me,' Gunnarstranda whispered in his excitement.

'At first I thought he was tormented by memories of people who were asleep when he blew them into smithereens.'

'Sabotage missions?'

Jespersen stared into the distance without speaking. 'God knows, he must have had a lot of terrible things on his conscience. Death and . . .' He faltered. 'But I found out it couldn't be anything like that.'

On tenterhooks, the policeman cleared his throat.

Jespersen was breathing heavily and leaned his head

back. The cat blinked again – and Jespersen gazed at the ceiling and stroked his chin with a low rasping sound. 'What is it they say . . .?'

'Who says?'

'The French. What is it they say when they're looking for the key to a mystery . . .?'

Gunnarstranda looked down at the photograph on the blue encyclopaedia. The winter sun, shining through the window onto the table, fell onto the picture and made it gleam like an old, matt mirror. '*Cherchez la femme*,' he whispered.

Emmanuel, his eyes still on a point on the ceiling, drew a deep sigh and repeated: '*Cherchez la femme*.'

Gunnarstranda swallowed, took the photograph and held it up. 'OK.' He sighed and took the plunge: 'What's her name?'

36

The Sauna

The most knowledgeable person in Police Inspector Gunnarstranda's circle of acquaintances was his brother-in-law. The problem was that it was getting more and more difficult to talk to the man as the years went by. For one thing, it was difficult to meet him without thinking about Edel. And for another, the conversation dragged for both of them as it seemed the distress of meeting was mutual. It always cost the Inspector quite some effort to get in touch. But now he had an excuse. Shortly after lunch he picked up the receiver and dialled the number.

His brother-in-law asked for time to think. For some unknown reason he seemed to be in a positive frame of mind; he almost seemed glad to hear the policeman's voice.

They arranged to meet after work.

At half past three the Inspector took his swimming things from the cupboard by the door, went out and caught the tram to the pool in Oslo West. Gunnarstranda always wore a bathing cap in public baths. If he didn't, his hair would trail after him like a wet sail after a boat. Tove Granaas had not yet commented on the way he combed his hair. But he knew a comment was not far off. He had bought his swimming trunks fifteen years ago, on Fuerteventura. He bought new goggles and a new nose-clip every year.

He stood for a few seconds looking at the green surface before bending his knees and diving in. He glided through without moving his legs – and noted with surprise that the water was not so cold – until his bathing cap, goggles and nose-clip emerged into the air. Then he swam 25 lengths, backwards and forwards, breast stroke, concentrating on his breathing and every single turn. Once that was completed, swimming leisurely on his back, he looked up at the clock to check his time. Two minutes faster than the previous swim, but still four minutes slower than his personal best.

Finally he hoisted himself out of the water, had a quick shower and went into the sauna. If there was room he always lay on the top bench. On this occasion there was room. The hot, dry air burned his palate. So as not to scorch himself on the wood he was careful to spread out his towel. But first of all he nodded to the others sitting there, then bent down for the ladle in a bucket on the floor and poured water on the stove. Four other men were there. A young, vulnerable-looking man in his early twenties, gawping at the others' sexual organs, was most interested in an athlete in his early forties – Will W – whom Gunnarstranda had arrested three times for GBH and extortion. Will gave the policeman a measured nod and continued to stroke his muscles with circumspection and wipe the sweat off his forehead with a towel. The other two men were elderly, part of a crowd which had been larger, and they often talked about their late companions. Today their attentions were turned to someone called Per who, according to them, had won the war single-handedly. They talked about Ronny, who was bullied when they went to Lakkegata School because he had gone to bed with his sister. They talked about Francis who had worked all his life in the Norwegian Parliament and had even disciplined the Prime Minister. Gunnarstranda lay back on the bench listening and waiting for his brother-in-law.

It was just after seven in the evening when he wandered back through his office door. He had been given three names to choose from. The first was a journalist in Trondheim who had written a number of popular science books about the area. The second a knowledgeable layman who could produce the most astonishing new facts from subjects which most considered exhausted long ago. According to his brother-in-law the snag here was that the man had links with neo-Nazi groups. Gunnarstranda opted to take his chances with the third name on the pad – a retired history professor.

He sat down on his office chair and drank a cup of coffee which his stomach told him he ought not to drink. He pulled out the lowest drawer with his foot. With the phone to his ear and his foot on the drawer, he listened to the phone ringing and contemplated the point where his black sock met his blue long johns.

'Yes,' said a woman's reedy voice.

'My name is Gunnarstranda,' the policeman said. 'I work for the Oslo police authorities. Have I got through to Professor Engelschøn?'

'Yes . . . Roar!' the voice shouted after a brief pause,

and the policeman heard the receiver being put down on a table. 'Roar! A call from the police!'

It was quiet and Gunnarstranda could hear heavy footsteps running over creaking parquet flooring.

'Engelschøn,' said a hoarse voice.

Gunnarstranda introduced himself.

'Delighted to meet you,' Engelschøn said expectantly.

'I've been told you are the person in Norway who knows most about the resistance movement during the German Occupation,' Gunnarstranda said, looking at the old photograph on the desk.

'By no means,' Engelschøn said, and repeated himself: 'By no means.'

'I'm trying to trace a woman,' the police officer said.

'Well, you police should be in a better position to do that than me.'

'This is connected with the period of the Occupation,' Gunnarstranda explained. 'The woman is Norwegian, but was supposed to be married to a gentleman of some prominence during the war. She was christened Amalie and her maiden name was Bruun with two 'u's, Amalie Bruun.'

Professor Engelschøn's house was the type of residence estate agents splash money on to advertise in newspapers. The house was in Snarøya. The roof ridge which towered over the trees bore two chimneys and overlooked a 1930s tarred, wooden house with intricately worked windows and pillars by the front door. The building reminded Gunnarstranda of Frognerseteren Restaurant and large farms in Gudbrandsdal valley.

Yet the house was different from most others in the district. There were no low-slung Italian cars next to it. There were no sleek setters running around in the garden, and there were no security company signs hanging over the entrance issuing dire warnings. In general there were no signs of the vulgar nouveau-riche culture which was hemming in the few remaining habitations with soul in and around the capital. The drive was covered with snow. Just one narrow, winding path had been cleared through the carpet of snow, stretching from the broad doorsteps to a rusty post box. The latter was secured with wire to a fence post which had been cemented in a long time ago. The steps were snow-free. A snow shovel and a piassava broom stood against the wall. The dry stems of a creeper clung tight to the round wooden pillars, waiting for the chance to transform the entrance into a green portal in the summer.

He was shown in by a stooped elderly lady with her hair in a bun who peered at him through two thick lenses.

The first thing that met Gunnarstranda when he entered was an aroma of green soap, lavender and lightly salted cod. It was a smell that took him back to his youth. At once he could see before him his mother's fat legs beneath her apron as she melted egg butter for the fish, and he saw the quiet nook in the flat where the black oak dining table was placed, between the stove and his father's bookshelf. As he stood there, struck by his confrontation with a smell from his childhood years, his eyes wandered around the house interior.

Two armchairs had pride of place in front of an old

TV. Some knitting had been casually discarded on one of the chairs. A pair of glasses with a broad black frame lay on the coffee table. Beside them an ashtray emblazoned with the design belonging to a long since forgotten brand of cigarette – Abdullah. A curved briar pipe with a chipped mouthpiece rested against the rim of the ashtray. On the wall, family pictures in oval frames hung around an embroidered motif of Norwegian nature: two elk drinking water from a pool in the wood. A wall clock struck a muffled chime to indicate that it was half past eight as Professor Engelschøn lumbered towards him.

The professor took him into a study in which every single square centimetre of wall space was covered with books. A computer with a flickering screensaver shone on to a desk awash with paper. Engelschøn's hair was grey and bristly and combed up rather than back. His complexion was pale and marked with deep furrows. The heavy chin hung like a digger's bucket under the sullen mouth. From behind his desk, his glasses down his nose, he resembled a protrudent bloodhound guarding a consignment of bones and meat from the slaughterhouse.

'In fact the woman you are searching for is rather interesting,' he growled in his hoarse voice and cleared his throat. 'I have found several pictures of her. Bruun was indeed her maiden name, Amalie Bruun. It was no easy task, but you put me on the trail. In 1944 she married Klaus Fromm, who was, as you pointed out, German. But not just any German. He was a judge, stationed here in Norway during the war.'

Gunnarstranda whistled softly.

'Klaus Fromm's details in the NSDAP and SS go back to 1934 when he was twenty-four years old.'

Gunnarstranda frowned as he did the arithmetic and said: 'And you're sure of this?'

Engelschøn lowered his glasses. The look he sent was cool and judgemental. 'Who recommended me, did you say?'

Gunnarstranda dismissed this question with a wave. 'What you've told me is something of a surprise, but we can come back to that. If this man Fromm was twenty-four in 1934, he would be ninety now – assuming he's alive.'

'Well, that's possible. I haven't been able to find that out. Do you smoke?'

Gunnarstranda nodded.

'Thank God,' the professor said and clamped his teeth round the mouthpiece of a Ronson pipe he produced from a drawer in the desk. He talked out of the corner of his mouth as he attempted to light up: 'Klaus Fromm had military and legal training, and in the late 1930s was appointed judge at the SS courts in Berlin. He came to Oslo in May 1940 where he took up a higher position in what was known as the SS und Polizeigericht Nord – which was a court that was in fact meant for Germans, but also sentenced Norwegian resistance fighters.' Engelschøn spread a sweet aroma of pipe tobacco around the room.

'Judge,' Gunnarstranda mumbled, lost in thought. 'What sort of rank would that be – in German?'

'He was an SS Obersturmbannführer.'

Gunnarstranda nodded. Encouraged, he lit his roll-up

and inhaled greedily. The atmosphere of this room was one of the most appealing he had come across for a long time.

'An Obersturmbannführer corresponds to a lieutenant-colonel,' Engelschøn explained.

'A high rank, in other words.'

'Indeed.'

'But the title of judge sounds somehow civilian. How high-ranking was he in practical terms?'

'How much do you know about the SS?' Engelschøn asked from his desk.

'Elite soldiers. And I suppose the story of Hitler's paranoia. The Night of the Long Knives.'

Engelschøn nodded. 'The SS was founded as a reaction to the growth of the SA, the Sturmabteilung. Röhm was the man in charge of the SA. And the more it grew, the greater the danger that it would challenge Hitler's authority – at least that was what he thought. In 1933 there had been 300,000 Brown Shirts under Röhm. That was why Hitler ordered the murders of a large number of SA officers in 1934 – the Night of the Long Knives, as you said. Thereafter, the SA was finished and the SS grew exponentially. The name Waffen-SS first came into official use in March 1940. Then this police division that Fromm worked in was established – along with a Totenkopfdivision which was responsible for guard duties and the administration of the concentration camps.'

'But until then hadn't the SS consisted of policemen?'

'Yes, indeed,' Engelschøn confirmed. He rummaged around the table, stood up and took a sheet of white paper from the printer on a stool beneath the window.

He sketched out a little organizational diagram on the sheet. 'The SS was administered by Himmler,' he explained. 'Himmler was the Minister of Internal Affairs in 1936 and the police were incorporated into the SS. The police had two sections: the Ordnungspolizei and the Sicherheitspolizei. This last-mentioned security organization was sub-divided into two further sections: the criminal police department, Kriminalpolizei or Kripo, and a secret state police, Gestapo. However, in addition to these there was a special police force – the SS Verfügungstruppe – which was closely linked with Hitler himself. You may have heard of Hitler's bodyguards – the Stabwache; they were subsumed under this Verfügungstruppe. Afterwards Hitler's bodyguards were re-named Leibstandarte SS Adolf Hitler. The difference between the Leibstandarte and the rest of the SS was that the soldiers had sworn personal allegiance to Hitler, which of course was done because direct allegiance to the Führer weakened Himmler's influence and power within the SS.'

'So Hitler didn't trust Himmler?'

'Shall we say that Hitler was aware that his authority could be swayed? As I'm certain you know, he was the victim of several assassination attempts. At any rate he made sure that the Verfügungstruppe constituted the cornerstone of every division that carried the name Waffen-SS. But the reorganization of 1940 was implemented first and foremost with the growth rate of the organization in mind. In total the Waffen-SS consisted of thirty-eight divisions. Can you imagine that? Hm? Of course, you know the Germans were dab hands at organization.'

Professor Engelschøn sat down again. 'Did I answer the question?' he asked and provided the answer himself: 'No, I didn't. Klaus Fromm bore the rank of Obersturmbannführer, but did not work in the field.'

'An *eminence grise*,' Gunnarstranda suggested, watching the lengthening column of cigarette ash and concentrating on not letting it fall.

'Yes. At least a man with civilian and military power.' The professor used the mouthpiece of the pipe to shove an ashtray across the ocean of papers separating them. Then he picked up the photograph the policeman had found under Jespersen's desk pad. He studied it thoughtfully while tapping the pipe against his temple. 'But Amalie,' he broke off, 'Amalie, née Bruun, grew up here in Oslo. She lived in Armauer Hansens gate 19 until she was married. She and Fromm got married on 12th November 1944. The ceremony took place in Kristinelundveien 22 – in what came to be known as 'Brydevilla' – where the SS court was accommodated during the occupation. Here,' the professor said, peering at the papers before holding up an A4 sheet: 'A copy of the marriage certificate: Klaus Dietrich Fromm married to Amalie Bruun.'

'In 1944. So he was thirty-four years old. How old was she?'

'Amalie was born in the maternity clinic of the Rikshospital on 3rd July 1921 – so she was twenty-three when she got married.'

'Eleven years younger than Fromm.'

'Yes, that sort of thing was not so unusual before . . .'

'But in the case I'm working on . . .' Gunnarstranda said, trying to blow a smoke ring but failing, 'there is another man I have reason to believe . . .' he started, staring at the ceiling before repeating himself: 'I have reason to believe that this man had a relationship or was in love with Amalie Bruun at some point . . . and he was also twenty-three years old in 1944 . . .'

'Is that right?'

'So this man was the same age as her. A well-known resistance fighter.'

The professor glared across the table. Gunnarstranda was reminded of dogs fighting over bones and scraps of meat. 'Who?' Engelschøn barked.

'Reidar Folke Jespersen.'

Engelschøn nodded. 'He was one of Linge's boys, wasn't he? No, he wasn't,' he added hurriedly, took the pipe out of his mouth and studied the ceiling. 'Reidar Folke Jespersen, no, he didn't work with Linge. He – yes, that was it – he was a saboteur. One of the toughest and most notorious in fact, though I'm sure you knew that, didn't you?'

Gunnarstranda shook his head.

'Trust me, Reidar Folke Jespersen was a man with a lot . . . a *lot* of blood on his hands.'

'He was killed just recently, a few days ago. I'm working on the case.'

'Yes, I read about it, about the murder. But I didn't connect . . .' Professor Engelschøn wore a worried frown. 'You think Folke Jespersen was in Amalie Bruun's circle? That would be . . . well . . .'

Gunnarstranda waited patiently while the professor searched for the right word.

'Sensational,' said the professor at length.

Gunnarstranda opened both palms again. 'She and Jespersen may have been childhood sweethearts for all I know. After all Oslo was not a big city. Well, forget it. It's Amalie I'm interested in.'

'Hm.' The professor shook his shoulders and began to riffle through the pile of folders in front of him. 'I had a photo of the married couple here,' he mumbled, lifting up the papers. Eventually he held out a large photograph. 'Here you can see a picture you'll find interesting – it's of an elegant German soirée.' The photograph was taken in a large hall or room. There were uniformed men together with women wearing long dresses. Some perched on chairs, others on sofas, and there were two men leaning against a mantelpiece in the background. 'Lots of shiny brass,' Gunnarstranda commented.

'Indeed, lots of fine folk . . .' The professor rose to his feet and, with stooped back, scurried round the table. He bent down and held a quivering, nicotine-stained, fat finger over the photograph. 'That one . . . that's General Wilhelm Rediess, the chief of police in Norway, and that one . . . that's SS Oberführer Otto Baum on a visit from Berlin . . . so it must have been an important occasion. Baum ended up as the C-in-C of the 16th Panzer division. He was one of the most decorated officers in the war. Look at all his medals – the photo's not that sharp, but you can see the Knight's Cross and the Iron Cross 1st class. You can imagine, can't you! And him. There you can see . . .'

Gunnarstranda nodded: 'Is that Terboven?'

'Of course, and he's sitting beside your friend – Amalie Bruun.'

Gunnarstranda adjusted his glasses. Even though the woman's face in the picture was partly turned away from the photographer, he recognized her by the mole on her cheek and the high forehead. He guessed she would have been the centre of this party – being as beautiful as she was – courted by these important men. He perceived a kind of determined wantonness in the look she gave the photographer. But her chin was longer and firmer than he had imagined. This was no shrinking violet – she was self-confident, she was witty and she dominated social gatherings.

The professor's trembling finger pointed to the right: 'Can you see the one with the side-parting and the thick lips . . .?'

'Yes?'

'That's Fromm, her husband – and he does indeed look *fromm* in this photo – it's German for pious. He must have just delivered a couple of death sentences.'

'I think he looks like the writer, Sigurd Hoel,' Gunnarstranda said and added: 'With those round glasses . . .'

Professor Engelschøn furrowed his brow for a few seconds. 'Well . . .' he mumbled, clearly not convinced, and pointed to a man and a woman on the right of the picture. 'And him, the one sitting next to the other blonde, him, you see, that's Müller – the German propaganda boss in Norway – and the one joining in the flirting, that's Carlo Otte himself, the man responsible for running the German economy in Norway.'

'Veritable VIP lounge.'

'Indeed. No small fry here.' The professor chuckled.

'As you can see, finding information about Amalie Bruun was not difficult. She had good connections, let's put it like that.' He toddled around the desk and sat down.

'And you have no idea what the occasion here was?'

'No. But there is a sense it is some kind of delegation, with the visitor from Berlin, Otto Baum, there.'

'But how did she – a girl of twenty-three – get here, get into such circles?'

'I'm not sure when this photo was taken, but I assume it must have been some time in late '43, or early '44,' Engelschøn chuckled, puffing on his pipe. 'One of the reasons for my conclusion is that I have seen Baum's list of decorations. And in this photo he's missing a couple of medals that he was awarded in 1944 – so . . .' Engelschøn straightened up, '. . . the photo must have been taken at least six months before she married Fromm. Hence she is probably his escort at this party, I imagine. But how . . .' Professor Engelschøn chewed his lip. 'How people find each other and get married is of course like the birds and bees, but they did find each other. You know they worked together?'

'Worked together?'

'At any rate she was employed as a secretary in the German administration. It's nothing new for work colleagues to be united in the bonds of matrimony.'

Gunnarstranda studied the photograph – the Germans with the insignia on their shoulders and self-assured expressions on their faces. He scrutinized Fromm. There was something that caught his eye. He stared at Fromm again. It was the same feeling you have when you are trying to remember a name that has slipped your mind. There was something about the way he stood that drew his gaze. But he had no idea what. The feeling was unpleasant. So he decided to study Amalie Bruun instead. He tried to imagine this woman being the centre of attention when the formalities were over and the band struck up. He asked: 'Was she an avowed Nazi?'

'I haven't a clue. But there's nothing to suggest she was a member of the Norwegian Nazi party, the Nasjonal Samling, if that's what you're wondering.'

Gunnarstranda sat gazing at the picture. His eyes were still drawn to Fromm.

'She had worked for a newspaper, *Aftenposten*, amongst other places, before she started her job with the Germans.'

'*Aftenposten*?'

'I beg your pardon?' The professor was taken aback by Gunnarstranda's exclamation.

Gunnarstranda's lips were trembling. 'When did she work for *Aftenposten*?'

Engelschøn shrugged. 'Until some point in '40 or '41. She was making use of her formal training – yes, you can guess what her qualifications were. Your lady had taken exams in German commercial correspondence – and she began shortly afterwards as an office help in the Ministry of Justice, but she packed it in and went to work for the German administration. But it's impossible to know why – I would guess her knowledge of German played some part in it.'

He took another look at the photograph and suggested:

'She's very presentable . . . that may well have had some significance.'

'So she had a background in journalism?'

'Not at all. She was office-trained. In those days women journalists were rare. I would presume she had had an office job.'

Gunnarstranda passed back the photograph. He sat looking into the distance as he planned his next question: 'What happened to these people after the war?'

'Well, good point . . . I suppose the same as other Germans. They were arrested, deported, some went back home. Some became lawyers – that I do know – in Germany. The propaganda boss, Müller, became a property developer. As far as Fromm is concerned, I have no idea what happened to him. But all the judges working in Brydevilla were arrested and put on trial here. But, you know, the Norwegian High Court decided that SS und Polizeigericht Nord had to be considered a military court in line with the Wehrmacht's own courts, so the judges could not be punished as they were only doing their jobs, so to speak. However . . .'

The professor scratched his head.

'Yes?'

'There was a case they tried to pin on these judges, you know. Well, you're too young to remember much from the war, but I am not. In February 1945 – just three months before the German capitulation – some Norwegian hostages were shot in a reprisal execution . . .'

'Why was that?'

'Hostages were often being shot in fact, but this time

the underground movement liquidated a Norwegian Nazi – Major General Marthinsen – the boss of the security police in the Nasjonal Samling. A number of Norwegian hostages were executed afterwards . . .'

Engelschøn stood gazing at the floor, lost in thought. He mumbled: 'One of them was the brother of a boy in my class. I went to Ila school, you see. And that was the worst school day of the whole war. Everyone knew, all the pupils, the teachers, everyone knew that Jonas's brother had been taken from his flat and shot. But Jonas didn't say a word about it. He sat quietly gazing into the air. None of us said anything . . .'

Engelschøn shuddered as though he were shaking off something nasty, then trudged back to his chair behind the desk. 'Yes, well,' he said, heaving a deep sigh. 'The end of the story was that it was decided that these court martial judges had not contravened international law.'

'All the judges were acquitted?'

'Yes, but this legal issue was not resolved until 1948. Fromm may have been in prison all that time.' The professor shuffled over to his untidy work station, sat down by the computer and typed something in. 'It will be harder to find . . . how long the man was in prison,' he declared, swinging round on the swivel chair.

'And Amalie?'

'Unknown.'

'She disappeared?'

'Well . . . I doubt it. If she had disappeared, the police would have investigated and that would have been recorded in the sources to which I have access.'

'But you don't have anything about her?'

'No.'

'But the treason trials? After all she was working for the Germans.'

'Members of the Nasjonal Samling were punished after the war, not people who worked for the Germans.'

'What do you think happened?'

Engelschøn shrugged his shoulders. 'As a woman she may be part of our bad conscience. A few German spouses were deported to Germany. Or she may have been sent to Hovedøya – the women's internment camp.'

'Imprisoned?'

'Strictly speaking, women's camps were not prisons – but institutions established for the safety of the Teuton tarts, as they were called. But this case is a little special . . . because Fromm's case had to be appraised in the light of international law. Either she was deported to Germany or she stayed here. I have to confess it is very difficult to say anything concrete about this.'

'But her husband, Fromm? You have no idea what happened to him?'

'He was released, wasn't he!' Engelschøn shook his head. 'What happened to him? It may be possible to find out, but . . .'

'Try,' Gunnarstranda urged, taking the photograph of the German soirée. He scrutinized Fromm again without quite knowing why. 'It wouldn't be possible to borrow this photo, would it?'

37

Hockey

'That's nice,' said Eva-Britt from another world as the stereo played the gentle opening tones of Nils Moldvær's *Khmer*. Frølich got to his feet and turned up the volume. Even though the woodburning stove in the corner was as hot as it could be, there was a cold draught coming from the large living-room window. The radiator under the window sill was unable to deal with the cold air. He stood for a few moments meditating in front of the window as he looked out on the illuminated ring road – yellow and snake-like – as it twisted its way through the winter landscape. Cars lost colour under the floodlighting. A shower of sparks moved down the mountainside. It was the electrical current collector of a late-night metro carriage scraping against ice. The moon, which earlier in the evening had hung like a large, yellow rice-paper lantern over the mountain ridges of Østmark, now looked like a bucket of white paint spilt over a watery surface.

He turned and watched Eva-Britt.

He was nettled that she had come. She would always sit and wait when she visited him. If she wanted something, she would wait until he got it for her. Would you believe it, he said to himself. We have been sleeping together for years and she still sees herself as a stranger in my flat.

She was studying the Ikea catalogue from an angle, with a sneer playing around her lips as she quickly flicked from page to page. She looked like someone sitting on a tram reading a tabloid. He caught himself wishing it wasn't her sitting there.

When the telephone rang they exchanged glances.

'Will you answer it?' she asked from the chair.

'Give me a good reason not to,' he retorted wearily.

Eva-Britt sat up and looked towards the bedroom door, and then at her watch. She conspicuously lowered her arm with the wristwatch. The telephone stopped ringing soon afterwards.

'I won,' she said, skimming though the catalogue. He watched her cross her legs and snuggle back into the large armchair, knowing very well that she was being observed. A second later her mobile phone began to ring. They exchanged looks again.

'Will you answer it?' he asked.

She stared from his telephone to her bag, the source of the ringing. Displeased, she frowned. 'If it's for you, I have no idea where you are,' she said with conviction, nimbly got to her feet and dug out her mobile from the bag by the door. He followed her with his eyes.

'Yes,' she said with arched back and mobile to her ear. 'No, he's . . .'

She turned to him and mouthed: 'Your boss . . .'

He sat smiling at her.

'I have no idea . . .' she said, listening.

Frølich had to grin when he heard Gunnarstranda's shouted orders crackle out into the room. Eva-Britt's eyes were beginning to glaze over and she pulled a face as if someone were forcing cod liver oil down her throat. She took three ominous, stiff-legged, aggressive steps forward and threw the mobile to him without a word.

Frølich caught it in mid-air. 'Hi,' he said.

'This is a wild goose chase,' Gunnarstranda said, skipping the preamble. 'You talked to Arvid Jespersen about his brother's career, didn't you? About why he started out as an antique dealer? Right?'

'Yes, I did,' Frølich said. 'But . . .'

'And Arvid said something about newspaper production, right?'

'No, not production. Reidar took the waste paper off the print rolls from a number of newspapers and . . .'

'Yes, yes,' Gunnarstranda interrupted. 'And these rolls were pieced together. Where?'

'Don't know.'

'And they were sold on. Who to?'

'Don't know either.'

'But the nitwit must have said!' Gunnarstranda's voice was cracking with annoyance.

'Take it easy,' Frølich said heavily. 'The paper was sold to printers in African and South American states. But why are you so fired up about this?'

'I have another connection with South America, Frølich.'

There was the dry click of a lighter at the other end of the line as Gunnarstranda took out a cigarette and lit up. 'Back to Arvid and this newspaper story. Did he mention a person by the name of Fromm?'

'No, I'm positive about that.'

'Mm, have you got any plans for tomorrow?'

Frølich looked across at Eva-Britt who had demonstratively planted herself in front of his large living-room window, with her back to him. The clock showed it was past midnight. 'I'll do whatever you ask. You know that.'

'Great. I want you to go to Reidar Folke Jespersen's office in Bertrand Narvesens vei. If no one's there, I want you to go through the records in the office in Thomas Heftyes gate with a fine-tooth comb.'

'What are we looking for?'

'One or more letters, or copies of letters, from a gentleman by the name of Klaus Fromm. Klaus with a "k" and Fromm with two "m"s.'

'How far back?'

'As far as there are records.'

'Anything else?'

'No.'

'Anything else you want to say?'

'Check the years when they were selling paper, in other words the '40s and the '50s.'

Frølich sighed. 'Anything else?'

'Do you think Reidar Folke Jespersen might have been a Nazi?'

Frølich broke off a protracted yawn. 'Are you crazy?'

'No,' said Gunnarstranda. 'But why is it crazy?'

'Jespersen was running an illegal printing press in Oslo until 1943 when an informer gave him away and he had to escape to Sweden. From there he went to a training camp in Scotland where he was shown how to carry out sabotage. He was sent on several jobs to Norway – sabotage and . . .'

'Liquidations,' Gunnarstranda added laconically. 'Right, my mind is at rest. Sleep well.'

Frølich put Eva-Britt's mobile on the table. He breathed in, got up and stood in the cosy heat radiating from the stove, observing her averted back while nodding to the beat of the music: a long guitar solo, throbbing drums and the pure flow of a synth meandering through the room. From the kitchen came the nauseous burnt smell of coffee that had been on the warming plate for two hours too long.

She started to turn round. Frank wondered what expression she would have on her face. Whether this was going to be an evening of rows and grumpy faces.

'You gave that idiot my telephone number,' she proclaimed.

Frølich did not answer.

The subdued combination of heavy rock and modern jazz was still oozing from the loudspeakers when his telephone rang.

He and Eva-Britt exchanged looks.

'He won't give up,' she muttered darkly.

Frølich knew. It had been in the air for a long time. This evening they were going to have a row.

He strode over to pick up the telephone.

'Richard Ekholt,' the voice said.

Frølich had seen a picture of Ekholt, a photograph showing an ice hockey player in the Furuset team many seasons ago, a club strip and a face with black stubble and short, black hair – with a fringe. The voice matched the image.

'It's late,' Frank Frølich said calmly.

'I hear you've been asking after me.'

'Come to the station tomorrow and we can talk.'

'Don't ring off,' the voice demanded.

'I'm going to,' Frølich insisted. 'Phone us tomorrow.'

'One-nine-five.'

There was a rippling sound in the receiver. The ripple of laughter, Frølich realized. The man was laughing at him.

'Like a password, eh? That's so good . . .' The stranger was wheezing and groaning with laughter: 'One-nine-five.' The laughter continued. It sounded like the creaking of a rocking chair. A low snort on the line told him that Ekholt was gasping for breath. He continued: 'That's so good . . . a hundred and ninety-five.'

Frølich met Eva-Britt's eyes. She was looking daggers at him.

The voice on the line whispered: 'I know something. You've been asking after me, haven't you? I'm ready now – to talk.'

Frølich was still watching Eva-Britt, who tilted her head in an aloof manner, as though to signal that she knew what he was thinking. Frølich had had enough of her sulkiness. 'Can you come here, to my place?' he asked Ekholt.

Eva-Britt tossed her head in the air.

'No, you have to come here,' the voice said, now clear and composed.

Liberation, thought Frølich, and asked: 'Where are you?'

The voice on the line hissed. Frølich tried to identify the other sounds he could hear, the background noise.

There was another voice. At least one. 'Are you in a pub?' he asked.

'Just listen,' Ekholt said. 'Come in one hour's time – on your own, to town.'

Frølich looked across at Eva-Britt again. She was shaking her head – slow, heavy, ominous movements.

'This is the only chance you'll get!' The voice seemed neither inebriated nor desperate now, but unemotional and business-like.

Frølich could feel that he wasn't quite in tune with the mood shifts. The other end of the line was silent now, no voices in the background, no noise. He said: 'How can I know whether you are who you say you are?'

'You have my number? My mobile number?'

'Yes.'

'Ring me and I'll answer.'

'Wait.' Frank found the telephone number on the notepad sticking up out of the pocket of his leather jacket hanging on the hook. 'Ring off,' he continued. 'Then I'll call you.'

'Just a moment,' the voice said and Frølich heard a hand being placed over the mouthpiece. Something I'm not supposed to hear, he thought, and tried to work out what was going on.

'I need to know who you are,' Frølich said. 'Ring off.'

He stood looking at the telephone for a few instants before making a move.

'You're not going out now, are you?' Eva-Britt said in a gentle yet forbidding tone.

'I just have to call this number . . .'

'It took me three hours to get a babysitter,' she said.

'It's weeks since we've had time to ourselves – all on our own. And I've killed myself to get it. You're not going to go and stay out all night, are you?'

Frølich tapped in the number.

'Yes, this is Richard,' said the voice.

Frølich stared at Eva-Britt who stood with her arms crossed, waiting.

'Where shall we meet?' he asked brightly.

Frank Frølich left the raised intersection known as the traffic machine, drove down Europaveien, around Bjørvika, past the old customs house and along Langkaia, one of the quays. It was deserted, it was night-time and still. His watch showed 1.33 as he approached the roundabout by Revierkaia. Frølich felt a resigned tiredness sneaking up on him as he was unable to identify a soul on the street. A nagging feeling of doubt throbbed at the back of his mind: the thought that he had been duped.

He thrust his hand in his pocket for his mobile. He was going to put it on the seat, but changed his mind and stuffed it back. Then he slowed down and let the car roll in neutral until it came to a halt alongside the fence that separated the road from the last strip of quayside. He switched off the engine and waited.

After almost a quarter of an hour he got out of the car. With his hands in his jacket pockets he ambled back towards the roundabout. It was like a film. A street lamp cast a pale circle of light over the agreed meeting place and at the same time created a transparent wall against the darkness of the night. The light was reflected in the windows of the ticket booths situated halfway along the road leading to the ships bound for Denmark. The water in Bjørvika was frozen – solid black ice with white waves of drifting snow. The ice caught and reflected the flickering lights of Oslo town centre behind the harbour front. It had to be at least minus 20. Frølich shivered, breathed into his scarf and tried to remember which film it was this scene brought to mind. Scattered lights from the buildings along Festningskaia gleamed on the roofs of the parked cars. He sauntered on, out of the glare of a street lamp and into the next. The cold bit into his legs, feet, ears, hands. He wondered what he had done with his gloves. Left them on the seat in the car, he supposed. He twisted his wrist to see the time. Five minutes more, maximum, he thought. The only cars to be seen were parked in a line, a bit further down, near the traffic lights in Festningskaia.

Apart from the noise of the traffic moving in and out of the tunnel, everything was quiet. He leaned his head back and breathed out, into the light from the street lamp. A circular rainbow in his icy breath stood out against the light. He breathed out again. Another rainbow. A game from his boyhood. The cold began to eat into his toenails. He jogged on the spot and beat his arms against his chest. It was now almost ten minutes past the agreed time. He took his mobile from his inside pocket and with stiff fingers tapped in Richard Ekholt's number. He was trembling, but pricked up his ears when he heard a telephone ringing. He ducked – a reflex reaction. He moved away from the street lamp and pressed the off button. The silence was now as threatening as the sound of the telephone he had just heard.

His eyes scanned the area. Not a soul in sight anywhere. It was obvious – if anyone had wanted to hurt him, they could have finished him off a long time ago. He looked down at his mobile. Tried to memorize the ring tone that had carried in the night air. It had been some distance away, but how far? He slowly raised his thumb and held it over the key that rang the last dialled number. He pressed and stood listening. Soon the muffled tone rang out. Frølich started moving. He followed the sound. Increased the tempo, stopped, held his breath and listened. The sound was closer, but still there was no one around. He loped across the deserted roundabout. A disembodied voice broke the telephone connection and informed him in metallic tones that the person he was ringing was not available at the moment. He glanced down at the mobile and pressed the same key as before. The display showed the number he was ringing. There was the ring tone again. He spotted the line of parked cars. The sound was coming from one of them. The silhouettes of the buildings along the quayside were visible through the rear window of the nearest car. The phone had to be in there. He disconnected. The silence reminded him that he was alone and that what he was doing was wrong. He imagined American films in which cars exploded when an ignition key was turned. He repressed the fantasy and instead saw a stranger putting his phone down on the seat and getting out of the car to meet him. But where was this man now? For a brief instant he considered calling Gunnarstranda, but moved towards the car. He didn't feel the cold now; he was sweating.

The car was a dark Mercedes with a cut-off ski rack on the roof. *A taxi*, thought Frølich. *Just a metal holder – a taxi with the licence plate removed.* He went to the left to walk in a large circle around the car, which no longer seemed anonymous or abandoned, but large and menacing. He stopped about five metres from the car. When he went alongside, he noticed the side window had been smashed. What he had at first assumed to be ice was the window itself, a white sheet of splintered glass. The front windscreen was also shattered. What he had thought to be bits of ice on the car bonnet were fragments of glass. He walked on a few metres and could see the bonnet clearly. There was something on top. It was too dark to make out the precise shape. He crouched down to see better. Then he realized what it was: a foot. Someone was sitting in the driver's seat. Someone had kicked out the front windscreen and their foot was still there. Frølich straightened up and rang the duty officer at Police HQ.

38

A Man and a Woman

Gunnarstranda asked the driver to pull in by the fence just before the roundabout. As soon as the taxi came to a halt, a uniformed police officer came over and stooped down. Gunnarstranda rolled down the window on his side. 'It's me,' he said to the officer, who nodded and withdrew.

Gunnarstranda rolled the window up and turned to Tove. 'Once again, I'm very sorry,' he said.

'Relax,' she said, stifling a yawn. 'It was me who insisted on getting up.' She forced a tired smile when the taxi driver involuntarily looked up into the mirror. 'I mean, I insisted on coming here with you,' she corrected herself and observed the scene on the other side of the roundabout where two police cars were sending blue lightning into the night sky. 'That looks exciting.'

'It was exciting at any rate,' Gunnarstranda said without emotion, leaning forward between the two front seats and passing the driver a 500 kroner note. 'I get off here, but she's going home,' he said, turning to Tove who shook her head indulgently. 'You old-fashioned man, you.'

'Thank you for a nice evening,' he said, meeting her eyes.

She took his hand. 'Thank *you*.'

'Well, I'll have to be off,' he said, turning round in the seat and looking out. Another car with a blue flashing light had arrived. 'Yes, it's getting busy here,' he said.

She squeezed his hand again.

'Yes, take care then,' he said.

'You have to open the door first,' she said.

'Mm, that's right,' he said and looked for the handle. At that moment the driver got out and opened the door from outside.

Gunnarstranda got out, buttoned up his coat and stood watching the taxi drive away. As he turned, he noticed at least five men look away that instant, some with a smile on their lips.

Frølich towered over the other four. 'Had I known you had company, I could have waited until morning,' Frølich said with concern.

Gunnarstranda responded with a grunt.

'But since it was Richard Ekholt who was killed, I thought you would want to see the crime scene.'

Two other police officers moved aside as they approached the parked car with smashed windows. A covered body lay on a stretcher on the ground. 'Sure it's Ekholt?'

'Ninety-nine-point-nine per cent.'

'And he was strangled?'

'Looks like it. Someone sitting on the back seat put a nylon rope around his neck and pulled. Ekholt went wild and kicked out the front windscreen and a side window before he died.'

'The taxi licence plate?'

Gunnarstranda peered through the smashed glass.

'It was on the back seat.'

'Could he have taken it off himself?'

Frølich shrugged.

'Purse and money gone,' Frølich said. 'But not the telephone. A mobile under the pedals. The killer may not have seen it.'

'When did he ring you?'

'Between twelve and one at night.'

Gunnarstranda yawned.

'He talked about his licence number,' Frølich said. 'He said a hundred and ninety five and was killing himself laughing.'

'A hundred and ninety five?'

'Yes.'

'Not nineteen and five?'

Frølich shook his head.

'And when did you find his body?'

'Five minutes before I rang you. At ten to two.'

Gunnarstranda wandered around the car.

'Almost had a shock,' Frølich said by way of conversation. 'When a lady answered your phone.'

Gunnarstranda said nothing.

'But that's just great. Seemed a nice lady . . .'

'Did he appear to be on his own when he rang?' Gunnarstranda interrupted.

'Ekholt? There was some noise. I thought he must have been in a pub.'

'He wasn't talking to anyone?'

'Possible. I had the impression he was holding his hand over the phone, on one occasion anyway.'

Gunnarstranda nodded and yawned.

'Was that your lady friend?' Frølich asked with caution. 'The one in the taxi?'

Gunnarstranda stared up at him with vacant eyes. 'Could he have rung from here?'

'From the car?' Frølich ruminated. 'I thought I heard several sounds, background noises, music maybe.'

'But it wasn't a CD player you heard or the car radio?'

'I have no idea,' Frølich said.

'How long did it take you to get here?'

'Forty minutes.' Frølich added as an apology: 'Eva-Britt was at my place. And she was not best pleased when she had to go back home.'

'I see,' Gunnarstranda said, lost in thought.

'I waited for about a quarter of an hour in the car without seeing anyone.' After some reflection, he said, 'And I found the body ten minutes later.'

'If it was Ekholt you spoke to, he was killed between twelve-thirty and one-fifty-five?'

'That sounds about right, yes.'

'Tomorrow we have a briefing with Fristad, the public prosecutor,' Gunnarstranda interposed, taking a swift glance at his watch. 'At nine. In six hours' time.' He looked up at the sky. Then watched all the officers busy at the crime scene. 'I'm sure we're in the way here. You should go home and get yourself some shut-eye.'

39

Orientation

Gunnarstranda arrived home at five o'clock in the morning. He slept until half past eight, got up, dressed and began to scrape ice off the car windows at five to nine. The meeting with the public prosecutor, Fristad, was supposed to be in five minutes. He ran through the case in his mind. Fristad was an academic with a childish attitude regarding his own status and therefore always took advantage of the academics' privilege of arriving a quarter of an hour late.

Gunnarstranda lit a cigarette while the engine warmed up and the defroster cleared the front windscreen. He tried to go through all the points that had some connection with Ekholt, but realized he couldn't think clearly. Instead he switched on the car radio and heard there was chaos on all roads leading into Oslo because of a demonstration by taxi drivers. He took his mobile from his pocket, rang Fristad's office and warned them he would be late. Soon afterwards he switched off the engine, locked the car door and strolled down to Advokat Dehlis plass to catch the first convenient bus.

Fristad was seated, as always, and stretched out a welcoming arm to a blue chair by the conference table. Police Inspector Gunnarstranda organized the pile of reports on the table in front of him, put on his rectangular mail-order glasses and began to hold forth in a low voice: 'The murdered man, Reidar Folke Jespersen, was placed in a chair in the shop window of his own antiques business. He was killed in an office behind the shop. His body was stripped naked and dragged across the shop floor and put in the window. The killer had tied red thread around the man's neck. The corpse was discovered by a passing newspaper girl, Helga Krisvik, on Saturday 14th January at six-thirty a.m. She is a housewife, works part-time and has been eliminated from further enquiries.'

'Suffering from shock?' Fristad was chewing his glasses.

'We assume so, yes,' Gunnarstranda continued dryly. 'As to the deceased's last movements, we have managed to ascertain the following: Jespersen got up at his usual time on Friday 13th January. He left home at the usual time – but without saying goodbye to his wife who was in the shower. A little later, that is, at approximately nine o'clock, he turned up at a café in Jakob Aalls gate where he drank coffee and mineral water, and read a number of magazines. The owner – Glenn Moseng – had seen him once before, but was unsure when. Folke Jespersen insisted on sitting at the only window table in the café, from which he had a view of the block of apartments where a certain Eyolf Strømsted, who is, or at least *was*, his wife's lover, lived. The owner is not sure when Folke Jespersen left the place, but we know he had been sitting there for a very long time – several hours. At a few minutes after twelve he appears at Arvid Folke Jespersen's flat where Emmanuel Folke Jespersen is also waiting – both of his brothers. A married couple, the Kirkenærs, are also there and they make a formal presentation of their offer to buy the shop owned by the three brothers.'

Fristad rocked back on the chair behind the desk and drummed the tips of his fingers against each other. 'And what is happening in the shop while all this is going on?'

'Well, Karsten Jespersen – the murdered man's son – opened the shop at ten. He wasn't on his own. It was a planning day at the kindergarten, so he had his son, Benjamin, with him in the shop. Later Ingrid Jespersen arrived with a pot of coffee and two cups. There were no customers. The two of them sat talking while the little boy played and did drawings until a quarter past eleven.'

Fristad nodded with closed eyes. 'Has Karsten got the hots for the widow? I mean they're about the same age, aren't they?'

'They get on well in each other's company; they have a few common interests.'

'Are they bonking?'

Gunnarstranda looked up.

Fristad gave an apologetic smile. 'I read in one of your reports that the victim was impotent. Were the son and the widow bonking?'

Gunnarstranda, poker-faced: 'I didn't ask.'

'But do you think so?'

Gunnarstranda: 'Perhaps we should concentrate on my account of events first?'

Fristad nodded: 'Right . . .' he said with emphasis. 'Right . . widow leaves son to sleep with this guy with the crazy name, Streamstead . . .'

'Strømsted . . .'

'Right. And the poor eighty-year-old cuckold sits waiting for the bitch to visit a real man to get her weekly fill . . .'

Gunnarstranda stared at Fristad as though he were waiting for a phase to pass.

'Go on,' Fristad said gaily. 'Keep going.'

'In the meantime Reidar Folke Jespersen joins his brothers . . .'

'Yes, right . . .'

Gunnarstranda looked up, silent.

Fristad waved the policeman on.

'We know that the Kirkenærs give their assurance that the Folke Jespersens' life-work will be carried on, and make a concrete offer for the shop, the shop's name and the warehouse – I believe it's called goodwill . . .'

'Yes, right, goodwill . . .'

'But they don't negotiate at this juncture. The couple make a kind of assessment of the shop's worth and give an overview of their plans before leaving the brothers to their own discussions. That's when Reidar Folke Jespersen is supposed to have been unsympathetic and aggressive.'

'Why the anger?'

'I think there was a lot of history. The man should have retired ten to twelve years ago. He lords it over the others; he is the eldest brother. According to one brother, Emmanuel, Reidar perceived the initiative to sell the shop as a conspiracy against himself.'

'Right . . . but this business with the wife and lover, could that be a factor?'

373

'Well, of course it's possible,' Gunnarstranda conceded. 'According to the brothers and the couple, Reidar Folke Jespersen had been given prior information about the background for the meeting. Well, it's hard to know what exactly annoyed him about the negotiations. We do know however that after leaving the brothers he rang the wife's lover . . .'

'Yes, I read that. Pretty strong stuff, eh? The scorned spouse ringing while the two of them are humping away . . .' Fristad guffawed through moist lips.

'True. At any rate Folke Jespersen didn't argue or have a row with the wife's lover on the phone. He just asked to speak to his wife and gave her an ultimatum.'

'No more fucking around, eh,' Fristad said in English.

'Quite so. At 2.30 p.m. at the latest he rings a young freelance actress by the name of Gro Hege Wyller and brings forward a meeting with her. This change of plan is in itself worthy of note. They had been due to meet on 23rd January, but instead he asks her to come that day, Friday 13th January.'

'Right – and this was to the tune of *The Way We Were*?'

'Yes, Gro Hege Wyller dresses up and pretends to be a figure we have to assume is a woman from Folke Jespersen's past. Wyller acts out a play with him – a kind of ritual with improvisation, sherry and Schubert.'

'No sex?' Fristad asked in English.

'Never gave it a thought.'

Fristad grinned. 'Are you a puritan, Gunnarstranda?'

The police officer sighed. 'Ingrid Jespersen has confirmed that Reidar Folke Jespersen was not – as you yourself pointed out – sexually active. Frøken Wyller maintains that Jespersen talked about this without any inhibitions. It is my impression that the old man was finished with these things.'

'No jar of Viagra in grandad's medicine cabinet?' Fristad gave another moist guffaw.

Detective Inspector Gunnarstranda took a deep breath.

'Sorry,' Fristad said.

'Now I've forgotten where I was,' said Gunnarstranda, irritated.

'The photo,' Fristad hastened to say. 'Wyller's role model. Who's the woman in the photo?'

'Her name's Amalie Bruun, but her relationship with Folke Jespersen is not entirely clear.'

'But I suppose he must have been in love with her once upon a time?'

'The relationship isn't clear.' Gunnarstranda, wearied, took off his glasses.

'Right, yes, well, on to the taxi murder. I assume that is the next line of investigation, isn't it? Frank Frølich's somewhat dramatic nocturnal ramble through Bjørvika.'

Gunnarstranda stared blankly at the papers on the table.

'No,' he said. 'Let's take one thing at a time. Before Wyller comes to the dead man's office, Folke Jespersen rings his solicitor and asks her to revoke his will.'

'Is that relevant?' asked a strained Fristad.

'It's relevant to the extent that Jespersen is now focused on his own death for reasons yet to be clarified.'

'But what effect does the revoking of the will have on the beneficiaries?'

Gunnarstranda raised a hand to restrain the other man. 'Just a minute,' he said. 'Dr Grethe Lauritsen, who is the cancer specialist at Ullevål Hospital, says Folke Jespersen rang her that day. He was given the results of some tests and discovered that he had malignant cancer, which the pathologists confirmed, by the way.'

'Do you think that was why he revoked the will?'

'We don't know why. But we do know that very little time passed between his phone call to Ullevål Hospital and then to his solicitor.'

'But what are the consequences of his revoking the will?'

'There are hardly any consequences at all because he didn't make a new will. According to the solicitor – and I have read the voided will myself – the man's last wishes were simply a division of goods, who would get what *after* the inheritance had been split along financial lines. We know Karsten Jespersen was interested in a specific wardrobe, but I find it hard to believe he would kill his father for the wardrobe.'

'Odd,' Fristad concluded. 'Bloody odd,' he repeated, gazing at the table.

'There are two big mysteries concerning the man's last hours,' Gunnarstranda said. 'And they are the calls to Wyller and to the solicitor.'

'But if he had found out he was going to die?'

'Then he should have come up with a new will if he had gone to the trouble of cancelling the first. But he didn't.'

Fristad brushed his jacket sleeve with his hand. 'Fine, go on.'

Gunnarstranda breathed in. 'As will become evident, Gro Hege Wyller's statement is central. Richard Ekholt lives in the same block as Wyller . . .'

'Lived,' corrected Fristad.

'I know he's dead,' Gunnarstranda said in a low, menacing voice. 'Would you stop interrupting me?'

Fristad opened his palms and said nothing.

'Well, Ekholt was an acquaintance of Wyller's and apparently interested in her – but they didn't start a relationship. Ekholt drove Wyller to Ensjø. Here he tried to force her to have sex with him in the car, but failed – according to her.'

'Do you believe that?'

'I can't see why she would make up the story. She ran off and found the key to the warehouse in a post box on the wall; this was a regular arrangement. She unlocked the door and got to Folke Jespersen's office at 5.15 p.m. She performed this . . . . this assignment of hers . . . and rang for a taxi just over an hour later. It arrived at 6.42. We have a print-out of that. When they got into the car, Wyller noticed that Ekholt was still sitting in his car parked outside the building. He must have been waiting for her the whole time. But she left in Folke Jespersen's taxi. She says she consciously avoided Ekholt because of the brutal incident that had taken place before.'

'Right . . .' Fristad waved Gunnarstranda on.

'Ekholt followed the taxi taking them to town. Wyller says she noticed his taxi when she was dropped outside her bed-sit. She also says that Ekholt followed Folke Jespersen's taxi home.'

Gunnarstranda stood up and went over to the Imsdal spring-water dispenser next to the mirror. 'My mouth has gone dry,' he mumbled, releasing water into a plastic beaker.

'And everyone agrees that Folke Jespersen went home in the taxi – and it stopped outside his house in Thomas Heftyes gate at 7.15?'

Gunnarstranda drank another beaker of water and stared thoughtfully at the bottom. 'Everyone agrees.'

'And this man from the woods was waiting for him – Jonny Stokmo?'

'Yes.'

'He's an old friend of ours, isn't he?'

'Yes, he is. Two convictions: one for receiving stolen goods and one for selling contraband.'

'What was the unsettled score about?

Gunnarstranda sat down again. 'Frølich questioned Stokmo. But Stokmo was vague and evasive about the outstanding issues between him and the dead man. The only thing Stokmo would say was that money came into the picture. We do know that they talked before Folke Jespersen went upstairs to his flat.'

'But you've spoken to the son?'

'Stokmo Junior claims the bad blood between them is a matter of honour and goes back to the war and Jonny Stokmo's father – Harry Stokmo – who was alleged to have been swindled out of a lot of money by Jespersen. Harry Stokmo led refugees across the border during the war and he . . .' Gunnarstranda wriggled two index fingers to suggest quotation marks . . . '*received gifts* from Jews he guided over the border to Sweden. Folke Jespersen, it seems, assumed the goods were stolen because Stokmo didn't dare to put them up for sale after the war. Folke Jespersen took them and sold them, but neglected to settle up with Stokmo. Jonny found this out a short time ago – via some old receipts, etc. – and that was why he had demanded a settlement from Folke Jespersen on behalf of his deceased father.'

'Do you believe Stokmo Junior?'

Gunnarstranda gave a tired smile. 'Why not? If this story has any truth to it, it gives Jonny Stokmo a motive, and that gives us a handy line of enquiry. Why would Karl-Erik Stokmo invent a motive for his father? Anyway, we'll have to question Jonny again. The son's statement is not worth much more than hearsay.'

'Right . . . Make a note of that,' Fristad said.

'Of what?'

'That we need to check the story.'

Gunnarstranda sent him an old-fashioned look.

'Yes?' Fristad said.

'Do you want to do my job?'

Fristad cleared his throat. The silence was oppressive.

'And then?' Fristad faked a casual cough.

Gunnarstranda took a deep breath and ran a hand through his hair. 'Folke Jespersen went up to his wife, son, daughter-in-law and two grandchildren.'

'And Stokmo?'

'We know that night he visited a prostitute calling herself Carina. She has been checked out. Stokmo left this woman at about an hour before midnight. She had to clear up and get ready for the next customer at midnight. Stokmo claims he drove to Torshov and went to bed at about eleven in a room behind his son's workshop. He didn't see or talk to anyone. And this was a Friday.'

'Lies, in other words.'

'Let us say that Stokmo *may* have arrived at Thomas Heftyes gate shortly after Ingrid went to bed on her own. We can also say, with certainty, that Stokmo had no alibi for the moment of death.'

They eyed each other. Fristad roared with laughter. 'I know what you mean. Stokmo's an interesting one, isn't he!'

Gunnarstranda nodded.

'And up in Folke Jespersen's flat they quarrelled over the evening meal?'

'No.'

'But did they quarrel after the meal?'

'No – according to the widow, who maintains she went to bed as normal except that she was alone. She took a sleeping pill and woke up in the middle of the night not knowing what it was that awoke her.'

'If she killed her husband, she wasn't very creative about procuring herself an alibi.'

'Let's focus on the murder,' Gunnarstranda continued blithely. 'It's most probable that Reidar knew his killer. Either he arranged to meet him in the shop or he was in the shop for other reasons when his killer came. But as the murder appears to have been planned, the most likely scenario is that the victim arranged to meet his killer in the shop.'

Gunnarstranda looked up. The public prosecutor was sitting quietly with closed eyes, as though he were meditating.

'We know that Folke Jespersen was busy on the phone all afternoon and evening. Gro Hege Wyller said he received at least one call in his office, but he may have made many more before she arrived. The widow said there were several calls for him during the evening. However, we have not managed to find out who the callers were. The only person who has admitted calling is his brother Emmanuel. He says he phoned late in the evening, but Reidar didn't want to talk to him.'

Fristad nodded to himself. His glasses fell on to his chest and he put them back. 'Anything else?'

'According to the prospective purchaser – Kirkenær – Arvid was supposed to have rung *to remove the small cloud on the horizon.*'

'Did he?'

'What? Ring or remove the small cloud?' Gunnarstranda asked dryly. 'No, Kirkenær said Arvid had tried to get through to his brother, but without success.'

The two men sat facing each other, ruminating, until the policeman resumed: 'Folke Jespersen was killed by a single stab from an antique bayonet which was on display in the shop. The choice of weapon is an indication that the murder was not premeditated. Provided that the killer had not known about the bayonet and had not planned to use it. Nevertheless, we have to assume the stabbing was carried out by a strong person. The blade penetrated deep into the man's body, puncturing one lung and grazing some vital arteries – the forensics report says the killer held the victim and the bayonet until he was sure the victim was dead. So there was no struggle. The murder victim was stabbed, held tight and then let down gently onto the floor. There are no marks on the body to suggest he was dropped. He was let down gently and left where he was. The crime scene investigators made one vital point. There was not very much blood on the floor and so the assumption is that the killer's clothes must have been drenched with blood.'

Fristad nodded and his glasses fell onto his chest.

'Karsten Jespersen has gone through the registered items in the shop and a uniform is missing. It appears this had been sent to the shop anonymously a few days before the murder. The uniform was still in the box on the Friday when the man was killed. If Karsten Jespersen is telling the truth – we have only his word for it that this uniform exists – then there is the possibility that the killer donned the trousers and jacket, put his own soiled clothing in the box and made his escape. So, if the killer sent the uniform to have a change of clothing in the shop, it tends to suggest it *was* premeditated murder.'

'Doesn't that seem terribly complicated?'

'Premeditated murder is always complicated.'

Fristad nodded. 'But wouldn't a soldier wandering around attract a lot of attention?'

'It was very cold out. The killer could easily have hidden the uniform under a winter coat.'

'At any rate the uniform offers a logical explanation for why no witnesses observed a man with bloodstained clothing,' Fristad said to himself. 'Has Karsten Jespersen any documentation to prove the existence of a uniform? Has he got a receipt from the post office?'

Gunnarstranda looked up. 'Would that stand up in court?'

Fristad splayed his arms wide in a gesture of ignorance.

Gunnarstranda went on: 'The killer then stripped the body.'

'And the bayonet?'

Gunnarstranda nodded. 'As I said, it was on display in the shop – it belonged to a rifle used by an English soldier during the Napoleonic wars. We've got it, but there are no fingerprints on either it or the gun. At the time of the murder the shop was in the dark, as every other night. By the way, we have an indelible pen – the bog-standard type sold in stationers up and down the country. We assume the killer brought it with him, because it was used to write this strange message on the body. The message also indicates that the murder was planned – if a man takes a pen with him to write something on the body, it suggests premeditation. By the by, there are no prints on the pen either.'

'And this was the famous J for Jørgen, one hundred and ninety-five?'

'J for John. Nineteen. Five.'

'All right, all right. We have the taxi licensing number.'

'Let's take one thing at a time.'

'Fine. When did the murder take place?'

'Somewhere between eleven-thirty in the evening and three in the morning.'

'And there were no keys in the dead man's pockets?'

'No keys. Cigarettes, yes. A lighter, coins, but no keys.'

'I take it no one else knows this?'

'Just you, Frølich and I know that the keys are missing.'

'I read that the widow says there was snow on the floor when she woke up.'

'Yes – if she's telling the truth. One possible scenario is that the killer, who still had snow sticking to the soles of his shoes, took the keys from the dead man, went upstairs, let himself into Folke Jespersen's flat, entered the bedroom and then left again.'

'Others?'

'My guess is that the snow on the floor was left by Folke Jespersen after an evening walk before he was killed.'

'Why do you think that?'

'Because the killer can hardly have had any snow on his shoes if he had changed into the uniform after wrestling with the body to get it into the shop window. In addition, the tread on the dead man's shoe soles was quite deep.'

'But the killer took the keys, you said? Why would he do that if he didn't use them?'

'The missing keys are a mystery. Either they have not disappeared and are still lying somewhere in the flat or the killer had something else in mind when he stole the keys.'

'You don't think the killer was in the flat?'

'If an intruder crept into Ingrid Jespersen's bedroom, it would only have been to see her sleeping and then to leave

– or to take something she knows nothing about, something she doesn't miss, in all probability something belonging to her husband. In short, the snow on the floor makes sense if Folke Jespersen popped in to see her.'

Fristad cleared his throat to ask a question, but Gunnarstranda was quicker: 'That's one possibility. Another is that Ingrid Jespersen made up the whole story about the snow on the floor.'

'Why would she do that?'

'Well, you tell me. I find it difficult to believe that she would make it up. Unless it was to give credence to the theory in our eyes that the killer pinched the keys.'

They sent each other a look. 'On the other hand,' Fristad reasoned, 'if the widow invented this business about the snow on the floor . . .' He left the sentence hanging in the air.

Gunnarstranda nodded.

Fristad completed his reasoning: 'Then it is very probable that she invented the break-in story because she was the one who killed her husband.'

'Your conclusion could be right, but the argumentation may be wide of the mark,' the Police Inspector concluded. 'I lean to the view that the husband left the snow on the floor.'

The public prosecutor and the police officer eyed each across the table again. 'But what do you think, Gunnarstranda? What does your gut instinct tell you? Did the widow bump off her husband?'

'Motive?' Gunnarstranda wondered aloud.

'Money, sex, heat of the moment,' Fristad said. 'Young woman marries much older man. He turns down a stack of money by rejecting the offer proposed by his brothers and Kirkenær. On top of that he puts an end to his wife's bedroom romps with the lover. These two factors cause a row. The widow is not short of motives!'

'Opportunity?' Gunnarstranda mused.

'Of course she's the one with the opportunity to bump her old man off whenever.'

'On her own or with help?'

'With the lover; she holds him, the lover stabs.'

'The lover has an alibi.'

'Bloody hell,' Fristad whispered in a hoarse voice. 'What sort of alibi?'

'He lives with a man – Sjur Flateby, who maintains that Strømsted was never out of his bed that night.'

'For me, as a prosecutor, that alibi does not stand up. A partner's statement is the same as a spouse's – worthless.'

'I agree. But it's better that the partner admits the lie in a statement to us than you destroy the man in a court of law.'

'Does this guy know Strømsted is shagging the widow?'

Gunnarstranda shrugged. 'He may have an inkling – as he was asked about Strømsted's movements that night.'

'Tell the partner about the infidelity and see how long Strømsted sticks to his alibi. Although the widow may have done it on her own.'

'Possible. But we mustn't forget the others. Jonny Stokmo hasn't got an alibi, either.'

'What's his motive though?' Fristad asked. 'No money

was taken, just this damn uniform, and we only have Karsten Jespersen's word for it that it exists. If Stokmo killed . . .'

Gunnarstranda nodded. 'The problem with Stokmo is that he doesn't stand to gain from Folke Jespersen's death. He doesn't get any money and his father's name isn't cleared. If Stokmo killed Folke Jespersen he must have done it in rage or he must have had a different motive from this story about his father's besmirched honour. Problem number two: the Stokmo theory doesn't square with premeditated murder. If Stokmo planned the murder, why didn't he have a plan to clear his father's name at the same time?'

'I see,' Fristad said heavily.

'Furthermore, there are the two brothers,' Gunnarstranda said. 'They have no end of motives.'

'But do they have the opportunity? I think I read in one report that they are ill, overweight and have difficulty standing up.'

'They have all the opportunity they need,' Gunnarstranda objected. 'They're old and white-haired like the victim. They own the shop with their brother. They can move around the shop without anyone raising an eyebrow. They have keys to the shop. They might have got in and waited for Reidar to come down. They don't have watertight alibis either – both claim they were tucked up in their beds – alone.'

'Are they physically capable?'

'Of what?'

'Killing their brother.'

'Now you're applying normative assessments, Fristad.

The rule is we stick to facts, motive and opportunity.'

'Fine. Go on.'

'According to these purchasers – Kirkenær and Varås – Arvid Jespersen said to them, before Reidar was killed, that . . .' Gunnarstranda formed quotation marks with his fingers . . . 'that there was a small cloud on the horizon which had to be removed.'

Fristad smiled. 'That sounds damned conspiratorial.'

'It does.'

'Fine. The brothers may have done it,' Fristad concluded.

'The widow rang Karsten Jespersen when she woke up that night. But Susanne Jespersen said Karsten wasn't at home.'

'But does that mean the son was on the ground floor killing his father? His wife swears he was in bed asleep when the widow rang,' Fristad said with a frown.

'The letter and the numbers only make sense if the son is the murderer.'

Fristad shook his head. 'If you're right that the coded message has something to do with St John's Gospel, well, we may perhaps be able to conclude something of that nature. But then you're overlooking the fact that a taxi was waiting outside with its engine running.'

Gunnarstranda sighed. 'I'm not overlooking that. The point is that we don't know if it was the same car that was seen every time. One witness saw a Mercedes taxi parked outside the shop, but it was at least four hours before the murder was committed.'

'But the taxi licence number was 195.'

'The witness didn't say that.'

'What are you trying to say now, Gunnarstranda?'

The policeman cleared his throat and braced himself: 'We know that Richard Ekholt drove a taxi with the number 195. But the witness who saw a mysterious taxi in Thomas Heftyes gate could not identify it – it was not necessarily Ekholt's vehicle. And we don't know if Ekholt parked in Thomas Heftyes gate . . .'

'But we do know that Ekholt followed Folke Jespersen that night!'

'Yes, we do.' Gunnarstranda smiled at the public prosecutor. He knew how much the man liked to destroy mere circumstantial evidence. 'The fact that Ekholt followed the murder victim in his taxi *might* suggest that it was Ekholt's vehicle parked in Thomas Heftyes gate an hour later. The fact that Ekholt had set his cap at Gro Hege Wyller and *might* have been jealous of Folke Jespersen that evening *might* suggest a motive. The fact that Ekholt followed Folke Jespersen *might* suggest that he is involved in the murder. Ekholt's licence number *might* even suggest a connection with the writing on the dead man's chest – since the numbers coincide. The strongest *indication* that Ekholt is involved is the fact that he rang Frank Frølich last night giving the number *one hundred and ninety-five* as a kind of password so that Frølich would take notice of him. However, unhappily, Ekholt is dead. If he had any involvement in the murder, we will have to turn to other witnesses to have this substantiated. We have plenty of circumstantial evidence, but . . .'

In a spirit of generosity Gunnarstranda opened the palms of his hands to allow Fristad the last word:

'But not a scrap of bloody proof,' Fristad rounded off sourly.

'You would like this taxi-driver to be involved, wouldn't you?' the policeman asked, lighting a cigarette he had in some miraculous way placed between his lips.

'No smoking in here,' Fristad said.

Gunnarstranda inhaled, half-opened the box of matches and held it in his hand.

'Yes, and I still believe it – that this taxi-driver is involved. If you don't stub out that cigarette, you'll receive an official warning.'

Gunnarstranda inhaled again and flicked ash into the half-open matchbox. 'Let's assume there is a link,' he said. 'We suspect a motive, which is that Ekholt has deluded himself into thinking that Gro Hege Wyller is his girlfriend. He gets a shock because he thinks she's having a relationship with the old man. Ekholt feels rejected and trampled on, and therefore follows the old codger to have it out with him. That's more or less what we think, isn't it?' He took another drag. 'If what we think is right, if Ekholt lay in wait for the old man when he was alone in the shop, why would he put the man in the shop window and write his taxi number on his chest?'

'Buggered if I know!' Fristad said, gesticulating with his arms. 'It's your job to know that! And now I'm getting nervous because you have the cheek to pollute my office with that stinking cigarette. Are you aware that I have a secretary who is prone to taking a fortnight off for an allergy?'

'Relax,' the policeman said, putting the half-smoked

cigarette into the matchbox and closing it. 'While we're considering whether Ekholt might have killed Jespersen, we must not forget our trump cards. The first is that the murder was planned, and the second is that Folke Jespersen must have let the murderer in and so he most probably knew him. I doubt whether Folke Jespersen knew the taxi-driver.'

'But if Ekholt had stood banging on the window, Folke Jespersen might have let him in,' Fristad countered. 'Ekholt was a taxi driver. He was wearing a uniform. He might have pretended he was enquiring after a customer . . .'

'You know best what line you will take in court,' Gunnarstranda answered, raising his palms. 'And we haven't even started to talk about the son's motives. I would like to discuss the inscription on the man's chest . . .'

At that moment they were interrupted; the door was thrust open and Frank Frølich walked in.

Frank felt quite stressed after running the gauntlet of tabloid journalists on his way to Fristad's office. Getting into the public prosecutor's room gave the same liberating feeling you had when you sheltered from a heavy downpour under a large spruce. Fristad and Gunnarstranda, each seated on a blue swivel chair, were silent and deep in thought.

'It smells of smoke in here,' Frølich said, sniffing.

'You see,' Fristad said accusingly and shook his head in irritation at Gunnarstranda. 'You see. Now you've done it.'

'Bloody hell,' Frølich breathed out. 'The press are

going wild about this taxi murder.'

Gunnarstranda swung round on his chair towards Frølich. 'They were saying on the radio that the taxi drivers in town had gone bananas,' he mumbled. 'It's the usual whinge. Screaming on about the crazy times we live in and the lack of security for taxi drivers. Early today there were a hundred taxis honking their horns outside parliament. Every bloody office worker in town got to work late – even those working here and in the Department of Justice. There was a jam right out to Gardemoen airport.' Then he added, 'The killing might be connected to our case, but it's not a foregone conclusion.'

'The mobile phone under the pedals,' Fristad said. 'The call to Frølich and the code number 195 . . .'

Gunnarstranda made a weighing motion with his hands: 'Licence plate or chapter and verse in the Bible. The choice is yours.'

Fristad stopped swinging on his chair and stamped both feet on the floor with irritation. 'But he rang and said the number. The man driving taxi number . . .'

'Yes, OK,' Gunnarstranda interrupted, annoyed. 'But you have to remember that Frølich has been searching for the driver of taxi number 195 for several days! He might have said the number just to identify himself.' He turned to Frølich: 'Did the man say anything about the writing on the dead body?'

'No,' Frølich confirmed. 'He just said the number. A hundred and ninety-five.'

'Nothing else?'

'No, apart from . . .'

'From what?'

'What I told you. That he knew something. I don't think he was alone when he rang.'

The other two men stared at Frølich, who gave an apologetic smile: 'He may have been in a pub or a café. I could hear quite a bit of noise. Background noise. And sometimes he seemed to be covering the phone with his hand.'

'Ekholt may have been in conversation with someone while he was talking,' Gunnarstranda explained to the public prosecutor, who pulled an expressive grimace.

Frølich hunched his shoulders. 'I'm not sure. But the thought went through my mind.'

'Who could it have been?' Fristad mused. 'Gro Hege Wyller?'

Frølich shook his head. 'If there was someone, it was a man.'

'Is this relevant?' Fristad asked.

'Since he was found murdered an hour later, it's relevant,' Gunnarstranda answered.

'But how can we explain the fact that Ekholt was killed after talking to Frølich?' Fristad barked.

'No idea,' Gunnarstranda said with a shrug.

'But this murder must be connected with the murder of the antiques dealer!'

'Must it?'

'He said he knew something, didn't he!'

'Everyone knows something. You do, and so do I!'

'But it would be perverse to believe anything else except that the murders are connected!'

Gunnarstranda shrugged. 'Well.'

'But you've got to be able to see that!' Fristad continued in a milder tone.

'Not necessarily.'

'Not necessarily? He drives a taxi with number 195. The numbers are written on the dead body and he even rings the police in fits of laughter as he says the numbers!'

'Just describe what happened,' Gunnarstranda suggested stonily.

'What happened? Ekholt went into the shop, he grabbed a bayonet and stabbed the man because he thought the old goat was humping his woman!'

Gunnarstranda and Frølich watched Fristad with interest. He had stood up and was standing by the table as he opened and clenched his fists in quick succession.

'Yes?' Gunnarstranda said, impatient.

'Yes, then he stripped the man, painted the number on his chest and sat the man in an armchair in the shop window.'

'Why?'

'Why? I don't bloody well know why.'

'And then?'

'And then what?'

'The keys.'

'Yes,' Fristad said, calmer now. 'He took the keys, went up to the first floor and . . .'

Frølich grinned.

Fristad sat back – crestfallen.

'That story's no good,' Frølich said. 'To me it seems more logical that it was someone who wanted to put the body on show. And, if that's right, I reckon the coded message is a reference to the Bible.'

'But why was Ekholt killed?' Fristad mused aloud.

'He may have been robbed and killed by a customer,' Gunnarstranda said in a soft voice.

'You don't believe that yourself, Gunnarstranda.'

'All the taxi drivers in town do.'

'But we believe the two murders are connected, don't we?'

'If there's a connection between the murders of Folke Jespersen and Ekholt,' the Police Inspector said, getting up to pack his papers away, 'it has to be because Ekholt knew something about the first murder. But we have no proof that there is a link. Anyway, Frølich and I cannot investigate the murder of Ekholt.'

Frølich coughed and said: 'I bet Richard Ekholt was killed because he saw the first murder!'

'If that bet is accepted, the odds will be poor,' Gunnarstranda said with a grin.

Fristad looked up: 'So you agree there's a link.'

'I didn't say that. But this murder must be investigated on its own terms. A whole profession in this town is demanding it.'

Fristad, dejected, watched Gunnarstranda packing his papers. 'What's your next move on this case?'

'I'll keep at it,' Gunnarstranda said brightly. 'I'm working my way back through Folke Jespersen's life.'

'How far have you got?'

'I expect to finish 1944 in a couple of hours,' Gunnarstranda answered, folding his glasses and putting them in his inside pocket.

40

From Thoughts to Deeds

Frank Frølich looked at his wristwatch. It showed a quarter past three. He glanced over at the front door of Reidar Folke Jespersen's warehouse in Bertrand Narvesens vei. He switched off the engine, pulled the handbrake and stepped out. The door was not locked and the light was on in the huge storage area. 'Hello,' the policeman shouted as the door slammed behind him. 'Hello,' he shouted again, moving down the corridor between all the objects.

'Over here,' answered a familiar voice. Anna was standing between two stacks of chairs. She was holding a large writing pad in her hands.

'Did you make it then?' he asked.

'What?' she asked, confused.

'Your visit. To Aker Hospital.'

'Oh, that.' She nodded. 'And you?'

'I did what I had to do, yes.'

They stood looking at each other in silence. A lock of black hair fell forwards. She wound it behind her ear with two fingers.

'And that was good,' he said, feeling foolish and unimaginative.

'And you?' she said. 'I mean what are you doing here?'

'Have to go through the files, if there are any.'

'There are two filing cabinets.'

'Where?'

She pointed to the staircase running up the wall to a door in the middle. 'Up there – on the first floor.' She assumed a sympathetic expression. 'The office is there. But there's a lot of paper. Enough for a doctoral thesis.'

Frølich sighed and looked at his watch. 'The evening is still young,' he said with forced irony.

She smiled back. 'The evening hasn't begun,' she said.

It was cold in the warehouse. Icy breath came out of their mouths as they spoke. He noticed that her fingers round the biro were pink with cold. 'And you?' he asked shyly.

She lifted the pad. 'I'm making an inventory.'

'I mean your back. How is your back?'

'Fine,' she said. 'Do you know what helps? Reflexology. Yesterday I sat in a chair while my feet were massaged for a whole hour. Wonderful. In the end I fell asleep.'

'Bloody cold in here,' he said.

She nodded and blew on her fingers. 'It's warm up there. What are you looking for?'

He shrugged. 'No idea.'

She blinked. 'You don't know what you're after?'

He turned to the staircase and tried a witty riposte: 'I never know what I'm after.'

'At times you do,' she protested through half-closed eyes.

They eyed each other again. He could feel his cheeks burning. 'Yes,' he sighed, moving towards the stairs. 'I'd better go and look.'

He stopped on the top step. Anna closed a wardrobe door and wrote something down. She must have felt his gaze because she peered up. They stared at each other.

He went into Jespersen's office. It was boiling. He stood with his back to the door and cursed himself for being thick-headed and clumsy and incapable of striking up a conversation.

He had been intending to ring her. Now that they had bumped into each other he hadn't a clue what to say to her. He traipsed over to Folke Jespersen's filing cabinet and opened the top drawer. A packed row of hanging files stuffed full with yellowing papers fought for space. He automatically took out an armful of files, carried them all to the desk, sat down and began to leaf through the papers. It was difficult to concentrate. He was thinking about Anna downstairs. He was thinking about his deficient social skills. Half an hour later he had taken off his sweater and jacket. One pile had become two and he was halfway through one drawer. He glanced at the door and wondered whether to go out and talk to her. No, he told himself. You'll just make a fool of yourself.

After an hour he heard a door slam. He checked his watch. It was past four. She had gone for the evening. He heaved a deep sigh and blamed himself yet again for not taking the chance when he had it.

He stood up, ambled through the kitchenette and onto the landing at the top of the staircase. The large hall was in darkness. The outlines of cupboards, chairs and indefinable junk stood out in the dim light from the row of windows high up on the wall. For the first time in many years he envied people who smoked.

By ten minutes past eight he had studied the paper-work from six out of eight drawers in total. So far the search had been futile. He was worn out and needed fresh air. He opened the window a fraction.

From the open window he heard the outside door close with a bang. He stood up and staggered through the kitchenette out onto the landing.

It was Anna. She was on her way up the staircase. With a six-pack of Frydenlund draught beer under her arm. She peered up and dangled the beer. 'Hope you don't have any other pressing engagements this evening?'

They divided the rest of the files between them and talked about seventies music, taking turns to suggest bands and songs which the other had to identify and date. If you couldn't answer, you weren't allowed to ask for clues. Anna was kneeling on the floor, flicking through the papers and drinking beer. 'Edgar Broughton Band,' she said just as he found the piece of paper he was looking for.

'What did you call that lot?'

She looked up, sure he hadn't a clue. 'The Edgar Broughton Band.'

He was reading the piece of paper he had just found. 'I went to the Edgar Broughton Band gig in Château Neuf in either '72 or '73. I was in the eighth class.'

'Proof,' she demanded.

'*Inside Out*,' he said. 'LP from '72.' He waved the piece of paper. 'We're done,' he said.

When he asked her if she wanted to go to his place and listen to records, she was standing, conveniently, with her back to him. She was looking out of the window, at the moon, and left the question unanswered. They locked the door behind them, and he left his car in the car park. They strolled towards the metro station. The quality of conversation was variable. At times it was serious.

She commented that they were going to the wrong platform.

'Wrong?' Frølich asked.

'If we're going to town, we need to be on the other side.'

'If we're going to my place, we have to take the train coming,' he said, pointing to the Lambertseter train roaring out of the tunnel.

When they alighted, both were in earnest mood and walking side by side, hardly exchanging a word. It was only when they were alone in the lift that he got to taste her lips. She pulled his neck down to her with both hands. They stood lost in dreams. They didn't let go until the lift started to descend again.

They listened to 'Heartattack and Vine' by Tom Waits while they made love. Afterwards he fell asleep but woke up when she pulled the duvet over them. Naked, they lay gazing at the sky through the large window in his bedroom. Visibility was sharp and clear. Red blotting paper covered almost the entire moon.

'Crazy,' he said.

'Lunar eclipse,' she said in a barely audible voice.

'Is it?' He drew her closer to him and pressed his chin

into her rounded shoulder.

'Your beard's soft,' she said. 'I would never have believed your beard would be so soft.'

He whispered: 'I've never seen a lunar eclipse before.'

'You may never see one so clear again,' she said. 'Conditions are very unusual tonight. Soon it'll be total.'

He intertwined his fingers through hers.

'In fact I should be by Tryvann Lake watching it through a telescope,' she said. 'I had arranged to meet a group of college friends.'

'Do you meet college friends to watch eclipses?'

'Astronomy was one of my courses.'

'If you want, we can take a taxi.'

'I can see it brilliantly from here.'

They lay close. Her back against his chest, her thighs against his. She stirred her feet, like a cat when it is getting comfortable, he thought, breathing in her hair and staring up at the sky. There was a tiny crescent of yellow still visible behind the pale red blotting paper.

He felt he had to do as she did, to whisper: 'That's the shadow of the earth, isn't it? Why is it red and not black?'

'Sunlight passing through the earth's atmosphere, which filters out most of the blue. Red is what's left.'

'Nice.'

'There are thousands of people at Tryvann. They'll talk about it on TV. People all over Norway wrap themselves up, go out and stare at the sky. Right now we tiny humans everywhere are captivated by what is going on above us.'

'No wonder,' he said. 'The earth's shadow, as it were;

the sun shining on the earth while the shadow covers the moon. That's a pretty big deal.'

'It's God moving,' she whispered and pressed her cheek against his hand.

41

The Ladies Speak

Once again Police Inspector Gunnarstranda drove to Haslum and the well-maintained suburban terraced houses to pay Emmanuel Folke Jespersen a visit. This time he had not warned him of his impending arrival. Hence the reaction when he rang the doorbell was a little slow in coming. He looked up at the frosty, blue sky which presaged another cold snap. He breathed in and at length heard the sounds of an elderly man tottering painfully to the front door. 'You again,' Emmanuel Folke Jespersen said when at long last he opened the door. 'Don't you ever get tired?'

He turned and trudged ahead of the policeman into the flat. Panting, he paused in the doorway to the living room as the detective slipped off his over-shoes.

Emmanuel slumped back into his wide armchair and looked around. 'Don't have any coffee,' he mumbled. 'Don't have any biscuits . . .' He took the remote control from the coffee table and raised it. 'We'll have to make do with Schubert.'

'How did they meet?' Gunnarstranda asked as the first sweet violin tones spilled into the room. 'Do you have any idea?'

'Who?' Emmanuel asked.

'Amalie and her husband Klaus Fromm.'

Jespersen threw his arms into the air. 'My God, you're persistent, and efficient.' He let out a deep sigh. 'Klaus Fromm was his name, that's right. And Amalie . . .'

'I'm annoyed that you have withheld this information from us,' Gunnarstranda interrupted with severity.

Emmanuel shook his head. 'Withheld? No. I know almost nothing about Fromm. And the name had completely escaped me. I know a little more about Amalie. She was Reidar's childhood sweetheart.'

He pointed the remote control at the stereo and lowered the volume. 'Reidar and Amalie were always together from very young. They were the same age. And they didn't live very far from each other – in St Hanshaugen. Arvid and Reidar and I – we lived over a shop in Geitmyrsveien, next to the sharp bend, you know the one, above Diakonhjemmet, the hospital. Amalie's family lived in a block closer to Ullevål. And they became lovers.' Emmanuel splayed his hands. 'It happens nowadays, too. But I don't know that we used the word *lovers*. Things change over time. What is certain is that Reidar spent more time with Amalie than with his friends. Amalie was Reidar's great love. They were inseparable. Like two magnets, they attracted each other and there was nothing they could do about it, it seemed.'

Emmanuel folded his hands over his stomach and leaned back. 'When you were leaving last time, I wondered whether I should tell you what I'm going to tell you now. But I decided you would have to make some progress first, at least winkle out the name of her husband. In a nutshell, if what I'm going to tell you should turn out to be relevant to your case, I thought you would first have to prove its relevance. Perhaps that can't be done – proving relevance. But at least you have proved how hard-working you are. I can't help you much with the story of Amalie's marriage. But I do know how they met. Amalie's family had connections in Germany. Her father may have studied there or they may have had distant relatives. I have no idea. Our family always went to Tjøme in the summer; Amalie and family went to Germany. She met her husband-to-be one summer, either '38 or '39. He was mature – much older than her. You can imagine it. I suppose Fromm had more to offer her than Reidar. And after that summer things were never the same between Amalie and Reidar. She finished it. But then there were those opposite poles, they were fatally attracted, and she was engaged to another man from another country.'

'Klaus Fromm?'

'Of course. The love between Amalie and this man was my brother's great torment during his younger years.'

Gunnarstranda writhed with annoyance. 'And you just kept your mouth shut about this?'

Emmanuel stared at the policeman with disdain: 'When she returned after the summer holiday – I think it must have been in '38 – the tragedy was, you see, that Amalie and Reidar continued to be a kind of couple. While she couldn't quite let go of him, it was clear that things were not as they had been once. She even wore a ring – can you imagine! Engaged to an older man living in Germany. Well, I don't know what to say. It was this magnetism between them that destroyed everything. Instead of two of them there were now three.'

'This lady betrayed your brother and got engaged to a German, whom she later married. Your brother risked his life fighting aginst the Germans.'

'Life can be like that,' Emmanuel said diplomatically.

'It's incomprehensible.'

'Mozart died a pauper. A lot of things are incomprehensible, Inspector.'

'Some things can be explained too.'

'Like what?'

'Yesterday I had an officer go through the files in Bertrand Narvesens vei. He found a strange document. It's an invoice issued in 1953. It was made out to a newspaper in Buenos Aires and addressed to a gentleman by the name of Klaus Fromm.'

Emmanuel frowned. 'Why is that so incomprehensible?'

The detective took a deep breath. 'I cannot comprehend how your brother could do business with Amalie's husband after the war!'

Emmanuel was breathing heavily. 'There's nothing to comprehend. Reidar was a down-to-earth pragmatist, through and through. He was no uncompromising Hamlet! He was Reidar Folke Jespersen. The war was over. There was no one to kill any more, nothing to fear any longer. What sense was there in remaining enemies – least of all with Klaus Fromm? What was the point of continuing hostilities after the war?'

'I can't make what you are telling me add up,' Gunnarstranda interrupted obstinately.

Emmanuel pursed his lips with exasperation. 'And why not?'

'Klaus Fromm was not just anyone. He was part of the German Occupation Forces in Norway. He signed the death certificates of innocent men – in retaliation against your brother's actions. This man was the personification of every man's hatred for the occupying power. Amalie Bruun chose this man. Your brother must have perceived this as offensive.'

'And how can you claim that?'

'It's obvious. She betrayed your brother and instead chose someone who represented everything he was fighting against, everything he put his life at risk to crush. She couldn't have done anything worse to him.'

'And you have the audacity to express an opinion about this?' Emmanuel's eyes were flashing with anger. 'You have the audacity to set yourself up as a judge over two people's love for each other, people you don't know?'

Gunnarstranda sat down and crossed his legs, struggling to keep his composure. 'But am I mistaken in anything I have said?' he asked in a gentler tone. 'Didn't she do what I said? Didn't she choose to marry Klaus Fromm? Wasn't he a judge during the war, in the most hated building in Norway, second only to the Nazi prison, Møllergata 19?'

'Yes,' Emmanuel said. 'She did all that. But does that mean you have a right to judge her?'

'Maybe I don't, but your brother must have felt he had that right.'

Emmanuel stared blankly at the policeman for a few moments. 'You're forgetting that Amalie and Klaus

Fromm loved each other. What do you think they should have done?'

The policeman fell quiet.

'Should she have taken my brother when she loved someone else? Have you ever thought what view of humanity you are defending? Should Amalie Bruun have lived on her own – gone into a nunnery just because she loved a German, a man who was born in the wrong place on the planet?'

'Klaus Fromm was a murderer.'

'No, he was no murderer.' Emmanuel shook his head with vigour. 'My brother was a murderer. Klaus Fromm was a German soldier doing an office job.'

'He was a judge, not an office worker, and he could have chosen different work.'

'Could he? The post in Norway was the job he was given – a job he chose to be near the woman he loved, to whom he was engaged.' Emmanuel leaned forward across the table. 'I understand your frustration. But the world is not always easy to understand. Sometimes things happen as they happen. The marriage between Amalie and Fromm would have been nothing out of the ordinary – had it not been for the war. Fates and dramas such as those Amalie, Fromm and Reidar experienced are enacted all over the world a hundred times every day. But on this occasion it went wrong. It was the war that destroyed Amalie and Fromm and Reidar. You can't blame any of them. There is no dishonour in love. People who fall in love are innocent, whoever they love and for whatever reason they love.'

Gunnarstranda clenched his teeth in annoyance: 'You

say she met Fromm in 1938. At that time Fromm had been a member of the NSDAP for four or five years. I know he has an SS record from at least 1934. The rosy idealized picture you were painting does not stand up. Amalie Bruun was, it is true, seventeen or eighteen when they met, but she threw herself into the arms of a man who in all probability was already a murderer, at the very least an avowed fascist!'

'But are you going to blame this young girl for that?' Emmanuel threw his arms into the air in desperation. 'Even Chamberlain had a naïve view of the German Nazis. And he was the English Prime Minister. How can you demand political awareness from a woman in love – a teenager? In Norway we had a free press and not just that – the general public refused to accept the true nature of the Nazis' aggressive expansionism and demands for Lebensraum in the 1930s. Amalie was a young girl who fell in love with a man; that was all. What do you expect of a teenager? You know that Reidar began his resistance work by printing an illegal newspaper, down at old Hammerborg, don't you? Well, do you know who wrote in that newspaper?'

Emmanuel paused for theatrical effect. 'You don't,' he said in triumph. 'You don't know who clattered away on the typewriter – the King's appeals, news from London – who crept down in the evenings, risking life and limb to write in the rag? You don't know. It was Amalie Bruun. She worked in the German administration, but she was a patriot. She risked her life for her country. It wasn't her bloody fault she was in love with a man who was not my brother!'

Emmanuel banged a clenched fist down on the table and sat gasping for air after his outburst.

Police Inspector Gunnarstranda gazed thoughtfully at the plump man leaning against the table and struggling to wipe away the sweat. 'Well, I'll give you that,' he said. 'I'm sure you're right, and as for what Amalie Bruun and the German felt for each other, it's neither my job nor anyone else's to pass judgement. But I do know that your brother never forgot Amalie Bruun.'

'No one would ever be able to forget Amalie Bruun. I haven't forgotten her either – even though I never had a relationship with the woman. You have to remember one thing,' Emmanuel said with solemnity. 'Amalie was an unusual woman, with regards to both beauty and intelligence. It's not so strange to yearn, is it? What about yourself? I've heard you lost your wife and you're a widower. Don't you yearn?'

'Keep me out of this!' Gunnarstranda snarled.

Emmanuel shook his head gravely. 'Well,' he said. 'Since you're not mature enough on that score, let me give you an instance from the drama of my own life instead. On 4th October 1951 I observed a dark-haired beauty on platform 4 of the old Østbane station. I walked past and we had eye-contact for four seconds. Not a week has gone by since then, not a single week in fifty years, when I haven't thought about the woman – on platform 4 – but I have never seen her again. The memory of the dark-haired woman is one of many instances when I took the wrong decision and allowed fate to lead me astray. I'm sorry, Inspector Gunnarstranda. The fact that my brother still had yearnings for

Amalie Bruun is of no importance. It's neither here nor there.'

'Last time you told me that Reidar was obsessed with ownership.'

'Owning things, not people.'

'Do you think he was always able to distinguish?'

'Yes.'

'I think you're hiding something.'

'Dear Inspector, have you ever heard the expression: let sleeping dogs lie?'

'I know you're holding back a matter of vital importance!'

Emmanuel wiped away more sweat. 'I'm holding back nothing.'

'Yes, you are,' the policeman said. 'The events in this love triangle must have been quite exceptional. Fromm came to Norway in 1940. Reidar was betrayed and fled the country in 1943. Amalie and Fromm got married in the autumn of 1944. In the period from 1940 to 1943 the eternal triangle is played out, a drama which you in your detachment flick onto the floor like a dollop of butter. But what are you actually saying? Yes, you do imply elements of jealousy, lies, grudges, envy, illegal activities, silence, secrets, deception – a whole cauldron of turbulence and passions which according to you stop bubbling and boiling as soon as peace is announced. For me this is totally incomprehensible. But why does it fail to make sense up here?' The policeman tapped his temple and went on to answer his own question: 'Because I have the feeling some information is missing, the information that would allow me to understand what actually happened.

But you were there. You saw them. You talked to them. There's something you're holding back. There's something you know that I don't.'

'Why are you so damned sure?'

'I can sense it.'

'There's nothing.'

'There must be something.'

'The reality of war is surreal at the best of times. You cannot comprehend war with peace as a reference point.'

'Well,' the policeman said, leaning forward in his chair, 'I can accept the story of Amalie's summer love at the end of the thirties. I'll buy the whole of the story about her meeting a virile man who was older, charming, worldly-wise, intelligent and who wielded power. I can understand her falling for him and rejecting the like-aged Reidar of whom she might have had more than enough. I can also understand your brother and feel sympathy for his spurned love. I can see the heavy cross of fate they have to bear. I can even accept that she is caught between two lovers. I know that sort of thing happens: two men fighting over a woman. I can understand Amalie Bruun's unhappiness – in the middle of an irreconcilable conflict – being torn between her love for her husband and loyalty to her country. But then there is this insurmountable hurdle, the mystery of why your brother maintained contact with Klaus Fromm after the war.'

'Klaus Fromm was an editor and newspaper proprietor. He bought the ends of paper rolls that Reidar was given by Norwegian newspapers like . . .'

'I know the story,' Gunnarstranda interrupted curtly.

Emmanuel, bewildered, gaped at him.

'I also know about his receiving stolen goods from a man by the name of Stokmo who smuggled Jews across the border. Some say it was these stolen goods that provided the basis for the business you and your brother lived off.' Gunnarstranda raised a hand in the air to prevent the other man from saying anything. 'Don't say a word,' he added in a frosty tone. 'The case has been shelved anyway. I can see that your guilty conscience makes you wary when an old flatfoot like me comes round digging up your past. I can see that, but I don't accept it. I am not appealing to your moral code now. I am merely asking you to show me respect. You see, I know it cannot be a coincidence that Fromm and your brother maintained their links. You're holding something back.'

Emmanuel raised his hand and placed it on his chest. 'Hand on heart, Inspector. There is nothing in all this business that I'm consciously holding back!'

The policeman scrutinized him – this sweaty, short-winded man with a look of suffering on his face. 'If,' he began. 'If you've told me everything you know, there must be something, some detail that has slipped your mind. Something important.'

'There's nothing. Your phone's ringing.'

Gunnarstranda started. He stuck a hand in his jacket pocket for his mobile phone.

'I've just been to see Eyolf Strømsted's partner,' Frølich said. 'Sjur Flateby. Do you know what he does for a living? He's a vet.'

'So?'

'You should see his patients. While I was in the waiting room, there were two nymph parakeets, a guinea pig and a forest cat with a bitten-off tail.'

Gunnarstranda stood up and grimaced an apology to Emmanuel before going into the hall to speak undisturbed. 'How did it go?'

'He didn't say a word.'

'Did you tell him his partner has been humping Jespersen's widow once a week for three years?'

'Yes, I did, but he's sticking to his story. He and Eyolf were fondling and smooching in bed until late into the night of Friday the 13th. They fell asleep from exhaustion at half past five in the morning.'

'What do you think? Is it lies?'

'No idea. I'm in the dark on this one. I also said that his statement would not be taken into account, but he didn't say anything then either.'

'Did his face drop when you told him about the widow's sex life?'

'Not at all. That's why I'm in the dark. He said he and Eyolf were keen to have freedom in their relationship and all that stuff. They've been living together for just one year. And he's always known about Eyolf and Ingrid Jespersen. He said they were both trying to find themselves. Then he began to talk about men's search for their sexual identity. This was Eyolf's big problem. It was all a bit too glib for my taste.'

'OK,' Gunnarstranda said, ready to finish the conversation.

'There is one more thing,' Frølich interjected.

'Come on then.'

'Someone has broken the seal on the shop door.'

'Which shop?'

'The antiques shop in Thomas Heftyes gate. The seal's broken.'

'Break-in?'

'No, someone had a key. Our police ribbon and seal have gone.'

'I'll meet you there in . . .' Gunnarstranda checked his watch. '. . . In half an hour,' he said and rang off.

Emmanuel's cat had taken his place on the sofa. 'What happened to Amalie after the war?' the policeman asked from the doorway.

'I have no idea.'

'Klaus Fromm was imprisoned after the war. What did his wife do?'

'I have no idea.'

'But that's damned funny – since you know other sides of the story.'

Emmanuel Folke Jespersen shook his head gravely. 'Peace was a happy time – but also chaos. I didn't think about Amalie much after the war. I hadn't given her a thought until you showed me the photo.'

'Once again I think we're moving into an area where you find it convenient to hold back the truth.'

'I have no idea what happened to her. Ask me in court and you'll get the same answer.'

'Have you seen her since then?'

'No. I've seen neither her nor Fromm since 8th May 1945.'

42

Stretched Resources

Gunnarstranda took Drammensveien into town. It was a bad decision. The queue of vehicles was slow-moving. He turned off at Skøyen where the traffic was just as congested. In Bygdøy allé he got stuck behind a bus that spewed out clouds of black diesel exhaust every time it braked. Evening was beginning to draw in. A frozen, stooped figure trudged along the pavement. Further ahead dark silhouettes stood waiting in shelters. Gunnarstranda was twenty minutes late when he turned left into Thomas Heftyes gate. He parked outside the window of the antiques shop, got out and waved to Frølich who came hurrying towards the car.

Gunnarstranda peered round for other police officers. 'Bloody hell,' he said in a low mumble.

'What's up?' Frølich asked nervously.

Gunnarstranda ran his eyes up the dark street.

'What are you looking for?'

'What's up? You can see as well as I can what's up. Not one of our officers is here.'

Frølich shifted feet, ill at ease. 'Hm,' he said. 'You may be right.'

'There's no one here,' Gunnarstranda stated.

'They must be . . .'

'You can see for yourself there's no one here. Hell,' the

Inspector snapped and plunged into his jacket pocket for his mobile phone.

'Who are you ringing?'

Gunnarstranda didn't answer.

Cars were parked on both sides of the road. Three youths ventured out of their local watering hole and stood on the steps shivering in the cold. Gunnarstranda's phone rang for a long time.

'Yes,' Yttergjerde said at the other end, at last.

'There are no officers outside Ingrid Jespersen's place,' Gunnarstranda growled.

'Thought you would ring,' Yttergjerde said.

'Why is there no one here?'

'Orders,' Yttergjerde replied.

'Whose?'

'Chief's. New priority apparently.'

'What are you doing instead?'

'Taxi murder.'

Gunnarstranda rang off. 'You knew,' he said to Frølich.

'Me?'

Gunnarstranda eyed him in silence.

'Of course I knew, but everyone knows you're scrabbling around with this photo of a woman from the war years. As a result it's difficult to make the case that we need someone to keep an eye on Ingrid Jespersen.'

'Has anyone asked you?'

'No.'

'How do you know then?'

'I was told we could keep an eye on her ourselves . . .'

'What do they need all these officers for?' Gunnarstranda interrupted and again stared into space.

'Questioning. All our witnesses have to be questioned about Richard Ekholt's movements.'

Gunnarstranda examined the main door to the shop. 'This seal is fine,' he mumbled, moving to the entrance to the flats. The door to the staircase was unlocked. They stopped in front of the door that led into the shop. The Oslo Police HQ seal had been ripped off and removed. The same applied to the police ribbons across the entrance. They stood contemplating the door for a few seconds. 'Doesn't look as if it has been damaged anyway,' Frølich concluded.

'Who reported this?'

'Aslaug Holmgren. An elderly lady living at the top. She rang Karsten Jespersen wondering whether the shop was going to open since the police had removed their . . . *barriers*.' Frølich made air quotation marks with his fingers, '. . . as she called them. Karsten Jespersen rang me. I came here and found what you see here.'

'You don't think Karsten Jespersen went into his father's shop?'

'Neither he nor Ingrid Jespersen have been in there, they claim.'

'Have you been in?'

'Not yet.' Frølich dug deep in his pockets for a variety of keys. 'I was waiting for you to come.'

He unlocked the door.

The room was dark. They went in. Frølich switched on the light. The shop looked much the same as before except that there were no forensics or crime-scene officers present. Gunnarstranda stood in the doorway watching Frølich open the office door, peep in and prowl around the shop. Frølich peered under the table, behind chairs, glanced at the shop window, thrust his hands into his pockets and turned to Gunnarstranda. 'Doesn't look like anyone has been here,' he concluded calmly. 'My guess is some young lads were up to their tricks.'

Gunnarstranda stood ruminating. 'When were our officers ordered away?'

'Yesterday, I suppose.'

'You don't know?'

'I'm pretty sure it was yesterday.'

Gunnarstranda went on ruminating.

'I've got quite a bit of paperwork to do,' Frølich said, waiting.

Gunnarstranda nodded. 'You go,' he said. 'I need to think.'

When Frølich had gone, he switched off the light in the shop and ambled into the little office. He paused in the doorway for a few seconds contemplating the desk with the ancient, black typewriter and the small radio and the simple hotplate on an old washstand with a marble surface.

Behind the desk was an old wooden swivel chair. He sat down. Beside the typewriter there was a beautiful wine glass covered in engravings. Gunnarstranda took out a roll of plastic gloves from his pocket, put one of the gloves on, then held the glass between his fingers and twirled it. The engravings were of animals: a fox and a hare. A fairy tale, he thought. He put down the glass, leaned forward, placed both elbows on the desk and rested his head on his hands. While sitting and meditating with his eyes half-closed, his eyes roamed from wall to wall: the old washstand, the typewriter, the telephone, the ink pot, the hotplate with the old-fashioned cloth-covered lead. He followed the lead with his eyes. At one end, next to the wall, something caught his attention. There was something glistening beneath the wall-socket.

Gunnarstranda rose to his feet, walked around the desk and knelt down to see better. It was a fragment of glass. He took the glass, stood up and held it to the light. It was a piece of crystal with engraved lines on. He stared at the wine glass on the desk. He bent down and compared the engravings.

The conclusion was obvious: someone had been inside. Someone had used the key to enter the shop. The same person had managed to smash one of two very valuable glasses.

43

The Missing Link

Late that evening there was a knock on Gunnarstranda's office door. It was Yttergjerde.

'I saw the light,' Yttergjerde stammered.

Gunnarstranda swivelled round on his chair. 'Have you got the time to come here?' he commented sarcastically. 'I thought you were working on the taxi case.'

Yttergjerde waved some loose sheets of paper. 'What the heck do you think these are?'

'Claims for overtime?' Gunnarstranda taunted.

'The list of calls from Ekholt's mobile phone.'

Gunnarstranda nodded. 'So you can prove that he rang Frank Frølich now?'

'Yes.'

'And that Frølich rang Ekholt?'

'Yes,' said Yttergjerde.

'Great news,' Frølich grunted from the sofa where he had been sitting reading the latest *Donald Duck* comic.

Gunnarstranda yawned.

'Don't pretend you're not interested in this list,' Yttergjerde sneered and checked the papers. 'There are a helluva lot of calls to a lady who turns out to live in Hegermanns gate . . .'

'Gro Hege Wyller,' Gunnarstranda said. 'You don't need to tell us. We know she didn't ring back.'

'Right,' Yttergjerde said with a grin. 'Like a copy?' He waved the copies.

Gunnarstranda took one. He sat studying the list. 'I know that number,' he muttered to himself, stretching out an arm, lifting up the receiver and tapping in the number.

The other two men watched him. Gunnarstranda recoiled when the answer came. Then he slammed down the phone. It was as though someone had run an electric current through his lean body. The tired figure slumped over the telephone became a bundle of energy and jumped up from the chair. Suddenly Gunnarstranda's sullen face split into a dazzling white smile.

'What happened?' Yttergjerde asked with caution.

'I rang the wrong number.'

'Who did you ring?' Frølich asked.

Gunnarstranda swung round to face him. 'Are you coming?' he asked.

'Where to?'

'National archives.'

Frølich stared at him in amazement. 'You rang the national archives?'

Gunnarstranda shook his smiling head. 'No. But I reckon we will have to ring them. I would guess they are closed.'

Frølich pulled on his military boots. 'But who did you ring?' he asked, grabbing his leather jacket.

'The Hotel Continental.'

It took a few hours to get in after closing time. The librarian assigned to them by the Permanent Secretary could not understand why the visit could not wait until the following morning. He seemed a desiccated old stick and had to confer with his line manager before he would meet them. Where his skin was not frozen or pink, he had red hair and freckles. He had pulled on a grey duffel coat over his striped pyjama bottoms. He drove up in a Ford Sierra with a ski box on the roof and let the engine idle while he unlocked the door and showed them into the library with the micro-fiche readers. It was almost midnight.

It took another half an hour to find the right film.

Frølich was hungry. When Gunnarstranda announced they were going to make an arrest, disappointment was the first thing he felt. An arrest meant he would have to wait – for food. Frølich scratched his beard and tried to work out where the nearest McDonald's was.

'Look,' Gunnarstranda said, straightening up.

Frølich bent down and looked into the machine that was reading the micro-film. He stared at a certificate of some kind. Illegible rounded handwriting. 'What is it?'

'It's a marriage certificate.'

'I can see that. But whose?'

'Amalie Bruun's parents.'

'And that's why we can arrest them? Are you mad?'

'I hope not.' Gunnarstranda was grinning. 'Now I feel like a smoke, Frølich.'

'I feel like something to eat.'

'Start smoking, Frølich, and you'll forget about food.'

'You always feel like smoking. Now come down off your high horse. What is it on that certificate that means we can make an arrest?'

'Have a look,' Gunnarstranda said with a smile.

'I am having a look. Please tell me at what.'

'The bride's maiden name. The name of Amalie Bruun's mother.'

PART THREE

An Eagle in the Hand

44

Awakening

I mustn't wake up, she thought. I want to sleep through until it is morning. As soon as she had formulated the thought she knew she would wake up because this night was quite different from any other. Her eyes closed, she lay rigid beneath the duvet. She was experiencing the worst thing in the world, waking up in the middle of the night, in the silence, alone.

When, at last, she dared to open her eyes, she was looking down at the floor where a strip of yellow light from the next room cut across the parquet and up the wall like a laser beam. She didn't move a muscle. Without making a sound, she tried to breathe evenly and calmly while thinking about the previous time she had woken up like this.

The important thing now was to lie still so that the duvet didn't rustle and she didn't make any noise. Why not? she thought. Because. There is no because, it is just a question of lying still, relaxing and accepting that everything is as it should be. A question of sensing sleep overtake her and then falling into oblivion again, finding release from these terrible hours, release from this loneliness – from being awake and alone in this room, in this bed without Reidar.

As soon as she thought of Reidar, she visualized the

white, lifeless body which was no longer him, which was dead. In death he had been transformed into an empty shell. A mortal frame with no tired, stiff, vain man; no more impenetrable armour. Reidar had developed into a man she feared to tell the truth because he would never accept the truth she asserted, because he always ended up treating her like a little girl. Ingrid Jespersen, fifty-four years old – a little girl.

Without thinking, and without noticing, she let out a sigh of self-pity. But on hearing the sound, she froze.

She had made a noise, and that was what she hadn't wanted to do.

I'm a failure, she thought. It all came out: I'm over fifty, a widow and still a child feeling sorry for herself. But it's not because I live alone; it's because I never managed to live my own life. I needn't have gone out of my way to satisfy others. I could have been myself. I needn't have been frightened. You're much too frightened, she told herself. And you thought Reidar would protect you. Look at you now. How can Reidar protect you now? The fear that was kept at bay by his presence has caught up with you in an instant. Now you are a prisoner of fear, and you will never be free.

Ingrid lay still and knew she was right. She had married Reidar because he gave her security. And now she was caught by the same fear she had fled.

It had been a mistake to choose Reidar. She should have chosen a man of her own age, lived happily and had children.

And now? It's too late. Now I can't have children.
You never wanted children.

No, perhaps I didn't want to have children. But I should have had children anyway. Someone should have forced me. A woman who says she doesn't want children is a child herself. She is not capable of becoming an adult. Look at me now. An ageing body mounted by men out of politeness or charity. I've always walked around like a trophy. I'm an American matron with blue hair. I'm a stork, a bird without the proportions of a bird, the woman who can carry her age with dignity – because I never found out what it was like to grow old. I'm the person young women despise and young men are ashamed of because I use any means at my disposal to keep myself young – which is to deny yourself. In the eyes of others I have no dignity.

A new sound caused her to freeze again.

She was lying on her side with her eyes wide open, staring at the floor and the yellow strip of light.

She was not alone.

The certainty of this began as a light chill across her skin causing nubbles to form. At the same time she felt the hairs on her neck stand up and the chill moved under her skin into her bones. The feeling spread from the small of her back, through her body, and was transformed into a numbing paralysis, draining life from her bones, divesting her arms of power, making her pupils widen and preventing her from breathing.

Slowly she moved her index finger up and down. It functioned. But she couldn't feel the rest of her body. All she could sense was the rush of blood streaming through her veins. She could feel her heart pumping blood around a body that was numb with terror.

She found herself thinking that she could hear regular breathing, and she was aware that the person breathing knew she was lying still and listening.

There was that sound again.

Someone clearing their throat. The sound freed something in her body. She could feel herself tensing up like a cat ready to jump, her legs coiled and her arms ready to launch herself. She didn't do it consciously. Her sole thought was an image of herself fleeing, sprinting across the floor to the front door and liberty. She girded herself. The blood swirled through her head, almost drowning the next thing that happened.

'I can tell you're awake,' a voice said. 'It's about time.'

45

Room 306

It was night. The cold was keeping even the hardiest of night owls indoors.

'I thought it was a bit strange,' Frølich said, stifling a yawn, as Gunnarstranda turned off Parkveien and continued down Drammensveien towards the city centre, 'that they lived the way they did.'

'You met them at the Continental?'

Frølich nodded. 'Temporary accommodation. They were looking at houses, they said. They live out of town.'

'They didn't give their home address?'

'Yes, they did. Tønsberg at that. But I didn't know . . .'

So as not to get caught up in the tramlines, Police Inspector Gunnarstranda parked on the pavement beside the National Theatre. 'Of course not,' he muttered, gazing up at the dark windows of the Hotel Continental before opening the car door and getting out. He stood breathing in the cold night air. Behind him he heard the dull sound of Frølich closing his door. It was cold on the ears and both men were exhaling icy breath. A patrol car crossed Karl Johans gate and drove slowly down Universitetsgate. In contravention of the rules, and cheekily, they switched on the flashing blue lamp when they encountered the traffic lights on red in

Stortingsgata. They turned left and disappeared round the bend by Stortinget.

Gunnarstranda looked across at the entrance to the Hotel Continental. It was a warm glow of welcome in the cold, dark night.

'Ready?' Frølich asked.

Gunnarstranda nodded. 'I'm ready.'

'Let's go then.'

They crossed the street. Frølich stayed downstairs in reception. Gunnarstranda took the lift up to the second floor. Three minutes later he was standing in the narrow corridor on the second floor and waited. Not a sound to be heard from inside. He raised his arm and checked the time. Three minutes later he raised the same arm and knocked. At that moment he heard the telephone ringing inside the room.

It took a while before Frølich's call was answered. Then the door was opened a fraction. The woman who opened it was wearing jogging bottoms and a faded T-shirt.

'Hermann isn't here,' she said, squinting sleepily into the bright corridor light.

'That doesn't matter,' Gunnarstranda said, taking a deep breath. 'It's you I've come to talk to.'

'Me?' She placed a sun-tanned hand against her bosom, her eyes quizzical but also disbelieving.

Gunnarstranda took another deep breath. 'You and I are going to talk about your husband,' he sighed. 'Your husband, his past and in particular his relationship with taxi drivers.'

46

The Masked Questions

'Where?' he asked.

Ingrid Folke Jespersen was sitting up in bed. She could make out the silhouette of a dark figure in the armchair by the window. A head and an upper torso stood out against the darkness outside. It was a man. She tightened the duvet around her body. She wanted to say something, but no sounds emerged.

'Where is it?'

All she could manage was a puzzled shake of the head.

'Where is it?' the man repeated gently. He stood up and, with slow steps, crossed the floor.

Now he's going to do something, she thought.

Light. He switched on the ceiling lamp. The light made her eyes smart. She scrunched them up, but not before she had seen that the man had a balaclava over his face, with holes for eyes and mouth. He looked like a bank robber. And he was holding a large knife in his right hand. The steel blade glistened.

'Where have you hidden it?' said the lips behind the woollen mask as the figure casually leant against the wall.

'Who are you?' she managed to whisper.

The lips behind the mask smiled. 'What have you done with it?'

She sat with the duvet wrapped around her.

The man took two steps forward. The hand with the knife hung against his thigh. He slowly moved towards the bed. There was a strong smell of scent.

The knife gleamed. She jerked her head back. It banged against the bedrail. There was a burning sensation where the knife scraped against her neck. She forced her head back as far as she could. The edge of the bedhead cut into her neck. The tip of the knife was pressed into her throat. 'Be careful,' she managed to breathe.

'Of course,' the voice said.

She tried to avoid looking at the red lips through the hole in the mask and stared at his eyes. This is turning him on, she thought, not daring to move a muscle.

'I just want to know where it is,' he said, taking hold of the duvet. He held it lightly in his hand. She was squeezing it tight.

'Let go. Let go,' he whispered.

She let go.

He flung the duvet onto the floor. Her nightdress had bunched up around her waist. She closed her eyes in shame. The man ran the tip of the knife down her neck. 'Mousey, mousey,' he said, running the knife across her breasts. 'Come out wherever you are . . .' he whispered and pressed the tip of the knife into her stomach. 'Not there,' he whispered.

'Please,' she breathed.

He ran the knife across her hips. 'Not there . . .'

He scraped the tip across her stomach and throat again.

Then he got to his feet. He stood with his back to her.

She lunged for the duvet.

'Lie still,' he commanded her.

Her stomach hurt. She wanted to get away.

He walked to the window.

He said something, with his back turned.

She tried to force her vocal cords into action.

Again he said something.

'What were you . . .?'

'Where is it?' he asked, spinning round. She saw only his eyes. They were flashing. She tried to pull her night-dress down over her thighs.

'Answer me!'

'I don't understand what you mean.'

He said nothing and glowered at her. She tried to avoid looking at his eyes through the holes of the mask. His eyelashes were grey and rigid. Then he was by her bed. He seized her wrist. The blade glistened in the light from the lamp. At the very moment she felt the skin around her wrist being twisted, she felt a stab of pain in the palm of her hand.

'Do you understand this?' he raged.

Blood coursed down her fingers and wrist.

'Yes,' she whispered, looking down at her hand which was covered with hot blood pouring out of the wound. Numb from the sight, she sat watching the blood flow out until she came to her senses, then wrapped a corner of the duvet around her hand.

'Don't make a mess,' he yelled and grabbed her leg to pull her out of bed. He let go of her ankle and she fell. He tugged at her and pulled her hair. She got to her knees, but stumbled again. She tried to get up and follow him. Once in the bathroom her sole sensation was the underfloor heating.

'Plaster,' he whispered in a panic. 'Where do you keep your first aid things?'

'There.' She pointed to the medicine cupboard beside the mirror.

'But we'll have to wash the cut first,' he whispered and kicked her head first into the shower cabinet. There was a crack as her forehead hit the tiled wall. A second later freezing cold water sprayed down over her body. She coiled up in the corner and screamed. In a flash she saw the blood from her hand mingle with the water and flow towards the drain. The pain shot up her arm as the icy water stung her back. She was unable to breathe normally. And at last the shower stopped. She couldn't stand up. She tensed all her muscles waiting for the boiling hot water, the water that would scald and burn her body. But it didn't come. After a time that seemed like an eternity she opened her eyes, blinked water from her eyelashes and stared at the man standing with his back to her as he rummaged through the cupboard. She dragged herself up.

She drew herself up onto one knee. The thin nightdress was drenched; it stuck to her stomach, her thighs and her breasts. She tried to find support. The glass of the shower cabinet was stained with blood where she had groped for a hold. She sniffed and wiped the mucus off her face with her good hand.

'Please don't make any more mess,' he said, turning round. 'Well, aren't you attractive?' he whispered, licking his red lips. He took a towel and passed it to her.

'Here, dry your face on this.'

She obeyed.

Seconds later he had placed a wad of gauze on her hand and bound it with a bandage. She looked down. But he grabbed her chin and raised it. She shut her eyes.

'Open!' he ordered.

His eyes were pale blue, almost grey. And she recoiled because she had seen those eyes before.

He began to laugh. But she had no energy left for anything except staring.

He snapped his mouth shut, then said: 'Where is it?'

She couldn't stop herself. She began to cry.

At that moment the telephone rang.

47

Discussion

Gunnarstranda first rang at 3.30 a.m. without getting an answer. At 3.56 the unit leader was able to say with certainty that there were people in the flat. A man's and a woman's voices had been identified. At 4.04 the Special Forces unit had their people in position. At 4.10 one of the officers had seen a glimpse of the man through one of the windows in the flat. The man was wearing a mask. Then the unit leader asked Frølich to draw him a map showing the layout of the flat. At 4.18 Gunnarstranda rang for the second time.

They had situated the centre of operations in Fritzners gate. Gunnarstranda was parked on the pavement in Bygdøy allé. In the car beside him sat two men, one the Special Forces leader listening to the conversation. It was blackest night outside.

Gunnarstranda counted eighteen rings before Ingrid Jespersen answered. 'Yes,' she said nervously.

'Police Inspector Gunnarstranda here,' he said.

'It's the middle of the night,' she replied.

'We have reason to believe that there is a Hermann Kirkenær in your flat,' Gunnarstranda said. His feet were freezing. The cold was coming through the car door.

She didn't speak.

'We have reason to believe you are in a hazardous situation.'

'Me?' she said.

'Could you go to a window facing Thomas Heftyes gate so that we can see you?'

There was silence for a few seconds before she spoke. 'I'm still in bed.'

'I can wait until you dress.'

'Why should I?'

'Dear fru Jespersen, answer me the following: Are you alone or is there someone with you?'

She cleared her throat. 'I'm alone.'

'May I speak to the man who is with you in the flat?'

'Don't you believe me? I'm alone.'

'Very well, fru Jespersen. We're coming up and will ring the doorbell. We expect you to let us in so that we can search the flat.'

'No,' she gasped.

'Why not?'

'It's impossible.'

'We have reason to believe that a wanted person is hiding in your flat. I can assure you that we . . .'

'You can't do that,' she interrupted.

Gunnarstranda glanced to his left and exchanged looks with the man listening. The man pulled a face and said something inaudible.

'Well, I think it would be best if you let me talk to Kirkenær,' Gunnarstranda said, unruffled.

This time the silence was a little longer. The sounds suggested a hand held over the receiver.

'He's asleep,' she said on her return.

Gunnarstranda glanced across at the two men in the car. They were grinning at her comment. 'Wake him up,' Gunnarstranda said calmly.

'Just a moment.'

'Hello,' said a man's voice.

The sound of the voice created a buzz of activity in the adjacent car.

'This is Police Inspector Gunnarstranda, Murder Squad. I'm leading the investigation into the killing of Reidar Folke Jespersen,' Gunnarstranda said, and went on: 'It's important that you understand I do not have overall authority in this situation that you have placed yourself. I therefore urge you to follow my instructions. That way we can bring this to a satisfactory conclusion.'

'If you have nothing else to say, I see no reason to continue this conversation,' Kirkenær said, unmoved.

'I know that your grandmother's name was Kirkenær,' Gunnarstranda said. 'I know your mother's name is or was Amalie Bruun. I know you have taken your grandmother's surname.'

Kirkenær coughed. 'You're putting me in a very difficult position.'

'Your position is very simple. Grant Ingrid Jespersen safe conduct out of the building and come out with your hands over your head.'

'Just a moment,' Kirkenær said.

Gunnarstranda exchanged a swift look with the unit leader in the adjacent car. The man motioned him to keep talking.

'Hello,' Gunnarstranda said.

Ingrid Jespersen came back on the line. 'Hello,' she said in a starched tone. 'We're fine here. Please don't disturb us. I invited this man here.'

'Fru Jespersen, leave your flat. That's the only thing you can do to make us call off the action. If you don't come out, there will be very grave long-term consequences, especially for the man with you.'

Another silence.

Kirkenær came to the telephone. 'Ingrid likes it here with me,' he said. 'Shall we say you ring back tomorrow?'

Gunnarstranda watched a policeman slowly releasing the safety catch of his weapon. He said: 'Grant her safe conduct.'

'Your request cannot be complied with,' Kirkenær answered in the same formal tone.

Gunnarstranda watched the armed policeman. He passed by the car where the unit leader was listening on the line and gesticulating.

'Grant her safe conduct.'

'Your request cannot be complied with,' Kirkenær repeated.

Gunnarstranda glanced at the other car. The man listening in gesticulated again.

'I repeat,' Gunnarstranda said, feverishly trying to think of something, 'either you come out with your hands above your head or you allow Ingrid Jespersen safe conduct out of the flat. You have ten minutes. Otherwise the matter is out of my hands. When suspected criminals take hostages, the case is automatically referred to a different department.'

'I'm not taking hostages.'

'The smartest move would be to comply with my request. It will save us a lot of bother, stress and unnecessary emotions.'

Kirkenær chuckled. 'Emotions. I like you, Gunnarstranda.'

'Ingrid Jespersen has gone through enough already. Let her go.'

''Fraid I can't.' Kirkenær sighed. 'The lady is my ticket out of here.'

'She's innocent.'

'She's not innocent,' Kirkenær said with force.

'Her husband was guiltless. Wasn't that so?'

'He was guilty until the day he died.'

'There was a witness who saw you that night,' Gunnarstranda said.

'You're bluffing.'

'No. There was a witness.'

Kirkenær's breathing accelerated. 'Who?'

'A taxi driver by the name of Ekholt.'

Kirkenær sniggered. 'The man's dead. I heard it myself on the radio.'

'But you didn't need to hear it, or read about it,' said Gunnarstranda. 'We know you killed Richard Ekholt. We have proof.'

'You're boring me, policeman.'

'You forgot to take the driver's mobile phone with you. It was in the car where he was found. It tells us as much as Ekholt could have told us if he had been alive. Why do you think I'm here? We've surrounded you, Kirkenær. We've painstakingly slotted in the last pieces of the jigsaw. I have a print-out from Ekholt's mobile phone company which proves you contacted him and he you – all the times too. I know Ekholt was watching you that night. I assume he did something to you he should not have done . . .'

'You're putting me in a worse and worse situation, Gunnarstranda.'

'No, you put yourself in this situation . . .'

'Shut up!'

'It's over now, Kirkenær. Come out. Ingrid Jespersen is innocent.'

'There are a variety of ways of approaching guilt, Gunnarstranda. I suppose, as a policeman, you are used to rationalizing, aren't you?'

'That may well be true, but you . . .'

Kirkenær interrupted: 'But hasn't it occurred to you that if you just use your mind you're constantly operating in relation to dreams and you never find out where you really are?'

Gunnarstranda craned his neck. Men in combat uniforms were running past the cars. A taxi had stopped and half parked on the pavement. The driver was following what was going on with interest.

'That's not how I see my situation, but I understand your reasoning,' he said on the telephone.

'Let's take the opposite case. Some people always have to feel; they're feelings people. Their problem is that by feeling they take in only what happens and never why things happen. Are you with me, Gunnarstranda?'

'I'm with you.'

'Some would say the logical approach is to think first

and feel afterwards. But if you think before you feel, you twist the reality to fit your dreams instead of turning your dreams and thoughts into reality – isn't that true?'

Gunnarstranda manouevred a half-smoked cigarette out of the ashtray and pressed the car-lighter. With the cigarette in his mouth he was unable to answer right away.

'Isn't that right?' Kirkenær yelled.

'Mm, yes, that's right.' Gunnarstranda took out the lighter and lit his cigarette. From the corner of his eye he could see the unit leader grimacing.

'That's why you and I have to choose the fourth method. Feel first, think afterwards: observe, feel and use your instincts to form rational decisions.'

'I'm sure you're right,' Gunnarstranda commented dryly and inhaled. 'But you don't take hostages to give a lecture on philosophy, do you?'

Kirkenær chuckled. 'You see, Gunnarstranda. You've been influenced by the method. You listened to my explanation, took what I said and your other dealings with me into account and then you came to a conclusion.'

Kirkenær continued: 'I don't expect you to understand. But if you had been through what I've been through, you would have known I did the only thing possible.'

'Really?' the policeman said, playing along. In the adjacent car two men were gesticulating to him. 'Murdering Folke Jespersen or the taxi driver who saw you?'

Kirkenær chuckled. 'Don't be so silly. If you continue

like that, I'll put the phone down.'

'But why all the bother, Kirkenær? Why first plan the buy-out, then send the SS uniform and finally put the body in the shop window?'

'He had to be crushed, bit by bit, and to know who was taking revenge on him.'

'But you could have just parked outside the shop and run him down, couldn't you?'

'I wanted to crush him, not kill him.'

'Why put him in the shop window?'

'So that others could see his guilt.'

'Why did you kill him?'

'I didn't kill him.'

'But he died.'

'His death was beyond my control.'

'Why did you come here?'

'To get my revenge.'

'And did you get it?'

'No, I'm getting it now.'

'I repeat,' Gunnarstranda urged. 'Ingrid Jespersen has nothing to do with this case.'

'And what do you know about that? What authority have you got in this matter?'

'You'll have to trust me,' Gunnarstranda said with slow precision. 'If I'm no longer . . .'

'I've wished Reidar Folke Jespersen dead for a long time,' Kirkenær interrupted. 'So long in fact that the dream has an entry in the annals of time. When he did die in the end, I felt no satisfaction at all.'

'There, you see . . .'

'That's why I've come to finish off what was started,'

Kirkenær interrupted.

'You mustn't even think of finishing anything,' Gunnarstranda said hastily with a glance to the left. One of the men in the car was nodding encouragement and pointing to his watch.

'Well,' the Police Inspector went on, 'the reason I've been on your heels is that you don't have the right to take the lives of others, however great the pain leading to the decision.'

The policeman was about to go on, but Kirkenær jumped in first: 'We are speaking two different languages. The morality that you are advocating doesn't interest me, in much the same way as I don't care about the system or machinery of power that you represent.'

'Everyone cares about something.'

'Like what for example?'

'Your mother and father.'

'Folke Jespersen was my father.'

Gunnarstranda was lost for words.

'Didn't you know?' Kirkenær asked.

'It was one of the hypotheses that has led to me sitting here. But has it not occurred to you that it might be a lie?'

'Why would my mother lie?'

'What makes you so sure she didn't? Why did she marry Klaus Fromm?'

The other end went quiet.

Gunnarstranda's mind whirred. He looked to the left and was met by two tense faces. 'You went to the meeting on Friday to let Folke Jespersen see you,' Gunnarstranda said. 'He recognized you. He knew you

446

were his son. He immediately revoked his will and arranged a meeting with your mother . . .'

'My mother's dead,' Kirkenær broke in angrily. 'Why are you trying to blacken my mother's name?'

'On no account would I dream of talking ill of your mother,' the policeman reassured him. 'I'm sure she was an exceptional woman. I believe, for example, that Reidar yearned for her all his life.'

Kirkenær was breathing heavily down the line.

'Did I say something wrong?' the policeman asked.

Silence at the other end for a few seconds. Gunnarstranda stared with growing unease at the telephone. Then, in a dry, staccato voice, Kirkenær began to speak: 'At the crack of dawn on 8th May 1945 Reidar Folke Jespersen kicked in the door to my mother's house and dragged her out of bed. Her husband had been led away after the Germans surrendered and was being held in prison. I was two years old, lying in a cot in the same bedroom. But the Norwegian heroes ignored me. It was four o'clock in the morning when Reidar Folke Jespersen and five other men drove my mother out of town to a lay-by in Maridalen. There they cut off her hair. My mother described it to me, several times. There were six of them. Three of them raped her, one after the other. Two held her down and one – I'm sure you can guess who – stood watching. Afterwards she was left to get back to town on her own, wearing a torn nightdress and with a shorn head. Her child was alone in an empty, ravaged flat in Oslo. It was a hike of almost ten kilometres. And every time she met people on the road, she was given a blow to the back or they spat in her face. But she walked tall. She was bleeding down below, her body was soiled by the sperm of unknown men, there were cuts all over her face and body, but she marched the ten kilometres back to town with a straight back, because she had no intention of accepting, she had no intention of using the same human concepts of guilt. Her love was defined as treason. As a woman she had broken her oath of allegiance to Norway during the German occupation; she had given her love and her body to a German soldier. Thus she had insulted her country and those who were insulted presumed the right to beat her with sticks, spit at her, defile her and humiliate her.'

'I understand both your mother's and your father's feelings in this matter,' Gunnarstranda began when Kirkenær paused.

'Thank you, but you are in no position to understand,' Kirkenær interrupted again. 'Historical facts have two sides. Even the mob had feelings of honour at that time. Distinctions were made between people. Distinctions were made between those who lived in and out of wedlock. Women who were married to Germans and had children were transported out of the country, to Germany. But my mother never received this protection. Why not? Right. Because of Reidar Folke Jespersen. He could have turned a blind eye; he could have even used his influence to give me and my mother protection. After all, her husband was in prison.'

'Don't you think your father received his punishment when he found out you were his son and that he had . . .'

'You understand nothing, Gunnarstranda. These weren't anonymous men drunk on the intoxicating air of liberation who humiliated my mother. This was Reidar Folke Jespersen, the war hero, who came home to find his sex object taken by the occupying forces. For him it was not enough to win the war. He also had to destroy my mother. For him the war was not over until she was dead and publicly stigmatized.'

'But he didn't take her life, did he?'

'She died by her own hand when I was twelve years old. The doctors treating her diagnosed her illness as a psychosis. But they didn't know what I know. My mother was taken from me and killed on 8th May 1945. The person who should be blamed, Reidar Folke Jespersen, is dead now and is therefore no longer burdened with guilt.'

'What are you going to do now?' the policeman asked with dread.

'I'm going to finish off what I started. I want to take my revenge.'

'I can't allow you to do that.'

'I'm already beyond your authority. You can't do anything, nothing at all.'

'You're forgetting that your actions affect others apart from you.'

Kirkenær fell quiet, and Gunnarstranda went on: 'I'm here because I've been talking to your wife, Iselin. I've just come from her now. She is clearly innocent. Do not cause her any suffering. I'm asking you at least to take her into account. For the last time I demand that you come out with your hands above your head.' Gunnarstranda looked to his left. The unit leader had opened the door and got out of the car. He had had enough of listening to the conversation. He was leaning against the car door and giving orders over the radio. 'If you don't, you will be talking to someone else,' Gunnarstranda sighed. But Kirkenær had already rung off.

48

Postlude

Police Inspector Gunnarstranda looked very tired and drawn as he parked in the drive to Tove's house in Sæter. A stranger in a blue dressing gown opened the front door when he rang. She stared at him in confusion. He went in and walked past her. He continued up the stairs to the first floor. He paused because he could feel he was being observed. When he turned round, the woman in the dressing gown darted out of sight. Whispering voices came from downstairs as he put a hand on the door to Tove's flat. It wasn't locked.

He stood with his back against the same door and met Tove's gaze from the armchair. Slowly she lowered the book she had been reading until it was in her lap.

'Aren't you asleep?' he asked, looking at his watch.

She rose to her feet. 'No, I was listening to the radio.'

He nodded and hung up his coat and jacket.

'Didn't you want to be there?' she asked.

'No,' he said, rubbing his face with both hands. 'Police raids and guns are not my thing.'

'They were saying on the radio . . .' she began.

'Yes,' he broke in. 'I heard. He was shot.'

Tove observed him and said nothing.

Gunnarstranda slumped down onto a low sofa by the window and rolled himself a cigarette.

Tove Granaas went to a corner cabinet beside the front door. It was brown and very old with small doors. She took out a bottle of whisky. 'You need a dram,' she said, filling a glass and passing it to him.

'Have you got to go to work?' he asked.

She filled her glass, then looked at her watch. 'In two hours.'

He took a sip.

'Now you can tell me,' she said.

Gunnarstranda sat staring at his unlit cigarette. 'He sent his stepfather's uniform to Jespersen through the post. As a warning, or a threat, I suppose. The idea must have been to conjure up Klaus Fromm's ghost. But unfortunately for poor Kirkenær it wasn't Reidar who opened the parcel. His son, Karsten, did. The next step in the planned murder was to appear in front of his real father. To appear in the flesh – to be Nemesis in person. And that must have gone as planned. Reidar must have known that Amalie Bruun's son was his child, but he obviously thought that the boy didn't know. The Friday reunion went off as planned. Reidar recognized his son. That's the only explanation for him bringing forward the appointment with Amalie's lookalike that afternoon. And it also explains why he rang the solicitor and revoked his will – he had realized that Kirkenær knew and he would have to consider a further beneficiary. It also explains why he torpedoed the sale of the shop and agreed to a meeting with Hermann Kirkenær that same night without a murmur. For Kirkenær this was the third and decisive confrontation – a private meeting. Late Friday night the prodigal son returned. The two of them met downstairs in the shop, and revenge took its course.'

'Revenge for what?'

'His own wretched life.'

'His life?'

'Reidar committed a brutal assault on Kirkenær's mother when peace was declared. His mother suffered from depression as a result and committed suicide some years later. Kirkenær was a war child without a home country, without a mother and father.' Gunnarstranda gazed into the distance. 'I don't think I have the energy for this roll-up,' he said and put it on the table.

'Has he confessed?'

Gunnarstranda raised his head. 'No.'

The policeman sat rapt in thought. 'After killing his real father he must have put on his stepfather's uniform and put his blood-stained clothes in the box. Then he took the keys from Reidar's pockets and went to the flat . . .' Gunnarstranda paused.

'Why did he break into Ingrid Jespersen's flat now, so long afterwards?' Tove asked.

A thoughtful expression crossed Gunnarstranda's face. 'He said he was going to extract his revenge, but I don't understand why he wasn't already satisfied. If I have anything to reproach myself for, it is because I did-n't press him harder on that point.'

'He didn't say why?'

'Not directly.'

'Did he want to hurt her?'

'It was a more grandiose plan than that. *I want my revenge*, he said. But he didn't say what he was aveng-ing, apart from his mother's suicide. It's a bit odd, though, that stabbing his father wasn't enough for him. Ingrid Jespersen had nothing to do with what happened to his mother. What would he be avenging by hurting her?'

'An eye for an eye, a tooth for a tooth,' Tove suggested.

Gunnarstranda sighed: 'But he had his revenge when the old boy lay dead on the floor, didn't he?'

'Where did Kirkenær go in the years after the war?' Tove asked.

'Fromm went to Paraguay after the war, as lots of the top German Nazis did. He set up a newspaper.'

'Amalie and the child?'

'According to Iselin Varås, Kirkenær's wife, Kirkenær grew up in Paraguay, Germany and Norway.'

'In Norway?'

'Yes, Amalie's mother was from Tønsberg – the Kirkenær family.'

The policeman's mobile phone hummed in the pocket of his coat in the hall.

Gunnarstranda struggled to his feet. He exchanged looks with Tove as he took out the phone. 'Please be brief,' he said with a yawn.

'Kirkenær will live,' Frølich informed him. 'His condition is stable and he's out of danger.'

'Well, that's something.'

'Do you think we've got our man, boss?'

'We'll have to hope so. Why's that?'

'Well, after the hostage drama went out on radio, a witness came forward and said he wanted to change his statement.'

49

Rorschach

Frank Frølich sat down in front of the computer screen and watched *Heat* on DVD – the long sequence where Val Kilmer and Robert de Niro shoot their way out of a police trap like commandos while Al Pacino, the cop, runs like a lame goat firing single shots from his automatic. He had the same feeling he always did when he watched the film; it had nothing to do with him not liking Pacino, but alongside de Niro and Kilmer he wasn't cool enough. At the same time it irritated Frølich that he supported the crooks every time he saw the film. He should have been writing a report on his interviews with Sjur Flateby and others, but he wasn't in the mood, and since he wouldn't be able to go home for another couple of hours yet, he made use of the computer's DVD player to give him the requisite sense of relaxation.

Something in the atmosphere made him lift his head and glance towards the door. Gunnarstranda was standing in the doorway. Frølich paused the film. He shoved back his chair, away from the computer table.

'There's light at the end of the tunnel, Frølich.'

Frølich didn't answer.

'Ingrid Jespersen says Kirkenær was searching for something.'

'In her flat? What?'

'I have a suspicion I know what,' Gunnarstranda murmured. 'But it might take an hour or two,' he went on. 'We need a scanner and a good photo-editing program.'

Frølich stood up.

'This,' Gunnarstranda said, showing him the photograph of a German soirée towards the end of the war. 'The first time I saw this I knew there was something familiar about it.'

'A face?' Frølich suggested.

'Maybe. At any rate, there is something in this photo that a voice inside me tells me I should subject to a closer examination.'

Two hours later Frølich had scanned in four photographs of a German party at Brydevilla during the war. He had printed them several times, rotated them on the screen, made them brighter, darker, improved the contrast and magnified them.

'I can see it's the same woman,' Frølich said, pointing to Amalie Bruun. 'But what do you actually want me to do with this?'

Gunnarstranda didn't answer straight away. He sat looking at the original photograph which showed Klaus Fromm in uniform, chatting casually to an unidentified person on a sofa.

'I want you to magnify it one more time.'

'To check out the lady?'

'All of them. I want to have a closer look at the men,' Gunnarstranda explained, chewing his lower lip in consternation. 'Him in particular,' he added, pointing to Fromm.

A further hour later they sat with a pile of prints in

front of them. Some looked like non-figurative shadow painting and experimental art. Black mists and grey hues gave way to white expanses with scattered, tiny, black dots.

'Reminds me of the Rorschach test,' Frølich said.

'Hm,' Gunnarstranda brooded.

'That's those inkblots forensic psychiatrists show their clients. They show one of these blots and if the guy thinks it looks like Queen Elizabeth's genitals, then he has got long-term impaired mental faculties and gets off.'

'Exactly,' Gunnarstranda said, miles away.

'The test's called Rorschach after some Swiss guy, I think . . .'

'Him,' Gunnarstranda exclaimed, pointing to Klaus Fromm again. 'I want you to enlarge this fellow, as sharp as possible.'

'What's the point? All you can see is grey porridge and inkblots.'

'Try anyway.'

'Ten more times,' Frølich said and moved the mouse up and across the image of Fromm.

'Stop there,' Gunnarstranda said, excited. 'Back.'

'What is it?'

'Back, slowly.'

Frølich obeyed. They saw an X-ray like silhouette of the man's shoes, trousers, his hands resting on his lap. 'There, yes,' said Gunnarstranda.

Frølich was lost. They were looking at a mass of grey with dark shadows.

'Can you enlarge it any more?'

'I'll try.'

The Windows hour-glass stayed on the screen until the greyish black mass of indefinable contours returned.

'Yes!' Gunnarstranda said in a reverential whisper. He was shaking with excitement. He almost dropped the lighter as he lit his roll-up. 'Look,' he whispered, pointing to the screen.

'I can't see anything.'

'Yes, you can.'

'But what am I supposed to be looking at?'

'At the picture.' Gunnarstranda held a quivering finger in front of one of the dark patches on the screen. 'Look at that, the medal. Can you remember seeing it before?'

'No.'

'Have a closer look.'

Frølich stared. 'I give up,' he said at length.

Gunnarstranda beamed. 'So near and yet so far,' he teased, not without arrogance. 'Print out what's on the screen anyway.'

Frølich obeyed.

Gunnarstranda stood up and held the paper as it slowly hummed its way out of the printer.

'So, what do we do now?' Frølich asked.

Gunnarstranda waved the print-out. 'Aren't you curious?'

Frølich gave a measured nod.

'If you have the inclination, and if you think you have the time, you can join me.'

'Where?'

'By the pot of gold at the end of the rainbow.'

50

The Boy, the Dog and the Wasps

He was running. The car went into a skid. Past him. The boy couldn't stop, couldn't turn round. The car skidded round and blocked his way. The driver's door was thrust open. Out jumped a young soldier with a grin. In his hands he was holding a machine gun. He smiled as he took aim. He smiled as he fired. The boy heard the bullets a hundredth of a second before the salvo rang out. By then he had thrown himself to the side. He rolled down the slope. Knowing he hadn't been hit. Sharp stones tore open his anorak and made his back bleed. Behind him he heard the soldier, and a dog was barking. He crawled through a thorn thicket. It hurt as the thorns scratched his face and hands. He lay on his stomach behind and under an almost impenetrable mesh of thorny branches. His heart was pounding. He could hear the pounding inside his ears. The dog came down the slope wagging its tail. It was an Alsatian. It was sniffing and whining. And running round in circles. It started digging with its front paws. Then suddenly it jerked back and let out a loud whimper. It growled and made snapping movements in the air. The leaves rustled. Gravel and pebbles rolled down the slope. The outline of the soldier filled out behind the thicket. The boy held his breath. The dog went on its knees with a plaintive squeal. The man with the machine gun turned and stared right at the place where the boy was hiding. The dog fell on to its side. The soldier raised his gun and took aim. The gun barrel moved slowly from right to left. The soldier shouted at the dog, which was emitting low whimpers. The soldier spun round, ran over to the dog and cursed. A swarm of insects was buzzing around the dog. They were pouring out of a hole in the ground like a gush of water from an underground spring. At that moment the boy felt the first wasp sting on his face. The pain was intense and it burned. He clenched his teeth so that he didn't make a sound. The soldier took three steps back from the dog and swore. He pointed the machine gun at the dog and fired. The volley was deafening. The dog's body shook. The boy felt sick. The wasps were crawling over his face. Light, ticklish wasp feet walking over his lips, his eyelids. He opened his eyes for an instant. A horde of wasps was stinging him again and again through his anorak sleeve. The soldier with the machine gun waved his free arm to chase the wasps away.

Another wasp stung the boy on the neck. The pain was so great that he let out a half-stifled sound from his mouth. The soldier immediately froze – and listened. The boy breathed through his open mouth. He breathed in a wasp and crushed it between his teeth. The gun barrel went from bush to bush. Suddenly the soldier cursed out loud and grabbed his cheek. The wasps were attacking the soldier, who let off another volley into the air, then retreated up the slope. The boy instantly crawled out. He brushed the wasps off him and again was stung in the neck. He gasped with the pain. Wasps were all over his

bare hands. They stung him. He cut himself on the sharp
stones. His whole body ached. He wriggled his way
under the branches and away, out of danger from the
insects. But the soldier was still standing up there some-
where. He and the others. They were longing to get back
to their bunks. The sooner they shot him, the sooner they
would be able to get some sleep, food and cigarettes.
They hated him. No. They didn't hate him. But he
annoyed them. His being alive made them angry.

Karsten Jespersen paused in the story. It was a natural
place to pause. Benjamin was looking at him with big
eyes. He had both arms round his little giraffe and all of
its neck in his mouth. Benjamin was waiting for the next
part. But at this point in the story most of the excitement
was over and Karsten was not sure how to go on.

He wondered why, and formulated an answer in his
mind. His story was about *the boy*, with no specific char-
acteristics, but the boy had been a young man. In fact
the story had been about his father – Reidar Folke
Jespersen.

What really happened was that the young man had
escaped from the soldiers and run across bogs and
heathland until he came across a smallholding surrounded by trees, a smallholding where there lived a
young logger of his age who helped Reidar to get safely
across the border into Sweden. It was easy enough to
make the escape exciting, but Karsten was more interested in allowing himself a few literary liberties. He was
planning to add another part about desperate refugees
being led across the border by Harry Stokmo. A group
of wretched figures between trees listening to twigs

cracking, and creeping under cover while trying to prevent their children from coughing or tiny sobs from escaping – and then it would turn out that it wasn't a patrol cracking twigs underfoot but the little boy crawling out from under the brush.

Karsten thought that with a small child as the protagonist the story would be timeless and universal. It would catch Benjamin's imagination, he thought. The story didn't need to be about the 1940–45 war in Norway, it could just as easily be a modern war, in Kosovo for example.

Karsten hoped that Benjamin would identify with the boy in the bushes – as Karsten had done when he was first told the story, imagining himself behind the bushes with the Alsatian sniffing around a few metres from him. It was now, at this very moment, while reflecting on the first action in the story that Karsten became a little unsure of himself. He remembered that he had been told the story by his father, as a first-person narrative. But he also remembered how he had identified with it. This fact, that he had enjoyed the story to the full even though it had been a first-person narrative, told by his father, rendered him pensive, distant. At this moment, while his gentle fatherly eyes rested on Benjamin's engrossed, impatient features, he realized that his edited story was not just unnecessary, it was also a little suspect. There had to be a deeper psychological *motive* for him to edit the story, he began to think. And he had palpably concealed his father's role. At some point in Benjamin's life he would be bound to realize that the protagonist of the story was his own grandfather. Then the natural response would be to ask himself why his own father would conceal this fact from him. Benjamin would wonder about his father's, Karsten's, motives in concealing the truth. And it wouldn't be long before he found an answer. He might not find the correct answer, the one Karsten considered to be correct, that the story had been edited *to give it a literary lift*. Benjamin might find other answers – for example that Karsten changed the story in order to sweep the truth under the carpet. Perhaps Benjamin would think that Karsten begrudged his father the hero's role. At this moment while Benjamin was waiting with bated breath for him to go on, Karsten had felt ashamed and fallen into a trance. And he didn't snap out of it until little Benjamin started shifting in his bed with unease. Karsten found himself sitting beside him with a distorted expression on his face.

'Daddy,' Benjamin said, impatiently waiting for him to go on. 'More.'

Karsten gave a start. 'It's late,' he said and got up. The curtain in front of the window was illuminated by a car coming up the drive. He went to the window and looked out. The headlamps blinded him, like two evil eyes, he thought, as the car parked a few metres from him and the lights were switched off. The evil gaze of two eyes hung on his retina as he watched the car doors open. The letters on the car door were unmistakeable. He read POLITI and it was like a déjà-vu experience. It reminded him of something he had dreamed. *They're coming*, he thought. He listened to Benjamin's congested breathing and watched two dark silhouettes coming towards the window. *They're coming to take me away.*

51

Divide and Rule

After Frølich had parked the car, they sat looking up at the windows in Ingrid Jespersen's flat. 'Third from the left,' Frølich said. 'There's a hole in the glass.'

'I can't see anything,' Gunnarstranda said.

'A single shot,' Frølich said. 'A round hole in the pane. Those boys are pretty good.'

'And her?'

'They had to sew up her hand. Five stitches.'

Gunnarstranda nodded towards the building on the other side of the street. 'There they are.'

Ingrid Folke Jespersen and Eyolf Strømsted walked out of the front door. They went over to a brown Opel Omega parked on the opposite side. Ingrid started the car while Eyolf waited in the passenger seat. Ingrid got out and scraped the ice off the windscreen when the engine was running. She scraped with her left hand. The other one was swathed in a bandage.

The two detectives stepped out.

'Oh, hello,' Ingrid said on catching sight of them.

'Have you got five minutes?' Frølich asked.

She looked at her watch with a frown.

'It'll be very quick,' Frølich said.

The passenger door opened and Eyolf Strømsted showed his curly head.

'Just stay inside,' Gunnarstranda said quickly. 'We need to have a few words with fru Jespersen.'

'Here?' she asked.

Frølich motioned towards the police car.

Gunnarstranda opened the rear door for her to take a seat and he sat next to her. Frølich took a seat behind the steering wheel. Some people on the pavement were huddled together. The engine of the Opel opposite them was running. Eyolf Strømsted was sitting with his head facing the front.

'That wasn't very nice,' she said.

'What's that?' Gunnarstranda asked.

'Being bundled into a police car like that. Look at the neighbours.' She pointed to two middle-aged women who had stopped to stare at the police car. 'I hope you know what you're doing.'

'Have you any reason to doubt us?'

'No . . .'

'There are a couple of untidy details,' Gunnarstranda said. 'About the course of events on the night your husband was killed.'

'I have nothing to add,' she said coolly.

'We haven't managed to get a statement from Hermann Kirkenær yet.'

'I suppose not.'

'He's in a coma.'

'So I understand.'

'Did he say anything to you about the night your husband was killed?'

'Nothing at all. I'd rather not . . .'

'We've spoken to his wife, Iselin Varås,' Gunnarstranda interrupted. 'She says Kirkenær left the Hotel Continental between one and half past one in the morning. He returned to the hotel at the latest at three with a uniform packed in a box, which proves that he had been to the shop to pick it up.'

He paused to let the words sink in.

'Is that enough proof?' she asked after a while.

'There are a couple of things we can't quite get to add up,' Gunnarstranda said, and turned to Frølich: 'Could you start the engine and get the heating going?'

Frølich obeyed. He stepped hard on the accelerator.

The curly head in the Opel opposite peered nervously in the direction of the police car.

'What things?' Ingrid asked stiffly.

'Well, Kirkenær returning home with the uniform in a box.'

'Mm. And what's strange about that?'

'Well, we were working on the theory that Kirkenær killed your husband and got his clothes covered in blood. Since he couldn't go out onto the streets with bloodstained clothing, we thought he had put on the uniform which he had conveniently sent to the shop beforehand. Afterwards he had packed his own clothes in the box where the uniform had been. But that doesn't tally with Kirkenær returning home with clean clothes and a clean uniform in a box.'

'Why do you believe everything the woman says? It's obvious she would protect her husband.'

'Of course, except that she knows nothing about her husband's real and much closer relationship with your late husband. But you can rely on us. We have seized the

466

box, the uniform and the clothes. No one would have been happier than me if we had found blood on these items. The next problem is this damned medal.'

'What medal?'

'The medal that Kirkenær was trying to get off you the night he was shot by the police.'

'Was he looking for a medal?'

'Yes.'

'I didn't understand what he meant. Anyway, he didn't find a medal in my flat.'

'No, he didn't. Because I've got it,' Gunnarstranda said, retrieving a little plastic case containing a bronze medal from his inside pocket. 'Karsten's son, Benjamin, was playing with it on the same morning as your husband was found dead.'

'How do you know?'

'Because we – Karsten, Frølich and I – saw him doing it. He even showed it to us.'

Silence in the car.

'Frølich,' Gunnarstranda said.

With difficulty, Frølich turned round.

'Could you go and take a statement from our friend in the other car?'

'Of course,' Frølich said, getting out and closing the door behind him.

The two of them on the back seat contemplated his large body towering over the car while he waited for two cars to pass. Then they watched Frølich cross the street and open the door for Strømsted to get out. The engine was left running. They saw Frølich order Strømsted into the rear and follow him in.

'Really,' said Ingrid Jespersen.

'It'll be interesting to read what he says later,' Gunnarstranda said.

'It's cramped in here,' Eyold Strømsted said with apprehension. He bent forward and stared past Frølich, towards the rear of the police car where Ingrid Jespersen's profile could dimly be seen. The defroster and the heater were on full. An oval patch on the front windscreen had opened up. 'What are you two up to?' Strømsted asked.

'We're taking a new statement from you,' Frølich answered laconically.

'Why's that?'

'Full name?'

'Eyolf Strømsted.'

'Born?'

'Fourth of the fourth, nineteen-fifty-six.'

'Marital status?'

'What are the categories?'

'Married, single, cohabitee.'

'Cohabitee.'

'Address?'

'Jacob Aalls gate 11B.'

'Is it true that you share a property with Sjur Flateby, born on the eleventh of the ninth, nineteen-forty-eight?'

'It is.' Strømsted looked across at the police car from which Ingrid Jespersen was watching them with a pallid face.

'Sjur Flateby has withdrawn his original statement.'

'What?'

Frølich searched through his inside pocket for some folded A4 sheets, which he passed to the other man. 'This is your partner's new statement. Would you be so kind as to read through it?'

Strømsted took the papers. He seemed bewildered.

'Bottom of page two,' Frølich said. He turned over the page and pointed. 'This is the bit that differs from his earlier statement. Sjur Flateby swears that you went out on the evening of Friday 13th January and didn't return until after five in the morning.' Frølich gave the man with the alluring curls a long, hard stare. 'Before,' he continued with a cough. 'Before, you both claimed you were snug at home in front of the TV until one o'clock at night, after which you went to bed and kept each other awake until half past five. What do you say now that you no longer have an alibi?'

'Back to the medal that Kirkenær was searching for,' Gunnarstranda said.

'What about it?'

'Look at it.'

Gunnarstranda passed the medal to Ingrid Jespersen.

'Nazi treasure,' she said, examining it.

'Guess where the boy found it,' the detective said.

She shook her head.

Gunnarstranda pointed to the window of the antiques shop. 'He found it in the shop. Benjamin found it while his father was working in the shop on Friday the 13th. You might remember. In your statement you said you and Karsten were drinking coffee in the office that morning from ten until just past eleven. During this time the boy was drawing and playing on the floor. He told me last night that he had been rummaging through a box containing a uniform. He had pinched this off the uniform.'

They looked at each other. 'So?' Ingrid said at last.

'There were no keys in Reidar's clothes when he was found dead,' Gunnarstranda said.

'Is that so?'

'We thought it strange because he must have let himself in that night.'

'Sounds reasonable,' she said.

'We know that Kirkenær came to the shop on Friday the 13th to meet Reidar. Our theory was that your husband let him in. Then Kirkenær killed him. We thought he wore the uniform so that his blood-stained clothes would not attract attention. We thought he took Reidar's keys after killing him.'

'Didn't he?'

'Oh yes, he took the keys.'

'So, what's the problem?'

'The problem is that stealing the keys is totally illogical.'

Ingrid stared at the policeman. 'Are you claiming . . .?' she said in a stiff tone, and repeated herself: 'Are you claiming the man who broke into my flat in the middle of the night and slashed my hand was sane, logical and in possession of his right mind?' She raised her bandaged hand.

'We assumed,' Gunnarstranda said, undeterred, 'that Kirkenær took the keys from Reidar after killing him, went into your flat, possibly leaving snow on the floor, and dropped the medal from the uniform. However, since Reidar's grandchild found the medal before Reidar was killed, Kirkenær can't have dropped the medal in your flat. Do you agree?'

Ingrid gave him a stern look.

'There are two logical questions which have to be answered here. If Kirkenær didn't drop anything in the flat why did he go back later to look for something? And why did he take Reidar's keys if he didn't need them? There is only one logical answer to the first question. Kirkenær took the uniform with him to remove any traces that might indicate his personal connection with this man. He didn't realize that the medal was missing until long after. But when he did, he knew the medal would be traced back to the war and to him. So it was handy for him to have your husband's keys. He could use the keys to get into the shop and look for the medal. But the answer to the second question is still problematic. Why did he take the keys when he couldn't know that he would need them? Can you recall that the seal we had put on the shop door was broken?' Gunnarstranda asked. He went on: 'The seal had disappeared but the door hadn't been opened. I went into the shop and found some fragments of a broken wine glass. But our officers had this glass down in the records as intact after the murder. So someone must have removed the seal after the murder and gone into the shop, then smashed the glass by accident. I think it was Kirkenær. He had your husband's keys and searched for the medal in two stages. First of all he unlocked the shop and searched it without success. In his confusion he knocked a glass off the desk. The next night he returned. And he broke into your flat. But why would he do that? He couldn't have guessed that the medal was there. The medal could have been at the bottom of the harbour as far as he knew. It could have been anywhere.'

He paused. She was looking away.

Neither of them said anything. On the other side of the street Frølich and Strømsted were involved in a discussion of the heated variety. Strømsted was gesticulating.

'Don't you think he was looking for the medal?'

'Yes, I do. But I believe he was after something else, something more important than finding the medal. I think he had a very special reason for stealing the keys off your husband. The medal was a secondary matter.'

She coughed. 'He was unhinged,' she said. 'He wanted to kill me.'

'Correct,' Gunnarstranda said brightly.

'Correct? What do you mean?'

The detective smiled. 'Haven't you guessed? The only logical explanation for Kirkenær stealing the keys from Reidar's clothes was to take his revenge. He wanted to hurt or kill the person who was close to Reidar. He wanted to hurt or kill you. And for that reason he wanted access to your flat. That was why he stole the keys.'

'At least we both agree on that,' she said nervously, peeking at the Opel. 'The man's unhinged.'

'No, he isn't,' Gunnarstranda said with a smile.

'No?'

'He wanted to kill you, not because he's crazy but because he had been deprived of the opportunity to kill

472

your husband. He had been planning the murder of your husband for months . . .' Gunnarstranda was interrupted by the ringing of his mobile phone. 'Yes?' he said.

'Strømsted refuses to make a statement until he has consulted his solicitor,' Frølich said into his ear. 'What do I do?'

'Arrest him,' Gunnarstranda said. 'I'll have a car sent.'

After ringing off he bent forward and took the radio from between the two seats. 'Your paramour on the other side of the street has just confessed that he visited you on the night your husband died,' Gunnarstranda said to Ingrid. 'So it looks as if you may have to give your third version of what happened that night.'

Ingrid grabbed his arm. 'Please don't take everything from me,' she whispered through rigid lips.

Gunnarstranda sat up to his full height and looked her in the eyes. 'Why are you frightened of telling the truth?' he asked in a gentle tone. 'We know Kirkenær came here that Friday night. We know he found the front door open, unlocked. We know he went into the stairwell and found the shop door unlocked. We know Kirkenær had one motive for coming here. He wanted to kill your husband. But he couldn't have done it. It wasn't him.'

'Why are you so sure?'

'Because your husband was already dead! Hermann Kirkenær found your husband dead on the floor. Since he was already dead all he could do was expose the body to public humiliation. Kirkenær stripped the dead man and dragged him to the shop window. We also know that he was seen doing that. There was an eye-witness.'

'An eye-witness?'

'Yes.'

Ingrid Jespersen opened and closed her mouth.

Gunnarstranda smiled like a fox smelling meat through an open pantry door: 'If the uniform jacket and trousers in the shop were not used to cover the trail of blood that night – how did the killer conceal the blood on his clothes and body?'

He looked straight into her eyes. 'I know the answer,' he said. 'And you know the answer.'

The silence persisted until Gunnarstranda cleared his throat: 'I've just asked Frank Frølich to arrest Eyolf Strømsted on a charge of murder. Do you really want to be charged with being an accessory?'

'It was almost three in the morning,' she said in the same monotone as before. 'I had rung Susanne and Karsten in total panic. Afterwards I heard steps on the stairs. A ring on the bell. It was Eyolf.' She went quiet.

Gunnarstranda coughed and stared at the front of the building, towards which he was beginning to feel a strong aversion.

'He looked terrible,' she started, wringing her hands.

'Blood?'

'Yes.'

'Go on.'

'Reidar's blood.'

'Go on!'

'He undressed and had a shower. I put his clothes in the washing machine.' She took a deep breath. 'Not everything came out clean, so he borrowed some of Reidar's things before leaving.'

'What did you do with the clothes that weren't clean?'

'I put them on the fire.'

Gunnarstranda turned his gaze onto the car where Eyolf Strømsted was keeping Frølich company. Strømsted's eyes had a hunted, fearful look. 'I think he knows you've spilt the beans,' he said, addressing her.

'I don't want to see,' she said.

'Why did he kill your husband?'

'He said he hadn't meant to.'

'What did you do while his clothes were in the washing machine?'

'Nothing.'

'When did he leave?'

'At about five.'

'Two hours without doing anything at all?'

'We talked.'

'What was your story for the police?'

'I would go down and see what had happened when it was light. Otherwise I would stick to the truth. But I didn't even manage to do that. The police arrived before dawn.'

'The body was seen by a newspaper girl because Kirkenær had put it in the shop window,' Gunnarstranda said. 'What did you think then? When your husband had been put in the shop window and was not lying on the floor as Strømsted had said?'

'I thought Eyolf had lied to me. I thought he had put the body in the window. Eyolf thought I had done it. He thought I had my own plans and was manipulating him. That was why he told your assistant that Reidar had rung us on the Friday. He wanted to punish me, in the same way as I wanted to punish him. We were wrong, both of us. Of course it was this crazy man who made a spectacle of poor Reidar. But we couldn't know that.'

52

Credits

'Would you believe me if I said it was his own fault?'
said Eyolf Strømsted.

'Probably not.'

'If I said I hadn't meant to kill him? Would you believe
that?'

'Of course.'

'With no objections?'

'Murder is rarely intentional.'

'What about if I said it was an accident?'

'That's more difficult, but it's no secret that accidents
have an easier passage,' Gunnarstranda answered.
'Death by misadventure is cheap for the state and it
helps us to sustain a belief in the essential goodness of
mankind. But don't make too much of it. I would advise
you to stick to the truth. Leave the legal side of things to
those who understand it.'

'He rang me and said he wanted to meet,' Strømsted
said.

'When?'

'He rang some time before midnight. Half past eleven,
I think. He insisted I went there as soon as possible.'

'Why did you agree?'

'Out of concern for Ingrid. She had been very dis-
tressed earlier in the day, after her husband's call – at my

place. So I put on a jacket and went. The door to the stairwell was open and he met me on the ground floor. We entered the shop. He started talking about my responsibilities towards Ingrid. He asked me if I was prepared to marry her. I asked if he would get divorced, but then he began to laugh. *I'm going to die*, he said and went on talking about Ingrid as if she were a little child. *It's important that you take care of her when I'm gone*, he said. I asked where she was. He said she was asleep in bed in the flat above us. He had just been in to see her. *The simplest thing would be if you killed me*, he said with this weird laugh. *Why do you think you're going to die?* I asked. He didn't answer. *Why?* I persisted. *Because death has finally caught up with me*, he said. Then he passed me the bayonet.

'I can't remember taking it. But I remember looking at it. I couldn't take my eyes off it. While he was talking about all those he had killed during the war and while he went into detail about the convulsions people suffered as life ebbed away – all that time I was staring at the black steel. I remember thinking about how elegantly it had been formed, how such a gruesome, evil intention had been moulded into an object. He said he wasn't afraid to die. I think he asked me if I would do him the favour of killing him. I don't know if I answered him. I think I did – I refused. I don't remember because I couldn't take my eyes off the blade.

'When I did, everything had gone quiet. But it was too late. I looked up. Something had happened to his eyes. I have never seen anything like it. As if he had snapped. *Prove it,* he shouted and threw himself on the bayonet.'

Strømsted raised his head.

'And that was it?'

Strømsted flashed a hollow smile. 'That was it? I didn't have a chance. I was standing in his little office, leaning against the wall, when he rushed headlong at me. I felt the steel sinking into his flesh. He put both arms round me, held on tight as his body quivered. We slid down the office wall. He was lying on top of me and kicking with his legs. Blood was spurting out. I had blood over my face, my hair and neck. It was running down the inside of my sweater. And you sit there and ask if that was it?'

'Were you holding the bayonet?'

'Of course I was. But this is the incomprehensible part. I can't recall it moving from his hand into mine.'

'What did you do afterwards?'

'I can remember freeing myself.'

'In the office?'

'After he finally stopped jerking. I rolled over towards the door.'

'Was the light on in the shop?'

'No, just in the office.'

'What happened next?'

'I remember standing there with the bayonet in my hand and looking down at myself. The old man was dead, that much was obvious. He face was white and his mouth wide open. I felt dreadful – warm blood inside my clothes – and looked dreadful. Don't remember what I was thinking, but I wiped down everything I had been near when I was in the office. Afterwards I went up to Ingrid's flat and rang the bell.'

'Did she open the door?'

'Yes. I told her what had happened.'

'What did you do?'

'I had a shower while she washed my clothes. We dried them in her tumble-dryer.'

'How long were you there?'

'Until five.'

'And then?'

'Then I went home.'

'Did you at any point consider calling the police or turning yourself in?'

'Yes.'

'Why didn't you?'

'We agreed it would be best not to.'

'Who agreed?'

'Well, it was my decision.'

'Why?'

'Friends, lots of people, knew about the incident earlier that Friday, his phone call when Ingrid and I were in bed. I told Sjur, as a joke, because it was funny. I know Sjur had told it to many more people. The phone call was already a good story doing the rounds. I knew that the police would find out sooner or later. But when Ingrid's old man died, the incident wasn't so funny any more. All of a sudden it seemed hard to imagine that I would be believed – that it was an accident.'

'Did you go back downstairs to the shop?'

'No. We agreed that Ingrid would "discover" the body when it became light. And call the police.'

'Did you go through the dead man's pockets?'

'No.'

'Did you notice anything as you were leaving?'

'Like what?'

'Like the shop window, for example?'

'No.'

'Where was the body lying when you left?'

'He was lying on his stomach in the doorway between the office and the shop.'

'And the front door was unlocked when you arrived?'

'Yes.'

'When would that have been?'

'I would reckon at around half past twelve, maybe closer to one.'

'And how long after did he die?'

'At half past one, maybe.'

'And Kirkenær?' Gunnarstranda asked as Frølich drifted into the office.

'Still in a coma.'

'Shame.'

'Will he go free?' Frølich asked.

Gunnarstranda shook his head. 'He desecrated the body,' he said. 'He went there during the night. We have Iselin Varås's word for that. He found the body, stripped it, penned his message and placed it in the shop window after removing the keys. Those acts on their own are theft and desecration – enough for a charge.'

'But can we be bothered?'

'No,' Gunnarstranda said, lighting a cigarette. 'We'll charge him with murder.' He waved the lists of calls from Ekholt's mobile phone.

Frølich observed him from under knitted eyebrows.

Gunnarstranda blew a perfect smoke ring. 'Ekholt was sitting in his taxi and saw everything that was going on in the shop window. He didn't see the killing because that happened in the back office and the shop was pitch black. But he did see who put the body in the armchair by the window. Ekholt put two and two together and got eleven. Of course he thought he was watching the murderer. Iselin Varås said Kirkenær took a taxi back to the Continental that night. She had no idea what was going on. But she was worried when they began to get phone calls from a strange man purporting to be a taxi driver. Kirkenær refused to talk to the man, and he refused to allow her to talk to him. Who else could the taxi driver have been if not Ekholt? Kirkenær thought he was hailing a normal taxi with a normal driver that night, not a witness. For his part, Ekholt thought that Kirkenær had killed the old man, so he made sure his taxi was chosen. According to Iselin Varås, Kirkenær seemed edgy and irritable every time the stranger called. Kirkenær slammed down the phone every time except for once. Iselin said that one evening he had agreed to meet the man and had gone out soon afterwards. I thought it might be interesting to find out which evening it was.' Gunnarstranda waved the paper he was holding in his hand. 'I showed her this list of calls from Ekholt's mobile phone. The stranger's calls matched the list exactly.'

'Kirkenær met Ekholt the same night Ekholt spoke to me,' Frølich said in a low tone.

Gunnarstranda flicked the ash off his cigarette. 'Ekholt must have had one single purpose, to blackmail

Kirkenær. The phone call to you was a sign that he meant business when he was threatening Kirkenær that he would tell everything he knew. What he didn't take into account was that Kirkenær was dangerous.' Police Inspector Gunnarstranda stubbed out his cigarette on the sole of his shoe and gave another sparkling white smile. 'When Hermann Kirkenær wakes up from his coma, he'll be staring right into your mug,' he said softly. 'And you will charge him with the murder of the greedy taxi driver – Richard Ekholt.'